I0727942

WAR BROTHERS MC - AXLE, REAPER, BOMBER

BOOKS 1, 2 & 3

BIANCA LEE WARD

This book contains adult themes and is not suitable for persons under the age of 18.

For information regarding possible triggers, please see www.biancaleeward.com or contact info@biancaleeward.com.

War Brothers MC: Axle, Reaper and Bomber

ALSO BY BIANCA LEE WARD

VIPER

War Brothers MC

I've got one month to convince her to be my wife . . .

Until I laid eyes on Sophie, I never planned on marriage. All that changed after our hot night together in Vegas.

Now she regrets our impulsive Vegas wedding and is demanding a divorce. But I'm not signing the papers. Hell no! I'll give up every single one of my womanizing ways for a woman like her.

Sophie thinks I'm only infatuated by her looks, except I see how everyone underestimates her. I'm not intimidated by her wealth, her modeling career, and the trail of broken hearts she has left behind. What we have is different.

I've lived my whole life unable to feel anything thanks to my rough childhood, but for Sophie I'll risk everything. Her rich father and the jealous women in my club aren't going to stand in my way.

If she wants a divorce, she'll have to spend one month with me at the War Brothers clubhouse. Sleeping in my bed.

Then we'll see if she still refuses to say I do . . .

Grab your copy of Viper now.

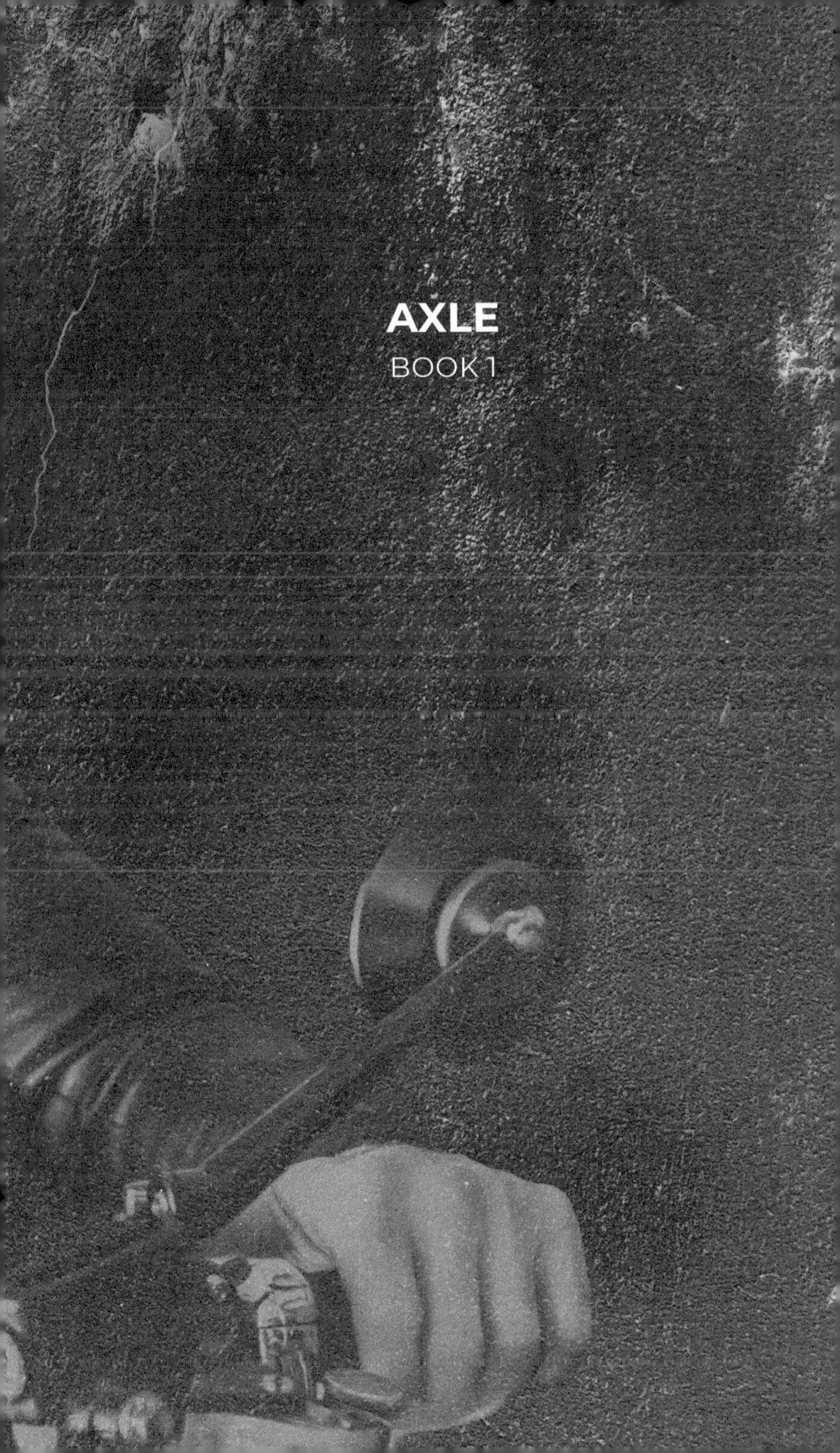
AXLE
BOOK 1

ONE
A NEW HORIZON

Elena

"You have reached your destination," my phone's GPS app says. I pull over, mount the curb, and cringe at my terrible driving skills. I scan my surroundings and sigh in relief—no one saw that. It's late afternoon. Despite using a navigation app, I still got lost and could have arrived earlier.

The two-story redbrick house is average looking. It will be my new home in Crown Village, a small coastal town with a lake and beaches. I already know I'm going to love it here. My previous town just didn't feel like home.

Closing my eyes, I recall the first time I told my parents I was leaving.

Mom's mouth is wide; her eyes bulge and then narrow. "No! You're not leaving."

I clench my shaking hands in front of me. "I got a job as a waitress at a respectable restaurant." I smile, thinking if my parents see how happy it'll make me, they'll be happy.

"Why are you moving away from us?" Dad asks. "You

gave up college . . . now you're taking up *another* waitressing job away from us and your sister?" His disapproving glare slices through me like a blade.

I frown. I'll miss my sister, Ava, but that's about it. I shake my head to get rid of these thoughts—I need to stay positive.

Two girls in bikinis, with towels around their shoulders, rush out of the front door of the house and dash past across the lawn. They're probably going to the beach; it's not far. That's what the ad said, at least. I'm renting a bedroom in a shared house because that's all I can afford in this town. It's so expensive here.

When I step out of the car on shaky legs, the breeze swirls around me, flicking my hair. I inhale the fresh, salty air. I could get used to this. I had to escape my small hometown and experience life while I'm still young. A sudden flicker of nerves makes my heart pump in my chest. I roll my shoulders back. "Pull yourself together," I mumble under my breath.

After closing the car door, I walk across the lawn and stand by the front door. I knock. "Hello," I call out. It comes out as a strangled whisper, so I clear my throat to try again. "Hel—" is all I can say before the door opens right into my head. Pain ricochets through my forehead and nose.

"Sorry," the guy in the doorway says. He chuckles.

A girl opens the door fully. "Are you alright?" She's attractive and also wearing a bikini, and her blond hair is tied back in a super high ponytail.

"Yes," I say. I smile tightly, even though it still hurts. "I'm Elena. I'm supposed to be moving in today."

She gives me a big smile. "I'm Lucy. The owner told me about you. Your bedroom is the first one you see when you get up the stairs. I'll go get your keys." She darts away.

I swallow and look at my feet, conscious of the guy's eyes on me.

"Want to join us at the beach?" he asks.

When I look up, I try to focus on his face so that I don't stare at his body. He's wearing only shorts.

I peer back at my car. "I've got to get unpacked . . . but uh, thanks."

He nods. "Maybe next time," he says, and smiles.

Lucy comes back with an outstretched hand. "Here are your keys."

I take them from her.

"The small one is the key to your bedroom. Just lock it when you leave to go anywhere, because we have parties occasionally. The big key is to the front door."

"Thanks," I say hesitantly. Is she insinuating that there are thieves or that random people will barge into my room when they are over? I consciously make a note to lock the door 24/7.

"I'll see you later," she says, then I watch as the two walk away in the same direction as the other girls went.

I return to my car, open the back door, and retrieve my heavy suitcase. I tow it along on its wheels while I proceed to the house. The front door opens on the living room, which is furnished with weathered green couches. A few beer bottles are scattered on the tables. The house is basic, with white walls, worn floorboards, and the bare minimum of furniture. As I walk in further, I see the kitchen toward the back and a staircase to my left.

I drag my suitcase over to the stairs. I go up one stair, pull . . . two stairs, pull . . . My suitcase is so heavy. This is going to take a while.

I'm breathing heavily when I get to the top, but at least the door is only three steps away. I knock first, just in case Lucy directed me to the wrong room. Silence. I push the door wide and see a white metal bedframe with a mattress on top, a white chest of drawers, and a nightstand.

Two and a half hours had passed by the time I'd dragged

my suitcase and bags of clothes, shoes, books, and toiletries up the stairs and unpacked. I'm straightening the spines of my books when I hear laughter and talking coming from outside the house. The voices move inside and the front door bangs shut.

I step out of my room to hear a guy say, "I wonder if that girl is still here or if she bolted after seeing us." He laughs. "The look on her face and what she was wearing . . . it looked like she was going to church."

I glance down at my long dress with three-quarter sleeves and my ballet flats. What's wrong with my outfit? To be fair, I have worn this dress to church on Sundays many times, but still . . .

"Her name's Elena. I'm sure she's in her room," Lucy says. She looks up the stairs. Her friends follow her gaze until all eyes are on me.

I give them a small wave. I've always been socially awkward.

Lucy waves me over. "Come down and have some pizza with us."

My stomach growls, reminding me I haven't eaten since breakfast. I go down the stairs and approach her.

"Come on, I'll show you around," she says with a bright smile.

I clasp my hands in front of me and nod.

Lucy steps over to her friends, who have taken a seat on the couches. "Everyone, this is Elena," she says. She points to the three attractive girls. "These are my friends Cindy, Jasmine, and Lia. They all live here too." Cindy and Lia have blond hair, and Jasmine has black hair. The girls give me a friendly smile.

Two guys are fighting over the remote. Lucy points at one and says, "Jeremy is my boyfriend." It's the guy I saw this morning and who made fun of my dress. He snatches the remote and then smiles at me.

"Justin is Cindy's boyfriend," Lucy says, gesturing toward the other guy. He salutes me.

I follow Lucy toward the kitchen. The kitchen cabinets are cream, but with plenty of scratches. A broken cupboard door hangs crookedly. It's clear that no one is taking care of this house. I suppose it's perfect for people our age.

"Pots, pans, cutlery, and cups are stored in the cupboards and drawers," Lucy says. "The grocery store is only a short drive away. Write your name on things in the cupboard and stuff like milk so that no one gets confused about who it belongs to."

I follow Lucy back to the loud voices in the living room. Lucy sits on Jeremy's lap, and I take a seat on the single chair.

"Where are you from?" Lucy asks. Everyone quietens and all eyes lock on to me.

"I'm from Meadowbank. It's a small town around a thirty-minute drive from here." My hometown isn't anything to be embarrassed about. I need to be independent from my parents, and I thought a beach town would be a great place to move to.

"Oh yeah. It is small. It takes what, five minutes to travel through?" Lia asks sarcastically.

"Something like that," I answer.

"What brought you to Crown Village?" asks Jasmine as she twirls her long black hair around her finger.

I was lonely and bored. "I landed a job at a restaurant."

"Which one?" asks Lia.

"Crown Village Seafood Restaurant."

"Our friend Cameron works there. His parents own it. The food there is so good," says Justin. Everyone else nods.

"So good, but so expensive," says Cindy.

There's a knock on the door. Both guys stand up and hurry to the door. "Pizza's here!" Justin yells out.

"Where do you guys work?" I ask them.

Cindy's face contorts. "I don't work. I'm at college studying economics."

"I'm studying tourism," Jasmine adds in.

"Jeremy and I are studying business management," says Lucy. "Justin, engineering, and Lia, social sciences."

"So, you all study and don't work?" I clarify.

"Yep." Lucy nods, and I feel an inch tall. Their parents must pay for everything.

The boys walk in and place the cardboard boxes on the table. When they open them, a heavenly smell wafts out. Jeremy takes two large slices and sits back down before he crams as much as he can into his mouth. As I take a small slice of pizza and a napkin, I marvel at just how different I am from them. While they're out partying and sleeping in, I'll be working.

After my belly is full, I say good night and go to my room. I lock the door before I lie down.

I could have been like them. Going to college was an option for me. I got the grades for it. I considered majoring in English, but in the end I wasn't certain. I wasn't going to get into that much debt without being one hundred percent sure what career I wanted. I thought I was doing the smart thing. Taking time off to consider my options. But according to my parents, I have the brains, so I should be going to college and making something of myself, not just being a waitress on minimum wage.

My phone beeps. The message is from Henry, my ex-boyfriend, who I broke up with a while ago. We had been together since high school. He got into a college on the East Coast and intended to live on campus, but I didn't want to have a long-distance relationship. Besides, we had grown apart long before we broke up.

The breakup had been amicable, and we still talk occasionally. I'm glad that there's no bad blood between us and that we can still be friends. We've been close for so long.

Henry

How did the move go?

Good thanks.

At least someone cares, I think to myself.

I've met my roommates, they seem friendly.

That's awesome. I look forward to hearing about it all.

I go back to my home screen. No phone call from my parents, asking if I arrived safe or if I've settled in okay. They were less than pleased about me moving and said I'm making a mistake. I wanted—no, I needed—to get out from under my parents' judgement.

When I was searching for jobs, I saw a position as a waitress being advertised in Crown Village. Excited by the opportunity, I immediately applied. I was tired of being comatose, living but not alive. My roommates seem to be friends with the restaurant owner's son, so that's a positive considering they seem like a friendly group of people.

I pick up my reading glasses and put them on, then grab a romance novel from the nightstand and start to read. Soon I'm lost in stories about love, book boyfriends, and happily ever after, which are far better than my reality.

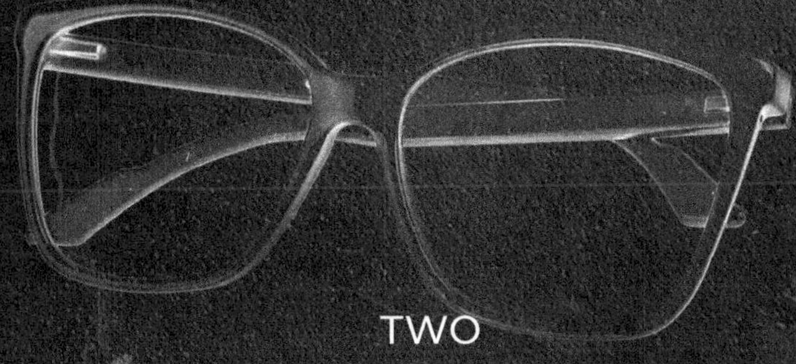

TWO
TRYING TO BE OPTIMISTIC

Elena

Gazing at my reflection, I gather my long blond hair and tie it into a bun before I apply tinted moisturizer, mascara, and strawberry lip balm. I expel a breath. This will have to do. I'm wearing a black three-quarter skirt and a white blouse.

Knock, knock. "Come on, I'm busting to go to the toilet." Jeremy's voice filters through the bathroom door. If these boys are going to live here, sharing one upstairs bathroom with seven people isn't going to work.

I push the door open, and he darts in and starts peeing in the toilet before I can even close the door behind me. I shudder. Gross!

"Tell Cameron I'll see him tonight," he calls out.

Back in my bedroom, I slip my handbag over my shoulder before I leave. I lock my door and go downstairs.

It's quiet compared to last night. When I woke up at two a.m., I could hear their voices and music. Empty pizza boxes and beer bottles and glasses from last night are scattered across the coffee table. I hope this isn't a daily occurrence, but I suspect it might be.

In the kitchen I pour water into a glass and take my anxiety medication out of my bag. I swallow my daily dose: two tablets. I've been on anxiety medication since high school, when I put so much pressure on myself to do well that my hands would shake.

"I've got this," I say, trying to convince myself that I'm confident before I head out the front door.

I walk to my faded yellow Mini Cooper. It's older than me, but despite a few bangs and scratches from my driving, it gets the job done. My seat creaks as I get in and settle while I open the GPS app on my phone. "Don't let me down," I mumble. My GPS says it's a seven-minute drive, but I'm leaving early, in plenty of time before my shift starts at eleven.

My heart beats faster the closer I get to the restaurant. The town's main road runs along the beach. The water is calm, and it lazily laps the shore. I see small shops to my left and palm trees scattered along the sidewalk.

The restaurant is just up ahead. As I approach, a car leaves an angled parking spot nearby. I put on my blinker, and after several attempts and a car horn blasting, I reverse park. When I get out of the car, I see that I parked a little too close to the line for comfort, but I ignore it and make my way to the side-walk, trying to control my breathing with slow breaths.

The restaurant appears modern, with floor-to-ceiling windows and a deck that wraps around the outside. A black sign with gold lettering proudly displays the name of the restaurant and my new place of employment: Crown Village Seafood Restaurant. It's fine dining, and I hope I'm not out of my depth. I'm not the most graceful person. I think the manager at my last restaurant gave me a good reference to get rid of me. I accidentally broke several plates and glasses. I always apologized, but I'm lucky I kept my job as long as I did.

A Closed sign hangs on the door, but when I knock lightly, a young man appears. He opens the door, and I say, "Hello, I'm Elena. I'm supposed to be starting today." I try to sound confident, though I don't feel it.

The man's eyes roam my body, making me shift uncomfortably. His smile widens when his eyes reach mine. "Hey, sorry," he says and opens the door further. "Come on in. The name's Cameron."

I carefully enter. My stomach rolls like crazy.

"You're more beautiful in person," he quips, and I pause. "I had to check out your Instagram profile," he says casually, and then he laughs when I don't answer. "My father makes me ensure I'm hiring the right people; he can't hire someone whose behavior will reflect poorly on the business. You know . . . our family restaurant's reputation is important."

As I exhale, my shoulders sag an inch. "Of course," I say and smile. He was doing his due diligence for his family's business.

"Come take a seat," Cameron says, glancing at the closest two-seater table.

He sits down opposite me, and I can't help but notice that he's handsome, with brown eyes and hair and a broad smile.

"Thank you for giving me this opportunity. I appreciate it." More than he will know—it allowed me to get out of my hometown.

His eyes light up. "It's my pleasure. About the restaurant, we serve seafood, obviously. It's fine dining, so the customers expect professional service. Your role at the beginning is to bring out food to the designated tables. Simple. I need you to smile and be professional and approachable." His eyes trail me again. "What you're wearing is perfect."

I clasp my hands together and sit up straight, trying not to show how nervous I am.

He takes a menu from the table and passes it to me. "We serve primarily high-quality, locally sourced and sustainable seafood and produce, and our prices match our ethos." He glances down at his watch. "The chefs and waitresses will arrive soon to prepare for lunch. I'll have one girl show you the ropes, and you can shadow her today. If you have any questions, just let me know."

His phone rings and he pulls it from his pocket. "Hey," he answers and puts a finger up at me, signaling he'll be a moment. I nod and give him a small smile before he walks toward the rear of the restaurant and enters a door that I assume leads to the kitchen.

As I wait for him to return, I survey the restaurant. Tables are separated evenly around and ringed with elegant chairs with timber legs and plush fabric seats. The real beauty is the full view of the ocean.

Members of staff come in through the front door; the men smile at me, and a bald one gives me a friendly wave. They head to the back of the restaurant. Women dressed similarly to me walk in, but they pay no attention to me. Not that I'm anyone important, but I was hoping to make a few friends while I'm here.

Cameron's been gone for a while, so I pull my phone out of my bag. When the women start setting up the tables, I stand up to help just as Cameron reappears and the front door opens.

"Mel, good to see you've turned up."

A girl around my age with a short pixie cut walks in. She gives Cameron a big smile, walks to him, and gives him a kiss on the cheek.

I'm surprised at the affection. I hope Cameron doesn't expect that from me.

"Miss me, did you?" she purrs.

"Always," he says playfully, and then he turns toward me. "Elena is new. She's shadowing you today." He turns back to Mel. "Be nice," he says sternly.

That is not an encouraging sign.

Cameron walks away and Mel moves toward me, her eyes scanning me up and down. "I can see why he hired you."

I clear my throat. "Why do you say that?"

"He only hires attractive waitresses." Her eyes drift over me again. "Come with me. I'll show you where to put your things."

As I walk behind her, I notice that she's dressed like me, although her skirt is a lot shorter than mine. I tap her on the shoulder and lower my voice. "I don't have to kiss Cameron on the cheek, do I?" I recoil at the thought.

She laughs. "No, but it'll do you a lot of good to be *very* friendly to him. The tips here are worth putting up with him. I encourage it, though, because I usually get the best shifts when I do."

I've already decided that that won't be happening. I guess I'll have to deal with getting the crappy shifts.

We walk past the tables, then through the large doors and into the kitchen area. Mel puts her bag on a shelf. "Put your bag up here."

As I put my bag away, Mel's phone beeps. She pulls it out, then laughs when she stares at the screen and types.

"Boyfriend?" I ask, making small talk.

She waves me off, then puts her phone away. "No, a guy from this dating app I'm on."

I blink a few times, unsure how to reply. "Cool."

Butterflies perform acrobatics in my stomach as I make every effort to take in Mel's instructions on the details of my job. Cameron was right. It doesn't seem too complicated, and I try to remember table numbers and the menu.

Apart from Cameron watching my every move, my first shift is a blur of friendly faces and the delicious aroma of food wafting through the restaurant. Once the last patron leaves, I help clean the tables and then grab my bag. Cameron leans against the wall close to me, making me take a small step back.

His eyes flick over me before he says, "How was your first shift?"

"Good, thank you."

He smiles. "I'll see you tomorrow at the same time. Can you also work the evening shift tomorrow?"

More shifts, more money. "I sure can. I live with Lucy and the girls. Jeremy said he'll see you tonight."

Cameron's brows lift. "You live with Lucy?"

I nod.

"Looks like we'll be seeing a lot more of each other. Are you coming out to the diner too?" he asks.

I'm not sure how I feel about seeing my boss at my house. "Early night for me tonight. Have fun though."

I follow Mel outside and glance around one last time. "Are there any other staff members I haven't met yet?"

"Only a couple of girls that do casual shifts," Mel answers.

At my last restaurant there was both waiters and wait-resses. "Aren't there any waiters?"

She opens the door and we walk out. She flashes me a smile. "You noticed that, huh? Cameron reckons women bring in more customers—therefore, more money—but I think he just likes to perve on us. I saw Cameron's got his eye on you."

A sense of unease twists knots inside of me, despite my attempts to stay optimistic. I don't want any special attention. I want to do what I do best—blend into the background. My introverted self doesn't enjoy going out to socialize. I'm happy being at home reading a book.

A loud rumble makes me jerk, and I pivot to the sound of motorcycles passing us. I count seven black bikes that, even for a person who knows nothing about bikes, look high-end. Their black and chrome parts shine in the sun. The men driving them, who are wearing matching vests, seem scary.

"That's the War Brothers MC," Mel says after they pass us. "They're the hottest men in town." She lets out a long sigh. "What I wouldn't do to become a sweet butt."

I turn around to face her. "What's a sweet butt?"

"The women who are allowed to live there with the men. They help at the clubhouse doing cleaning and cooking, but they're in it for the sex and to live there rent-free. I'm so jealous!"

I'm disturbed by that revelation and realize I grew up very sheltered.

Her phone pings, and she pulls it out and smiles. Her eyes return to mine. "Do you have a boyfriend?"

"No." Henry and I are just friends now. He has always treated me well, but our connection seemed more like a friendship than a romantic relationship.

"Have you thought about setting up a profile on a dating app?" she asks enthusiastically.

I shake my head. "I recently got out of a relationship. I'm not interested. Anyway, aren't the guys on them only after sex and hooking up?"

"No, you can put what you're after on your profile. Everyone's rich here. You have to agree that it would be lovely to go out and be wined and dined for a night. It's whatever you want it to be."

I shrug. "It doesn't interest me." I just moved here. I have next to no experience with guys and the thought sends my heart racing.

She tilts her head. "You're weird, you know that?"

I chuckle. "Yes, I'm well aware." I've always been shy; I can't help it. I live vicariously through the books I read.

"I'll see you tomorrow," she says over her shoulder as she walks away.

"See you then," I reply and walk over to my car.

A new town, a new job, and an unspoken hope for a new beginning.

THREE
THE BET

Axle

Viper, Cash, and I are hanging out at the clubhouse bar. The music is pumping, and one of my favorite bands, Motionless in White, is playing. I join in, singing to the chorus.

"Shit, you sound terrible," Viper says, smirking.

I sing louder just to spite him, using my hand as a microphone. I scream at the end until he throws a dirty tea towel at me and scores a direct hit to my face.

I gag, rip it off, and throw it back at Cash, who's standing behind the bar. "That stinks!"

He laughs. "It shut you up, didn't it?"

Viper's squinting at me. "Can you hear your own voice?"

I nod. "Sure can."

"Then you must hear how shit you sound."

I gasp dramatically. "You must have a hearing problem then," I say to Viper, fighting off a grin.

He shakes his head as he chuckles.

"Did I just hear something dying?" Reaper, the president

of our club, is walking toward us with an expression of disgust on his face, which makes all of us laugh.

"You mean the sound of an angel," I clarify.

"If the angel was being brutally murdered," Demon chimes from the pool table, where he's playing a game with Twitch.

I roll my eyes. "Well, I've got to entertain myself somehow."

The other men return to their conversations. Grace sashays over to me, giving me a flirtatious glance. I groan. Prime example number one of why I'm bored—no more casual sex with the stage-five clinger. I shake my head. "Not now," I call out to her over the music, loud and clear.

She pauses, but then keeps walking toward me while Viper chuckles next to me. I grit my teeth and plaster on a smile, trying not to lose my shit at her.

"Oh, come on, baby," she coos, pushing up her boobs, which are about to burst out of her bra-like top.

She's hot . . . amazing body, but she needs a big fucking wake-up call. We will never be anything but fuck buddies. My nonexistent patience vanishes. I raise my voice and stress, "I said, *not now*."

Her eyes widen. She fakes a tight-lipped smile and retreats.

I blow out a breath. "Fuuuck! I'm trying my best not to be a dick because she's a sweet butt and lives here, but she's making it really fucking difficult."

Viper looks at me with a raised brow. "What's up with you lately?"

"She's in full stage-five-clinger mode. Even started asking me if I would ever get married." I shake my head while Viper laughs.

He cringes. "That's heavy. She realizes she's living at a motorcycle club, right?"

"*Exactly*. I knew I had to stop the casual sex right away. Next she'll be poking holes in condoms, trying to get pregnant."

Viper throws his head back, letting out a loud laugh as Cash asks, "Does anyone want another drink?"

"Another beer," I say.

I thought going for a long ride on my Harley today with all the club members would lift my spirits and calm my restlessness, but it was a temporary fix. "We need to have a massive party here. Spread the word for chicks from nearby towns and girls who recently moved here for college."

"I'm keen," Viper replies, upbeat. "Is that's what's up your ass? You want new pussy?"

I shrug. "This town is pretty small, and we've been through a lot of the women here." A *lot*.

He raises his brow. "What exactly are you after?"

My eyes wander over the women in the clubhouse, and I grimace. "The opposite of them," I say, and tilt my head toward the sweet butts. Vera, Grace, Candy, and Mercedez are dancing to the music and rubbing up against each other.

"I don't want an easy girl. I want someone to keep my interest . . . I want . . ." My lip twitches. "Innocent."

Viper puffs out a breath of air. "Keep dreaming. Have you ever even met a nun?"

I chuckle. "She doesn't have to be a nun."

"Virgins want relationships. Good luck finding one that doesn't."

I don't want a relationship. She doesn't have to be a virgin either. A challenge is what I'm after. Viper has a point. Biker parties aren't the place to find someone like that. But then inspiration strikes. "I'm going to go on one of those dating apps."

Viper's eyes brighten. "That is going to end up being some

great entertainment. You'll have to show me who you find on there."

I pull my phone out and search for dating apps.

One hour later, I've signed up to three. The chiming of message notifications makes my smug grin stretch wide.

"See . . . the ladies flock to me."

Viper shakes his head, trying to smother a smirk. "Not the lady you're after."

My smile vanishes.

"Did you put on your profile that you're a member of a motorcycle club?"

"Yeah, of course I did." It always attracts the ladies.

"Idiot! Delete that part, and don't use any photo of you that shows your cut," he says while pointing at my War Brothers MC vest.

"Do I have to take a picture with my hair parted on the side like a good boy as well?" I say, my voice dripping with sarcasm.

He chuckles. "No, I'm just saying if you want to attract a different type of woman, you're going to have to change it up a bit, at least for the first part, anyway."

This is going to be harder than I thought. I crop one of my photos so that it shows only my head and shoulders and nothing about being in a motorcycle club, and I change my occupation to mechanic. Even though I'm not qualified as one, I'm just as skilled.

Next I browse profiles, choosing women within a two-hour drive from here. I'm not driving any further than that to see them. I want to open the net as wide as possible because I'm sure the women who live here know my face. A few of the women who have matched with me are local. "Nope"—swipe. "Nope"—swipe. I delete their requests.

An hour later, as I'm flicking through the women on the app, I find a pretty little thing with long blond hair and a sweet smile. "Fucking perfect." In her profile picture, she's wearing jeans and a fancy long top. I click on her profile. There's not much information about her. Just that she works in Crown Village at a restaurant. I've never seen her before. I frown when I see she doesn't have any other photos.

"Do you think this one's a catfish?" I ask Viper. I give him my phone.

"Ohhh," he says, amused. "She's hot! You'll never know until you talk to her." He zooms in on the picture and laughs. "You've found your nun."

"Why do you say that?" I ask.

"She's wearing a gold cross around her neck."

Excitement buzzes through me. *Fuck yeah.* That's a sign right there!

I'm halfway through my beer when my phone chimes. When I look down at it, my heart jolts. "She matched me!" I cheer. "If I spend some time with her, that should make Grace leave me alone too. I'm just saying . . . two birds, one stone." Grace can move on to one of my brothers.

Viper throws his head back. "Ha! The only way you're going to get into that pussy is in your dreams!"

I pull at my cut, then mockingly run a hand through my hair like he usually does. "We all can't be as pretty as you."

He laughs. "She looks young and classy. Take another look at her picture! Her clothes cover most of her skin. I'm sure she has a chastity belt on too. I'm telling you—she will never go out with a biker."

The photo of the innocent woman glows from my screen.

"You want to make a bet on that? I guarantee I can get into a relationship with her, and I'll take it one step further and make her fall in love with me." Because I'm pretty sure that's the only way I'll be getting into those sweet panties. I can't help myself. I'm spurred on by the thrill of the gamble and of getting with someone I've never been with before.

Viper's smile widens and his hand shoots out. I grip his hand and shake it. "Easiest money I've ever made," he says confidently.

My eyes tighten. "You're wrong, and I can't wait to wipe that smug smile right off your face."

"Don't forget," he remarks with a cocky smirk, "she probably won't have sex till marriage."

My eyes bulge and I swallow hard. "She better not! That's old school anyway." I wave him off. "No one does that anymore."

"Yeah, they do," he says, and chuckles. "And here's another thought. You'll be talking to her through messages. How's she going to understand your dyslexic ass?"

A sigh escapes me. I'd forgotten about that. I'm going to have to download an autocorrect app on my phone to double check everything I write because I'm terrible at spelling—well, anything related to writing and reading. I'm good at fixing shit, which is why I'm a mechanic.

"I'll work it out. I've never seen her before. Her profile says she lives in Crown Village. She must have just moved here."

He shrugs. "Talk to her and find out."

"Oh, I plan to." I might even get Twitch, our club's tech guy, to stalk her online for me.

FOUR
DATING APP

Elena

Focusing on the glasses of wine on my tray, I stroll to the table that ordered them. *Nearly there . . .* Someone at a table nearby scoots their chair out in front of me. I gasp, then trip over the chair legs. I stagger and, with a high-pitched clatter, the glasses of red wine shatter on the wooden floor. For a second I seem to regain my balance, but then I fall next to the wine and broken glass.

My face is on fire as I assess the mess. When I look up, everyone in the restaurant is staring at me. "I'm so sorry," I stutter, not sure who I'm apologizing to. "I'll clean it up," I say in a rush. I turn to the customers who ordered the wine. "I'll get you another two glasses."

The woman who pushed out her chair doesn't even apologize—she just turns her nose up at me and walks away. So rude!

Then Cameron is by my side, wearing his customer service smile. "I'll get you your drinks right away," he says to the couple whose drinks are now on the floor. "Can you two clean this up?" he points to Mel and another waitress. Mel's eyes widen and her mouth twists.

"Sorry," I mouth as Cameron grabs my elbow and ushers me away to the kitchen. I close my eyes when he turns to me, waiting to be yelled at.

"Are you okay?" he asks.

I open one eye. I was not expecting that. "Uh . . . yes."

His eyes wander over me, and he smiles wide. "I'm glad."

Guilt pricks me. "I'd better go help them clean it up." I take a step away, but he grasps my elbow again and with his other hand waves it off. "Don't worry about them. I said they can clean it." I glance at the door, then at him. He's the boss, but Mel was scowling at us as we left. She did not look happy.

AFTER OUR SHIFT, MEL AND I TAKE SOME LEFTOVER FOOD IN containers and go to the beach to eat it. Sitting on a chair, I slurp up my noodles. "This seafood marinara is to die for."

Mel smiles. "I love every dish on the menu."

"If I didn't work there, I'd never be able to afford it," I point out, remembering the eye-watering prices.

"Cameron has taken a liking to you," she teases. "You might be stealing my shifts." Her voice is carefree, but I'm not fully convinced she means it.

"No," I say as I shake my head. "I just started. He probably felt bad for me. I embarrassed myself in front of everyone." I take another bite.

She giggles. "You certainly did."

I flinch.

"Luckily, it's not carpet," she points out.

"I agree." It would have left a lovely stain.

"I heard you live with Lucy and her sheep," Mel says.

I pause. My eyes widen at her nasty comment. "I live with Lucy and her friends, yes. Do you know them?"

"People get to know each other quickly in this town. Cameron is always saying how hot they are. Were they bitches to you?"

I slowly shake my head. "The opposite. They've been friendly since I arrived."

She frowns. "I thought they'd be like the mean popular girl group from school, you know."

Well, this is awkward. "Not at all."

She shrugs. "I'd say they talk about you behind your back then because you're so . . ."

My lips press into a line. I'm quite sure I have no interest in hearing what she's got to say next. "Because I'm a bit of a nerd." I finish her sentence for her in the nicest possible way.

"Yeah . . . like night and day opposites. Soooo . . ." she says, peering at the ground, then back at me. "I may have done something . . . to, you know, help you meet new people."

My stomach drops. I don't like the sound of that. "What did you do?"

She winces. "Can I have your phone to show you?"

My breathing speeds up as I cautiously offer her my phone. I try to think why she would need my phone, but I can't think of anything.

"Now . . . don't be mad at me . . ."

"O-kaaay," I say.

She passes me the phone. I frown when I see a picture of myself that was taken when my parents and I went out to dinner for my birthday last year. As I scroll down, it hits me. "You made a dating profile for me?" I screech. "I'm deleting it now!" I'm horrified.

She grins a little. "Give it a chance. Live a little. You should consider meeting new people."

I look more closely. She has Elena as my profile name; "Just moved to Crown Village, where I'm working at a restaurant. I'm looking to meet new people" is the bio.

"What if my parents see this?" I ask, then flinch. Why should I care what they think?

She gives me an odd glance. "I didn't realize you were fourteen years old."

Annoyance simmers. "I grew up in a strict family." I just moved here. It's hard to click my fingers and change my thoughts after years of worrying about my parents' opinions. I'll be defaulting to that for a while.

"And you still let your parents dictate what you do?" She chuckles.

"I don't get it . . ." I stare at her, confused. "Why would you do this? You're already on the app, and you hardly know me."

Her pout makes me think I shouldn't have said that. "I was trying to do a *nice* thing."

Oh dear. I think I offended her. I swallow down my irritation. I bring my phone to my face again. "Where'd you get this photo from?"

"I got it from your Instagram account. See, fifteen guys want to connect with you already."

I blink slowly. I'm waiting for her to say she's joking, but she doesn't. "You didn't . . .?" is all I can say because I'm reeling.

"You need it. Meet some new guys. Have fun." She glances away. "I may have already swiped yes on one of them."

My jaw drops. It just gets worse. "Who?"

"A guy called Axle."

I scoff. "What an absurd name."

"I've been on the app for a while, and I've never seen his profile. He recently joined, like you. He's from Crown Village, and he's so sexy. Trust me, you want to talk to him."

"Well, why don't you talk to him then?"

She pauses, then says, "It's my gift to you. I've heard he's good fun." Her critical gaze runs over me again, but then she smiles. "You're not getting married to the guy. Just talk to him."

"How do you know him, and why do you say he's fun?" I ask.

"I've seen him around. It's a small town." She takes a moment before she says, "He sticks to himself and his group of friends."

"So he's not some frat guy?"

She laughs. "No, definitely not . . . quite the opposite."

The message icon at the top of the screen shows the number one above it. I hold my breath and let my finger hover over it for a second before I press on it.

Axle

Hey, how are you doing?

I just stare at the message.

"See . . . it's not the end of the world," Mel points out.

I get out of the message and click on his profile. He's very handsome, and I'm sure he knows it. Short brown hair and a beard. His profile is minimal, like mine. It says he's a mechanic and, according to his bio, "looking for someone special." I melt a little at that. Maybe there are nice guys on the app after all.

I can't deny I'm curious to talk to him. No one as handsome as him has ever shown an interest in me. "But I'm not looking for another relationship," I say. I shove my phone back in my bag with more force than necessary. He must have gotten my profile mixed up with someone else's.

When I get back to the house, it's quiet. Everyone must be at class. After a shower, I lie on the bed. My stomach churns. I glance down at my bag beside the bed. I'm itching to grab my phone. My fingers tap on the bed until I can't resist the urge any longer and give in to the temptation. I pull out my phone and with a deep breath, I unlock it and tap on the dating app.

I look at Axle's profile picture once more. I should just delete the app, but I can't stop myself from responding to his message:

> I'm good, thank you. How are you?

I stare at the screen and place my phone on the night-stand, face down. I can't believe I just did that. I replied to a stranger. I run my hand over my face. Mel could be right, even though it's out of character for me. I should step out of my comfort zone and try to make friends.

My phone buzzes on the table. Here goes nothing . . .

> Fantastic now that I'm talking to you

I stare blankly. I start typing and then delete it.

> You're beautiful babe. Your profile says you just moved here. Are you enjoying it?

My face heats.

> The people are nice.

> I'm nice.

I laugh. I bet he's *nice* to all women.

How old are you?

Early twenties. How old are you?

Ha . . . don't give too much away now. Early twenties.

I'm getting banter and sarcasm vibes.

What brings a pretty little thing like you onto a dating website?

I decide not to go with the truth.

I want to make some new friends.

I'm an amazing friend. You're so lucky you replied to me.

I giggle.

Someone is full of himself.

Only stating facts, babe. I'm funny, I'm sexy as fuck, I'll listen to all your problems, and I'll be your shoulder to cry on. Trust me, we are going to be good friends.

I smile. Maybe the app isn't too bad after all.

FIVE
HALF-TRUTHS

ALL THE MEN ARE OUTSIDE CLEANING THEIR MOTORCYCLES. After replacing the back tire on mine, I hear a chuckle, then peer up to see Cash looking at me, amused.

"What?" I ask him, wondering why he has that stupid look on his face.

"Didn't you just replace the back tire?"

A smile curves across my lips. "Yes, I did." I love doing power skids, burnouts, and wheelies. It's who I am. The adrenaline rush is pure ecstasy.

"Are you ever going to grow out of your daredevil ways?" he asks, though the smile pulling at his lips suggests he already knows the answer to that question.

"Never! You should know that by now."

Cash and I spent years in the military together. It's how we met. He knows me well. I'm always doing reckless things, especially on my motorcycle. I've never cared about my safety —I'm always searching for the next thrill.

After cleaning my motorcycle, I step aside. "What a sexy beast," I say.

"Mine's sexier," says Viper.

I laugh loudly. "You wish . . . My exhaust is louder." My phone chimes inside my pocket. "Oh, look out, it's the wife," I say, ensuring Viper can hear.

He scoffs. "Oh fuck off!"

"It's true," I say smugly, then glance at Elena's profile picture again. Dayum, she's hot. She's much too innocent for me, but I don't give a shit. "Check it out yourself then."

Viper steps over to me and snatches my phone. I see him swiping and going through the messages.

He laughs. "You sound like an absolute pussy. Though I guess that's the point." He keeps swiping. "Jesus, you have been talking a lot. Did you ask her how church was?"

"Yeah, I did actually . . ."

His eyes flash wide. "You didn't?"

I chuckle. "No, but I told her I liked her necklace. I told you Viper—you're losing our bet."

"We'll see," he says. "Are we still organizing the party here?"

I nod sharply. "We sure are."

"What did the messages say?" Cash asks as he steps toward us. The whole MC knows of my bet with Viper. I've been bragging about my charm to anyone who will listen. Viper's going to lose. I'm going to make sure of it.

"She just moved here," Viper answers. "She works at a restaurant and enjoys reading." Viper's smile is huge. "She might be able to teach you."

"Really funny, aren't you?" I say sarcastically to the prick.

"Yep," he says. "She's into happily ever afters . . . you're going to break her virgin heart."

Virgin? Shiiit. I don't know whether it would be a good thing or a bad thing . . . not that I've asked yet. A weird sensation flickers through my chest. Perhaps it's guilt, but it leaves as quickly as it came.

Viper carries on reading, then peers back at Cash. "Axle makes a lame joke about him only reading motorcycle magazines. The nun has a sister blah blah blah. Just basic shit." Viper passes me back my phone. "The messages mean nothing."

"It's only been a few days," I tease. She's eating up all the attention I throw at her. This is surely going to be a breeze.

"Until she finds out you're a biker," he mocks.

I raise my brow. "That could be my way in. Good girls love bad boys."

Elena

WE HAVEN'T STOPPED MESSAGING. AS SOON AS I FINISH WORK, I'm back on my phone. He's addicting and charming. I smile stupidly at the screen.

Axle

> Where do you work, so I can come and say hi?

I rub my arm. Messaging and meeting up are two very different things.

> I hardly know you.

> Well, then you can get to know me 😊

> I want to see your pretty face and I'm dying to see your smile.

I blush. If this is how I'm behaving over messages, I could only imagine how hard it would be if I met him. He's a lot, but I can't stop myself from messaging back.

> Where do you work, then?

I'll tell you when you tell me.

I shake my head.

> You're cheeky!

You have no idea. 😊 At least give me your phone number, so I don't have to message you on this app. C'mon, I want to hear your voice.

I snicker as I stroll from my car toward work. I swiftly reply.

> You give me yours first and I'll decide if I want to talk to you. I've got work. Talk to you later.

I put my phone away.

"Hey," Mel says as she falls into step with me.

"Hey," I reply cheerfully.

She tilts her head and points at me, her mouth gaping open. "You've been talking to Axle, haven't you?" She doesn't allow me to reply. "Tell me all about it! I want details!"

I can't help but smile back. "He's really nice, very charming."

She scrunches her nose. "What did you just say? Did you say he's nice?"

I inch back, surprised at her reaction. "Yes, he is. He wants to meet me, but I've just started talking to him." I can't stop the thought of my parents' disapproval if they knew I was considering meeting up with a stranger.

Her eyes dart away before she glances back at me. "Did you want me to meet up with him first to, you know"—she smiles—"check he's decent."

I give her an odd look. "I thought you have met him?"

She shakes her head. "Only seen him and heard about him from others."

"Um, no, thank you. I haven't decided what I'm going to do yet."

We walk inside the restaurant, put our bags away, and put on our aprons. Cameron walks toward us, his eyes sparkling. "Good to see you, ladies."

I give him a tight smile and squirm under his gaze as his eyes run up and down our bodies.

Mel steps to him and kisses his cheek. "Hey," she says in a flirty tone, but his eyes stay on me.

"Hello," I reply to Cameron. I need the money, and apart from his wandering eyes, he's a kind boss and he gave me an opportunity to leave my hometown. He could be a lot worse, and I've made a friend in Mel.

"How's it living at home with Lucy and the gang?" he asks with a smirk and a raised brow.

"They're out a lot at college during the day and partying at night, so we haven't crossed paths often, considering I'm working."

He chuckles. "They sure love to party. Study hard, play hard. You should come to one of the parties. It'll be fun."

I draw back. "I'm not a big party person." Or a big socializing person. My kind of big night is staying up late to finish a book.

His eyes flash and his smile widens. "Well, we'll just have to bring the party to you. I'll get the girls to organize a party at your house."

Oh fantastic! I force a smile, but deep down I'm dreading it. At least at someone else's party I can leave when I want to. If it's at our house, I'll have to lock myself inside my room. "Oh, you don't have to worry about throwing a party for me."

When he leaves to go talk to the other waitresses, Mel leans in close to me. "I told you. He's got his eyes on you."

I put that uncomfortable thought to the back of my mind.

She laughs. "He's flirty and sometimes can get a little handsy, but just think of the money."

My head whips to her, my eyes bulging. "Handsy?" I squeak.

She brushes me off with a wave. "Don't stress. It's only minor touches; like, he doesn't grab my ass or tits or anything. Just sly feels—like, he brushes against me, stands too close and touches my hip and stuff. Nothing you can't handle. Trust me, I've had worse."

My breathing and heartbeat have accelerated. I've got to find a way to be polite to Cameron while ensuring I don't flirt back to provoke him and I'm firm if he does touch me. I can't lose this job. I don't want to go back home. I'm learning and getting a bit more confident in the position each day.

I work hard during my shift, and when I finish and am walking out the door, I pull out my phone and see Axle's number in the dating app messages. I'm in two minds about it. What if he ends up being a stalker or some guy who won't leave me alone? Then he has my number. I guess I could block it.

I wish I had my sister, Ava, or someone apart from Mel to talk to. I want to talk to Ava so bad . . . but I'm not sure if she'd even answer my call. We used to be so close, but everything changed when she met her husband. I need someone to talk some sense into me because I'm clearly not in my right mind.

When I arrive at home, I dash up the stairs. I shower and then lie on my bed. The reason I moved here was because I needed a change. My life never moved forward in my old town. My heart surges as I try to decide whether to call Axle.

I heave a sigh. *Just do it!* I give in to my intrusive thoughts, pick up my phone, and dial the number.

"Hello," a husky voice answers. There's loud music in the background, and I freeze. My mouth opens, but nothing comes out. It gets quiet. "Hello . . . Elena?"

"Hi."

He chuckles. "About time you called," he says playfully.

I can't help but smile. "I was at work." Did he miss talking to me? I shake my head. Don't be ridiculous.

"Hold on a sec, I need to go to my room." It makes me wonder where he lives and if he's living in shared accommodation like me.

There's a shuffling sound of movement, then a bang, as if a door was slammed closed. The music quietens. "Are we going on a date tomorrow?" he asks boldly.

I choke on nothing. "A date?"

"Yeah . . . a date . . . with me. Come on, I know you want to," he purrs.

He's a massive flirt. I'm in way over my head.

"Does your silence mean yes?"

I chuckle nervously. "I've only just started talking to you. I can't meet you yet."

"Why? We're friends, remember? Friends spend time together." He pauses. "Are you too good for me? That's not very nice, you know."

I huff. "I am not too good for anyone." Damn it, a wave of guilt washes over me. "I'm a nice person."

"Prove it!"

Still uncertain, I say, "I'll think about it." It's a big risk on my part.

"I'll take that as a yes," he's quick to respond.

I gape. "I never—"

"See you tomorrow, Elena," he cuts in, his tone seductive. He hangs up and I'm left staring at my phone. He must be joking . . . He doesn't know where I work.

I put my phone down. Surely, he won't find me. I pick up my reading glasses and book and open it at the bookmark. I try not to think of Axle, but my thoughts keep drifting back to him.

SIX

SURPRISE!

Elena

MY PHONE CHIMES, WAKING ME UP. I GROGGILY BRING IT TO MY face and see a message from Axle.

Axle

> Hey Babe, I hope you had a great sleep. I'm excited to see you today 🌝

I shift and sit up.

> Morning. I think you have me confused with another woman.

> I'm not talking to anyone else. Are you talking to another guy?

My cheeks flush slightly, and a soft smile tugs at the corners of my lips.

> No, I'm not.

I've been ignoring the requests on the dating app, and I haven't talked to anyone else apart from the people I live and work with.

> Great! What time are we meeting? When's your lunch break?

He's persistent.

> How do you know I'm even working?

> You always seem to be working.

> I need to get to know you more before I meet you.

Even though I'm curious, I'm not ready . . . my shy self may never be ready. I go back to the dating app again and tap on his profile. Short, thick brown hair, trimmed beard, full lips . . . and that jaw. He's so handsome. In his photo he's wearing a leather jacket.

After changing into my workout clothes, I pull out my yoga mat, unroll it, and begin breathing work and stretches. Then I select the yoga app on my phone and begin following the directions of the voice on the app. I should take the time before and between my shifts to explore the town. I make a mental note to start tomorrow. I need to get out of my comfort zone, even though just the thought of it makes me queasy.

When I finish doing yoga, I shower and head downstairs for breakfast. It sounds quiet again. I guess they're sleeping off their hangovers. I woke up at three to loud voices. Everyone sounded drunk, and they mentioned the word *party*, so I assume they had just gotten home from one.

Downstairs the girls are sitting on the couches. They're in

their pajamas, huddled under blankets, their hair ruffled. I try not to laugh at them. "Big night?"

Lucy nods at me slowly. "My head hurts."

"At least you weren't up vomiting," says Lia, who appears to be a pretty shade of white.

"You should come with us next time," says Cindy.

Jasmine laughs. "She won't go to a party." Jasmine is correct.

"I seem to work the evening shifts anyway." Not that I would. So many people drunk together in a small space . . . *no thank you*. I gaze at them. They look sick, and I'd prefer not to waste a whole day being hungover.

"We'll make Cameron give you a night off," Lia replies. "How's it working with him?"

I pause. "He's friendly." I'm a little uneasy with him, but he could just be overly flirty, and that's just the way he is, while I'm socially awkward, anxious, and overthinking everything. I smooth my skirt. "I'd better get going to work. I'll see you girls later." With a round of byes, I'm out the door and off to work.

I reverse park outside. You'd think that after parking the same way every day I'd get better at it. I absolutely am not. Inside the restaurant Mel and Cameron are talking by the counter toward the back. She's straightening his shirt. He shifts his gaze from Mel to me and his face lights up. It's only me. I have no idea why he seems to get excited.

"My girl Elena," he says with a bright smile.

My shoulders stiffen at the comment. I smile at both of them, say hello, and slip through the kitchen doors. As I'm putting my bag away and getting ready for my shift, I turn to find Cameron standing behind me. I jerk back.

He grasps my upper arms. "I didn't mean to startle you."

"That's okay," I reply, though my heart thuds in my chest.

"I got a message from Lia this morning. Am I working you too hard?"

My face falls. She messaged him. "Oh no," I stumble over my words. "They said I should go to a party with them," I rush out. "I told them I work at night, but I didn't say you worked me too hard." It was my excuse to stop everyone from asking me. I didn't know it would backfire.

He laughs. "I'm joking. I'll give you this Friday off. You can come with us. The parties here are fun. You're missing out."

Dread fills me. I don't like parties, and it doesn't sit well with me. He's giving me the night off only so that I can spend it with him and his friends. I glance away and fix my ponytail. "Maybe," I say offhandedly.

When Cameron walks away, Mel comes over. "Did Cameron say you're not working Friday?" she asks quietly.

"He did."

"I love my weekends off. You can work mine if you want."

I'm looking forward to my day off. She must notice my expression because she says, "Don't worry about it."

"No, no, I'll do it." It's an excuse for not going to the party, I guess.

She smiles. "Awesome. Thanks. You don't want to go to a party with them anyway. All they do is get drunk and hook up."

That's why I don't want to go. "Can you show me around town after our shift?" If someone else shows me, then I shouldn't get lost. I'm hopeless with directions.

"I'm busy . . . Maybe another time?"

Disappointment hits me, but I smile anyway. "Yeah, perhaps next time." I really have to meet more people.

The lunch rush is busy. I haven't stopped. Fortunately, no glasses were shattered. I'm wiping a table when I hear the front door open. The room goes quiet.

"Oh. My. God!" Mel says in a high-pitched voice. Before I have time to look up, she rushes to my side, grabs my shoulder, and gives it a shake. "It's him!"

I frown. "Him who?"

"It's Axle!"

Suddenly, I can't breathe. I freeze as all the air is sucked out of my lungs in one big breath. *How did he find me?* I briefly gather courage before stealing a glance at him. He saunters in, surveys the restaurant. His face is passive until his eyes find me. A broad grin spreads across his face. With a confident stride, he approaches. My heart pounds with such force that it might crack a rib.

Axle checks me out with no subtlety whatsoever. He's wearing dark jeans, a fitted white shirt, and a vest. This is the part where I should run, but my limbs are frozen solid and my feet are bolted to the floor. Anxiety courses through my veins.

Axle stands right before me. I swallow hard and stare up at his big hazel eyes and crooked smile. I'm so small compared to him.

"Don't I get a hug?" he asks cheekily, with a raised brow. "We're good friends after all."

I'm trying to smile, but I think it might look more like a grimace. *He's flirting. Eek!*

He steps closer and leans in, and the scent of pine and cedar washes over me. His hot breath makes goosebumps travel up my arms. "You have no reason to fear me. I don't bite . . ." He pauses. "Well, I do, but only if you want me to."

A shiver rolls through me and my jaw drops, hitting the floor with a thump because . . . he did not just say that. "How did you find me?" I squeak, finally finding my words.

He chuckles. "It wasn't difficult."

"I'm Mel," a seductive voice comes from beside me.

I forgot she was standing there. As I look out over the

restaurant, I realize that all eyes are on us, and my cheeks redden.

"Axle," he says to her with a chin lift.

I've never seen Mel smile so wide.

"I was hoping to order," he says before he glances back at me.

"We have a seat available right by the window. The best view in the restaurant," Mel's quick to respond.

"He's not staying." The words seem to fall from my mouth. I flinch. I didn't mean to say that aloud. He's caught me off guard, and I'm a blabbering mess.

He raises his brow, his smile wide. "I want to spend some time at the place you work to convince you to go out on a date with me. So, yes, I am eating in."

I shake my head and lower my voice. "No, you're not. I'm working."

"Is everything okay over here?" Cameron asks quietly. He stands to the side, alternating between looking at Axle and the floor. He seems scared of Axle. Should I be too?

"He's leaving," I say at the same time Axle says, "I'm ordering."

"This way," Mel says and ushers him toward a table. I shake my head at her. Why isn't she listening to me?

Axle says, "I want *Elena* as my waitress."

"Of course," Mel answers and makes her way over to me.

"I heard him," I say before she repeats what he said.

He's just like any other customer. I slowly walk over to him and put on my best customer service smile and play the part. "Are you ready to order?" I keep my tone professional.

His eyes scan me. "I would like to order," he purrs, "but I don't think what I want is on the menu."

I stare at him with bulging eyes. My face burns furiously. Oh my goodness! The confidence and cocky attitude are unlike anything I've ever had to deal with before.

He fights a smile, but his eyes are dancing with mischief. He's enjoying the effect he has on me. I have no idea what I expected, but he is tenfold the personality and I'm struggling to cope. Hell, I can barely talk. I just stare at him like an idiot.

"What do you recommend?" he asks as he glances down at the menu.

"The seafood marinara is good." But I should have answered with, "The food tastes horrible. You should leave because I'm shocked and embarrassed that you found me, and the whole restaurant is staring at us, and my boss is watching our every move." I momentarily close my eyes. I hope I don't get in trouble from my boss for Axle coming here.

Axle bops his head. "I'll have that then."

"Would you like something to drink?"

"A cola, thank you, *Elena.*"

I give him a tight nod and bolt through the restaurant and to the kitchen, where I give the chefs the order and take deep breaths.

"You are so lucky!" Mel says loudly.

"Shhh!" I say, not wanting the whole restaurant to hear.

"You lied to me. I thought you weren't meeting him."

"I didn't lie. I don't know how he found me. All I mentioned was that I worked at a restaurant, nothing more."

Cameron walks toward us with narrowed eyes. "What's a War Brothers Motorcycle Club member doing in my restaurant?"

"What are you talking about?" I ask. "I didn't see one."

Mel laughs. "You didn't see Axle's club vest?"

The vest. I cover my face with my hands. He's in a motorcycle club. The situation just went from bad to worse. My next thought is that he doesn't look like a scary biker. He's all charm and crooked smiles.

I drop my hands and give Mel a pointed stare. "Why didn't you tell me?" She had to have known.

She giggles. My lips press into a thin line. I'm seeing nothing funny about this.

"Do you know him?" Cameron asks accusingly.

I flinch. "I don't *know him* know him." I'm pretty sure that didn't make sense, but I'm going with it.

Cameron's lip curls. "Are you dating him?"

"No," I'm quick to answer.

He nods sharply at me. "Good. He's nothing but trouble. I don't want him in my restaurant again. He'll scare away our customers!"

Mel rubs Cameron's back. "It's okay. He's by himself, just having lunch."

"I don't want criminals in my restaurant," he says, then turns to me. "You should be more careful who you make friends with in this town."

When Cameron leaves, I'm left wondering why he seems to dislike Axle so much. "Is he a criminal?" I ask Mel.

She shrugs. "Not that I know of." Not quite the answer I was after. "He's a good type of trouble," she says, and winks. "And you need to take one for the team."

I stare at her confused. "Huh . . . what team?"

She points at each of us in turn. "We're a team. You're friends with Axle, so you can introduce me to all the members of the club. I've wanted to for years."

She's rushing things. I've only just started talking to Axle, and I literally just met him, but yes, he certainly is trouble.

I roll my shoulders back, gather myself, go to the bar, and pour him a cola. I sneak a quick glance. Yep, he's still staring at me. I gaze at him, shake my head, and deliver his drink. As I hand it to him, our fingers briefly touch, making me inhale sharply. Judging by the delight in his eyes, it was intentional.

He takes a sip, and then asks, "When does your shift finish?"

Him asking to see me outside of work makes my pulse quicken. "Why do you ask?"

"Why are you so defensive? I thought we were friends."

Is that what we are? "You turned up at my work."

"I told you I'd see you today," he teases.

"I thought you were joking!"

He tuts. "You shouldn't have assumed. Oh, I get it."

I study him, puzzled. "Get what?"

"You realized I'm a biker, and now you want nothing to do with me."

My lips press into a thin line. I know nothing about bikers. The unknown is what makes me feel uneasy.

"Who told you? Was it the boss who wants to bang you or the chick who wants to bang me?"

I look around. "Shhh! Keep your voice down." What he said irks me. "My boss does not want to bang me," I whisper-yell.

Axle cackles. "Trust me, he does."

I just shake my head. He's impossible.

Mel arrives at the table. "Here you go, your seafood marinara." She puts his plate in front of him, giving him a wink before she goes. She seems keen on him and the MC.

Axle digs his fork into the noodles. "I told you she wants to bang me," he says with a smirk before taking a bite.

I think he's right, which makes me wonder why Mel told me to talk to him. "She was the one who created the dating account. I wouldn't have talked to you if it wasn't for her."

With a thoughtful look, he asks, "Really? Are you free tomorrow?"

"I'm working," I say.

"What about after work?"

I bite my lip. "I'm busy."

"Yeah, you'll be busy."

I watch him curiously while he lounges in his chair.

"You'll be busy going on a date with me."

A laugh breaks out from my lips. "And if I say no?"

He shrugs. "I'll turn up here every day until you say yes." He peers over my shoulder. "Your boss isn't going to like that." He chuckles. "Though pissing him off every day will be amusing."

I know Axle will keep returning. "I don't think you're welcome back here at the restaurant."

His hazel eyes flash with amusement. "He'll never say it to my face."

I glance back at my boss, who abruptly looks away and walks back into the kitchen. I think Axle's right.

"I'll come get you. Tomorrow, before you start your lunch shift, then. Let's say nine?"

I shake my head, the collar of my shirt suddenly feeling too tight around my neck.

His eyes light up at the challenge. He leans in closer to me and looks into my eyes as he says, "Well, you better book me this table for tomorrow."

I don't have any other options. He'll keep turning up at my work. Emotions battle inside of me—excitement, anxiety, and curiosity. It's only in the morning. "I'll think about it. Now I'd better get back to work. I can't lose my job. I only just started here."

While I continue to collect plates and cutlery from other tables, I steal a brief glimpse back at him. He's still staring at me as I head into the kitchen.

After I set the plates near the sink, Mel is beside me once more. "What have you two been talking about?"

I don't have anyone else I can talk to about this. "He asked me out on a date."

She inches back. "Axle doesn't date." Her tone suggests she doesn't believe me.

"He said a date. I'm just repeating what he said."

She pouts. "Maybe he just meant spending time together."

I shrug. "Probably."

"Did you say you were going to have sex with him?"

"No!" I shriek, offended. Does she honestly believe I would pimp myself out to spend time with a guy?

She rests her hand on her hip and glances away, lost in thought. I step around her, only to be met with Cameron.

"How long's he staying for?" Cameron asks sternly.

I blink at him. What is everyone's problem? "I don't know. I gather until he's finished his meal."

"He's finished his meal, and he's asked for *his* waitress."

I wipe my hands on my apron. "I'll go see him now." Then I step around Cameron, feeling both his and Mel's narrowed eyes on me as I leave the kitchen. I know I'm new to the town, but their reactions have me wondering why they have such intense reactions to Axle.

"Are you finished?" I ask. Axle's plate is empty—spotless, in fact. Did he lick the bowl clean?

He slowly nods. "I am."

"The restaurant closes in the next thirty minutes." As in hint hint, nudge nudge, please don't get me into trouble with my boss.

"I'm staying until *you* finish."

I stare at Axle. He chuckles. "And when you start work tomorrow, I'll be here for lunch." He peers behind me. "And dinner." He inches forward, closer to me. "Every day, until you go on a date with me."

I close my eyes. I need this job. When I open them, he looks smug, like he knows he'll follow through. Any girl in my position would have already accepted.

"One date," I warn, though excitement shoots through me.

He rises to his full height, and I have to take a step back because he's so close and much taller than me. The combination of cologne and leather is divine. I peer up. He cups my chin with one hand, making me take a deep breath. "See you tomorrow, *Elena*."

My knees nearly buckle at his sexy, deep tone.

As he's walking out, I realize I can't have some stranger come to my house, especially one who's in a motorcycle club. "I'll meet you here at work," I yell out in a rush of words.

He pauses and looks over his shoulder, the smug smile back in full force. "I'll pick you up from *your* home."

"No, I'll meet you here," I object.

"I'm picking you up from your home, end of discussion."

I open my mouth to argue.

"Uh," he says, "I know where you live."

I blink in disbelief. "How can you possibly know that?" He just met me, and I've just moved here. It's not like I have friends he could have asked.

"I have my connections," he says with a wink. He swaggers aways while I stand still, dumbfounded.

A shiver rolls through my body. What just happened? How did I end up getting conned into going on a date?

"What happened?" Mel asks.

"I'm *apparently* going out on a date with him."

"You sure he said the word *date*?"

Annoyance bubbles up. "You know, you're really not helping my already low self-esteem." I take Axle's plate and walk to the kitchen, Mel following close behind.

"Sorry, the Axle I've heard about is different from the one I've seen today." She places her hand on my arm. "Good for you, getting out there and meeting new people."

I flash her a faint smile, even though I'm terrified about tomorrow.

After our shift, we step out of the restaurant and go our

separate ways. "Good luck for tomorrow," Mel calls out over her shoulder.

I'll need it!

I drive the short distance home and park outside. When I get into my room, I call my parents, needing to hear a familiar voice.

"Hello," my mother answers.

"Hey, Mom."

"Oh, so you haven't forgotten about us?"

They could have called me to check how I was, but I dismiss it. "I thought you'd like to know I've settled in well. The people I live with are—"

"I still can't believe you live with random people. I bet they're doing drugs and drinking, and God knows what else. Are *you* drinking?"

It's not like I could afford to rent a house here by myself. Sharing a house was my only option. "No, they aren't doing drugs." Well, not that I know of. "And no, I haven't been drinking. I've just been working."

"You know you act like who you hang around, so I hope you're making responsible decisions with people you meet there."

I flinch. I've always been one to believe in the good in the world. I strive to be a positive person and be kind to people who are good to me. "Everyone's been nice to me. I'm getting more comfortable in my job too. I get a view of the beach every time I'm at work."

"Oh, Elena, it's waitressing. It's not hard."

Heaviness weighs on me. There's no need to be nasty. "I'm going to bed; I've had a big day. Say hi to Dad for me."

After I finish the call, I grab a grilled cheese sandwich. I'm left wondering what we'll do tomorrow. Where will Axle take me? Nine in the morning is early, so it can't be too bad . . . Well, I hope so, for my sake.

SEVEN
TAKING A CHANCE

Elena

My mouth is dry . . . Sahara Desert dry. I'm outside on the front porch, pacing. I run my hands over my jeans, up, down, up, down. It's only a date . . . but did Axle mean it's a date like let's hang out or a *date* date? Imagine if my parents or anyone at home discovered I was going on a date with a biker. This is borderline insane. I should just message him to cancel.

"Uh . . . are you okay?"

The voice makes me jump. Lucy and Cindy are at the door with their bags over their shoulders. "I'm okay," I say with fake confidence.

"You sure?" Lucy asks with a raised brow. "It doesn't seem like it."

"Hmmm . . ." Because I'm not okay—I'm low-key terrified. "It's early for you two, isn't it?" They usually sleep the day away.

"We have assignments coming up," Lucy answers. "The

library is quiet, but the real question is, what are you doing?" Suspicion lines her voice.

The thunderous roar of a motorcycle gets louder. My heart thumps harder the closer it gets. Both girls are staring down our street. I turn to see Axle pulling up in front of our house. I used to think that men on motorcycles were scary, but Axle has changed my mind. His personality is anything but scary.

Axle turns his bike off and swings his leg over it. When he gazes at me, there's a wicked smile on his face. I'm getting the impression that it's his signature grin. The girls gasp behind me, and I don't blame them. He is all man and a far cry from my ex-boyfriend and Lucy's boyfriend.

I take hesitant steps toward him as he strides toward me.

"Elena," he says with outstretched arms.

I'm conflicted, both scared and fascinated by him. He must see my apprehension, because he says, "Don't look at me with those eyes."

I shake my head. "Like what?"

"Like I'm some sort of serial killer luring you onto my bike."

That makes me smile.

He grins. "Much better."

I like how he puts me at ease.

"Have you had breakfast, babe?"

I enjoy being called babe a little too much for my liking. "No, I haven't," I reply shyly. It's not like I could eat, knowing I was spending time with him.

"There's a good café in town you'll like. Have you been on a motorcycle before?"

My eyes widen. Why didn't I realize I would be riding with him on his bike?

"I'll take that as a no," he replies, filling the silence for me. He wraps an arm around my shoulders. I tense up a bit, despite the soothing warmth and the enticing scent of his cologne.

"You'll love it," he says as we walk to his motorcycle. It's black and chrome, and it looks fast.

"What if I fall off?" This is me, the clumsiest person on earth. I step out of his hold. He frowns. "This isn't a good idea," I mumble.

"Scared of enjoying yourself, huh?"

The amusement in his voice irritates me, and I narrow my eyes at him. "No," I clip out defensively.

He straddles his bike. "Well . . . get on then," he says, passing me the helmet.

"Okay," I reply, but my breathing is chaotic and I'm silently freaking out. I slip the helmet on and do up the straps under my chin. I peer around his bike. "Where's your helmet?"

"You're wearing it."

I start to unbuckle the helmet. "You can have it back."

"Elena, keep the damn helmet on. You're precious cargo. Now stop making excuses and get on my bike."

"Bossy," I murmur under my breath, though guilt about his safety makes my stomach roll. I fumble onto the bike behind him.

He turns his head. "You're going to have to *actually* touch me. Put your arms around me, hold on to me tight. Keep your legs away from the exhaust and lean when I do."

Simple instructions . . . I'm sure I'll mess it up somehow. The engine roars to life, startling me as I shift slightly in my seat. "You have nothing to worry about," he shouts over the engine. Easy for him to say. I'm the one risking my life on a death trap with a stranger I've just met. Oh, times have changed.

I inhale deeply, allowing the air to calm my nerves. I firmly wrap my arms around him, and I can feel the defined muscles of his abs through his shirt. When I press my cheek against his back, a sense of warmth flows through me at being so close to him.

I catch a glimpse of my roommates, who are staring at me with bulging eyes, their mouths agape. This whole situation is a shock to me too. I glance at the sky, uttering a prayer to protect me and keep me safe on this death trap.

We accelerate and I let out a squeal. He doesn't go fast, moving with the traffic at a safe speed, which I'm grateful for. We drive down the main street by the beach, where people are walking and exercising on the sidewalks and others are on the beach. We pass my work, and he slows down, pulling off to the side to park.

I swing my leg over the bike and wait for him to get off to pass him the helmet.

"See," he says cheekily, "you didn't die."

It was only a short ride. My legs still feel unsteady. Much to my surprise, it wasn't as awful as I had imagined.

The small café has a checkered black-and-white floor and posters of Elvis Presley and Marilyn Monroe on the walls. We wait in line, and as we approach the counter, I notice the cashier pull her shoulders back, push her boobs out, bat her eyelashes, and give Axle a flirty grin.

"Hey, Axle," she coos.

He grins. "Morning." He turns to me. "What would you like?"

I peer up at the menu, which is on the wall. I open my mouth to ask what's good here, but as my eyes land on the server, she's looking at me with a pinched mouth. I peer back at Axle. "Pancakes, please."

He nods. "What flavor?"

"Buttermilk with honey."

He nods again, then peers back at the server. "Buttermilk pancakes with honey, and I'll have the big breakfast."

"Sure, and drinks?"

"Coffee and"—he peers at me—"a cappuccino please."

He steps closer to the register as she reads out the price, pays, and then leads me outside to a two-seater table, where we take a seat. I lift my bag to my lap and pull out my wallet. "Here," I say as I unzip it. "How much do I owe you?"

He waves me off. "Put it away. You'll never pay when you're with me."

I follow his instructions, then put my bag down. It's nice of him to pay.

"I want to get to know you," he says.

I clasp and unclasp my hands. "Why?"

He gives me a funny look. "What do you mean, why?"

"Out of all the girls on the website, why did you want to meet me?" I'm pretty sure he could have had any woman on the website, and it's clear from my brief interactions with him that women love him.

He gives me a thorough once-over. "Because you're fucking hot." Heat rises from my chest, up to my neck, and to my face. "And you seemed like a cool person to get to know."

I snort, then cough. *Real smooth* . . . "No one has ever called me cool."

"Who cares what anyone else says or thinks."

He has a point. It sucks that I care.

"My question is," he says, "why did you move here?"

"I wanted freedom, I guess you could say. I wanted a chance to experience what life has to offer outside of my hometown . . . It's my turn." So many questions run through my brain. I peer at his leather vest, which has a 1% and a War Brothers MC patch on it. "How did you become a member of a motorcycle club?"

"Most of my brothers, who are club members, were in the military. Me and Cash served together. When we got back from the war, we struggled to fit in."

It pains me to see the deep frown on his face as he pauses and looks away.

"We heard of a few veterans who were starting a motorcycle club, so we came to Crown Village to check it out. That's where we met Reaper, Bomber, and Viper. We all just clicked, so me and Cash never left. Then a few more members joined, and now there's seven of us."

A surge of shock courses through me. He's so much more than I thought.

He grins mischievously. "What do you do for fun?"

I pause, trying to find my words. I'm boring as hell.

"You know what fun is, right?"

My eyes narrow at the amusement in his voice. I lift my chin. "Yes."

He leans back lazily. "Then what do you do?"

"I read—"

He bursts out laughing.

"And I enjoy yoga," I add, making him laugh louder.

He slaps his thigh. "Aw, babe, you're so innocent. Don't you go to church too?"

I pout. "I used to. How do you know that?"

He leans over and touches my neck. I suck in a deep breath. I peek down as he pulls my necklace out and lies it on top of my shirt. My parents gave me the gold necklace with a cross pendant on my fourteenth birthday.

"Just a guess," he comments with a smirk, and then he leans back in his chair. That cheeky smile is addictive.

The server comes over and places our plates of food in front of us. My pancakes look delicious, with a swirl of cream on top and strawberries on the side. But as I inspect the pancakes further, I notice a pink tinge, which makes me think they're strawberry rather than buttermilk and honey.

"Here's my number," the server says seductively, "in case you lost it. You didn't call me back."

Axle's eyes narrow. "You can see I'm having breakfast with Elena. And anyway, if I didn't call you, it was on purpose." He waves her off.

The server and I flinch at the same time. I'm feeling secondhand embarrassment.

"Fucking rude bitch," he says under his breath as he watches her leave. Then he looks back at me. "What's wrong?" he asks, staring at my plate of food before looking back at me.

"Nothing."

"No, there's a problem with your food. I saw it all over your face before that chick started carrying on."

"I ordered buttermilk pancakes," I say softly. I hate making a fuss. "I think this might be strawberry."

He leans over and takes my plate, but I grasp the other side of it. "Don't worry, it's fine," I whisper, not wanting to make a scene.

His nose crinkles. "No, it's not okay."

His unwavering gaze makes me let go of the plate. He's not the type to give in. I shrink in my chair with my head bowed as he goes back inside the café. I sit up when I hear his heavy footsteps return.

"You weren't going to say anything, were you?" he asks. "You were just going to eat them, knowing it wasn't what you ordered."

I grudgingly nod. People pleaser . . . that's me.

He shakes his head. "Don't be shy. If there's a problem, say it. Don't let people walk over you."

I offer him a small smile, appreciating that he stuck up for me. I already know it's something I need to work on. Being constantly criticized by my mother has left its scars.

"You want some of my food while you're waiting?" he asks. His enormous plate of food includes ham, sausages, eggs, bacon, a hash brown, and toast.

"No, thank you."

He picks up a piece of the crispy bacon and takes a bite. "Good, I'm not one to share."

This man has no filter, but he's a giant goofball. "Are you really going to eat all that?" I ask in disbelief.

His smile answers my question. "You bet I am."

"Your profile said you're a mechanic. Where do you work?"

"I'm the road captain of the War Brothers MC and I service, fix, and modify our motorcycles. I'm not a qualified mechanic, though, so I just do it for our club."

"What's a road captain?"

"I plan our rides, ensure our safety, service our bikes. That type of thing."

I tilt my head. "And you get paid to do that?"

After taking a huge bite of egg on toast, he replies, "Sure do."

Wow . . . he's pretty lucky. "What do you mean, you're not a qualified mechanic?"

"Ah-ah-*ah*," he says, wagging his index finger from side to side. "My turn to ask a question."

A sliver of annoyance flows through me. I'm greedy for more information. He's intriguing. I've never known anyone like him.

"Why'd you talk to me? Am I just a one-night stand to brag to your friends about?"

"No!" I shriek, utterly insulted. "Mel created the profile."

He snorts. "It's okay. You don't have to lie. I know you think I'm sexy."

I open, close, then open my mouth. I'm lost for words, and I blush. He's very good looking with that square jaw, piercing eyes, manly beard, and permanent devilish grin, but I'm not telling him that. His head is already too big for his shoulders.

"It's true," I say.

He chuckles. "Whatever helps you sleep at night," he coos.

I laugh, but then I remember what he said. "And I do *not* have one-night stands."

He adds a cheeky wink. "I'm just teasing."

After a moment of silence, I ask. "What did you mean you're not a *qualified* mechanic?"

"I'm just as skilled," Axle says confidently. "I was never good at school. I think I'm dyslexic or whatever it's called, so I suck at anything that has to do with reading or writing." He pauses and looks away. "The only reason I learned about fixing bikes was because I stole parts from an old man up the road from our trailer who owned a mechanic shop, and I sold them. When I did it again, he caught me and said he wouldn't call the cops if I paid him off by helping him in the garage, so I did. After the cleaning jobs, he saw I was interested in the bikes he was fixing, so he taught me things, and after that I helped him every day. I loved it."

His bright smile warms my chest. "Do you still spend time with him?" I ask.

His face falls, and I'm immediately filled with regret for asking such personal questions, but I want to get to know him.

"No, he's been dead for a while now."

I'm floored by his honesty, but grateful he shared it with me, nonetheless. "Did your parents care that you spent all your time there?"

"God, you're just going straight for the jugular with these questions." He snorts. "I could have been dead and my parents wouldn't have cared. Too busy getting high in the trailer we called a home."

I lean over and lay my hand on his. "I'm so sorry to hear that," I say sincerely. My heart aches for him. Something flashes across his face before he masks it with a smile, though there's still vulnerability in his eyes.

"I'm okay, babe. It was a long time ago, and I wouldn't change it for the world, otherwise I would have never met Victor, the owner of the garage, or built a life in the MC."

He's an open book, and I'm really liking that about him. He speaks his mind, and it's refreshing. "Thank you for sharing." I mean it. He looks like a badass biker, but he's more than that. Behind the vest are many layers of who he is as a person. I'm captivated by him. Even though I shouldn't be getting involved with him, I crave to know more.

My pancakes arrive and I smile at the server, whose head is bowed. She promptly turns on her heel and goes back inside.

Axle lifts his cup to his mouth and drinks. I watch his Adam's apple bob up and down. I have no idea how that's attractive, but it is.

He leans back. "Let me guess, you were a good girl and, being the book nerd that you are, you did well at school."

I cringe. "Maybe . . ." He's exactly right.

Axle chuckles. "Oh yeah. You're pretty much the opposite of me in every way."

I gnaw on my lip, not sure whether it's a bad thing or not.

After I eat my pancakes, we chat briefly before we get up. He wraps an arm around my shoulders, pulling me to his side, where I smell his cologne mixed with the leather of his vest, and I suppress a moan. Even though I'm startled for a second, I smile up at him. My heart is hammering, but his playful grin disarms me. Surprisingly, I feel a level of ease I never imagined I would experience with him.

We get on his bike, and I smile during the short ride home. Once home, I get off the bike and hand him the helmet, he grabs my arm and pulls me in close. He groans. "I don't kiss women, but I'm fighting the urge to kiss you right now."

My eyes go to his lips, craving a taste. "Well, don't," I whisper. Kissing him is my first instinct. I want to be soaked in his sin.

His eyes widen, then darken. My heart beats heavily. He grasps my necklace, pulls me to him, and captures my lips in a firm kiss. Sheer desire fuels me and I press my lips against his. Hard.

Time freezes. I'm leaning against him and his bike. My hands slip around his neck, my mouth parting. His tongue slides in and meets mine, holding me hypnotized. I whimper into his mouth. His arm tightens around me as my body heats up. With each movement of his tongue against mine, a rush of lust courses through my body, traveling from my veins to my groin. His kiss is demanding and authoritative. I'm at his mercy.

The long, lingering kiss makes my lips crave his as soon as he pulls away. I'm left panting, my head spinning.

His eyes are dark as his thumb caresses my bottom lip. "Looks like an angel, kisses like a demon."

My eyes latch onto his lips again. Axle is trouble, but I can't stop the way my body reacts to him.

I step backward and watch as he revs his engine, pulls out, and does a burnout, his tires leaving black skid marks. My eyes narrow. He shouldn't put himself in danger like that.

I touch my now-plump lips. There's cheering and clapping behind me. I turn my gaze toward the house and notice my roommates. I walk over to them.

"You never mentioned that you know Axle! That's so exciting!" Lucy exclaims, bouncing enthusiastically beside me.

I give her a small smile.

"All those motorcycle club men are hot," Cindy chimes in.

"So where did you meet him?" Jasmine asks, not sharing her friend's enthusiasm.

"Uh, the restaurant." I don't want them to know it was on a dating app.

I like the attention Axle is giving me. Getting attention is new to me, and while he's talking to me, I don't want to share him, regardless of whether they have boyfriends or not.

"Cameron would have hated that," Lia says with a laugh.

I think back and flinch. "Yes, he did. I'm going to go upstairs and relax before I start my shift."

I dart up the stairs, close my bedroom door, and lie on my bed, confused. Axle's a conundrum. A small part of me is still wary of him, but a much bigger part of me wants to learn more about him. He's friendly and warm. There's more to him than what a motorcycle club vest says. That he told me about parts of his life in such a vulnerable way has only increased my curiosity.

I don't know what came over me, but I wanted to kiss him, and as soon as our lips touched, I couldn't stop myself. I was drenched in his scent, his touch, his lips. A wave of euphoria unlike anything I had felt before surged through me. It was as if every cell in my body was buzzing, a sensation so intense that it left me breathless.

I wonder what he meant by not kissing women. He doesn't seem like one to lie, so I gather it's true, but it has me questioning why he kissed *me* then.

I wish I was close to my sister Ava again so that I can talk to her about it. She got married and I guess she got busy. She doesn't reply much anymore. I miss her so much, especially at times like this. While I don't generally hate people, I'm angry at her husband for taking her away from me.

At work I'm just going through the motions. My mind is elsewhere. I'm quiet when Mel asks about the date, even though she's persistent and asks me loads of questions. I keep it to a bare minimum and don't dare say anything about the kiss.

After my shift, I get into my car and pull my phone out of my bag. There's a message from Axle.

Axle

> Hey babe, I enjoyed spending the morning with you. Your kiss was the sweetest thing I've ever tasted. When can I see you again?

I gasp, panicking. What if I gave him the wrong idea? I hastily respond.

> I'm not having sex with you.

> Hahaha chill, babe. I want to spend time with you again.

I gaze up and peer at the ocean. I wanted to experience life . . . It's only another date. I refuse to look back and regret not taking a chance. It's not often I'm noticed by a good-looking man like him.

I take a deep breath and type.

> Okay, I'll see you after work. Pick me up from my house.

EIGHT
LOSING CONTROL

Elena

My roommates were quiet last night, but as I creep down the stairs, I hear them. Of all the days I was hoping to sneak out of the house without seeing anyone, they just happen to all be awake. The girls are at the kitchen counter, Jasmine with a coffee and Lucy and Cindy eating cereal out of bowls.

As I walk in further, I spot Jeremy. "Here she is," he says, and all eyes are on me. I swallow hard and smile.

As I walk to the coffee machine, Jeremy steps over toward me. "Axle from the motorcycle club, hey? I heard the War Brothers Motorcycle Club parties are epic. You'll have to invite us when you go."

"Oh yes," Cindy chimes in.

"Woah!" I say and lift my hand. "I've only just met Axle." Would I like to get to know him more? Possibly.

"Lucy said you were kissing him," Jasmine says, pouting.

My eyes flick straight to Lucy, but she looks away, avoiding eye contact.

"I'm just saying, we're all friends, so don't forget about us," Jeremy says.

"I can't believe you went on a date with him. Those bikers don't date. Are you seeing him again?" asks Jasmine.

I'm not a liar, but a part of me wants to lie to them. "I'm seeing him today, after work." Lucy and Cindy squeal in unison, making me flinch.

"I've never known any of them to go on dates. They only have sex," says Jasmine matter-of-factly. Lucy swats her arm.

The coffee machine beeps, signaling that my coffee is ready, but the conversation has put me off, so I grab the mug and empty the drink down the sink. I'm not sure whether Jasmine was suggesting that I was lying or that I was sleeping with him, so I say, "Well, I told Axle I'm not having sex with him, and he still wants to see me."

Lucy shakes her head. "Don't worry about Jasmine. She's jealous. I've heard Axle's a wild one, but have fun, and I want to hear all about it when you get back from your date."

Cindy sighs. "He's got heartbreak written all over him."

"If you think he wants anything more than a quick fuck, you're sorely mistaken."

I step back, puzzled by Jasmine's snappishness.

"Just let her have her fun," Lucy pipes up.

Jasmine rolls her eyes. "You're heading for disaster. Don't say I didn't warn you."

I give them a forced smile and hurry out. My breaths are shaky as I get in my car and pull the door closed. They've made me doubt myself, but it still doesn't make sense. Why would Axle waste his time when I've said I won't sleep with him if that's all he wants? He evidently has no issues getting women.

After my short drive to work, I walk into the restaurant to see Mel and Cameron at the counter. When they look up at me, Mel's eyes narrow and Cameron shakes his head. My stomach drops. What have I done wrong? I frantically think back to the last shift. I don't recall making any mistakes.

Despite the leisurely pace with which I approach them, my heart races. I need this job. I'll just apologize and tell Cameron that whatever I've done wrong, it won't happen again.

"You're a liar," Mel says bitterly.

I sharply inhale. "What did I lie about?"

"You said your date was uneventful. I didn't realize hooking up outside your house with Axle was uneventful for you. If he's so boring, I'll have him."

That's what they're annoyed about. I was stressed out, thinking I had done something wrong at work. I exhale slowly. She's testing me, even though I hate conflict. If she likes Axle so much, I can't understand why she told me to talk to him.

"I didn't feel it was necessary to share every detail about the date."

"I'm surprised you'd associate yourself with the likes of him." Disgust drips from Cameron's every word. "He's a criminal . . . the whole MC is bad news."

Mel scoffs. "You don't know that. What do they do to make them criminals?"

Cameron crosses his arms in front of him. "Everyone knows they are."

Mel gives him a pointed look. "You can't even answer the question. You don't know what the MC does."

When Cameron turns to me, his gaze softens. "I'm worried about you. I don't know why you'd put yourself in danger like that."

Mel puts her arm around my shoulders and walks me away from Cameron. "Just ignore Cameron. He's jealous that the MC members get more ass than him. If I thought Axle was dangerous, I'd tell you. It surprised me that you're going on dates with him because I didn't think he dated." I experience a slight sense of relief until she says, "The good girl falling for the bad boy. God help you!"

"I'm not falling for him."

She raises a brow. "Are you planning to see him again?"

I hesitate before I answer. "After work."

A slow smile curves across her lips. "You wouldn't see him again if you weren't interested."

BACK HOME AFTER MY SHIFT, I SIFT THROUGH MY WARDROBE WITH a growing sense of dread. I have no idea what to wear. He'll be here any minute. My hands tremble slightly as I pull on my favorite light-blue jeans and a pale pink T-shirt.

I've straightened my long blond hair, and I'm wearing lip balm and light makeup. With each step down the stairs, my nervousness intensifies. My hands feel clammy. He's probably used to being with confident, beautiful women, and I'm nothing like that. I peer down at what I'm wearing and wince. I hesitate and think about changing, but then I hear the familiar rumble of a motorcycle. This will have to do.

I bolt down the last few steps and outside, grateful that all my roommates are at college. As I walk out the door, Axle's pulling his helmet off. I quicken my pace, and his eyes meet mine. He smiles, making me smile right back. Excitement and nerves collide within me while I head toward his bike. I should take others' opinions lightly and decide for myself about him.

With his wicked trademark smile, he says, "Ready to go for a ride?"

"Sure," I answer as I glance down at his bike, remembering how fun the last ride was. But then I whack him.

He rubs his arm, exaggerating the pain. "What was that for?"

"The burnout you did. Don't do it—it's dangerous. You could have been hurt."

He stares at me a while before he says, "I've been doing tricks on bikes my whole life. I know what I'm doing."

I shake my head, then jut out my chin. "It's reckless and I don't like it."

He grants me a genuine smile. "I won't do it around you. How's that?"

"I'd prefer you not do it at all." Why risk the chance of getting hurt?

"Hmmm . . . bossy. I like it." He slips the helmet over my head and fastens the straps under my chin, then takes a step back as his eyes caress every inch of my body. "You're sexy as fuck, babe."

"Thank you," I murmur, my voice barely above a whisper. I felt underdressed before, but the hunger in his eyes makes me feel truly seen for the first time and strangely validated. "You look good too," falls from my mouth. *I'm so lame.*

He chuckles. "Yeah, I do." He's oh so modest.

I climb onto the bike and shuffle closer to him. I lace my arms wrap around his torso. His body feels lean and athletic. It stirs a curiosity in me about what he might look like shirtless, a thought that starts a small thrill fluttering in my stomach. The sensation is both exciting and frightening, and I'm acutely aware of the danger he represents—in more ways than one.

"Hold on tight," Axle says over the rumble of the bike. He pulls the motorcycle out onto the road.

The gust of air on my face and the road rushing beneath me have me smiling widely. With my cheek pressed against his back, I peer out as we pass by the beach and ride further along to the lake, where he parks in the closest parking spot.

When I get off the bike, my smile comes naturally. "That's so much fun!"

After he gets off the bike, I pass him the helmet, and he hangs it over one handlebar. "You're easy to please . . . No need to thank me."

He pulls me into him, his arm around my shoulders, and we walk across the grass to the sand. As we stroll along, I gaze up at him. "Are you trying to woo me, sweep me off my feet with a walk along the water?" I tease.

His lip twitches. "Is it working?"

I press my lips together, not wanting to sound too eager. Since I've met him, it's been a whirlwind of surprises. Walking along the lake was not what I expected we would be doing. Everyone was so wrong about him.

"I'll take that as a yes," he says, grinning smugly.

I don't argue the point. "What made you choose the lake?" I ask instead.

"I prefer not to be surrounded by civilians." He chuckles as he peers down at the sand. "Dating is new to me, so I didn't know where else to go."

"Next time, it would be great to just hang out at home. Watch a few movies or something."

"Next time?" he smirks. "Netflix and chill," he adds in an overly sexual voice. He chuckles. That sounds like so much more than just watching Netflix.

"Well, yes . . . just hanging out watching TV."

He grabs his chest like he's in pain. "Don't sound too enthusiastic. You're breaking my big biker heart," he teases.

I've come to learn it's just him. Everything is highly amusing, and he's got no filter. He says it in a way that's not sleazy, but everything's a joke to him. He's cheeky and quick-witted.

I playfully elbow him. "I'll hang out with you . . . but I'm not having sex with you," I say with my chin high in the air as I smother a smile.

"You're missing out," he quips. "I'll fucking ruin you for every other man."

My body heats and my cheeks burn. I rub my forehead. I need to snap out of it. I like the attention, but what sane, straight woman wouldn't like the attention of a sexy, fun biker with a killer smile?

"Where do you live?" I ask.

"At the clubhouse with the rest of my War Brothers MC brothers."

"Do you guys have parties there?" I ask, since everyone keeps talking about them.

His smile kicks up. "Yeah, we do."

I wonder what his friends are like. If they are anything like him, I think I'll like them too. "Will I get to meet your friends?"

He stops walking, so I pause. He's giving me a strange look. "Let me get this straight. You want to meet my friends . . . the bikers?"

I'm curious, but also a little scared. "I'm interested in learning more about you." He seems close to his friends.

He laughs and pulls me in tighter. "You're always surprising me."

That goes both ways. I remember all of them riding down the street, dressed up in black and leather, on their motorcycles. I frown. "What are they like? Will they hurt me?"

"What? Hell no. We don't hurt women."

"Do you all have orgies? I know you do illegal stuff, but how illegal? Do you kill people?" The word vomit is unstoppable.

He laughs. "Some people have sex with more than one person at once."

So that's a yes.

"And no, we just don't go around killing people." He didn't say he hadn't, though. "I can't tell you about what we do. It's club business. Being in our motorcycle club means we don't answer to anybody but ourselves when it comes to our brothers and our club."

"I've never experienced having friends who are like family. It must feel great to belong somewhere."

He picks me up, wraps my legs around his hips, and puts his hands on my ass. I squeal, then laugh in surprise.

"I think you're belonging somewhere right about now." His voice is raspy and seductive, but his eyes remain playful.

Stupidity and lust drive my arms around his neck, my hands snaking to the back of his head, into his hair, while I lean in and touch my lips to his. It starts off slow, but in true Axle fashion, it takes no time to become heated. My skin burns as our tongues duel and the passion intensifies. He squeezes my ass. I softly tug his hair, enticing a groan from his lips.

A phone rings faintly in the background, making him pause. "Fuck," he mumbles. He gently places me on my feet and brings his phone to his ear.

"Yeah," he answers. "Now?" He growls. "*Fine.* I'm on my way." He peers back at me. "Sorry, babe. I've got church."

I can't help but laugh. "You go to church? Really?"

"Not that type of church. It's where we hold club meetings."

My shoulders drop. Our date has been cut short. "Oh, okay."

He cups my jaw and searches my eyes. "Are you sure you want to meet my friends?"

Axle isn't as bad as people say. I'm sure his friends are the same, but I'd be silly not to feel some apprehension. I mutter, "Sure," trying to mask my uncertainty.

"You're going to see shit you're not going to like, and the

men cuss like me." He's giving me an out, but I still want to go.

"You and your friends can cuss in front of me. I'm not a saint."

He flashes me a sexy smile. "I know that. Take tomorrow's lunch shift off, and I'll bring you to the clubhouse then."

I bite my lip. As much as I'd like to, I can't lose this job. "I can't. I'm working."

His brows furrow. "The night shift too?" he asks.

I nod. "I'm new. I need to make a good impression."

"Oh, you've made an impression alright," he says, sarcasm lacing his voice.

"What's that supposed to mean?" I ask defensively.

"I. Told. You. Your boss wants to bang you. The guy's a creep and a pussy. Don't trust him."

I still. Axle's tone is mainly playful, but there's an edge to it I haven't heard before. I have Cameron warning me about Axle, and Axle warning me about Cameron, which is a little confusing. But I want to be independent . . . That means I get to choose who I'm friends with based on my own opinions and nobody else's.

"The atmosphere is different later in the night at the clubhouse. Don't yell at me when you hate it."

I scoff. "I won't yell at you."

I get on the motorcycle, and we ride back to mine. Every minute, disappointment festers. I yearn to get to know him. The short dates haven't been enough, and I still have so many questions. It's been eye-opening getting to know someone so different from me. We might be opposites, but we get along like I've known him for years.

After I get off his bike, I remove the helmet and pass it to him.

"I'll see you tomorrow night," he says softly.

I lean in to kiss him, but he pulls back. One of his hands is twitching by his side. "I only have so much self-control. I want to stay with you, but I really need to get back to the clubhouse, and the way *you* kiss . . ." He shakes his head. "Let's just say, your halo doesn't fool me."

I'm smiling a big, cheesy smile right back at him.

NINE
MEETING THE MC

Elena

I STARE DOWN AT THE DRESS I'M WEARING THAT I BOUGHT during my lunch break. It's a far cry from what I usually wear, with spaghetti straps and a hem that falls above my knees. It's no minidress but look out—I'm living life on the edge. I chuckle to myself.

I'm not sure if a dress is appropriate to wear. In my determination to look good for Axle, I didn't consider that a dress may not be practical on the back of a bike. But I can't ask anyone now, and anyway, I want to look and feel sexy. I'm sure he's used to glamorous women. I can't remember a time when I ever felt sexy. Henry made me feel pretty, but never sexy. I slip my sandals on, then stand up straight.

"Oh crap! Oh crap!" I grasp my racing heart. What if Axle wants me to stay the night? I didn't ask about my ride home. I pace. I didn't think this through. The rumble of a motorcycle makes me shriek in panic. I grab a bag and throw in some pajamas. I rush out to the bathroom and grab my toothbrush.

My breathing is out of control as I walk downstairs. Everyone's out, so the house is quiet. I open the front door to go outside. I can do this. I can do this . . . *No, I can't do this.* I retreat and start closing the front door.

"Hold up," Axle calls out, pulling the door open wide. "First"—his eyes ravish my body, making me blush—"you look fucking hot, babe. Second, you're not going anywhere. You committed to meeting my friends, so get your sexy self on my bike." He reaches over and takes my hand in his. "I'd never let anyone hurt you." He pulls me in for a brief hug.

I embrace his warmth and feel a sliver of relief. I believe him. He places a gentle kiss on my forehead, making me swoon and smile up at him. My stomach churns with mixed emotions.

When he sees the bag on my shoulder, he asks, with a wicked glint in his eyes, "Staying the night, are you?"

"I didn't know," I stutter out. "We didn't talk about when or how I was getting home."

He chuckles. "It's okay—I get it. You're keen to see me naked."

I scoff and choke at the same time. "That thought never came to my mind. I told you I'm not having sex with you."

He points to the corner of my mouth. "You're drooling just at the thought of it."

I'm tongue-tied before I can even contemplate a response. He lifts his shirt, displaying his fit body. My mouth drops open at the display of muscles. He pulls my hand to the top of his abs and slowly drags it down his torso. His skin is warm and taut. I yank my hand back before it reaches the top of his jeans. It felt so good, but I glare at him while I scold myself. Before I can utter a word, he tips his chin and says, "You loved it," and then kisses the air.

I blow out a breath, puffing out my cheeks. I take a slow step outside, trying to gather my wits about me. I turn and lock the door before we walk to his bike. He's out of control, but I always end up smiling or laughing at him. He's not the typical broody, intimidating biker. With his playful and flirty nature, it's no surprise he's popular with the ladies.

"Excited for your first club party, babe?"

"Hmm . . . party?" I ask, hoping I misheard him.

"It's just a quiet one, chill out . . . breathe . . ."

My heart is in my throat. I feel a storm of emotions swirling inside me. Am I anxious about the party or irritated by his condescending tone? Maybe it's both. My hands tremble slightly, and I catch myself clenching my jaw, trying to mask the frustration that's creeping onto my face. All I wanted to do was casually meet his friends, not be surrounded by drunk people. I don't do parties . . . *ever*.

After he gets on his bike, I stay standing. I look at him, his bike, and then the ground. "You're going to keep me safe, aren't you?"

"I've got you," he says soothingly. "I'll be with you the whole night. My friends are good people. You'll see."

I decide to have an exit plan just in case. "I'm only going if I drive my car."

He shrugs. "All good. You can follow me."

I appreciate that he didn't argue the point. He turns the ignition on and the bike roars to life. While I walk toward my car, he calls out, "I knew you wanted to see me naked."

I chuckle as I walk to the car. He's impossible.

As we drive through town, it's mostly quiet. Past the residential area and the shops, he speeds up before veering off on a dirt road. They must live on an acreage. He slows when we reach a huge two-story farmhouse. He leads me through the gate and drives off to the side and into an open shed. When he turns the bike off, there's loud music coming from the house.

There's a light on in the shed, so I can see a line of motor-cycles, a big black truck, and a van. I remain in my car just outside the doors. "Where do I park?" I ask as he walks toward me.

"Park it in the shed next to the van."

I give him a cautious glance. *Park* . . . I cringe. Not that there are any lines, but still. "My car won't fit in there."

He walks around the car and opens my door. "Move over."

I take my seat belt off and shuffle over to the passenger seat. When he gets in, I fight back a laugh because he's doing me a favor. He has to just about fold himself in half to fit in my small car and is nearly kissing the dashboard.

He adjusts the seat, closes the door, and shoots me a look that says not to say a word. I press my lips together to hold back my laughter. I relax in my seat as he smoothly maneu-vers the car into the parking spot. And there's something sexy about a man who's a confident driver.

"Trust you to have the world's smallest car . . . and what's this crap?" He gestures toward the speakers.

I huff. "It is *not* crap. It's Cardi B."

He turns the car off. "It's crap. You listening to rap is funny as hell, though."

Outside the shed, he puts an arm around my shoulders, pulling me to his side, and ushers me toward the house. My pulse skyrockets, and I'm seriously questioning my life choices.

"Tell me if you're going to faint and I'll catch you."

I tsk. He laughs.

"I'm not going to faint." I don't think I am . . . Well, I hope not.

"I'm just teasing you," he replies with the devilish grin he wears so well.

I peer up at the farmhouse. I'm walking into the lion's den. I lower my head as we walk through the front door. He leads me through a hallway that opens into an open-plan space. I pause, unsure of where to direct my gaze. My heart beats in sync with the heavy beat of the music.

My eyes bounce from one man to another. These guys are not what I'm used to . . . They're all tall, masculine men wearing similar clothes: jeans, a shirt, and the club vest. I'm not used to this much testosterone. Two intimidating men are playing pool. Further behind them, at the bar, sits a man with black hair, his back to us. A few people are playing darts.

One wall is adorned with a large black flag that bears the same logo that's on the club vests: a skull set over two crossed guns, with "War Brothers MC" written above it. At the rear of the room, a literal motorcycle is recessed in the wall . . . they really love their motorcycles. My eyes wander further. I squint. Is that . . .? I squeal and turn on my heel so damn fast.

Axle gently holds my face and raises my head to make eye contact. "What's wrong?"

I blush furiously. "Two people are having sex on the couch." I never imagined I'd say this, but here I am.

"Fuuuck." He looks over to them. "I'll be right back."

"Viper, put your dick back into your pants," he yells over the music.

I wince. I've never wished to fade into the background as much as I do at this moment. The music quietens, and I hear the hum of conversation.

Axle is by my side again. "All good now—he's got his pants on," he says casually, as if having sex in public is normal.

We turn around to face his friends. I keep my eyes closed for a moment before chancing a look.

"I told them to calm it down a bit, but"—he looks up, his

eyes fixed on his friend—"it looks like Viper didn't hear me," he says loudly.

"Sorry, man," his friend calls out. The apology sounds half-hearted, more teasing than sincere. I can't even look at his friend Viper now.

Axle drags me over to his friends at the pool table. They both pause and glance between us. Since my body is frozen, all I can manage is a stupid stare. I thought Axle was tall, but the man closest to me is enormous—I'm shorter than his shoulders. "This is Reaper, our president. We call him Reaper or Pres."

Reaper tips his head to me in greeting. "You sure you know what you're getting yourself into with him?" he asks in a deep, rough voice, tilting his head in Axle's direction.

My gaze shifts from Axle to Reaper.

Axle just laughs. "Oh, Pres has got jokes." But Reaper's not laughing.

I kind of wished I'd stayed home. Meeting Axle's friends is a car crash of embarrassment.

The other man has made his way to us. He's good looking, with dark features. His warm smile puts me at ease somewhat. "My name's Cash."

I smile back. "Oh . . . you're Axle's friend he went to the military with. My name's Elena," I say enthusiastically as I put my hand out. *I put my freaking hand out to shake a biker's hand.* I could hit my forehead right about now. Cash shakes my hand and I'm grateful he didn't embarrass me, but I don't miss the odd look and raised brow he gives Axle.

"I bet he's keeping you on your toes," Cash says.

"What does that mean?" Axle asks, the accusation clear in his tone.

"That he is," I answer Cash, and he chuckles.

Axle tugs me to the back of the room. "Cash is our treasurer. He's really smart. Manages all our stuff and does whatever a finance person does."

"What's with all the unusual names?" I ask. I watch the man by himself at the bar finish his drink, slam the glass on the counter, and leave. He does not seem happy.

Axle snorts. "Everyone calls each other by their road name, not by their actual name."

I pause. "So your real name's not Axle?"

He chuckles. "That's right."

I'm about to ask what it is, but we reach the dart players. A man wearing a cap that's been turned backward throws a dart and nearly hits the bullseye. "Hell yeah," he chants. When he sees us, he gives us a cheery smile. "Hey, I'm Twitch."

Another player, an attractive woman with long, dark hair, puts an arm around his waist. She gives me a quick up and down glance. "I'm Mercedez."

"Twitch is our security and IT expert," Axle says.

Before I can reply, a heavily tattooed man makes his way over to us. He has a mohawk and an eerie aura that makes me take a step back. I gasp when I see the shine of a blade and watch in horror as he throws his knife at the dartboard, hitting the bullseye.

"And that's Demon, our enforcer," Axle says.

I don't know what that means, and I'm pretty sure I don't want to find out.

Twitch scowls at Demon. "You're a cheat!"

Demon smirks and walks away.

I'm at a loss for words as I stare wide-eyed at the dartboard. Who in their right mind throws a knife near people? I plan to keep all my limbs, so I'm staying far away from him.

"My girl here is mute," says Axle, amused.

I playfully shove him. "I am not." I turn to Twitch and

Mercedez, say, "Hi," and give them an awkward wave and a tight smile. Why am I incapable of being normal?

Two women off to the side are giving me the death stare. One, her hair in a bob, is dressed classier than her red-haired companion, who is wearing similar clothing—or a lack of clothing—as the other women. I lean closer to Axle. "Who are they?" I ask.

He turns his head, then his eyes narrow. His arm around my shoulder tightens. "They're no one . . . Come on, let's go get you a drink." He pauses. "You do drink, right, or are you all work and no play?"

"Just one drink," I mutter. I peer back to see both women still glaring at me, looks of disgust on their faces. I exhale noisily. I have no desire to get involved in any drama. Do they not like me or is it because I came here with Axle?

Axle leads me deeper into the house, to the back, where there's a large kitchen. He pulls open the fridge door, leans in, and grabs two small bottles, one with a brightly colored label. He takes the lid off one and hands it to me. The drink is purple. I take a mouthful to ease my nerves.

"See?" Axle's smile is goofy. "I told you it would be fine meeting my friends."

"How was that fine?" Public sex, knife throwing . . . not to mention my incessant need to embarrass myself. "This is a quiet night?" What would a big party be then?

The couple that was shamelessly having sex walk in. They are smiling as they walk toward me. No embarrassment whatsoever. I'm blushing enough for the two of them.

"This is Viper, our vice president," Axle points out.

Viper is handsome and has a beard. He wears the same devilish grin Axle wears. The girl is short and petite like me, sporting the same long blond hair. I thought I was showing a lot of skin in my new dress, but she's wearing short shorts that are undone at the front and a bikini top that barely covers her nipples.

"It's good to meet you. I've heard *all* about you," Viper says, his voice heavy with inuendo. His eyes slowly drift over me.

The woman steps closer to me with a bright smile. "I'm Candy. You've been the topic of conversation around here."

I peer at Axle. He's waving his fingers in front of his throat, gesturing for her to stop talking. That's rude of him. I bring the bottle to my lips and take another gulp to hide my discomfort. I hate being the topic of conversation.

"You alright?" Viper asks me.

I stiffen, surprised at how observant he is. "Yes, I'm just getting a little tired." Minor lie for the greater good. Being with them . . . it's overwhelming.

Axle takes my drink and sets it on the kitchen counter. "Come on, let's go upstairs."

Viper laughs. "You're going to bed now? The party hasn't even started yet."

In that case, I'm glad we're leaving.

"Whatever my girl wants, she gets."

Axle is smiling down at me with warm eyes, and I melt into a puddle by his feet.

"Your girl . . ." Viper's voice is loud with disbelief. "So you're together?"

"No," I reply. I like Axle, but I just got out of a relationship and I don't know if Axle could commit.

Axle clicks his tongue. "Not yet," he says, then gives me a wink.

Axle's charm . . . his humor . . . his looks . . . deadly combination. He's trouble with a capital *T*. It both scares and excites me.

As we pass by the couple, Candy says, "Good night."

I pick up on Viper muttering something about money as

we walk by. Axle kisses my temple, looks over his shoulder, and says, "Yeah, you will."

As we leave the kitchen by the opposite door, we pass by a wall decorated with mug shots. I try to look at them, but Axle pulls me closer, encouraging me to walk faster. But then I spot Axle's photo. Even in the picture there's a smugness in his eyes and the slight tilt of his lips.

"Why is your mug shot on the wall? What did you do?"

He lowers his head. "Nothing. Stress less, babe. Keep walking."

As we make our way up the staircase, I gaze down at everyone. Being here is like being in another universe, though I'm not sure what I expected. I spot the motorcycle recessed into the wall again. I shift my eyes to Axle. "Why do you have a motorcycle inside the clubhouse?" It makes no sense.

His shoulders tense and he falls silent. When we reach the top of the stairs, he says, "It was Victor's."

The solemnity of his reply startles me. In a rare moment of vulnerability, his face softens and a frown tugs at his lips. Guilt hits me.

We walk to the end of a hall that's lined with bedroom doors, most of them closed. As he opens one, I say, "I'm sorry. I didn't mean to pry."

He ushers me into the room, closes the door, and gives me a smile that doesn't reach his eyes. "No need to say sorry."

His answer doesn't ease my guilt. He might be all smiles, but when it comes to losing his father figure, he can't mask the hurt in his eyes.

I look around. His room has a navy-blue feature wall. Against it stands his black bed frame, and his bed is made with black bedding. Another War Brothers MC flag hangs on the wall opposite the bed.

Axle is observing me closely. He slips off his leather vest and sets it down on the cabinet below the TV.

My breathing is erratic as he walks toward me. "I'm not having sex with you," I say again, not quite sure who I'm trying to convince at this point.

He laughs. "I know," he says, then grabs his chest as if someone shot him. "No need to keep reminding me, you're going to hurt my feelings."

I scoff. "I highly doubt that."

He fights a smile and sits down. He pulls off his boots, then shuffles over and lies down on his side. I admire his face. That square jaw . . . those full lips. It's criminal how attractive he is.

He pats the bed beside him. I give him a cautious stare.

"I'm not going to have sex with you," he says, his grin mischievous as he throws my words back at me in the same tone I use. "Unless you want me to," he purrs.

I struggle to hide my smile, but I stay standing. His bed looks daunting . . . lying down . . . next to him. After that kiss we shared, I question my self-control. He's watching me, but he's not forcing the issue, so I take a deep breath, though my heart is pounding, and slowly sit, then lie beside him. My breath catches in my throat when he shuffles over, closing the space between us. A blend of anticipation and nervousness ripples through me.

"You're too trusting."

I become rigid and try to sit up, but he pulls me back down.

"You came back to the clubhouse with me . . . you're in my bedroom. I wouldn't do anything if you didn't want to, but if I was someone different, you could have put yourself in a bad situation."

I turn away and stare at the wall. Am I so desperate for a connection with someone that I'd trust so blindly?

Axle grasps my chin and turns my face toward his until our eyes meet. "What are you thinking about?"

"Everything is new to me . . ." I never had the chance to make poor choices. I surrounded myself with like-minded friends and a like-minded boyfriend. We were the quiet, studious group that did well at school and kept to ourselves. "I've never had reason not to trust someone."

Something flashes across his face, then his brow furrows. "Promise me you'll be more careful." He's serious.

"So I should be more careful around you?"

His lip lifts. "Around everyone." His gaze quickly shifts to my lips, then back to my eyes. "But especially around me," he says before he leans down and presses a soft kiss to my shoulder, muting the voices inside my head. He plants a trail of kisses from my collarbone up my neck. A moan slips from my mouth as shivers rack my body.

His lips meet mine, and I'm helpless under his voodoo. I can't fight my attraction to him. My body flares to life, every part of me awakening. He slides his tongue into my mouth, shooting searing need through my body.

He pulls back an inch. "I'm obsessed with the way you taste," he growls, then his mouth is on mine again.

I lift my hand and gently run my fingers through his hair. He leans closer, pressing his weight against me, and an overwhelming need fills my mind. Bliss blankets me, while a deep longing pulses within. Our tongues dance together, and his grip on my hip becomes more insistent, pulling me closer.

He groans and eases back, dragging his teeth over my bottom lip. It's new to me, but the seductive way he did it . . . I liked it. I'm watching as his head falls back.

We both gasp for oxygen.

"Fuuuck. You can't kiss me like that," he murmurs, though his gaze lingers on my lips, betraying his words. He leans forward slightly, caught between resistance and desire.

I touch my tingling lips. The warmth of his kiss lingers, leaving behind a sensation of longing. I've never felt such desire for anyone . . . And I've never been kissed so passionately.

His eyes search mine, then his face softens. "I'm poison. You're going to regret meeting me."

Maybe . . . maybe not. "I'll make up my own mind." He never forced me into anything against my will. I wanted—no, I craved—his lips on mine. "I've enjoyed getting to know you." He's so different.

He lets out a sigh, leans down, and pulls the blanket up over us. "Turn around," he says, his voice still rough.

I roll over and he lies back down, pressing his body against mine. His chest is against my back, his arm encircling my body, cradling me against him. Warm and content, I smile. I shouldn't feel safe, but I do. I should be running away from him with what everyone else is saying, but I can't. I promised myself I'd make up my own mind about everyone I meet. In the short time I've known him, he's evoked emotions in me that I've never experienced before, which only compels me to spend more time with him.

The music from downstairs gets louder. I feel the vibrations from the bass. The voices have risen too. Maybe more people have arrived. My mind goes back to the motorcycle. "Can I ask you a question?"

"Sure, babe."

"Why is Victor's motorcycle inside?"

He's silent. I wait patiently.

"It's rare. Victor built it himself. I've never been able to bring myself to ride it—it's too important to me. So I asked the club if it could remain in the clubhouse, where it would be close by and I could always keep an eye on it."

He may wear a joker mask, but there's a loving man behind it. He isn't this horrible criminal and player everyone labels him as.

"What's your real name?" I ask.

"Jake."

"Jake," I say, tasting his name on my tongue. "Tell me more about yourself."

"Eh . . . what do you want to know?"

I pause. "Anything . . . Why did you steal parts from Victor, and what made you stick around and not go back to what you were doing before he caught you?"

"No one ever cared enough to teach me something. He helped me find something I was good at, and he looked after me."

Oh, my aching heart.

"I stole from him because I needed the money to eat and to help my parents pay the bills, but if I hadn't stolen from Victor, God knows where I would have ended up."

My parents may be unbearable, but I always had a roof over my head, clean clothes, and all the basic necessities. "What do you mean by not knowing where you may have ended up?"

"I was a menace to society." He chuckles. "I broke into people's houses and stole things. When the police found me with the stolen goods, I hopped on my motorbike and they had to chase me around in their vehicle. I loved the chase. To see how long it took them to get me. It happened a few times. I'd go to juvie, then get let back out."

Well, I see nothing has changed apart from the stealing. "And then you went into the military and met Cash?"

"I was angry when Victor died and hated the world, so yeah, I went into the military. Cash was my lifeline and just like me. We weren't in the military for long, though. We went overseas, served, and did our time, and that was enough for us. I think we're lucky that we left when we did. I see some of the others struggle with what they saw and experienced . . . especially Reaper. That shit haunts him."

Tears prick my eyes. "That's horrible."

"Awww, babe." He places a soft kiss on my shoulder that warms my heart. "Don't get upset. Life happens. Every club member has a shitty life story, but that's also what brought us together. Family is who you choose it to be." He hugs me tighter. "Now get some sleep."

"Bossy," I mutter.

"Damn straight. Night, babe."

TEN
SURVIVAL OF THE FITTEST

Elena

My eyes flutter open to sunlight filtering through the curtains. The music from downstairs has turned into a quiet hum. My thoughts drift back to last night. I survived meeting his friends . . . barely. It's a different lifestyle here. I've never witnessed people having sex in public.

I need to go to the bathroom. I shuffle out of Axle's hold and peer back at him. He reaches for me, but then he drifts back off to sleep. He looks so peaceful. I don't want to wake him.

I crack open the door. I don't see anyone, so I step outside. Heavy footsteps approach. Viper comes jogging up, drenched in sweat and with his shirt tucked into the waistband of his shorts. He gives me a head tilt. "Mornin'."

"Good morning," I say with a smile. "Can you please tell me where the bathroom is?"

He points down the hallway. "The door right at the end."

"Thank you." I tread softly, trying not to wake anyone.

After going to the bathroom and washing my hands, I stare at my reflection in the mirror. The responsible version of me says I shouldn't have stayed overnight. The new, you-only-live-once version says screw it.

I cautiously open the door and creep back into Axle's room. He hasn't moved and is still fast asleep. I walk over to my bag and rummage through it, searching for my anxiety medication. I can't take my tablets without water, but the kitchen is downstairs. I peer back at Axle and wonder whether I should wake him. I'm only going downstairs to grab a glass of water.

I leave his room, then pause at the top of the stairs and listen to the blend of soft music and quiet snoring from below. My eyes sweep across the room, landing on three people sprawled awkwardly on the pool table. I wince; that can't be comfortable. Empty beer bottles and cans litter the space. At the bar a few men sit hunched over their drinks. With a deep breath, I start my cautious descent, feeling the cool handrail under my fingertips. I just need to reach the kitchen, and then I can retreat back to Axle's room.

The men at the bar make my pulse accelerate. I try to creep by, but their gazes pierce me. One whistles, making me recoil. Perhaps I should have convinced Axle to come downstairs with me. I lower my head. Maybe if I ignore them, they'll get the hint.

I rush to the kitchen, where I search the cupboards for a glass that looks clean. I find a glass and fill it from the tap. I really don't want to walk by the men in the bar again. My hands shake as I grip the glass. I just need to get past them and get upstairs to Axle.

I exhale sharply and dash out of the kitchen and through the house while trying not to splash my water. I hear footsteps. My heart beats wildly. A large, intimidating man is blocking my way. I don't recognize him.

His eyes roam me with greedy delight. My stomach drops. "Can I please get past?" I murmur. I just need to get up the stairs.

"Come dance with me."

My grip around the glass tightens. I wait for him to move, but he doesn't, so I answer, "No," and try to sidestep him.

He leans down and grabs my hips.

"Let go," I say, my voice unsteady.

His hands tighten. "Just dance with me."

"Elena?" Axle is standing at the top of the stairs, his face set in stone.

The relief that washes over me eases the tightness in my chest. Axle's eyes are darting to me, the guy . . . His gaze turns deadly when he sees the guy's hands on my hips. The guy jerks his hands off me and takes a deliberate step away. I shuffle backward until my back is against the wall.

"Sorry, man," he blurts out, "I didn't know she was with you."

Axle races down the stairs with incredible speed. "I'm sorry, I'm sorry," the man pleads, but Axle doesn't hesitate. He tackles the man to the ground, the impact echoing on the wooden floor. With urgency, Axle straddles him, pulls back his arm, and delivers a punch that lands with a sickening crunch.

Startled by the sudden violence, I jump. My medication and the glass of water slip from my grasp. The glass shatters on the floor, breaking into tiny shards. The crash catches Axle's attention, and he stops and glances up at me. When he sees my concerned expression, he slowly rises. The guy underneath him rolls to his side, groaning and holding his nose.

Cash and Twitch rush in as Reaper storms down the stairs.

Axle takes cautious steps toward me. "Everything's

okay . . ." he says soothingly as the glass crunches under his boots.

"What happened?" Reaper booms.

The weight of the gaze of everyone in the room makes my skin prickle, but my throat tightens, leaving me unable to utter a single word.

"Piece of shit put his hands on Elena," Axle spits. He looks like he's holding himself back from going another round with the man on the floor.

Reaper's eyes cut to the man and his two friends, who have come over to help him up. "You three are never getting patched in . . . get out."

Axle wraps his arms around me. "I'm sorry," he says softly into my neck, his words muffled.

"Everyone out!" Reaper yells. Twitch and Cash start moving around the room, waking people up and telling those who are awake to leave.

Axle leans back and observes me. "Are you okay?"

My breathing is still heavy, but I nod. "I am . . . He just startled me." I couldn't decide what frightened me more: the man who believed it was acceptable to grab me like that or Axle's talent for rapidly switching from zero to death row.

"Can someone clean this mess up?" Axle yells.

"I'll do it," Mercedez says, then scurries away.

He looks down, bends over to pick up the pill bottle, and reads the label. He takes a step closer to me and gently asks, "Are these yours?"

"Yes."

He passes them to me. Mercedez gets to work with the broom, cleaning up the glass.

Axle frowns. "I'll pick you up so that you don't get cut by glass."

I nod, and he picks me up with ease. I wrap my legs around his waist.

"I've got you," he says as he walks through the mess to the kitchen. He sets my feet on the floor before he opens the fridge to pull out a bottle of water, which he passes to me. He peeks at the pill bottle in my hand, tilting his head. "What are they for?"

"It's my anxiety medication," I say before opening the lid and pulling out two tablets and taking them with a gulp of water.

Even though I'm wary of Axle, the deep frown on his face makes my heart contract. I go to him and touch his arm. "Please don't hurt someone like that again. It was a shock . . . to see you like that."

He blinks at me, then chuckles briefly. "You see my cut, yeah?" He points to the patch on his vest.

I bite my lip and nod.

"I won't let anyone touch you." He directs his attention to my bottle of tablets once more. "And now you're going to be scared to come back thanks to that trash."

Cash walks in and leans against the wall. "Are you okay?" he asks me.

"Yes, thanks." I'm not, but I appreciate his kindness in asking.

Reaper walks in. "No more parties for a while. I've had enough of randoms coming to our clubhouse." His eyes meet mine. "Did he hurt you?"

I shake my head.

Reaper turns to Axle, his eyes narrow. "I mean it. No more parties."

Axle is the one who organizes the parties . . . That doesn't sit well with me.

"Last night was all Viper, not me," Axle tells Reaper.

"I'll be sure to tell him that too, then."

"I'm going to go home," I say to Axle. I need some downtime. It's been chaotic.

Disappointment flashes in his eyes before he offers me a small smile. "Sure."

As we walk through the clubhouse, I bow my head. People are probably staring at me after what had happened earlier. When we get to Axle's bedroom, he leans against the doorway as I put my tablets away and hook my bag over my shoulder.

"You're not scared of me, are you?"

I pause, my eyes scanning his face. "I'm not scared of *you*. Just how you reacted."

He folds his arms across his chest. "He put his hands on you!" he says defensively. "I'm not one of the *boys* you would have hung around. I'm a man . . . a biker. I handle business, and I'm not letting a piece of shit hang-around make you feel unsafe in my own home."

I sigh. I was relieved he was there to protect me. He's right—he's not like anyone else I've met, and I should take that into account and accept that he won't react the same way either.

"Can I come back to your house with you?" he asks.

I smile at the knowledge that he still wants to spend time with me. "Yes, okay."

Once we reach the shed, I frown when I see my car's tight fit. "Can you reverse my car for me?"

"Pass me the keys," he says with a grin. "I'll move your car and ride behind you on my bike."

I move off to the side as he reverses my beat-up car. I still find his capability sexy. My car stands out among the lines of shiny motorcycles. The van is the only other thing that looks as crappy as my car.

I walk over to the driver's side as he's getting out. He stifles a laugh.

"What?"

"A good Christian girl like you listening to a woman rapping about pussy."

I cringe at the word, then glance at my car. "It doesn't sound as bad when she's rapping."

He steps aside, lets me get in, and then closes the door. "I'll see you at yours."

"Ride safely," I'm quick to reply. The motorcycle might be fun, but it's still dangerous.

He pauses and gives me a strange look and then a slight nod.

As I'm easing away, I hear the rumble of his bike. It isn't long until I pull up outside my house and he's parked behind me.

When I step out of the car, I notice that the driveway is full of cars. Everyone's home. I patiently wait for Axle to get off his bike before I say, "We can go somewhere else."

With a slight head shake, he asks, "I thought you wanted to come back to your house?" He looks confused.

I peer back at the driveway. "I think everyone's home, though."

He shrugs. "So?"

"I'm not sure how they are going to react, and if the guys are here, I don't want them annoying you."

His head inches back as his eyes grow cold. "You live with guys?"

I cringe. "Not technically."

"What do you mean, not technically?"

I'm not one to cause conflict, but I'm not going back to the negativity I had to deal with when I lived with my parents. "They stay here occasionally because *their* girlfriends live here with me."

"Like that matters," he says with attitude. "They're still staying the night here."

I put my hand up. "Stop." I straighten my back, standing

up taller. "I live with a group of friendly people and . . ." I pout. "At least I've never walked in on them having sex."

His lip twitches as if he's fighting a smile. "Okay, okay," he says, but I'm not entirely convinced. He puts his arm around my shoulders like he always does and pulls me into him while we head to the house. He allows me room to walk in first.

I hear voices coming from the living room. "Shh . . . Shh . . . they're coming inside."

I tilt my head toward my roommates. "I'll introduce you."

He grasps my hand and links our fingers together. I smile at him, but his body's still stiff.

When we walk into the living room, all my roommates and their boyfriends are sitting wide-eyed on the couch. "Hey . . . this is Axle," I say and look back at him.

Axle is no longer his playful self. He's drawn himself up to his full, intimidating height. He gives them a "hey" and a chin lift in greeting. I squeeze his hand.

I point to each roommate as I say their name. "That's Lucy, Jeremy, Lia, Jasmine, Cindy, and Justin."

"We've met," says Jasmine.

Axle tilts his head and looks at her. "Have we?"

The boys cackle. "Ouch!" one says. Jasmine throws a pillow at him.

I pull Axle toward the kitchen and let them talk among themselves. "Do you want a drink?"

"Nah . . ." he says. He stands by the kitchen counter. "I'll have food, though. What are you cooking for me, babe?"

I laugh.

He pulls a comical face. "It's a serious question," he deadpans. Him and his precious food.

"Sorry, I can't cook."

His face drops and he points to the front door. "Get out."

I break into a smile. "What . . .? Why?"

"You can't cook. I want a refund."

I lean over and playfully swat his arm. *Cheeky!* "How about some peanut butter on toast?" I suggest with a hopeful smile.

He lets out an exaggerated sigh. "Yeah, I suppose that'll do."

I know he's joking, and I chuckle. I pull out the bread and the peanut butter.

"Why do you take the tablets?" he asks, his voice laced with a hint of sadness.

I pause as I put the bread into the toaster. "It's complicated."

"Uncomplicate it for me. Help me understand."

"I've been taking them since high school. My parents had high expectations of me to excel at school—and I put a lot of pressure on myself too. I think by the end of it I just burned myself out, and if you haven't noticed . . ." I look down before making eye contact again. "I'm shy and super awkward. I struggle socially and with groups of people, but I'm trying."

He steps over to me, grips the back of my head, and gives me a chaste kiss on the lips. He peers over my shoulder. "I think my toast is burning."

It takes a moment to understand what he's saying. I whirl and press the button. The toast pops up. It's only slightly blackened—we saved it just in time.

I put our toast on plates, then spread the peanut butter. We eat in a comfortable silence, though as per usual he takes next to no time to eat. "How was it?" I say, trying not to laugh.

"Legendary," he says with a chef's kiss.

I laugh and playfully swat him again. "Liar."

My phone buzzes in my pocket. I pull it out to see Mom calling. "Hello, Mom?"

Axle leans in closer to me.

"I'm just calling to say I've booked a reservation for dinner for your birthday."

I frown, not sure whether I want to go back home, but I guess it's better than celebrating it by myself. "Okay, thanks."

"Henry will also be home to visit his parents, so I've invited their family to join us."

My eyes bulge. I take a few steps away from Axle.

"We're not together anymore," I say quietly. I get along with Henry and his family, but it's my birthday and I'd prefer them not to be there. It should be my choice, not hers.

"I can't comprehend why you ended it with him," she says in a clipped tone.

I groan, not wanting to have this discussion. "I'm busy . . . I'll talk to you another time."

"Too busy for your own mother," she pipes up.

Well, it's not like she's been checking up on me, but I bite my tongue. "Yes, Mom, I'm busy right now. Bye," I say before disconnecting the phone.

"What the fuck is up with your mom? She sounds like a bitch."

I flinch but don't disagree. "She's always been full-on and controlling like that. Just not as bad. It's only become a problem now because they don't agree with any of my life choices after school."

"You need to set her straight. Don't put up with her bullshit, with treating you like that . . . What are you doing for your birthday?"

I sigh. "Going out for dinner, I guess."

He snorts. "With your ex?"

I look down at the ground, then back to him. "I guess so."

His eyebrows are raised high. "Well . . . that ain't happening, and who cares what your parents want you to do? What do you want to do?"

I don't think anyone's asked me that before. I shrug. "I don't know. I haven't given it much thought."

"You tell me what you want to do, and I'll make it happen."

My heart flutters. Henry never offered that. In fact, no one ever has. I don't know Axle that well and he's offering. It's a big deal.

I glance down at my phone. "I've got to get ready for work." My buzz fades. I don't want to leave him.

"Then I might start heading out. I'll see you tonight."

My smile grows. "I'm seeing you tonight, am I?" I ask coyly.

He grabs my arms and swings me around until I'm in front of him. "Damn straight you are." He kisses me and smiles against my lips. "I better go, before I decide to keep you tied to me."

I laugh, though I don't know whether he's serious or not. I wouldn't put it past him. As I walk away, I feel a shooting slapping pain on my ass, making me gasp and jump. I turn to face him with narrowed eyes. My first thought is, *How dare he disrespect me.* My second thought is, *Oh, I actually didn't mind it.*

He groans. "Don't look at me like that." He shakes his head. "I'm out of here."

ELEVEN
PRETTY LITTLE LIE

Axle

I'M AN ASSHOLE . . . IF I WERE A BETTER PERSON, I'D QUIT THIS now, but I'm not a better person. I've gotten a taste of her, and now I'm hooked. She's addictive, and I feel high every second I'm with her. Every moment with her feels exhilarating, like an intoxicating rush I can't escape. I'm not giving that up. I'm going to hang on to her as long as I can.

I thought she'd be boring, make me go to church, get angry every time I cussed, but she's a cool chick. She's like a breath of fresh air. I don't kiss women, but my mouth waters thinking about the taste of her. Those seductive eyes when I smacked her ass . . . *oh shiiit*. I just wanted to drag her ass up to her room, but she's not that type of girl. The thought of getting between those creamy thighs, devouring her . . . giving her what she's never experienced . . . I'm hard. I groan . . . My dick and balls are going to be aching every time I see her.

I gently run the cloth over my bike. The front door creaks open, and Viper's voice cuts through the air. "Axle, church!"

After draping the cloth over the bucket, I walk inside. The door swings open to reveal Viper waiting for me.

"What happened this morning?" he asks.

I grind my teeth. "Some drunk put his hands on Elena. She looked terrified, and I lost it . . ." I shake my head, trying to get the frightened look on her face out of my mind. I feel an immediate impulse to hit that guy again.

"I gathered"—he smirks—"by the blood that was pouring out of the guy's nose that he had pissed you off."

"He's lucky that's all he got. I should see if Twitch knows where he lives."

Viper puts his hand on my shoulder. "Let it go. They aren't allowed back in the clubhouse. I haven't seen you like that since the early days . . . Are you all right, brother?"

As in when I was out of control . . .

We walk toward church. "She's a sweet girl. The thought of someone putting their hands on her or scaring her . . . I wanted to rip the guy to shreds." The need to protect her has me clenching my fists.

"I get it. I've just never seen you act like that over a chick."

I've never felt the need to.

We put our phones in the bowl outside church before we walk inside and take our seats. Reaper sits at the head of the table.

Once the door is closed, Reaper, our president, begins. "Cash, how are our finances?"

"Fridges are stocked, bills paid. Everything's good on our end," Cash replies.

Reaper nods and looks around the table. "I want to make it clear, like I said this morning, no more parties." Reaper holds eye contact with me and Viper.

Viper frowns and turns to me. I shrug. I no longer give a shit. Not after this morning.

"One of our fighters approached me asking if he could be a prospect," Reaper declares.

"Who?" I ask.

"Theo," Reaper replies. "The young man they call Rage who's been winning all the fights."

"He's been killing it," says Viper.

"The kid looks young. How old is he?" asks Bomber. We won't take on anyone as a prospect under eighteen, but the guy is a ruthless fighter. I'll give him that.

"Nineteen," says Twitch.

I raise a brow at him. Of course he knows. He's the computer guy—he can find out anything. Thanks to him, I found Elena.

"Did you look into Rage?" Reaper asks.

Twitch nods. "Certainly did."

"Has anything turned up in his background?"

"No, he only recently got out of school. He was brought up by a single mom. He has a younger brother. No red flags."

"He's a fucking good fighter. He'll bring in some serious coin," says Viper.

"If you're in agreement with Rage being a prospect, raise your hand," says Reaper.

Everyone around the table does.

Reaper glances at Cash. "Can you organize a War Brothers MC cut with a prospect patch for him?"

Cash nods. "Will do, Pres."

Reaper looks at me. "We've got a run soon. Axle, can you organize the best route to get there?"

"Sure, I've already started." I need to ensure we can get the shipment of pot there in the quickest time while avoiding public attention and the police. That includes traveling at night and paying off police officers in some counties to ensure safe travels.

"Once we confirm a date and time, Bomber, can you please check with your uncle to ensure it won't pose any problems?"

Bomber nods, while I roll my eyes. Our town is pretty much owned by Bomber's uncle, who has a hand in everything. Bomber has to speak with him to move our shipment of pot through Crown Village and the surrounding towns. His uncle extorts us for a cut of our profits, as if he isn't rich enough. He owns a lot of businesses in town, and we must get the go-ahead so he can make sure the police won't give us any hassle.

It's not like we deal hard drugs to the people in town. We just grow pot and sell it to a couple of motorcycle clubs, and then they distribute it between their clubs. That and the illegal fights earn us money. We're tame compared to a lot of motorcycle clubs. Some of them do things that are a lot worse to earn money.

"Has anyone got anything else they want to bring to the table?" asks Reaper.

The room is quiet. Then Reaper slams down the gavel to show it's the end of church.

As I stand, I glance at Twitch. "I need you to do something for me."

"Axle," Reaper says, making me turn. "Can I talk to you?"

I smile. Judging by the intensity of his expression, I doubt it will be a good chat.

I turn back to Twitch. "I'll meet you at the computer room."

As I step over to Reaper, he asks, "What are you doing with that girl?"

I jerk my head back in surprise. "I don't know . . . I'm just getting to know her."

He raises a brow. "I heard about the bet between you and Viper. I'm telling you now, it will not end well for you or the girl."

Nothing I don't already know . . . but I'm not willing to give her up. "It's not just about the bet anymore." I like spending time with her.

He searches my eyes and gives me a slow nod. "A word of advice? Keep your emotions in check. She's attractive and is naturally going to draw attention. You can't lose control every time some man shows interest in her, and from what I saw, she wasn't just scared of the guy who touched her—she looked worried about how you reacted."

"Yeah, yeah, I will." *I'll try.* "But the man touched her."

"I know. The guy deserved it. I'm not saying not to protect her. Just keep yourself in check."

Reckless is my middle name. I give him a tight nod before I leave and go to the computer room to Twitch.

"Hey, man," I say.

Twitch spins around in his chair to turn his attention to me.

"Can you look into Elena's boss for me? Dig up some dirt. I don't like the guy, and I want to make sure it's safe for her to work there. There's something off about him . . . I just want to know what it is."

"Of course. Why, what are you thinking?"

Usually nothing bothers me, but I'm on edge after this morning. "Elena is too nice . . . too trusting. I don't want a repeat of this morning, so I want to check him out since he's working with her every day. I've just got a bad feeling about him."

I leave the room and start walking through the house. Perhaps I'm paranoid, but I've seen the way he gazes at her, and I know that look. He wants to bang her for sure. I growl in annoyance, then pause. *Why do I care so much?* I'm the one

Elena should run far away from, but I tell myself I'm just looking out for her. Elena's out of my league, but she doesn't think so or she wouldn't be hanging out with me.

Viper catches up with me. "Did Reaper give you a lecture about Elena?"

"Reaper just said I've got to keep my emotions in check." He has a point, but saying and doing are two completely different things. "As long as no one touches Elena"—or looks at her—"I'm sweet."

"I thought she was going to be a bit of fun for you. I honestly didn't think you'd last after the first date. I know you wanted to win the bet, but I thought you'd be bored out of your brain. That's why I took the bet. But after this morning, watching you lose it like that . . ." He shakes his head. "You two aren't good for each other. I can see it now. If anything happens to her, you're going to lose it."

I glare at him, my body tense. "Why does everyone suddenly have opinions about the girl I'm with? I'm not giving her up." Hell to the no.

"Because she's not like the other women you've been with. I don't see her being able to handle being in the clubhouse."

"She'll be fine, and it won't kill you to keep your dick in your pants when you're outside of your bedroom." And anyway, Elena's handled everything so far.

He sighs and looks past me. I turn to see Grace and Candy walking toward us. Now it's my turn to sigh. For fuck's sake . . . I wish everyone would just give me a break. Grace sways her hips as she walks to me with that same so-called seductive smile she always gives me.

"No!"

Both girls stop, their eyes wide.

"I'm not in the mood to deal with you right now." I look

directly at Grace. "Turn your ass around and go shake it at one of my brothers."

Grace gasps. "Why? The nun clearly isn't giving you any."

I turn to give Viper a pointed glare. He gave Elena the name that Grace is using now. He winces.

Grace pouts, crossing her arms over her chest. "Tell me I'm lying? She's never going to be enough for you . . . Uptight bitch."

My jaw clenches as I stride toward her. She swallows hard, taking a few steps back. "If I hear you"—I turn my deadly stare to Candy—"any of you disrespect Elena"—I look back at Grace—"I'll show you exactly what fucking rude *really* is." My voice is deep, the threat clear. "Then I'll ban you and you can go back to wherever the fuck you came from."

Grace mutters, "Asshole," as she turns and leaves, and it makes me smile. *Yes, yes, I am,* but I'm not putting up with her shit. She's a guest living in my home.

I take my phone out and check the time. I'm counting down the hours to see Elena. I'm strung out. I like pretending she's mine even though it's a pretty little lie.

"Axle."

I turn to Twitch.

"Come see what I found." The intensity in his eyes unsettles me. "It's not good man."

TWELVE
WHIPLASH

Elena

"What's up with you today?" Mel asks.

I peer up at her, then finish wiping the table before I speak. "I stayed the night at the clubhouse."

Her mouth falls open, and she just stares at me for a moment. "Really? How was it? You'll have to invite me next time!"

"It was eye-opening." To say the least.

She steps closer to me. "Why? What happened? What were all the men like?"

"They seemed normal at first. Men playing pool and a few people playing darts, but then I saw two people having sex out in the open on the couch." I wince at the flashback. "Then someone playing darts used a knife instead of a dart to win. It was crazy how good his accuracy was . . . kind of scary."

She lets out a deep sigh. "You're so lucky . . . I want to go so bad."

There's such yearning in her voice that I cock my head. "Then why don't you?"

"I've never been, and I'm not willing to take the risk of being kicked out. That's why I created your profile. Axle didn't accept my request on the dating app, so I hoped he would accept you and you'd be my in. Did you talk to any of the other bikers or . . .?"

So, she used me. "I met most of them. The MC men look intimidating but seem surprisingly nice and down-to-earth." Well . . . most of them.

I step over to the closest table and start wiping it down, then flinch when I remember what happened in the morning.

"What's wrong?" she asks, her curiosity obvious.

I blow out a long, drawn-out breath through my mouth. "In the morning after I woke up, I went to get some water—"

With wide eyes she cuts me off. "Did you have sex with him?"

"No," I clip out.

I open my mouth to speak, but she's not finished. "Why not? You're not going to keep him around by teasing him. He'll get sick of that in no time."

Frustration claws at me. "I told him I'm not going to have sex with him. He already knows how I feel about it." I know he's a biker, but not everything's about sex . . . *or is it?* I shake my head, dismissing the thought.

"As I was saying, when I woke up, I went downstairs to get some water. They must have had a party after we went to bed. Some people were still awake, though none of them had the War Brothers MC vests on. One guy grabbed me, trying to get me to dance, but when I said no, he wouldn't listen. Axle saw it, ran down the stairs, tackled the guy, and started punching him." Thinking back to the blood splattering makes me flinch.

"Oh wow. I wish a guy came to my defense like that."

"Axle was hurting the guy . . . because he touched me." A sliver of guilt pierces me.

She subtly rolls her eyes. "You were staying at a clubhouse full of bikers and people that like to party . . . What did you expect to happen if Axle saw you were getting hit on or hurt by a stranger? I think it's hot he came to defend you."

"I guess." He's a biker. He won't act like the people I'm used to being with, and I know that if I'm going to spend time with him, I need to make peace with that.

After I finish cleaning, I get ready to leave. "Elena." Cameron is waving me over from a hallway at the rear of the kitchen.

I walk in his direction. I've never been in this part of the restaurant. I see a room off the hallway to the right. An unsettling sensation begins to grow in my stomach. I pause at the door and look around the office.

Cameron is sitting behind his desk. He gestures at the chair opposite him, so I take a seat.

"How are you doing? Are you enjoying working here?"

I smile. "Yes, I'm learning new things on every shift." I'm proud that I haven't dropped any more trays of food and drink. It must be a new record for me. "The tips are great." So much better than my last job. "While we're here . . . would it be possible to take tonight off?" I need a break, and it would be great to relax and not have to worry about work.

He gives me a leisurely nod. "I can't see why not. Why don't you have tomorrow off too, since you've been working hard?"

Staying in pajamas all day to relax or exploring the town both sound great. "Thank you," I reply happily.

"Why don't you come out with me, Lucy, and our group of friends instead? You'll enjoy yourself."

And there it is . . .

"We're always at the beach, hanging out, going to parties. Before you say anything—it's just people our age hanging out, listening to music, and having a few drinks. You'll like it."

This time I force a smile. I'm sure he's just trying to be nice, but he keeps asking me, and it's starting to feel a little pushy. My smile might mask the slight discomfort I'm feeling, but it doesn't change the fact that his persistence is starting to wear on me.

"Just have a think about it."

"I will," I say and stand, striding to the door and into the hallway.

"Elena," Cameron calls out.

I turn and he moves toward me. I back away because he's too close and in my personal space.

"Why are you so hesitant about hanging out with us, but you'll hang out with a biker?"

The malice in his tone as he emphasizes the word *biker* makes me take another step back.

"Where is she?" a loud male voice booms.

I startle . . . Is that . . .? My boss gasps and darts into his office, closing the door. I suck in a breath and hurry out into the kitchen.

When Axle's eyes land on me, his shoulders fall. He strides to me, his face set and his jaw ticking. I rack my brain as I try to work out what's wrong with him, but nothing comes to mind.

"Where's your boss?" he asks, his wild eyes searching the kitchen. All the chefs have stopped cooking and are standing still, watching us wide-eyed.

"Let's talk outside," I say soothingly, hoping I can calm him down out there, though inside I'm raging. I want to know what has him so upset at my boss, but another part of me wants to yell at him for disrespecting me at work.

"You're quitting," he demands as we walk, further intensifying the searing burn of anger.

We stride out of the building, Axle ushering me out with a hand pressed against my lower back. I keep walking until we're beside my car. For someone so easygoing, he surely gets angry . . . or is it jealousy?

I whip around to face him. "What was that about?" I hiss.

He growls. "I knew your boss was shady." He looks at the restaurant, his top lip curling up. His eyes flick back to me. "Has he touched you?"

I freeze and stare at him mutely.

He turns and starts marching back to the restaurant, so I dash to him and grab his hand with both of mine, pulling him close to me. "No, he hasn't." He has touched me lightly, but he hasn't touched my bum or anything, which I think is what Axle is talking about.

He's clenching his other hand. "What's wrong?" I ask.

"He was accused of sexual assault but paid the girl off. You're no longer working here."

My stomach drops. I gulp. It makes sense now why I was uncomfortable. "Cameron hasn't done anything. I promise. I'm at work surrounded by other people." My eyes soften. "I need this job."

"No fucking way!" he says with a savage bite.

I nibble on my lip. "I hate that it happened to another woman, and it's wrong on so many levels, but I need this job," I whisper. "Independence is important to me. I need to have it. I'll start searching for other jobs in town, but I can't just leave this one. I need the money, and I've only just started. I don't know whether anyone would hire someone who just left their job when they haven't even been there for long."

He shrugs. "People quit all the time, and I've got money."

"First, I don't want your money. I want my own. Second, I moved here because I wanted to be independent. I know you're worried, but I can't leave . . . not yet, not until I have another job. And third, we're not together."

Axle stands tall. His face is still stern. He's not budging.

"I can't have someone trying to rule my life again . . . It's a deal-breaker for me."

With a brief shake of his head, he crosses his arms, making his biceps bulge. "First," he says, copying my tone but injecting more attitude, "you *are* my woman."

I can't stop my lips from curving into a slow smile. "Am I?" In the back of my mind, I know I should be alarmed, but I really like him, and that overrides any doubts.

He nods his head sharply. "Yeah, you are." He steps toward me and pulls me to his chest. I put my arms around his waist, but he's still rigid. He leans back, cups my face, and lifts my head. "With you going to work, I don't fucking like it. Your safety and my sanity are more important than a job."

I stand on my toes and wrap my arms around his shoulders. "I promise I'll keep looking for jobs," I say before my lips touch his in a tender kiss.

"As long as I pick you up and drop you off at work. And you can't be alone with him ever . . . or go to work when it's just you two."

"Bossy!"

He nods. "Sure am."

"I'm capable of driving myself, but yes, I promise I won't be alone with him."

The side of his lip twitches. "Are you staying over at mine tonight?"

"Uh . . ."

"There won't be any more strangers at the clubhouse," he's quick to respond.

A little relief filters through. I'd rather not be home, where my boss can show up unexpectedly. It makes me question how my roommates are friends with someone like that. "Okay, I'll get my things." I lean up on my toes. His eyes slightly soften, but there's still an edge to him.

I get in my car and glance at him, but he stands off to the side, waiting for me to drive off. I put my key in the ignition, but nothing happens. I take the key out and try again. It doesn't start. "Great . . ." I mutter, then open the car door. "My car just died. Can you check it out for me?"

He smirks, appearing thoroughly amused with himself. "It's so old. The parts will cost a fortune, and you'll probably just have to buy another car."

My stomach drops. I can't afford that. He opens the hood and looks at the engine. My head falls back against the head-rest. How will I manage to travel to work now? I refuse to move back home with my parents . . . I just can't.

When I hear the hood shut, I look up at Axle optimistically, but the shake of his head all but crushes my hope. "There's probably something wrong with your fuel pump. It seems I'm taking you to work every day now," he says proudly.

I stand, shut the car door, and lock it. "You must be happy that you're getting your own way."

"You bet I am," he replies with complete and utter smugness, but his cheeriness doesn't reach his eyes. He puts his arm around my waist and draws me closer, and exhales deeply. "We'll go to yours and pick up your clothes. You should bring a big bag. I don't know how long the part and fixing the car will take."

"Okay, but I have to make it to every shift on time."

"I can do that."

I peer around. "Where's your bike?"

He points to the van a few parking spaces away. I'm grateful. That means I don't have to carry my bag on my back.

"We'll grab some dinner on the way," he suggests.

After we arrive at the clubhouse, he parks the van in the shed. I thought he'd be happy I'm staying with him, but he still seems distant. He was quiet on the way over. He takes my bag from the back seat and takes my hand.

Carrying our takeout in my other hand, I walk toward the house. I listen for loud music or any signs of a party, but there are none. My body becomes rigid and I cower as we walk inside, but when I steal a glance at the living room, I don't see anyone having sex. I exhale gratefully.

"Disappointed, are you?" Viper is at the bar, smiling widely, a beer in his hand.

"I'd say I'm relieved," I reply, making him chuckle.

"The fights are on tonight. All of them will be out," says Axle. He tugs on my hand, so I follow him up the stairs.

When we walk into his room, he sets down my bag by his wardrobe. I frown. "What's wrong?"

"Nothing," he says, but his voice is emotionless and he's not making eye contact.

I know something is wrong. I'm getting whiplash from his mood changes today.

"You want to go and grab a drink with dinner?" he asks, tilting his head toward the door.

I release a ragged breath and follow him out, down the stairs.

"Go take a seat in the living room, and I'll get us some drinks. What do you want?"

I want him to be happy. "Just water, thanks."

He walks toward the kitchen while I walk into the living room, where all four sweet butts are seated with Twitch. All of them focus their attention on me. Grace huffs, then rolls her eyes. She peers around me—I assume she's looking for Axle

—and then stands and gestures toward the couch. "Here you go, your highness."

Heaviness cloaks me. I hate conflict.

She storms away. "Grace," Vera calls out and then runs after her. Mercedez sighs, while Candy smiles up at me.

"Take a seat," Twitch says, gesturing to the seats the girls just vacated.

Axle comes up behind me and sits down, so I cautiously take a seat next to him. He puts a bottle of water next to me and I pass him his burger and fries.

"Are you going to the fight tonight?" Twitch asks, looking from me to Axle.

Axle takes a big bite of his burger and shakes his head.

"Are you going?" Mercedez asks Twitch. She's lying next to him, rubbing his leg.

"If they want me to, I will, but I'd rather stay here."

Mercedez smiles up at him.

I wonder if Twitch and Mercedez are a couple. They act like they are. It makes me wonder about me and Axle. Are all bikers who are in relationships with women doing what they want—having their cake and eating it too? I hope not.

"What are the fights?" I ask.

All eyes go to Axle, like they're waiting for him to answer.

"The MC runs illegal fights."

My shoulders tense at the word *illegal*. "Why?"

"It earns us money," Axle answers bluntly.

I eat a few chips while I think about that. "Do *you* fight?"

"None of us do."

I'm left wondering whether I've said something wrong. I relax on the couch, happy to know it's not Axle fighting. I briefly wonder about the MC's additional earnings, but I push the thought aside. I don't think I want to know.

"Well, the prospect will be," Twitch says.

"He isn't wearing our patch yet," Axle replies.

"What's a prospect?" I ask.

"A guy who wants to be a full patched member of the club but he has to prove himself first. Later on, we vote on if we want to patch him in," Axle answers.

"I've heard he's handsome," Candy says.

"Ooh . . . I can't wait to meet him," says Mercedez excitedly.

Twitch doesn't bat an eye at Mercedez's interest. I can't grasp how they can do that. They really must be with whoever they want at any time. I don't know how they don't get jealous . . . but then I think back to Grace. That could be why she's so upset with me. She was with Axle and envies me spending time with him. It all makes sense.

I watch a movie with them about a huge killer shark and a male hero that saves the day. After the credits roll, I hear the deep voices of the MC men. They're all heading for the front door. "Are they going to the fights now?" I ask.

"Yeah," Axle replies.

"I need to go to the bathroom. Can you point me in the right direction?" I ask him. I don't really need to go—I just need some space. Tension's rolling off Axle in waves.

"Mercedez, can you show Elena where the downstairs bathrooms are?"

Mercedez pouts and reluctantly gets up.

Oh crap! "It's okay, just tell me where it is."

Mercedez ignores me, so I follow her down the hallway. She points in the direction of the bathroom. I pause outside the door when I hear Grace's and Vera's voices inside.

"No more parties because of her. Who does she think she is? Axle was taken from me, now other men aren't allowed here anymore. For what . . . a guy touched her, who cares. She's not an ol' lady. The nun should go back to wherever she came from. She doesn't belong here." I can tell by the voice it's Grace speaking.

I flinch. That proves my theory. Nun? *Ouch!*

"I agree," says Vera. "But I think Reaper and a few of the men don't like the parties, bringing people they don't know into the clubhouse. I think it was a long time coming, but don't worry. Elena's not going to be here long. As soon as Axle's done with her, he'll be yours again."

I backpedal, regretting my decision to leave Axle. My chest aches. Grace sounds hurt and angry.

"I just don't get what the big deal is about her," Grace says. "She's got small tits. She's practically a virgin saint. He liked it when we fucked, and he fucked me hard. There's no way she's allowing him to do that to her."

Another blow to my chest, but this one hurts more.

Mercedez walks into the bathroom and clears her throat. I hear the soft hum of voices but can't make out what they are saying. Grace and Vera walk out, glaring at me as they pass by. Mercedez is walking out as I'm about to walk in. "What do you think about me and Axle?" I ask her.

She gazes at me with sympathy. "You sound like a nice girl, but . . . they have a point. You don't fit in here, and Axle is Axle."

My heart sinks.

"For your own self-preservation, I'd consider seeing someone outside of the MC. Grace really likes him, and I can't see her letting him go easily."

My shoulders fall. "Thanks for your honesty."

After I take a moment, I walk back to the living room, though I'm dragging my feet, feeling deflated by what the women said. I try my best to shake it off. When I meet Axle's gaze, I say, "I might go rest for a while."

"Are you alright?" asks Axle, frowning.

I glance at Mercedez, but quickly divert my gaze back to Axle, giving him a tight smile. "I'm fine."

Mercedez stands and grabs Twitch's hands in hers, pulling

him up. "Let's go lay down too," she says, her tone rich with innuendo.

We follow them out of the living room, but once we get to the far side of the room, Mercedez pushes Twitch against the wall and kisses him. In slow motion they swivel around, and Mercedez's arm falls back. She hits the motorcycle that's on the podium in the wall.

As it falls, I launch myself and catch it against my shoulder so that it doesn't crash to the ground. It's heavy, and pain radiates from the point of impact. A few seconds later Axle is pushing the bike upright. He carefully checks the bike for damage.

"Oh shit, we're sorry," Twitch blurts. Wariness is etched on his face, and he and Mercedez take a step back.

"Watch what you're fucking doing!" Axle lashes out, but the fear in his eyes is unmistakable. His heavy breaths pain me, so I gently grab his hand in mine and pull him away from them, through the house and into his bedroom.

Axle sits down on the bed and puts his head in his hands. We're silent as I kneel in front of him and undo his laces. His eyes are soft. He lifts first one leg and then the other so that I can tug his boots off.

His hands fall from his face as I stand up. He encircles me with his arms and pulls me between his legs. "It means a lot; you saved my bike tonight."

The vulnerability in his voice and his adoring gaze makes my eyes glassy. Clearing my throat, I run my fingers through his thick hair. "I know how much it means to you." I appreciate being privy to his past.

"I've been a cranky dick." His brows knit together. "Sorry, my head's not in a good place."

"Do you want to talk about it?"

"The thought of you going to work . . ." He shakes his head. "The more I think about it the angrier I get."

Remorse weighs heavily on my chest, so I lean down and give him a gentle kiss on the lips. "It won't be for long." It seems as though everything is against us and we are in constant battle with the rest of the world.

I step away from him and pull my pajamas out of my bag. I'm not sleeping in my clothes again. I clear my throat and give him a pointed look. The side of his lip lifts in a smirk, making me feel lighter. His smile is contagious. He slowly covers his eyes with his hands to give me some privacy.

I change into my pink satin pajama set. As I'm doing up the buttons on the pajama top, I glance at Axle. His dark hazel eyes are filled with lust and hold me captive as they travel slowly from my head to my toes, like he's committing what he's seeing to memory. When his eyes meet mine, they hold a promise of passion, which makes my heart hammer. I avert my gaze and busy myself with folding and repacking my clothes. I sense his eyes stalking me as I make my slow journey into the bed beside him, feeling a mix of butterflies and giddiness from the way he looks at me.

Axle slides his arms out of his vest, kicks off his jeans, and pulls his shirt over his head, revealing his tanned and taut skin, which is stretched over muscle. My eyes greedily study his body. My hands twitch—I crave to touch him—before my eyes land on his face, where I see a knowing grin. He knows I'm checking him out.

Axle's a storm of charisma and chaos, but I can't fight the feelings I have for him. He hides behind jokes and laughter, but behind his tough exterior, he bleeds like the rest of us.

He shuffles into bed next to me. My skin breaks out in goosebumps from the way his warm skin touches mine. I'm lying on my back, while he lies on his side, facing me.

"Why do you kiss me if you said that you don't kiss women?"

He smirks. "I seem to break all my rules with you."

I chew my lip, half smiling at his declaration.

He pulls the blanket down and runs his fingertips over my stomach, on top of my pajamas. My eyes close.

"Where did the motorcycle hurt you?" he asks softly.

My eyes connect with his adoring ones. I lift my hand to my shoulder.

With infinite gentleness, he places open-mouth kisses down my neck, eliciting a moan from me. His lips travel across my collarbone in deliberate, soft movements. He pulls at the neck of my pajamas, revealing my shoulder, where he presses a soft lingering kiss on the tender spot where the bike landed on me. My heart races wildly at his tenderness and at how he treasures my body.

"Were you hurt anywhere else?" he asks in a low, husky voice.

My breathing is heavy. It was mostly my shoulder, but I want him to go further, so I point to my lower stomach. His hands brush against my top and his eyes fixate on mine. He slides his hand beneath the bottom of my top and gradually lifts it higher. He watches me intensely, as if giving me a chance to say no, but I give him a brief nod because I desperately need his touch.

As his hand touches my breast, my thighs clench together. He massages one with his large, warm hand. Desire shoots through me. He pushes up my top and leans over, feasting on me. Sucking, pinching, teasing my nipple until my head falls back in pleasure. He plants open-mouth kisses down my stomach, making me shiver. He presses another lingering kiss to my lower stomach, where I said the bike caught me.

He props himself up on an elbow and lifts his head, his eyes surveying mine as his fingers delicately dance back and forth across my skin at the top of my shorts. His eyes search mine, and I brazenly spread my legs. My eyes are begging. I want more. Then his fingers made their way over my shorts.

"Are you a virgin?" he asks in a gravelly voice.

I can't speak, so I shake my head.

He growls. "I hate that some's had you before I have." His possessiveness edges on my raw ache. His hand slides under my shorts. I gasp, heart thumping. His hands go to my core and his finger teases my opening. I tense as his finger enters me, but as his lips meet mine, I relax. I trust him.

He slips in another thick finger, filling me, stretching me, and drags them slowly in and out. Pleasure courses through me. His tongue becomes more frenzied as his fingers thrust in and out, picking up speed. My back arches off the bed as I silently beg Axle to push me over the edge.

I've brought myself to orgasm before. Three-pump Henry never did it for me. When Axle's thumb meets my clit, I buck as it swirls in slow circles. My breaths come short and quick. Throwing my head back, I clutch the bed sheets. Pulling back, he watches me as I writhe under his touch.

"Come on my fingers," he demands as he increases the pressure on my clit. My ears are ringing. I struggle to draw in air.

"Let go and come for me, baby." The deep rumble of his voice and the added pressure of his thumb splinter my last shred of restraint. My muscles contract and release as spasms throw me into bliss. Lights dance behind my eyelids as I ride the waves of ecstasy, one after another, until I lie limp.

My eyes flutter open. His pupils are so dilated that his eyes are almost black, but there's a hint of a smile on his lips. "You're gorgeous when you come."

I glance down at his throbbing erection, my hand instinctively moving toward it. He tightly grasps my wrist. "Tonight is about you."

A new ache starts. I want him inside me. He lifts the fingers that were inside me and puts them to my lips, so I open, and he slides them into my mouth. Without hesitation I suck on his fingers, tasting myself, not caring.

He kisses me once more, this time slow and deliberate, each movement tender and full of warmth. With the gentle pressure of his lips, the slight tilt of his head, and the way his eyes soften when he looks at me, I know nothing could ever compare to the way he makes me feel.

THIRTEEN
HE'S A STORM OF CHARISMA AND CHAOS

Elena

Last night I lay awake long after Axle's breathing level out. I think I've only had a few hours' sleep. His arms are still as tightly around me as they were when he fell asleep. His vulnerability bled through when Victor's bike fell, and seeing him tormented because I'm working at a place he doesn't perceive as safe stirs up inner turmoil.

I told him I wouldn't have sex with him, but I think I was trying to convince myself of that. There's been no pressure from him, and he seems happy to just spend time with me. That only makes me want him more. I can't help but compare him to my ex. Henry was a three-pump kind of guy, and I'm convinced that Axle isn't like that. The thought shoots straight to the juncture between my thighs, making me wiggle my butt.

"I wouldn't be doing that if I were you," a deep, sleepy voice murmurs behind me, making me smile.

"And if I do?" I tease. My mouth slams shut. *Who am I?*

His arms tighten around me. "If you want something, babe . . ."—his husky voice drifts off for a moment—"all you've got to do is tell me."

"I'll keep that in mind."

When he rubs himself against me, his hard thickness presses into my behind. My breathing deepens and I shiver with lust. I'm desperate to have sex with him, but the warnings I've gotten from everyone give me pause. I shuffle over to get out of bed, until big arms lunge and swoop around me, pulling me back into his chest, making me laugh.

"Nah, you're staying here with me, baby girl," he says seductively. His voice is tinged with playfulness.

My phone rings, so I jokingly smack his arm. "I've got to get my phone."

His arms tighten. "No, you don't."

"Please, Axle," I say, trying to keep the amusement out of my voice.

"Beg again for me," he purrs.

"Axle!" I warn, then he chuckles and lets go. I reach over quickly and grab my phone. It's Mel calling.

"Hello," I answer.

"Oh, hey," she says. "Someone mentioned you have today off."

"Yes," I reply slowly as Axle shuffles closer to me. "I do."

"Any chance we can swap shifts?"

I let out a sigh. I really wanted the day off.

Axle snatches my phone from my hand. As I'm about to object, he says into the phone, "No, she's not changing shifts."

He pauses while staring at me, then disconnects the call and passes me my phone.

I drill my displeased eyes into him. "You shouldn't have said that."

He gazes at me with one brow raised. "You let people treat

you like shit. If you're not willing to stand up for yourself, I will."

My heart seizes, and I smile at him. He's right. I probably would have given in and said yes to swapping shifts. It's nice to know someone's looking out for me.

The aroma of bacon wafts through the room, making Axle sit up straight. With a long moan, he rubs his hands together. "Are you ready for breakfast?" he asks.

I smile at his eagerness for food. "Certainly."

We both get out of bed, and as I walk to the door, he strides forward and stands directly facing me, blocking the door. He directs a sharp glance at me.

"What's wrong?" I ask.

He tuts. "Hell no. You're not leaving this room until you're wearing something . . ."—he gives my shorts a long stare—"something that covers more of this up." He squeezes my thighs.

I try to hide a smile at his overprotectiveness. I take one step to the side of him, making out like I'm trying to get past him and to the door. With one quick movement, he picks me up, steps over to the bed, and throws me down. I bounce as I land on the mattress and squeal with laughter.

"Don't test me, baby girl," he warns, then picks up his shirt from last night and throws it at me.

"There . . . wear that. It should cover more of your skin."

I get off the bed, stand, and pull his shirt over my head. It smells so damn good. The hem of the shirt falls below my knees. It covers more skin, but I look like a mess in it.

He steps toward me, grabs a fistful of his shirt, and abruptly yanks me to him until I'm glancing up into intense stormy eyes. "You look so fucking sexy in my shirt," he says before briefly crashing his lips to mine. I love how he takes control. His lips curve into a smile against mine. "Let's get some food. I'm starving to death."

I chuckle as he takes my hand. It's quiet when we descend the stairs, but while we navigate through the house and toward the kitchen, I hear voices outside. Axle leads me out the back door. Everyone is sitting at a long wooden table in the back yard. Platters of food have been set out along the center of the table. I recoil—everyone is staring at us. I give them a tight smile as a blush creeps up my face.

Grace and Vera are sitting together between Reaper and Candy. Grace says something to Vera and they both stand, their chairs scraping back. With heads held high, they grab their plates and walk past us. I haven't been disrespectful or suggested they can't be near Axle and me. They've made it clear they don't want to be around me.

Axle tugs on my hand, and we sit in the chairs Grace and Vera vacated. With Axle now seated next to Reaper, I sit next to Candy, who gives me a small smile. Axle loads his plate with bacon and eggs, toast, and hash browns. I follow his lead but dish up only one-third of his plate of food.

"What?" he asks me.

My eyes flick from his plate to his face. "Nothing," I murmur. I smile, wondering where all the food goes, because he's fit.

There's chatter around the table.

"Nice shirt," Viper muses.

I peer down at the black War Brothers MC T-shirt that's hanging off me.

"Yes," Axle answers for me. "She looks hot in it." Then his eyes narrow. "You take your flirty eyes off her."

Viper chuckles. "I haven't seen this overprotective boyfriend side of you." He raises his brow. "I must say, it's highly amusing."

The chatter around the table changes to a lingering silence. I sense everyone's eyes on me, but I calmly savor my meal and focus on my plate. I look up just in time to see a slice of toast, tossed by Axle, hit Viper in the head, which makes Viper laugh even harder.

Candy inches close to me. "Are you two in a relationship?" she asks quietly.

I slowly nod at her.

She cringes before she smiles. "Congratulations."

"What's wrong?" I ask warily.

"Oh . . . ah . . ." She lowers her voice to a whisper. "I guess I'm just shocked that out of all the MC members, it's Axle that's in a relationship. Like him . . . of all people."

"Aren't you with Viper?" I ask.

She frowns. "I wish . . . well, not yet anyway."

I chew my toast, my mind drifting off, wondering why everyone is so surprised by the way Axle acts around me. Is it because he likes me more than others . . . or is there something else I'm missing? And why has no other biker got a partner? It strikes me as odd.

"When are you checking the bikes?" Reaper asks Axle.

"Today," Axle replies.

Reaper nods. Even sitting down, he's an imposing man. He has broad shoulders and carries himself with authority.

My eyes wander over the table to Bomber. He has black hair and a thick beard. Every time I've seen him, he's always seemed crabby and in his own world.

Cash is next, and there's a noticeable ease in his demeanor compared to the others. He offers a genuine smile, his eyes crinkling warmly, and I find myself mirroring his expression. His calm presence makes me feel more comfortable and at ease.

Twitch sits next to him, with Mercedez on his other side. She seems to be by his side all the time.

Demon is last. His skin is covered in tattoos that extend all the way to his neck. He sits back casually in his chair, observing. He rarely speaks, but there's something not right about him. I watch him flick open a switchblade and then press the lock on the bolster before snapping the blade back into the frame. I shiver and shuffle closer to Axle.

After breakfast, as we're leaving the table, Axle asks, "Mind if I take a couple of hours to inspect the motorcycles? I want to make sure they're running smoothly for our ride."

I smile. "Yes, okay."

He grabs my hand and pulls me through the house, outside, and to the shed. He walks toward the back, where there's a workbench with tools set out and a stack of tires next to it. The space in front of the workbench is stained with oil. I lean on a table while he goes out the back and wheels one of the large black motorcycles into the space.

"When will you start working on my car?"

"I've been too busy." He grins.

I scoff. "You haven't been too busy while I've been here."

"Some pretty little lady's been taking up all my time."

I chuckle. "Can I ask you something?" I have a lot more questions than one.

He pauses, looks up at me, and then shrugs. "Go for it."

"Why aren't the other MC members married or in relationships?"

His head falls back as he cackles loudly. His laughter echoes through the shed. I stare at him, waiting for a response, but he carries on laughing. The MC men are a bunch of good-looking guys, and from what I've seen, the women go crazy over them.

He sighs, smiling. "Oh, you're serious? Okay, so let me give you the rundown. Viper's pretty and he knows it. Scores heaps of chicks but has Candy on the side. She'll hover over him and take whatever he has to give her."

I frown at Candy being Viper's last choice. It's sad.

"Reaper, our president, has sex with Vera and is pretty picky with women. He's too busy focusing on leading our club." Axle chuckles to himself. "He won't let any woman stay the night in his bed, which I find damn funny. So every night they have sex, Vera must leave afterward. You should see the sour look on her face, but Reaper has rules."

Axle takes a breath. "Cash . . . he has sex to pass the time. I've never seen him interested in anyone. He won't admit it, but he's clearly not over his ex. She must have done something terrible. He's usually such a chill guy, but whenever she's mentioned in conversation, he goes cold as ice.

"Bomber, the angry-looking man," he says mockingly, "with the I'm-so-serious-every-second-of-every-day vibe has ex-girlfriend drama too. Bomber won't have sexy time with anyone but escorts because he's that devoted to her. Pretty lame . . ."

I think Bomber is sweet in that way.

"Twitch is having a fling with Mercedez, but we think he has a hard-on for Reaper's sister Milly, which is funny because it will never ever happen."

"Why not?" I ask curiously.

"Because she's *Reaper's* sister, the one he's protected and supported since they were young. And Milly's shown no interest in anyone at the clubhouse. Twitch needs to get that out of his mind."

I bop my head in understanding.

"Then we have Demon. The rumor is he goes to the city for sex. I'm not sure what he gets there that he can't get here. Probably some kinky shit. He's a pretty closed-off guy. I think only Reaper knows his story. I don't know what woman would go for a sociopath anyway."

"Do you think something bad happened to him and that's why Demon is the way he is?" Scary as hell.

Axle's smile fades. "We've all had bad things happen to us, but sometimes it's like there's nothing behind Demon's eyes. He's always been loyal to the club and has done whatever has been asked of him. I know without a doubt that if I need him, he'll be by my side, no questions asked."

They might be bikers, but I find myself fascinated by their morals and ethics. If anything, I've learned that the MC is about loyalty, friendship, and sacrifice. I decide to lighten the mood, so I tease, "You know a lot about your friends' love lives. You're a gossip."

His grin spreads wide. "Oh yeah, baby," he says as he steps back over to the bike with a tool in his hand.

I remain quiet as I watch him. I have no idea what he's doing, though he appears confident.

"Can you go over to the corner of the table? There's a dusty black stereo. Can you turn it on? That should turn on the radio."

After I turn it on for him, I say, "I have another question." I try to keep the anxiety out of my voice.

I obviously fail, because he says, "This isn't going to be a good question, is it?"

I puff out a breath of air. "Did you have anything going on with Grace?"

He laughs. "We used to have sex . . . nothing else."

Unease cloaks me. He just used her . . .

"Don't give me those judgy eyes," he says with attitude, and when I look at him, his brow is raised. "She knew the deal. I ended the casual sex, and she's pissed."

"Angry at me, you mean . . ."

His face turns stern. "Has she said anything to you?"

"No." Just passive-aggressiveness every time we cross paths. I'm just going to be the bigger person. "So that's it between you and her?"

"Yes, I'd rather shut my dick in a car door than go back to that."

My hands fly to my mouth as I try not to laugh at his rude comment.

"This song is a fuckin banger," Axle says happily while he works on the bike.

"I'm Sexy and I Know It" by LMFAO plays in the background. He dances from side to side, swinging his hips, making me laugh. It's somehow sexy and goofy at the same time.

He lifts his shirt over his head, and my eyes bug out of my head. I can't get over his muscle definition. His jeans hang dangerously low on his hips, and I'm pretty sure he's not wearing anything underneath them. He has the body of a god, and I crave him. "I just want to . . ."

He freezes. When my eyes meet his, he prowls toward me and picks me up, his hands under my ass. I wrap my legs around his hips and our bodies press together. His eyes search mine. "What do you want?" he asks in an urgent, deep voice.

I'm tongue-tied and suffocating from his closeness, but I snake my arms over his shoulders. His mouth hovers over mine, his warm breath caresses my skin, but he doesn't move. I'm burning up without his lips on mine. My eyes flick to his lips and back to his eyes.

"I'll ask again, babe . . . What do you want?"

I want him with a desperation I've never felt before, but the words don't find their way out of my mouth. Instead, my body aches as he slowly lets me down onto my feet. Disappointment slices me. He cups my face in his hands, crushing his lips to mine. I thread my fingers through his thick hair while I demand entrance into his mouth, granting me a low rumble from his chest.

Our tongues spar. Every nerve ending lights up. As I pull his head down harder, he inches back, nipping at my lip, sending a bolt of pleasure down lower. Then he's smiling against my lips. As he pulls away, he runs his hands slowly down my cheeks. I squint at him while his eyes dance with mischief. I step back. Something seems suspicious. "What did you do?"

He cackles to himself. He grabs my chin, gives me a hard peck on the lips, looks me dead in the eye, and says, "You look sexy with grease on your face, babe."

"You didn't," I say, but the smugness all over his face already answers his question for me. I step over to him and whack him. "This better come off!"

He shrugs. "Maybe . . . maybe not."

I look down at my jeans, then try to turn around to see if there's grease on my ass from him holding me up.

Whack! I squeal.

"What?" he asks coyly. "I'm just adding another handprint to the collection."

I curse under my breath.

"That's not very Christian of you," the smartass remarks.

I give him the finger as I walk out of the shed. I hear his hyena laugh while I'm walking.

When I step inside the clubhouse, Grace is cleaning up the table near the stairs. I'm surprised. From what I've seen, the house is a mess most of the time. With my head down, I try to dart by her. But as I pass her, there's a pull on my arm and I'm yanked back.

"Is it true?" she searches my eyes. "Are you and Axle together?"

I pull my arm out of her grip and take a moment to observe her. There's a slight tug at the corner of her lips, like she's smothering a smile. I don't like it, but I answer her. "Yes."

She shakes her head at me. "Are you really that clueless?" She giggles while my stomach churns. "You think it's a coincidence you're with him? Like you're going to reform a player. People like him don't change."

I peer at Cash, who's joined us. "What are you two talking about?" he asks. His eyes harden when he looks at Grace.

"Nothing," she hastily responds.

He clicks his tongue. "It doesn't look like nothing."

She clears her throat, her eyes darting around. "I better get back to cleaning." Then she leaves.

Cash's eyes search mine. "I don't know what she said to you, but for what it's worth, I've never seen Axle as happy as he is with you."

I smile up at him. "Thank you."

"Is that grease?" He laughs when I reluctantly nod. "I can't take you seriously with the grease on your face. Come into the kitchen. I'm sure we have something that'll help you get it off."

Once Cash has helped me remove the grease, I have a long shower and get into Axle's bed with one of my favorite books. My mind wanders back to Grace, but I put it down to jealousy. I berate myself for even thinking about it because it only puts me in a bad mood. I refuse to lower myself to her level.

I glance at my phone and sigh deeply. My parents haven't reached out to me, and the weight of their silence hangs over me. Yet when I'm with Axle, a comforting presence fills the void, making me feel less alone.

I focus on my romance novel, and soon I'm immersed in the story and thoroughly enjoying my time relaxing while I wait for Axle.

I'VE CORRUPTED HER

Axle

"How are you doing with the bikes?"

I look up to see Viper. I stand, reach for a cloth, and wipe my hands. "Good for tomorrow's run. No major repairs and nothing out of the ordinary."

He peers around the shed. "You and Elena are getting close. Has she said she loves you yet?"

My body vibrates with tension, but I plaster on a smile. "Not yet . . ." I answer, but for once, I don't want to talk about it.

His unwavering stare drills holes in me. "You like her," he says. A knowing smirk plays at the corner of his lips.

I frown. I don't know how I feel, so I'm not saying shit.

He mashes his lips together. "Okay, I'll drop it! Tomorrow, what will you say to her about where we're going?"

I shrug. "Just that the club has business to take care of."

"And when she asks what that is?" he probes.

"She's curious about the MC, but I don't think she's ready to know what we do, and that's fine."

"Are you dropping her off at home before we ride out?"

"No!" My answer is fast and sharp. My fists clench at the thought of her roommates' boyfriends and her boss. "Fuck, man, what's with all the questions?"

He gives me a funny look. "So you're going to leave Elena here . . . at the clubhouse . . . with the sweet butts and Twitch."

My head falls back. Not a great idea either. Twitch will be fine, but he's not one to get involved in girl drama if Elena needs help, and I don't trust the sweet butts to not tell her about the bet. "When's the prospect start?" I ask.

"Reaper said he's ready to start whenever. Cash said his War Brothers cut came in yesterday. We can organize a church meeting to discuss it."

I nod. "Let's get it done now. Rage can start before we leave, and his first job can be to watch over Elena."

Viper lets out a small chuckle. "You mean stalk her every move."

"Sounds about right." I need Rage to watch her here at the clubhouse and at her job and at her home. "If something had to happen and I wasn't there, at least Rage would be there, and he can fight."

Viper chuckles. "Elena's not going to like that."

"I don't care." If I didn't make that bet and she didn't work for a creep, I wouldn't have to go to these lengths . . . or would I have anyway? I seem to be a jealous psycho where she's involved. If I don't have to worry about all the bullshit drama because Rage is by her side, I won't have any distractions while riding.

"You go rally the troops. Meet you in church," I say, wanting to check up on Elena first.

He nods, and we head into the clubhouse.

When I reach the door of my bedroom, I peek inside. She's reading a book with a couple kissing on the front cover. I don't know how she has the patience to read. I can't sit still for that long! Not to mention that it would take me years to get through it. Her long blond hair curtains her face. I take a step further . . . Is that . . .? "Fuuuck, babe," I say, and groan. "You look sexy as hell with those glasses on. You're giving me naughty librarian vibes."

She peers up and smiles sweetly.

I make my way to the bed with furrowed brows. "How are you holding up? Sorry for being late; servicing the bikes took longer than I expected." I feel a pang of guilt as I realize she's been waiting for hours. It's strange, this guilt emotion. Can't say I've felt it often.

She slides the bookmark into the book and puts the book down beside her. "It's been a relaxing day. I needed it after all the working I've been doing."

"Good . . . good." I glance down at her book on the bed, then lean over and snatch it. She lunges at me, and I'm eating that shit up. I step away and open the book at the bookmark.

"Give it back!" she snaps, scrambling to get out of bed.

I squint at the black text on the light, creamy page. "When his tongue swirled around my core, I screamed." I chuckle, half turned on and half curious.

Elena is out of bed, jumping at the book, so I raise it higher above my head, to where those little hands can't reach. "Axle!" she yells.

I read another random line. "He kept up a slow, steady rhythm that was pushing me to climax." I laugh while Elena pulls at my arms. "I closed my eyes and burst apart," I say dramatically. "A wave of bliss washed over me." I bring the book down to her, where she grabs it from me with a bright red face. She gets embarrassed so easily. *I fucking love it.* "Here

I was thinking I got an innocent Christian girl, but she kisses like the devil and reads porn."

She scoffs, giving me the evil eye, but I can tell she's trying her best not to smirk at me.

"I've got church now, but I'll be back up soon." I walk back to the door, but I can't stop myself from peering over my shoulder, which is not a good idea. She looks so inviting on my bed. I got lucky with her. I grab my dick through my jeans and playfully narrow my eyes at the sexy vixen. "How am I supposed to go to church with a hard-on?"

She blinks. Her eyes go to my dick, then she licks her damn lips. I growl. She's not helping. I uncomfortably make my way out of the room and down the stairs. I deserve a gold medal for how long I've waited to have sex with her. Seems I won't have to wait much longer, thank fuck! I still can't get over that damn book. I should have known it was porn.

After putting my cell phone in the bowl outside, I walk into church, where everyone's seated around the table, with Reaper at the head. I close the heavy door to ensure club privacy and take my seat on the right, between Viper and Cash.

"Who organized this meeting?" Reaper asks.

"Me," I reply. "Since we have the prospect's cut, can he start like . . . today?"

"Why today?" Bomber asks, his face serious. It won't kill him to smile every now and again. Cranky bastard.

"Because I'd like another guy here to protect the women when we're gone. Give Twitch a chance to focus on the product. It's a good test to see if the prospect is serious about the job."

Demon snorts. "Since when do you give a shit about the women?"

"Since he's in love," Viper says mockingly.

Dickhead! "I am not," I declare, then shove him. He flashes a smirk. "Just shut up," I cut in before the asshole has something else smart to say.

"All in favor of the prospect starting today?" Reaper asks.

I raise my hand, along with everyone else at the table. I let out a shallow breath. That worked out well for me.

"He starts today then," says Reaper. He looks to his right. "Viper, can you call Rage?" Then to his left. "When he arrives, I'll introduce him to everyone, but Bomber, I'd like for you to tell Rage the bylaws of the club and what's expected of him in his role as a prospect."

Reaper looks around the table. "Anyone else have anything to discuss here?" There are subtle head shakes all around, so Reaper bangs the gavel to signal the end of the meeting.

As we walk out, I put my phone back in my pocket and, with a smile, walk back up the stairs to my woman. In my bedroom I grab a clean shirt and jeans from my wardrobe and say, "I'm having a shower, babe."

The hot water soothes my shoulders, which are tense from leaning over the bikes. I roughly dry my body, put on cologne, get dressed, and head back to the room.

I pause when I see the bedroom door is closed. That's weird. When I open it, I drop my clothes on the floor, the same time my jaw hits it. My eyes bulge and all the blood rushes to my dick.

Her shirt is lying discarded on the floor. The blanket just covers her nipples, leaving her creamy skin on display. The only thing around her neck is the gold necklace with the cross on it. She's not even naked and I'm drawn to her. I've never felt this type of powerful pull to a woman before . . . like if I don't touch her or taste her soon, I might die.

I gulp and peel my shirt off my body and throw it on the floor. My heart pounds faster with every step I take toward her. Her chest rises and falls heavily. She looks so angelic, so innocent, but I know better. I crawl into bed. With other women, I just wanted to have sex and get off, or get my dick sucked, but not with her. I want to savor every moment and fuck her so good that she'll never forget about me.

"Lay down, beautiful," I murmur thickly. I'm panting with anticipation as she shuffles down, her big blue eyes resting on me. "I'm dying to fuck you."

She bobs her head, biting her lip. She looks nervous. I kiss the bruise left by the bike falling on her. I clutch the blanket and pull it away from her, gradually lowering it to expose her perfect skin, delicious curves, and perky breasts. I want to burn her body into my memory. I don't know if this will be the only time I see it.

She's still wearing panties, but that's all. When my eyes reach hers again, she's avoiding my gaze. "Hey," I say and cup her chin to lift her eyes to mine. "You're gorgeous . . . you know that?"

Her lips tip up. I kick my jeans off, and her eyes latch on to my dick, making it throb painfully. I lean over, grab a condom, and put it down near her. I grip the thin straps of her underwear and tug. She lifts her hips, granting my request, and I drag her panties down her luscious legs.

I need her mouth. My lips meet hers before I pepper kisses down her neck, along her collarbone to the top of her breast. She squirms, making me grin. My lips close over her pebbled nipple, and her sweet little moan is the best sound I've ever heard. My mouth is watering for more. I don't think I'll ever get enough of her.

Her fingers thread through my hair as I kiss between her breasts, then down her flat stomach. I'm enjoying exploring her body. My hand traces her hip, then I press a soft kiss there. She rubs her thighs together, and I can't stop the cocky grin on my face, knowing she's aching for me.

"We can go as slow as you want," I murmur. I'm drunk,

overcome with need, but I'm holding myself back for her, giving her what she needs.

"I want you to kiss me," she says breathlessly. I crawl up her body. Her arms go around my shoulders and I press my lips to hers. My tongue slips through her parted lips, sending scorching heat through my body. Our tongues move together in a sweet rhythm. When she sucks on my tongue, I let out a low moan.

My fingers work their way down and into her pussy. She's soaking wet. This time I put my fingers to my mouth, tasting her. She licks her lips. My hand goes back down, and this time I push a finger inside, which makes her back bow.

"Oh God . . ." she mutters through heavy breaths.

"Not God, just me, baby."

Two fingers work inside of her now, then my thumb presses on her sweet spot and she bucks. With a swift motion, I reach over, snatch the condom, rip open the packaging using my teeth, and effortlessly roll it onto my erection. I rise over her and her legs open wide for me. I move between her thighs and rest the bulk of my weight on my elbows.

With our bodies pressed together, our lips meet again. The hunger in our kisses is intense. I grab my cock, align it to her, then slowly push it in. She sucks in a harsh breath. "I've got you," I say reassuringly, allowing her to stretch, then slowly rocking in and out of her until her body relaxes.

I slip my hand under her and cup her ass cheek, pulling her against me so that I can go deeper inside of her. I moan aloud; she's hot, wet, tight—perfect. Her fingers dig into my shoulders, and I take that as a sign to speed up. I lick the sweat from her neck.

Our bodies move slickly together. She's throbbing around me. *So fuckin' good.* I drive into her again and again, her cries getting louder. Her fingernails claw my back. Our movements become faster, deeper, harder. She thrashes underneath me.

I'm lost in the moment as her walls constrict around me and she screams. I let out a guttural groan as I follow her over the edge and release into her.

Our breathing is heavy as I drop my face into the crook of her neck. I give us a moment before I pull out, get up, and get rid of the condom in the trash can. When I turn to face her, I nearly step back. Her messy blond hair surrounds her face, her heavy breathing makes her chest rise and fall, and her lips are plump. She tenses when she sees me looking at her and leans down to grab the blanket. I sit on the bed beside her. "Don't be embarrassed, babe. I fucking love your body. You're a dream." I've never been good with words, but I know I could never explain to her how beautiful she is.

Her eyes soften. I pull the blanket back up and lie down next to her. She shuffles into my side and rests her head on my chest. I soothingly stroke her arm until she falls asleep. I want to wake her up and ravage her body again. The way she looks at me, holds on to me, kisses me. I want to hold on to this feeling forever, holding her tight, enjoying the warmth of her in my arms.

I know she has strong feelings for me and knowing that someone like her likes me has made me so happy. Maybe she loves me . . . Wait a second . . . back the fuck up. Do I want her to love me? *I'm not good enough to be loved.* Can I love her? *I don't know.* It's possible what we have is real. Her being here feels right. I close my eyes and drift off to sleep.

I'm woken by a light knock on the door. The room is dark. I yawn. I hear another three knocks, so I gently settle Elena on the bed, shuffle over, then grab my jeans from the floor and get into them, doing up my zipper as I open the door to see Reaper, his face stern.

My guard goes up. "Is everything alright?"

"We've got to do the trip tonight. Everything should stay

the same. The police will stay out of our way, and the Kings of Chaos are meeting us by the Crown Hotel."

I peer over my shoulder at Elena. Damn, I really don't want to leave her. "Is Rage here?"

He gives me a sharp nod. "He's downstairs."

"I'm coming down now." I step inside, grab my shirt, and pull it over my head while I follow Reaper. As I walk downstairs, the men at the bar stare at me. Viper has a smug-ass look on his face. I make my way over to them. "What?"

"Have a good *night*, did you?" asks Viper.

I play stupid, but he knows what happened. I open my mouth, but nothing comes out. I don't want to brag, so I'm unsure what to say.

Viper raises a brow. "Cat got your tongue?"

"How do you know?" I ask.

"The whole MC heard you two having sex. Not exactly quiet," says Cash, smirking.

I ignore their chuckles as I point to Rage and walk to him. His eyes widen, but he stands his ground. "Your first task as prospect is to watch Elena."

"Who's Elena?"

"Short, long blond hair, quiet, absolute stunner. Wears more clothes than the rest of them."

He nods.

"Protect and watch over her at all costs. I mean around the clubhouse, apart from my room. Tell the sweet butts to fuck off if they start any shit. Any mention of a bet—I need you to shut that shit down right away."

"Okay," he answers.

"Oh, there's more. Elena will need to go to work. Take the MC truck. The keys are on the table by the front door. It's important." I put my finger to his chest. "Take her to and from work and sit in the restaurant with her. Keep an eye on her. Her boss is a creep."

He jerks his head in a nod. "Got it."

"I'm not done . . . If Elena wants to go back to her house, follow her inside too. If she wants to sleep there, you sleep on the couch, and you tell her to lock her bedroom door."

"Anything else?" he asks, hiding a smirk.

"Don't be a smartass, prospect." The guy needs to learn his place in the MC. "Yes, there's one more thing." I grab his vest, pulling his head close to mine. "You try to get onto Elena or even look at her the wrong way, I'll chop your dick off and feed it to you." I see the fear in his eyes . . . good. I let go of him. "Well, I won't chop your dick off, but"—I tilt my head in Demon's direction—"he'll do it for me."

Rage's eyes follow mine to Demon, who's playing with his butterfly blade, and then Rage eagerly nods his head. "Understood."

"Hey, Viper," I say with a crooked grin. He turns my way with raised brows. "I think the kid is taking your place as the sexiest club member." The chicks must love this guy.

Viper snorts, but I don't miss him running a hand through his hair.

"Axle." I turn to see Elena, who's now dressed, walking down the stairs toward me. "I woke up and you were gone," she says, frowning sleepily.

I pull her close and kiss the top of her head. "We've got club business on, and we've got to leave tonight."

Her shoulders fall and her body slumps. "Tonight?"

"Yeah, sorry, babe."

She wraps her arms around me, hugging me tightly.

"Time to go," Reaper says, and we all follow him out through the house and out the front door. Everyone's getting on their motorcycles, and engines are roaring to life around me. As I walk to my bike, Elena has a tight grip on me. I chuckle. She's cute.

"Don't leave," she says softly, with pleading eyes.

I turn to her, cup her ass, and lift her until her legs wrap around me and she leans down and presses her lips to mine.

"Come on, lovebirds," Viper yells over the roaring motorcycles.

I set her down on her feet. Sadness shows on her pretty face.

"I've got to go." *Not that I want to.* I could lie in bed with her forever. "Rage, the new prospect, will take you to work."

Elena nods. I lean in, give her one more chaste kiss on the lips, and walk to my bike, start it, and slide my helmet on. There's a gentle touch on my shoulder.

"Be safe," she says, serious now.

"Will do, babe."

Her eyes narrow. "No burnouts!"

I chuckle. "Okay, babe, no burnouts."

It's weird having someone care about me like that, wanting me to be safe, being worried about me . . . it feels good . . . really good. I've never cared about myself, just the club and my brothers. I couldn't care less about my existence.

I reverse my bike and glance back at her one final time, then follow my brothers out of the clubhouse gates.

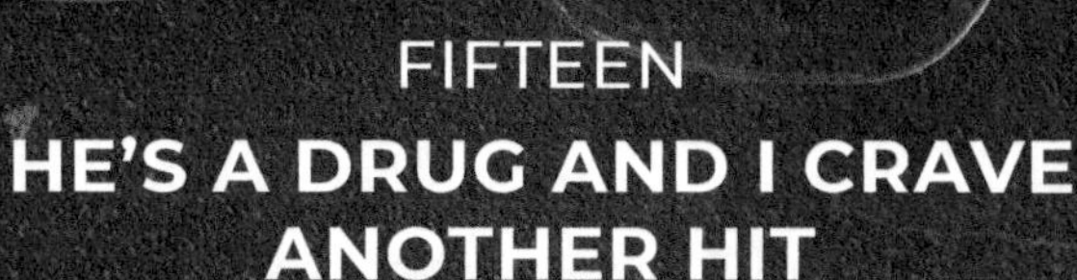

FIFTEEN
HE'S A DRUG AND I CRAVE ANOTHER HIT

Elena

Yesterday's happiness has been dwindling since Axle left. I haven't moved from his bed, although I know I must get ready for work. I grab my phone and message him.

Axle

How is your trip? Did you get there safe? xx

I wait for a reply, but it doesn't come. My stomach churns.

I go downstairs and see the new guy stocking the bar fridges under the watchful eyes of Grace and Mercedez. When he turns, I see the girls weren't wrong—he is very handsome. He's clean-shaven, and I can see the indent of his biceps through his shirt.

"Elena is it?" he asks with a friendly smile.

I smile back. "Yes, and you must be the new prospect."

"The name's Rage." His eyes flick over me, but not in a sleezy way. "Are you ready to leave for work now?"

"I am."

"I'll take you," he says.

I follow him to the front door, but he stops at the computer room. I sense the intensity of Grace's death stare as I wait for him.

"Hey," Rage says to Twitch, who's sitting at his desk. "I'm taking Elena to work. Do you need anything while I'm out?"

"I'm all good, thanks," Twitch replies.

I follow Rage to the shed. The truck beeps, signaling that it's unlocked. I move to the passenger side and stare. With my short legs, how am I supposed to get up?

"Is everything alright?" Rage asks from the back of the truck.

I flush. "Do you mind helping me up?"

He smiles. "Sure." He steps over to me, opens the truck's door like a gentleman, and picks me up like I weigh nothing so that my feet reach the step.

I take a seat and close the door. He gets into the driver's side. As we're driving down the dirt road to town, I glance at him and make small talk. "So . . . why did you want to become a prospect?"

He looks at me for a second before his eyes return to the road. "I got to know the guys through the fights. After school, I never knew what I wanted to do other than fight, so I thought it would be cool to be part of something."

"The women at the clubhouse have taken a liking to you."

"Yes." He chuckles. "They have."

He's been here for only a day, which makes me wonder what the girls have said to him already. "Grace is available."

"Which one's Grace?"

"The one with red hair." Passive-aggressive queen B.

He bops his head. "Thanks for letting me know."

It will make my life easier at the clubhouse if she likes someone else.

Once we get into town, Rage asks, "Where do you work?"

"Crown Village Seafood Restaurant, on the main road."

After he parks outside the restaurant, he comes over to my side of the truck and holds out a hand to help me down. "Thank you," I say, but then I hear the beep of the truck locking. I peer over my shoulder to see Rage following me. "What are you doing?"

He puts his hands in the pockets of his jeans and glances down before making eye contact. "I'm coming with you."

My stomach drops. Of *course he is.* "Axle is forcing you to watch me, isn't he?"

Rage doesn't reply. His lips are set in a firm line. Rage seems harmless, so I decide not to make his life difficult and walk inside.

"She's back," Mel says, her eyes wide. I smile at her, but she looks over my shoulder, her smile brightening ten-fold. She comes over and whispers, "Who's that?"

"Rage. A new prospect for the MC."

"Wow! He's fiiine."

I grin at her and turn to Rage. "Take a seat anywhere. I'll be setting up and assisting in the kitchen."

"I've got to follow you into the kitchen, though."

I blow out a calming breath. "You're literally going to follow me into the kitchen?" I ask, unable to keep the disbelief out of my voice.

"Yes, I can't see you from out here."

He's taking his job too literally. "Trust me, I'll be fine. Axle never followed me in there." Well . . . he did once, but I won't tell Rage that.

Rage gives me a suspicious look.

"Go sit down. You'll find a menu on the table, and you can order something to eat. Would you like a drink?"

"Water, thanks."

I leave, go into the kitchen, and get my apron out.

Mel's at my side. "He's like . . ." She flaps a hand in front of her face, fanning herself.

Cameron comes out of his office with his hands up. "Is that another War Brothers MC member?" He looks me up and down with a sneer. "How many are you with?"

I scoff. Even though I try not to let it, his words still cut. "Axle's got something on, so Rage has decided to . . . join me today."

Cameron straightens his spine. "I told you I don't want any MC members here. You've disappointed me," he says, shaking his head. "If my parents see the security cameras and see you've brought them here, I can't stop them from letting you go."

If I can get another job, I don't really mind, apart from missing out on the good tips. There'd be less bickering between Axle and me.

"Don't you think it's too much?" he asks, but before I can answer, he carries on talking. "It's harassment, and it's not healthy."

"It's not harassment," I'm quick to point out. Unhealthy, maybe . . .

"Oh, they can harass me," Mel says in a sultry voice. I try not to smile at her. Cameron's eyes narrow.

"What? If anything, you'll get more female customers. The cougars with their ugly rich old husbands are going to enjoy perving on him while eating their meals. In saying that, I'm going to go talk to Rage and work my magic." She hastily leaves, and I'm left with Cameron, who's staring at me.

"Your roommates have been asking about you. You should spend some time with them."

I think they only want to talk about or see Axle, not spend

time with me. I don't know how to respond. "I'm busy," is all that comes to mind.

He steps toward me and lifts his hand, but I step back in time before he touches my hair. It seems too personal. Having to be hypervigilant of my boss's actions every time I'm at work is a sickening feeling.

"You're beautiful and deserve so much better than the likes of a club member can offer you."

He just crossed a line! I force my face to be passive because I don't want to cause a scene, especially since Rage can walk in at any moment and I haven't found another job yet.

"Umm . . . I'd better get to work." I briskly walk out and busy myself with work. Time passes and I'm lost, just going through the motions. Menacing thoughts filter through my brain. *Is Axle safe? What's he doing?* Do I want to know? As long as he's safe, that's what really matters.

Mel stops at Rage's table as much as she can. He always smiles at her. She's loving it.

"Where's Axle?" Mel asks when she reaches me.

I frown. I miss him. "He's out with the MC. He'll be back soon."

"Aww . . ."

I raise my eyes to meet hers.

"You really like him."

There's no point denying it. "I do."

The sympathy in her eyes bugs me. "Just be careful. He'll hurt you."

"Thanks." I sigh. "It's not the first time I've heard that."

She lays her hand gently on my arm. "Leopards can't change their spots."

I pull back my arm with more force than necessary and stride toward my bag. "Bye everyone," I call out and go to Rage, who stands.

"Ready?"

"Yes." I follow him to the truck. After being helped inside, I pull out my phone to see messages from two people. Axle and Henry.

Axle

Everything's good babe. We should be back tonight.

Relief floods me.

How's everything been going there? How's Rage?

He's really nice. There was really no need for him to follow me.

Yes. There was. Have you missed me babe?

Yes, I have.

I've missed you too. I've got to go. But I'll see you tonight.

Be safe xx

I gaze through the window of the truck, recalling last night. The way Axle looked at me, like he was starving. Goosebumps travel up my arms. The way he made me feel good and didn't rush me. I appreciate that more than he'll ever know. Everyone portrays him as a player, but he's been attentive, protective, and caring.

I remember that I have a message from Henry.

Henry

I let out an audible sigh. I prefer not to meet him and my parents for my birthday. He's nice, but he's not who I want to spend my birthday with.

"What was that big sigh for?" Rage asks.

"My ex messaged me. My mom has organized for my parents and his family to go out with me for dinner for my birthday."

"Your ex?" he clarifies, looking disturbed.

"Yes."

"Axle doesn't seem the type to let you spend time with your ex. He's very protective of you."

"I've decided I'm not going to go because I want to spend it with Axle instead. I haven't told my parents or my ex yet." I recoil. "My mom will be mad."

"Just tell them. You'll feel better once it's done." He's right.

"I'll do it when we get back to the clubhouse."

Upon our return, I walk through the door and head to the kitchen for water. Vera is pulling the dishes out of the dishwasher while Grace is drying them and putting them away. Mercedez and Candy are seated at the counter.

I give them all a small smile. "Did you screw Rage too?" asks Grace.

I blink at her, taken aback by her words. "I didn't screw him!" I'm offended. "I went to work." *You know, like actual work.* It's on the tip of my tongue, but I keep my cool.

"Well . . . I'm sure Axle won't mind sharing you around," Grace says with a mocking grin.

I scrunch my nose. "He'll care. He gets jealous easily."

Mercedez and Vera are watching us. Candy is looking anywhere but at us, trying not to get involved.

"Why don't *you* spend time with Rage," I say offhandedly, wishing she'd give me a break.

She giggles. "Oh, I will be, but don't get that twisted. I'll be waiting for Axle when you dump him, and you will. It's only a matter of time."

Rage walks in, and his head tilts as he watches me closely. Then it comes to me. Rage is checking on me, making sure I'm alright. I give him a small smile back.

"Hey, Rage," Grace says, trying to sound sexy. She sashays over to him, rubs her hand down his stomach, and then grabs his hand. "Come have a drink with me?"

"Are you alright?" Rage asks me.

"Sure, you go and have a drink." Take her away from me. She's a horrible person.

Grace looks at me, her grin even wider. "Don't forget, whatever happens on a ride, stays on a ride."

I stand and watch Rage and Grace walk to the bar. I'm left wondering what Grace meant by that comment. Vera and Mercedez finish up and leave. Candy remains. "Try not to let them get to you," she mumbles.

"Hmm . . . easier said than done."

"Hopefully, Rage will give Grace someone else to obsess over."

I like Candy. She's always bubbly and positive. "I hope so. What did she mean by whatever happens on a ride stays on a ride?"

Candy cringes. "Well . . . it's a rule with most motorcycle clubs. If the men leave the clubhouse to go to a different town, they can have sex with anyone. So it's not classified as cheating."

Heaviness weighs on my shoulders. I grab my bottle of water and go upstairs to Axle's room. After having sex with me last night, would he have sex with another woman? I'd like to think he wouldn't.

Dread washes over me. I grab my phone from next to the pillow and call my parents.

"Hello," my mother answers.

"Hey, it's me, Elena."

"You have been ignoring us," she says. "No phone calls."

"You know you can call me too." My mouth slams shut. It slipped out before I could stop it.

"What did you say to me?" she asks.

"Nothing," I mumble. "I'm just calling to say I'm not coming home for my birthday."

"You're not what?" she screeches. "Yes, you will. I've organized dinner, made plans with Henry's family. Don't you embarrass me like that! You're coming and that's final."

"Actually . . . I'm not. I appreciate the dinner; send Henry and his family my regards. I've decided I want to have a quiet birthday here."

"You *will* come home!"

"I'm not arguing with you. I told you what I'm doing. See ya, Mom." I disconnect the call and send Henry a message that I won't be seeing him, but I hope he's well.

My phone rings, alternating between my parents' number and his, but I let it ring and lie down, knowing I've got another shift in a couple of hours. I take the time to rest, though my brain won't shut off from the negative thoughts.

Reluctantly, when the time has come, I pull on my uniform, preparing for my next shift. My heart's heavy, and it's hard to shake the unsettling sensation in my stomach. I take a deep breath, forcing a smile that doesn't quite reach my eyes. I'll need to put on a customer service smile tonight.

I go searching for Rage. He's in the living room, Grace on one side, Mercedez on the other. I groan. I'd rather not go to him, but I need a lift.

"Excuse me, Rage. It's time for me to go to work again."

He's on his feet in a second, but the girls whine. I dart out to the truck before I hear what they're saying.

The drive over is silent. He parks outside of work. "Don't you drive?" he asks.

I point over to my sad car that's still sitting there. "That's mine. It's not working."

He chuckles. "Isn't Axle a mechanic?"

"Yes, he is." That reminds me: I need to get onto him about fixing it.

Work goes by slowly, my eyes flickering back to the clock constantly. I'm relieved once my shift is over.

After Rage drives us home, and once I'm out of the truck, I say, "Do you know when Axle will be back?"

Rage replies, "I think he'll be here within the next hour."

Anticipation bursts through my chest. "Finally!"

He chuckles. "You two seem great together. I hope I can find something like that one day."

Oh . . . he's so sweet.

When we go inside, the sweet butts don't affect me . . . nothing does. I'm glowing and have a bounce in my step. Closer to the time Axle's due to arrive, I stay by the front door and wait. My stomach is doing flips, but adrenaline is firing through my veins. He's a drug, and my body aches for another hit.

As soon as I hear the rumble of motorcycles, I run out the front door and impatiently stand on the porch. As they all pull up, I wait until I see Axle, then I hurry down the steps to him. He gets off his bike and takes his helmet off just in time as I launch myself at him and wrap my legs around his waist. I pepper his face with kisses while he laughs.

His head inches back. "I missed you too, baby girl," he says, then presses his lips firmly against mine.

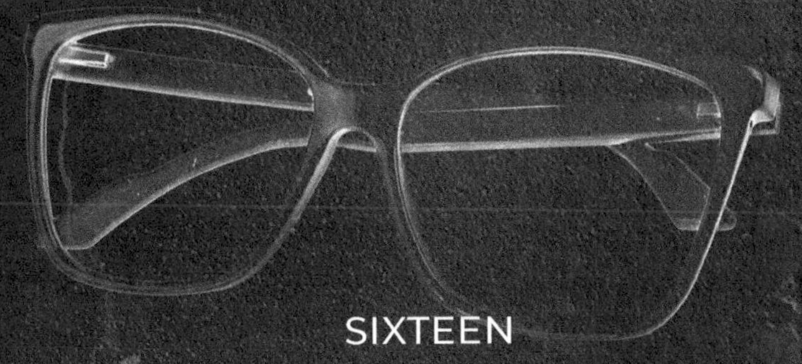

SIXTEEN
PERFECTION

Elena

leaning over me.

He inches back. "Happy birthday, babe," he says with a big goofy grin.

I smile back, because how could I not? I know I made the right decision to stay home with him. Axle makes me happy. "Thank you," I reply, my voice still sleepy.

"I'm taking you out to lunch, then I have a surprise for you."

My chest warms and excitement bubbles inside of me. I wonder what it could be. "I've got work today, so we could have breakfast and do everything in the morning."

He shakes his head, smiling mysteriously. "I called your work to say you're having the day off for your birthday. Seriously, who works on their birthday? And you're not having something like ramen noodles or a grilled cheese sandwich for lunch."

I'm a tad annoyed he called my work, but I know he just wants to make today special for me. "A poor person like me still has to work. But I'll enjoy my day off for my birthday with you."

A small frown tugs at the corner of his lips. "I told you I've got money."

"I want to work."

"But . . . you don't have to. I've got heaps of money."

I raise my brow. "Hmm . . . being an MC member earns you a lot of money, does it?"

He averts his gaze, so I put both hands on his cheeks, the way he does to me when he wants me to look at him.

"I have plenty of money because Victor gave me his business when he passed away."

Oh, my heart cracks open for him. "Why don't you run the business if he gave it to you?"

With a subtle shake of his head, he says, "I struggle to read and write. I know nothing about running a business and I'm not a qualified mechanic, so I can't do it. I sold everything but kept his pride and joy—the motorcycle that's in the clubhouse."

I put my arms around him, pull him to me, and hug him tightly. He leans in, and his mouth grazes the side of my neck. He chuckles. "I'm okay . . . It's just difficult to talk about him sometimes." Beneath the cocky exterior, Axle knows pain all too well, but he masks it with quips and an I-don't-care attitude.

He pulls back. "I think you should move in."

I giggle and lightly whack his arm. "Yeah, right."

He smiles wickedly. "You belong in the clubhouse . . . in my bed . . . with me."

I stare at him, waiting for him to laugh or say he's joking, but he doesn't. My heart races. "We haven't been together long enough, and I'm sure you'd get sick of me."

He scoffs. "Get sick of you, baby girl? Never!"

I haven't stayed at home with my roommates for a while now. If I stayed here at the clubhouse, I'd get to see Axle every day. We're like Velcro, spending as much time together as we can. When I'm with him, everything feels right.

"Since it's my birthday . . . how about you inspect my car again," I suggest.

He scrunches his nose. "Nah . . ."

My lips part. "What do you mean, nah?"

He raises his head higher. "I enjoy taking you to work and picking you up."

"I need my car fixed. Please look at it for me." I'm being polite, but my voice holds a warning. He's a mechanic, after all.

Axle rolls his eyes. Cheeky devil. "It's time for your first present."

I tilt my head. "First present?"

He nods slowly, licking his lips, then I feel the heat of his hand between my thighs, making me buck. As his fingers tease my opening, he lowers himself and crushes his mouth to mine, full of all-consuming passion. This is what he does to me. Nothing else matters but us.

His groan vibrates against my lips. "I'll never stop wanting you," he says, and trails kisses down my neck, sparking a fire within me. He slides lower, leaving a trail of kisses until he moves to the middle of my thighs. I can't catch my breath as he places his hands on my legs, opening them wider.

He settles between my thighs, his mouth on me, and I suck in a harsh breath. As he sucks and his tongue dances over my most sensitive spots, I writhe beneath him, one hand curling around the bed sheets, the other tightening my grip on his hair. His stubble only enhances the pleasure.

He sucks on my clit harder and my head sinks into the

pillow. "Oh, Axle," I say through pants. "I can't take it any longer. I want you inside me."

He stops, chuckling. "Damn, babe. Those words coming out of your mouth . . ." He lets out a low whistle, then crawls up my body, his eyes feasting on me. He stops at my necklace. "You know what necklace would look better?"

"What?"

He smirks. "A hand necklace."

"A what—" My words are cut off by his lips colliding with mine. Hard. Demanding. Desperate. I moan beneath his bruising assault.

He pulls back. "Are you on the pill?" he asks.

I can't speak, so I nod. My body burns and my core aches. I want his body pressed against mine. As if he can read my mind, he does just that. My hands slide over his heart. "I love you," I murmur.

He stills, searching my eyes as if trying to determine whether I'm lying.

"Why would you love me?" he asks sadly.

There's a heaviness in my chest at the thought of him not valuing himself. "How could I not love you? You make me feel seen."

His gaze wanders across my face. He looks at me adoringly. "I love you too," he says, and it's the most genuine words I've ever heard him say. I melt into oblivion. I never dreamed of falling in love with a biker, but here I am.

His lips find mine again. He thrusts his tongue into my mouth and kisses me like he needs me like the air he breathes. Desperate for him, I kiss him back just as ruthlessly until his hand goes to his cock. I watch as he pushes himself inside of me. He's so big, but I'm soaked, so he glides into me, even with the tight fit.

His thumb strokes my clit as he sinks to the hilt. He's not gentle this time. Every slam of his hips, every punishing stroke of his cock drives me to orgasm. Over and over, he pounds into me. The rougher he gets, the more turned on I am. Our bodies slap together as he thrusts over and over again.

My muscles tense, my feet curl, and I detonate, screaming in pleasure. I contract around his cock. A moan rips from his chest, echoing through the room. He slams home, pumping his hot cum inside of me. Shaking and pulsing, I ride out the waves. I never imagined I would like sex as rough as that, but with him, I do.

He pulls out and lies beside me, so I shuffle over and rest my head on his chest, listening to the out-of-control beats of his heart. He affectionately presses his lips against the top of my head.

We lie in bed together for hours. I lie in his arms, warm and content.

After we shower, I put on a summery pale-yellow dress. I want to look pretty on my birthday. When we walk downstairs, Cash and Viper are sitting at the bar, talking. They look up at us. "Happy birthday, Elena," Cash says.

My smile is wide as I reply, "Thank you."

Viper leaps off his stool and strolls toward us. When he wraps me in a bear hug, Axle loudly clears his throat. "Happy birthday, darl'," Viper says.

"Thank you."

As Axle and I walk outside hand in hand, I'm elated at the fact that Viper and Cash remembered and said happy birthday to me. I don't recall Henry's friends ever saying it. The men at the MC are different. I'm glad I met them and got to see who they really are.

Axle helps me into the truck, and as I shut the door, I hear Cardi B. My mouth drops open as I shift my gaze from the stereo to him and back again. "I thought you hated my music."

He shrugs and turns it up, making me laugh. When the chorus comes on, he sings it with me. I point to him, my mouth in a perfect O. "You know the lyrics. You're a secret Cardi B fan!"

He scoffs. "I wouldn't go that far." He shrugs. "The song's catchy though."

We drive into town. I smell the salty breeze as it drifts through the window, flicking up my hair. Axle's hand finds mine in my lap, and he gives it a gentle squeeze, a soft smile on his face. He takes me to a café along the main road that I haven't been to before.

The whole time we're there, he's fidgeting with more energy than normal. He seems more excited about my birthday than I am, and it's the sweetest thing.

I take a sip of my cola, appreciating the fine specimen in front of me. Broad shoulders, masculine beard, and the club vest. It's the whole sexy bad boy vibe. An indecent grin is permanently etched on his face, and he makes me laugh every day. Spending time with him is fun.

He's eating his burger, one massive mouthful at a time, and it makes me giggle. I love that he eases my anxiety. I've never had anyone support me like this and remind me not to be taken for granted. Even though we are opposites, we fit and ground one another, encouraging each other to be better people.

My phone rings, distracting me from my thoughts. It's my sister, Ava. "Hello," I answer in a rush, eager to talk to her.

"Hi, Elena, happy birthday!" she says cheerfully.

"Thank you!" I say and smile.

"What are you up to on your birthday? Mom mentioned you weren't having dinner anymore."

The only person I miss not seeing is Ava. "I'm spending my birthday with my boyfriend. We've just had lunch. Now he's got a surprise for me." I peek up at Axle, who has a soft expression on his face.

"I'm so happy to hear you're having a great day. A boyfriend . . . wow, congratulations. We'll have to catch up soon so you can tell me all about him."

"Sounds like a plan," I reply, even though I doubt it will happen because she's so busy now. I make a mental note that if I get married, I mustn't get too caught up with married life and must make time for friends and family. *Not that I have many friends or family members.* I love my sister, and it hurts that we aren't close anymore.

"I miss you," slips out of my mouth, and there's a second of silence.

"I miss you too," she says softly and sincerely. But I wonder, if she shares my feelings, why has she been so distant? All I want is for us to be close again.

Axle twirls his finger in the air, signaling that I should wrap up the call.

"I'll speak to you later. Thanks for calling me." My mood lifts after having talked to Ava. I know she cares about me. She's just busy being a wife now. Maybe I'm just being too needy.

"I don't get it . . . if you miss her, why don't you just talk to her more?"

I shrug. "Ava became distant after she got married. I'm surprised she called for my birthday."

He reaches over and covers my hand with his. "Her loss. Are you finished?" He gives my plate a pointed look.

I laugh. "Yes, I am."

"Second surprise time." Then his face turns serious. "I had no idea what to get you, so I thought I'd take you to one of your favorite places and let you choose what you want."

I smile wide. "Okay, let's go."

He pays, then comes back and takes my hand in his,

kissing the top of it. As we step outside, I walk toward the truck, but he pulls me forward onto the sidewalk. "It's further down there," he says, so I follow him.

We pass a few more restaurants and cross the road. As soon as we reach the corner, I see where we're headed: Crown Village Bookstore. I squeal and bounce on the spot. He laughs, as now I'm pulling him toward the shop. When I open the door, a little bell above it chimes.

"Get as many books as you want," he says with a grin.

I wrap my arms around him tightly. As I pull back, I stand on my toes and kiss him on the cheek. "Thank you, thank you, thank you. This is the best birthday present ever."

His face lights up at my words, and I make my way to the romance section. I pull one book out at a time, check the front cover, turn it around, and read the blurb. I open one of the new releases wide and breathe in the scent of new book, almost getting high on the smell.

When I put the book back, Axle's giving me a weird look. "Don't give me those judgy eyes," I tease him.

He chuckles and shakes his head.

I stack the books in Axle's arms as we go around. I notice the girls around us giggling and checking him out—not that I blame them. If I was in a bookstore and a sexy biker came in and carried around books, I'd be giddy too.

After my shopping spree, a twinge of guilt sets in, but Axle continues to reassure me that it's for my birthday.

When we go back to the clubhouse, we have sex well into the evening. My birthday is perfect.

SEVENTEEN

RIP MY HEART APART

Elena

Yesterday was amazing. I'm excited about reading my books, but I don't know which one to start with. I sit up in bed and read the titles on their spines.

Axle groans. "Lay back down with me." His voice is husky and sleepy.

He tugs on my arm, but I shoo him away. "I want to read one of my books."

He groans again, more dramatically this time, making me chuckle.

"I should have realized giving you books would take your attention away from me."

"Aww . . . poor baby," I coo, trying not to laugh that he's jealous of me reading.

The moment I catch the glint of mischief in his eyes, I brace myself for what's to come. In an instant, he leaps up and gently pushes me back onto the bed. He grips my wrists firmly, pinning them down. I can't help but chuckle, but my laughter quickly fades as his lips meet mine, and suddenly, he becomes my entire world once more.

After breakfast I help the women clean up, even though there's an awkward, silent tension between us. Halfway through, Grace throws the tea towel down on the counter and leans over to whisper something to Vera. How much longer will this continue? Will Grace ever accept that Axle and I are together and just move on? I'll never tell Axle about the way they treat me. I can't expect him to fight all of my battles.

After we finish, Candy turns to me. "Why don't we go watch a movie and let the men do whatever they're doing?"

I nod, giving her a small smile. It's good that Candy seems to be nice and tries to include me, despite the other two being passive-aggressive.

Once we're seated on the couch, Candy grabs the remote and glances at me. "You're very happy today."

Vera comes in and takes a seat on the other side of Candy. I give her a wary stare.

"Absolutely, I am!" I beam. "Axle made my birthday yesterday a very special day."

"Oh. My. God. Happy birthday for yesterday!" Candy says joyfully.

"Thank you."

"So you two are serious then?" she asks curiously.

I nod.

She looks cautiously from me to Vera. "Have you said the *L* word to him yet?"

"What *L* word?" I ask, confused.

"Have you said 'I love you' to him yet?"

Vera's inching toward us to better hear our conversation. "Keep going. I want to know your answer," she says with an evil smile that sends a shiver down my spine. I wonder why they're so interested.

"Yes, we've said it to each other."

Candy gives me a forced smile. "I'm so jealous."

"Does Viper know?" Vera asks me.

I frown. I thought she'd be angry to know that me and Axle are serious, but she's not. I cock my head. "How would I know if Viper knows about me and Axle's discussions?"

"Axle would tell Viper," she says, pouting. "I can guarantee that Viper's not happy about it."

Candy bites her lip and shakes her head at Vera.

My stomach drops. I thought Viper liked me. I wonder why he wouldn't want me and Axle to be together. "What's going on?" I ask, my eyes darting between the two of them.

Raised voices make me turn my head toward the kitchen.

"It's showtime!" Vera says, then looks at me. "Follow me if you want to know what I'm talking about."

Anxiety shoots through me. I should stay exactly where I am if Candy's deep frown is anything to go by. Nothing good could come of what Vera has to say, but I don't like secrets and I want to know what she's referring to.

Vera walks down the hallway and I follow. She's smiling smugly and my stomach is queasy, my heartbeat erratic.

"You know you're not the only one Axle's slept with since he's been talking to you," Vera says in a hushed voice.

I shake my head. I don't believe her, because I don't trust her.

She nonchalantly shrugs. "I just thought you should know . . . because if you love him . . . I know I'd want to know if he was cheating on me."

I yank at the collar of my shirt, which has constricted around my throat. We keep walking until we reach the kitchen. We're behind the wall, so no one else can see us. There's yelling. The voices belong to Grace and Axle. I start to step forward, but Vera grabs my arm and shakes her head.

"I thought she was a bet . . . a joke, but you're the one that looks like a fool because you've fallen for her!" Grace yells.

My body grows cold. My mind spins . . . a bet . . . a joke. *No!* This isn't happening. I grab my heart that's now gaping wide open.

Axle laughs coldly. "You know nothing about how I feel."

Why isn't he calling her a liar?

"Yes, I do," Grace says. "You never looked at me the way you look at her." She's furious, but her voice is tinged with sadness.

"Do you listen to a word I say?" Axle bites back. "I don't know, maybe the one hundredth time I said we were only having sex. Stop your jealousy bullshit and get over it."

"Of course I'm jealous!" she screeches, making me jerk. "I wanted to be your ol' lady."

He scoffs. "Well . . . that was never going to happen. I didn't even know I wanted an ol' lady until Elena."

"Does your Saint Mother Teresa know about the bet with Viper yet?"

I assume I'm the Mother Teresa she's referring to.

"If you dare say a word to Elena . . ." His voice is threatening.

Bet . . . A wave of nausea hits me. I fight back the urge to vomit. Tears fall fast, wetting my cheeks, but I don't wipe away these tears of pain.

"Congratulations," Grace says in a sickly-sweet tone. "You won the bet—you made her fall in love with you."

And with that the knife goes through my heart and I can feel the jagged end slice right through me.

She giggles loudly. "Have you collected your money from Viper yet?"

And the knife continues pushing through my back. I clasp my hands over my mouth, trying to stop the sobbing.

"That's enough!" Axle shouts.

"I don't want to break her little heart," she mocks. "But I

can tell you right now she's going to find out. Secrets don't stay hidden."

"Yes, they can," Axle says harshly.

A cry tears from my mouth. I can't stop it. My chest burns. It's like I'm underwater and trying to breathe. I turn the corner. Grace and Axle look up, startled.

Grace's smile is triumphant. She clicks her tongue. "Oops . . . looks like she knows now!"

Axle's hands go to his head. "Elena . . ." He looks distraught, but I don't believe it. He grabs at the base of his throat. "Let me explain," he says, taking a cautious step toward me.

"All this time you were pretending . . .?" I ask, my voice breaking at the end. "How could I have been so stupid?"

He takes another step, but I move back. "Don't come near me," I cry out through sniffles and a flood of tears.

"That bet was only at the beginning . . ." he says in a rush of words. "Then I met you, spent time with you . . . and it all changed for me." His eyes are glassy and he sounds sincere, but all I hear is more lies. Being with him was an illusion. He's exactly the person everyone warned me about.

"I don't believe you!" I yell at him with disgust. "I trusted you . . . I loved you . . . How could you?" My voice softens at the end, laying bare the excruciating, raw pain within me.

I turn and leave. I can't even look at him. I run through the house, past people staring at me with open curiosity, with Axle's heavy footsteps behind me. He grabs my arm. I yank it back. "Don't *ever* touch me again." My voice reverberates through the space, tinged with hurt but also rippling with anger.

"I'm sorry . . ." He tugs at his hair. "It was before I got to know you . . . You have to believe me."

I pause to meet his pained gaze. "I've got no reason to

believe anything you say anymore." I wipe the tears from my eyes, but it's no use. They keep falling.

He reaches for me again but stops and drops his arm to his side. "I'm sorry," he says again. "I hate that I did this to you. You mean everything to me. You know you do."

I thought I did. I don't know what to believe anymore. A storm brews within me, where sorrow and rage collide. I keep walking up the stairs and still hear him behind me. "If you've ever had any respect for me at all . . . *don't* follow me," I hiss. I need to escape this place. I'm suffocating.

He stops and I dash upstairs and to his room. I shove my clothes and books into my bag and swing it over my shoulder. Cash is outside Axle's bedroom when I rush out.

"I'll give you a ride home in the truck," he says.

I realize I'm stuck here otherwise. "Thank you," I whisper, appreciative of his kindness. I follow Cash until we meet Axle, who hasn't moved. I refuse to look at him. How could he be so callous?

"I'll get her home safe," Cash says.

I follow Cash down the stairs and we dart outside, where I struggle to draw air into my lungs. My body is as cold as ice, and my heart constricts. It's alarming how effortlessly Axle lied to me. He told me he loved me, wanted me to move in with him . . . Devastation and disbelief bleed out of me with every step to the truck.

EIGHTEEN
WOLF IN SHEEP'S CLOTHING

Elena

Deceit. Betrayal. Pain.

I'm lying in my bed, on my stomach, holding my pillow and looking absently at the wall, when I hear a light knock on my door.

"It's Lucy. I just wanted to check you're okay."

When I arrived home, Lucy, Cindy, and Jasmine were chatting in the living room. Their conversation halted as they saw me bolt upstairs, my face flushed and eyes brimming with tears.

"Of course she's not okay," Cindy says. "I bet Axle dumped her."

I shut my eyes for a moment. Everyone doubted our relationship.

"Shhh! You don't know that," Lucy says.

"Oh, come on. You didn't believe Axle was going to change," Jasmine says arrogantly.

"I'm fine," I say, though the tone of my voice says

otherwise.

"Okay . . . well, I'm here if you need to talk," Lucy says.

I have no desire to. Especially to Jasmine, who will give me the I-told-you-so speech. And I would rather avoid seeing the sympathy in their eyes. I'm pathetic. Someone gives me an ounce of attention and I'm hooked. I give them everything, to my detriment.

I roughly rub my tears away. I shouldn't have gotten involved with Axle. His presence tricked me into thinking I meant more to him, but everything was fake. I was just a victim of his manipulation. He worked me like a puppet and showed no mercy. Axle said he loved me. He's nothing but a wolf in sheep's clothing.

My phone rings again, but I let it ring out because I know who it'll be. Axle ripped my heart out. Now he's got blood on his hands. I can't bring myself to talk to him. Not now . . . not today, possibly never. He's just going to say all the right things like he usually does.

Perhaps Axle's hazel eyes, crooked smile, and easy charm were what put me at ease and made me lower my guard. He said I trust too easily. I thought I knew him. I never imagined him to be so heartless. Vera said there were other girls . . . how many? I feel so stupid. Everyone warned me about him. I guess some people don't change.

I snuggle into my pillow and close my eyes, taking deep breaths. I need sleep to take the pain away because I need peace, and moments later, I finally get it.

My eyes open to the buzzing of my phone and the bright light of its screen. It's dark outside. I check my phone and see eight missed calls from Axle. It's getting late—it's eight thirty. Mouth dry, I rise and drag myself to the door. I take a second to get myself together to face my roommates before I open the door and go downstairs.

I had hoped they'd all be in bed, but voices are coming from the living room.

"Elena," Lucy calls out. I pause and slowly pivot to see them sitting on the couches. Then I spot my boss with them. *Could it get any worse?* I fake a smile, then turn and go to the fridge to get a bottle of water. I don't even get a sip down before Lucy and Jasmine are standing directly in front of me.

"What happened?" Lucy asks in a small voice.

"It's Axle, isn't it? I told you he'd break your heart," Jasmine says in the same tone Grace used. "He slept with me, then ignored me like I never existed. Don't take it personally —it's just who he is."

Don't cry. Don't cry. I clear my throat. "We broke up." Lucy places her palm on my arm. "I'm going to go back to sleep," I tell them. "Have a good night, you two."

As I walk away and reach the bottom of the stairs, Cameron calls my name, making me halt and internally groan as he walks over.

"Is everything alright?" he asks.

I nod. "I'll be okay." I try to sound like I'm fine, but I'm not and I don't know if I ever will be. Cameron puts his arms around me and hugs me tightly. I cringe, feeling uneasy, but to not make it even more awkward, I pat his back with one hand.

He pulls back with a smile. "If it's about the biker, I've always known you could do better. You don't want to get yourself mixed up with those types of people."

"Those types of people" make me narrow my eyes. He has no idea what the MC stands for and who they are. Axle might have broken my heart, but I refuse to listen to people bad-mouth the MC because I know they are good men. I pull myself out of his hold. "You don't know them. They served our country in the military and are a friendly bunch of people. I have no idea why you think so poorly of them, but I'd appreciate it if you said nothing negative in my presence."

His eyes widen. The silence is loud. He rubs the back of his neck. "Sorry."

No, he's not. I look at the stairs. "I'm going to bed."

"Are you coming to work tomorrow?" he asks.

Just the thought has me cringing. "Sure, I'll be there tomorrow." I've had time off. I can't afford to give up another shift.

"Both shifts?"

At least it will keep my mind busy. "Yes," I reply. "Good night." I dash up the stairs before he keeps talking to me. My shoulders are heavy and my chest aches. I don't feel like discussing it with anyone, so tomorrow is going to be hell with Mel. I go into my room, then change into my pajamas.

After I lie down, I grip my phone. My thumb hovers over the notifications. I don't think I could talk to Axle now, but I do want to read the messages. *No!* I force myself to turn the vibration and sound off before turning my phone upside down, the screen facing the nightstand. I drift off to sleep.

FROM THE MOMENT I WAKE UP, I SEE AXLE'S FACE. I SWALLOW forcefully and rub my chest, recalling Grace's words. Axle warned me he's poison. I should have listened. I so easily ignored the red flags that kept popping up with everyone warning me about him.

After I shower, I change into my work clothes. I feel slightly better from the hot water and the fact that it hid the tears that silently flowed. I walk down the stairs and bolt out the door, trying to avoid my roommates. When I step onto the porch, I freeze. The War Brothers MC truck is outside, with Cash behind the wheel.

Of course. My car hasn't been fixed. My head falls back. How am I going to get to and from work every day? I stroll to the truck. "Thank you for picking me up. You didn't have to."

He grins, though the sympathy in his eyes is unmistakable. "Yes, I did. Axle's working on your car now."

My stomach plummets. "He's fixing my car now? Out the front of my work?"

"Yes," he replies.

"I would rather not see him." I blink furiously, trying not to cry. But I know I need my car fixed and I have to go to work right now.

"Do you still want to go?" Cash asks.

"Yes," I reply with a heavy sigh. I don't want to, but it's not like I have a choice. I stare out the window on the short drive.

Cash parks the truck. Before I get out, I say, "Thanks for the ride." As I'm closing the door, I peer up at my car and see Axle jogging over to me. I turn away from him and quickly walk toward the restaurant until I feel a hand grasping my arm. When I turn to him, I shake my head, glaring at him.

He's clutching me desperately, but his hand then slips away. "Sorry." He's breathing heavily and frowning. He has bags under his eyes, and his hair is sticking up like he's been tugging at it. "I've sent you a bunch of messages."

"I got them, but I haven't read them." I lift my hand in a stopping motion. "I can't do this right now. I've got work." I step to the side, but he does too.

"You need to listen to my side of the story."

Hurt turns to irritation. "Why should I?" I raise my voice. "So I can listen to more lies? Haven't you stolen enough from me?" *My heart . . . my time.* But maybe he needs to hear the pain he's caused. "How could you lie to my face?" I don't let him answer. "You have no respect for me. You just play mind games, and I'm the idiot who fell for it."

His head jerks. "No, I love you," he insists, his voice thick with emotion. "You felt it too, didn't you?" He lowers his voice. It's almost a whisper now as vulnerability washes over his features. "I was never fake with you."

I laugh rudely. I might be losing my mind. "You don't love me. You'd never be able to hurt someone you love the way you've hurt me."

He looks down, then back at me. "I'm sorry I hurt you. I'm an asshole and I fucked everything up, but I made the bet before I met you. Then things changed. I didn't take the money."

I grit my teeth at his words. "Do you want a pat on the back for not taking the money?" I'm burning up as anger pours out of me.

He raises his hands defensively. "No."

I see Mel and Cameron standing by the front door of the restaurant. I need to just walk away, but I can't help myself and ask, "What about the other girls then? How many were there?"

He frowns and cocks his head to the side. "What other girls? What are you talking about?"

"Vera said you were cheating on me with other girls."

He swears under his breath. "She's a fuckin' liar."

"Seems you two have that in common."

He paces. "I was never with anyone while I was with you. The last time I was with a chick was literally the night we spoke on the phone for the first time. That was it! And anyway, you were the one talking to your ex."

Rage told him. "We have only texted. At least I don't *live* with my ex," I bite back. I hate that I'm yelling at him, but at least I'm standing up for myself.

Mel walks toward us. "I'm coming," I say to her and brush past Axle.

"I love you, and I'm not just going to let you walk away from what we have."

I stare up at his handsome face. My vision blurs. "You can't fix us . . ." I whisper and walk to Mel.

I dart inside the restaurant with Mel close behind. I rush into the bathroom and go to the basin to wet my burning face. At least Axle looks like he's in pain, so there might be a part of him that's upset too. But is he upset because he got caught out or is he truly upset about what he did to me? Now I'm questioning everything.

Mel rests her hand on my back. "What happened?"

I rub under my eyes and clear my throat. "We broke up."

"Oh no." Her voice sounds sympathetic, but the smile tugging at the corner of her mouth reveals that her true emotions are quite different. She reminds me of Grace and Vera.

"I'm fine," I say before she says anything else. "We'd better get to work." I square my shoulders and plaster on a fake smile—fake it till you make it. But Axle's words haunt me as I work. I do my best to keep my distance from Mel and Cameron, but at the end of my shift Cameron calls me over.

When I reach him, I say, "I'm sorry I dropped the plates." Luckily, there were only two and they just had leftover food on them.

"No need to apologize." He tucks a stray strand of hair behind my ear.

My muscles tense and my heart accelerates. He drops his hand to my shoulder and rubs my arm. I'm so mentally exhausted I can't bring myself to say how uncomfortable he's making me.

"You should come have a few drinks with me after work one day. Loosen up and forget about everything."

To forget and not experience pain sounds appealing. I muster up all my energy and give him a small smile. "I'll think about it."

Once my shift finishes, I grab my bag. Mel is by my side.

"What happened? Did he break up with you?" she asks.

"I don't want to talk about it." The shortness of my reply should signal that I mean it, but she keeps going.

"Why won't you talk to me about it?" she asks, sounding irritated.

I stare at her dumbfounded. The nerve of her. How is she making this about her? "It's none of your business," I say sternly. I'm sick of people manipulating me and being fake.

Her mouth slams shut and her eyes widen.

I ignore her and peek out the front door. The MC truck is waiting outside, in the closest parking space. Mel walks past me, straight to the driver's side. Annoyance flares. What if it's Axle? Would she go there even though we broke up yesterday? I don't trust her, so I swiftly walk to the truck. When I open the door, Viper smiles at me.

"Nice to meet you," he says to Mel.

"You too," she says, batting her eyelashes.

I snort. Viper puts the car in drive, and we pull out. My eyes are on my car as we go.

"Axle said it is working fine now, so you can drive it home after your shift tonight," Viper says, like he knows what I'm thinking.

"Hmmm . . . I bet he's the one who broke my car."

No response. I whip around to glare at Viper. When Axle learned about the sexual assault claim against my boss, my car *suddenly* stopped working. "I can't believe him!" I hiss.

Viper chuckles.

My eyes narrow. "It isn't funny!"

He shrugs. "It's his way of trying to protect you."

"Protect me?" I huff. "You mean manipulate me?"

When we pull up outside my house, Viper turns to me. "He really loves you."

I roll my eyes. I don't think any of the men would know what love is if it hit them in the face.

"I never thought any of us would have an ol' lady, let alone Axle. But I've never seen him so torn up. It was my fault too. I shouldn't have been a dick and goaded him, but after he spent time with you, whenever I mentioned the bet to him, he always got defensive and was short with me."

The fight within me dwindles, leaving only a deep sense of exhaustion. I release a long, weary sigh. "It's not your fault," I whisper, though the words feel heavy as sorrow threatens to engulf me entirely. "He broke me, Viper, and it hurts all the way to my soul, knowing I can't trust him or be around him anymore." Pain tinges every word as my tears fall.

Viper leans over, puts his arm around me, rubs my back. I'm grateful for his compassion.

NINETEEN
WAR OF GUILT

Axle

I've asked Viper to tell Elena her car is fixed, because I know she won't answer my call. I sense the stares of the other men as I walk straight to the bar, grab a full bottle of whiskey, twist off the cap, and take a gulp. The burn of the liquor matches my burning rage. I do it once more, then sit down. "Can you grab me a beer?" I ask Rage, who's behind the bar, giving me a cautious look.

"Uh, sure," he says. He grabs a beer for me and puts it in front of me.

I take a swig, craving the numbness brought by alcohol. I rub my eye and wonder how everything got so fucked up. I had one fucking job . . . one job . . . win the bet . . . don't make it personal. Noooo, not greedy me. I'm always searching for the next high, so I gave in to temptation. I had to fucking taste her . . . then I was a goner. I messed up one of the best things in my life. I chuckle. I'm good at fucking things up . . . no, I'm a master of fucking things up. All we had is gone, and I'm the one to blame.

After ten beers, the pain has lessened but I still feel like shit. Memories of the pain in Elena's eyes and the sob. I groan. That fucking sound of her crying. It guts me. And to think I did that to her? I cracked her smile . . . I was the one who broke her.

The men are talking around me, but I hear nothing they say. I stare off into space, thinking about Elena. Those seductive eyes, that rockin' body . . . She was nice to me—not that I deserved it. It's hard to find someone as genuine as she is. She's rare. She didn't care about the cut; she wanted to get to know me . . . and no woman has cared to get to know me before.

I peer down at my phone, press the home button. No messages or phone calls. What did I expect?

Viper sits down next to me and slaps me on the back. "I hate seeing you like this, brother. I thought I'd let you know I spoke to her."

"What did she say?" I inch toward him, hanging on his every word.

"She was crying, and I could tell she misses you. Tell her how you feel, then give her time to process it."

This was coming from the biggest player of us all.

"I tried to explain everything to her the other day when Cash dropped her off. I told her we made the bet before I met her. Everything changed afterwards. Vera said I was having sex with other women." I pause, then mutter, "Bitch," under my breath. "I was exclusive with Elena, and it still somehow gets thrown in my face that I was cheating."

"As I said . . . give her some space," he says.

Not possible. "You know me. How am I going to give Elena space?" My mouth twists at the idea. "She needs reminding every fucking day that she belongs with me and that I want her back."

Viper shakes his head. "It's not about you, it's about her. At least give her a few days."

I grab my phone, then stand and shove it into my jeans pocket, knowing not talking to Elena is going to be torture. We've grown so close. I bring the bottle to my lips and drain the remainder of the beer. "I'm going to lie down for a bit."

He nods. "Take it easy, man."

I stumble through the clubhouse, aware of the men's penetrating stares. Hanging on to the handrail, I climb the stairs, make it to my bedroom, and collapse onto my bed. Elena's scent on the pillow is like a punch to the face. Fuck, I miss her. I don't know how I'm going to last even a few days without her.

I WAKE, GASPING FOR AIR. I'M DRENCHED IN A COLD SWEAT. I reach out, desperately searching the bed for Elena, but she's not there. Reality is brutal. I see her shadow everywhere I go, even in the dark, but I'm alone. I've never understood the true meaning of relationships until I met Elena.

Three whole days I've waited. I find comfort in alcohol, sleep off the hangover, then eat and sulk. Going from my bedroom to the bar and back again. Cash, Viper, and Reaper have tried to talk to me, in whatever way they can, but nothing helps the crushing guilt that weighs heavy on my chest, every goddamn day. I roll over and stare at where Elena used to lie. I don't know how much longer I can take this.

Back in the bar, I'm swirling beer around in my glass, watching as it slides around. I hear women talking and shift my gaze to Vera and Grace. Their eyes widen when they see me, and they hightail it out of here. They've been avoiding me, which is a smart move on their behalf, because I just want to let loose on them for destroying the best thing in my life.

Every day the tension in me rises. I feel it in my shoulders. The anger gets worse daily. I fist my hand tightly. I'm going to snap soon. I can feel it.

I roll my head back. My neck cracks. *Fuck this!* I stumble through the clubhouse and grab my bike key off the table. As I walk toward the front door, I hear, "You're not fucking riding like that. You're wasted."

I turn at the sound of Reaper's voice. I respect Reaper, but for the first time, I don't want to abide by his rules.

"Rage," Reaper calls out, "can you take Axle wherever he wants to go?"

"Sure thing," Rage answers and walks toward us. "Where are we going?" he asks as we walk outside.

"Elena's house. I'll give you directions."

His eyes widen, but he keeps his mouth shut.

When we arrive, I say, "Park behind that car." I point to Elena's car. At least it's running now, so she doesn't have to rely on anyone for a lift to and from work.

My heart's slamming against my ribs, and just for a second I wonder if I'm doing the right thing. *Does she hate me?* I clench my fists again. I need to pull myself together. I take a moment, sitting in the car in silence, before I get out and walk toward the house.

I open the front door and walk inside. Four girls are staring at me from the couch. "Where's Elena?" I point to the stairs. "Is she in her room?"

The black-haired one jumps up, rushes over, and stands between me and the staircase. I have to woosah myself to calm the fuck down. "What are you doing?" I snap. "Let me through."

She jerks, but then smiles smugly at me. Maybe this is karma for sleeping with heaps of women.

"Elena doesn't want to see you."

The self-satisfaction in her voice irritates me further. "Let me be the judge of that."

She pouts. "No. She wants to be left alone."

"Who are you to say anything?" I chuckle darkly. "You hardly even know Elena, let alone are friends with her. What . . . I fucked you, now you're trying to get back at me?"

The girls in the background let out a gasp. The girl standing in front of me drops her shoulders. Perhaps I shouldn't have lashed out, but she's standing between me and Elena right now.

The blond girl walks over. "Uh, I think it might be best if you leave. I'll tell Elena you were here."

Breathe in . . . breathe out. I storm out of the house, then get into the truck with Rage. "Let's go home. I need another drink."

TWENTY
BROKEN TRUST

Axle

MORE DAYS PASS. NO MESSAGES, NO MISSED CALLS. I THOUGHT about turning up at Elena's doorstep again or going to her work, but I don't know if it's going to make the situation worse. Every second of every day, I'm haunted by her. I'll never forget the taste of her lips. I remember how my fingertips dragged across her smooth, soft skin, over her curves.

It's Friday night and Viper's organized a clubhouse party. I think he just feels bad for me. Everyone is outside, huddled together, talking in groups, while the music's blasting. I gaze down at my still-full beer. I am not in the mood to drink tonight. My body has had enough.

A girl sits close to me. I glance at her face. She's smiling widely. "I know you," I say, though I can't put my finger on how or where I know her from.

"I work with Elena."

Elena . . . just her name is enough to cause me pain. "How's she doing?" I have to ask.

"Quiet . . . sad. Comes to work and goes straight home." She puts her hand over mine. "And how are you doing?"

I pull away from her, curling my lip. She's fooling herself if she thinks I'd have anything to do with her.

"I wouldn't worry about trying to get back with Elena if I were you."

Here we go . . . "Hmmm . . . and why's that?"

"I'm sure she's getting drunk right now, trying to get over you."

My chest is tight. All senses on high alert. "What did you just say?" I sneer, hoping I heard her wrong, because Elena hardly drinks.

The girl pouts. "They're having a party at their house tonight. I was told it's going to be huge, so I'm sure she'll be finding someone to try to get over you."

She reaches for me, but I shove her hand away. *Elena drunk . . . her boss . . .* "Fuck!" The tension in my voice cuts through the air. I take a few quick steps over to the clubhouse and punch the window. It shatters with a high-pitched crack, shards of glass falling to the ground. My hand aches. Blood drips down but I barely notice.

Demon is closest to me. He walks over and looks at my hand. "What's going on with you? Is everything alright?"

The anger swells inside of me. My body is on fire. "No, I'm not. Come with me?" I pause. "I need to check on Elena, so you might get to have some fun if anyone dares to touch her."

A sardonic grin envelops his face. "I'm in."

I knew he would be. He's twisted. We're both a little unhinged. I'm reckless, but he's higher on the psycho scale than me.

Viper and Cash are watching me closely. Cash stands, but as he walks toward me, I mumble to Demon, "Quick. Let's get out of here before they try to stop us."

Demon gives me a sharp nod. "I'll get the keys. Meet you in the van."

"Get me a tea towel from inside for my hand."

As Demon walks away, I glance at Cash. "I'm alright. Demon's just getting something for my hand."

He gives me a slow nod.

I hurry along the side of the house and to the van. If Elena's boss is there with her . . . if he tries anything . . . My hands ball into fists. I swear I'll kill him.

Elena

THE HOUSE IS FULL OF STRANGERS. SOME DANCING AND OTHERS talking. I cough from the cloud of cigarette smoke.

"I'm so happy you could join us," Lucy says with a wide smile, and then she bumps her hip against mine.

I give her a fake smile in return. I regret agreeing, but after a long week I need this distraction. I just don't want to think about Axle. He's under my skin. It pains me to know I still love him, even with all the heartbreak he's caused me. I don't regret the time spent with him, because he made me happy. No matter how hard I try, I can't hate him.

"Here," Lucy says, handing me another full shot glass. This time there's red liquid in it. She raises hers and we clink our glasses together. "To getting over Axle."

"Cheers," I say and swallow in two gulps. Instantly a sharp burn hits my throat, making me cough and my face twist into a grimace. "Oh, that one's strong." It warms my belly, but my head spins. Someone grips my shoulders, and I turn to see Cameron.

"You need to relax," he says softly, gently working his fingers into my shoulders.

My body stiffens slightly, but I'm too sluggish to move away from him. "I am relaxed," I murmur.

He laughs. "Not relaxed enough. How many shots have you had?" he asks, then looks between me and Lucy.

Lucy shrugs. "We're still standing," she says, then giggles. "Alcohol will help her forget . . . at least for tonight, anyway."

I peer down at the empty shot glass. "Well . . . pour me another."

"That's the spirit," Cameron says.

Cameron pours me another shot and reaches over to pass it to me. I blink a few times. I see two shot glasses, though I'm pretty sure my eyes are playing tricks on me.

Cameron laughs and brings the glass to my lips. I swallow the shot down.

My head falls to the side. Everything's spinning. I grab the kitchen counter to stay upright.

"Are you alright?" Lucy asks, sounding worried.

I rub my forehead. *No, I am not.*

"I'll take her to her bedroom so she can lie down," says Cameron.

Hmm, bed . . . seems like such a good idea right about now.

"Are you sure?" Lucy asks him or me. I'm not exactly sure at this point. I just want to be in my warm, comfortable bed.

"It's fine. I'll get her there safe and tucked in bed," he replies.

Cameron grabs my hips, helping me stand. "Woah . . ." I mutter. We walk around the bunch of bodies. I put my arm over his shoulder as we step up the stairs. He wraps his arm around my waist, pulling me tight against his body. When we reach the top, he wiggles my bedroom doorknob.

"It's locked. Do you have the key?"

My eyes are heavy, but I point to my pocket. He dips his hand into my pocket. It lingers there, and then he rubs the edge of my privates. I take a step back, nearly losing my footing. "What are you doing?" I slur.

He smirks. "Helping you into your room." He unlocks the door and guides me inside and eases me down on my bed. He leans over and brushes my hair out of my face.

"Mm," I grunt. I want to go to sleep.

He leans over me. "I'm going to make you forget that piece of trash. I'm going to make you feel good." His lips crash into mine.

Shock turns my body to stone. *No . . . this can't be happening. I don't want him.* I squirm, trying to pull away, but I'm struggling. His body is heavy. I'm drunk, but I know I don't want this. He grabs my boob roughly.

"Don't," I say, but he doesn't listen. He kisses down my neck while I'm struggling beneath him, my heart racing, my stomach queasy.

"Get off me!" I say, louder. I try to push him off, but he's so strong.

He's frowning. "What, you can take dick from a biker, but you don't want mine?"

I blink at him. Worry clutches at me. *Will he hurt me . . . rape me?*

The door crashes against the wall with a loud thud, jolting Cameron upright. He leaps off me, eyes wide with panic, and hurriedly backs away to the far corner of the room. His voice is shaky as he protests, "It's not what it looks like."

Axle's chilling gaze is aimed at Cameron, the hostility radiating off him. Instant relief eases my heavy heart. *He's here. He will protect me.* Axle darts to Cameron and grabs him by the throat. Cameron's feet are dangling. "I'll fucking bury you!" Axle screams in his face.

Demon kicks the bedroom door closed. His smile is amused, and a wicked glint dances in his eyes. A dull crunch pulls my attention back to Axle. He's out of control, throwing punch after punch at Cameron's face. Demon creeps toward him, his smile curving higher. He pulls Axle off Cameron.

Axle glares at Demon. "Get the fuck off me."

Demon doesn't flinch. "I'll take care of him." He peers at me and his gaze softens. "You tend to her. I'll meet you at the van in ten."

Axle turns to me and his shoulders fall. He takes cautious steps toward me, then takes my shaky hand in his and helps me sit upright. I notice the blood and redness on his hands and knuckles. He scoops me up, one arm supporting my legs and the other my back and pulls me to his chest. His heart is hammering against me, and his breathing is heavy. He kisses the top of my head.

As we walk out, Demon says, "You're mine, motherfucker."

The terrified scream that follows makes me flinch, but I have no sympathy for Cameron because I know he would have tried to rape me if he'd had the chance. Axle closes the bedroom door behind us and carries me down the stairs. His body is stiff, as if violence is still coursing through his veins, but his need to care for me outweighs that part of him.

The screams fade away, drowned out by the blaring music. I burrow deeper into the comforting warmth of Axle's chest, choosing not to meet anyone's gaze. He kisses the top of my head again.

"I'm so sorry," he says just loud enough that I can hear it.

It's not your fault. I want to reassure him, but the words catch in my throat, leaving me unable to speak.

Outside, he opens the van door and ever so gently places me down on the seat. His eyes drift over my face and body. With a pained expression, he asks, "Did he hurt you?"

I shake my head. Physically, no . . . I tug at Axle's shirt, needing him to stay with me. He sits on the seat beside me and pulls me down so that my head is resting on his lap. He strokes my hair and whispers, "I've got you."

Tears well up as I imagine what might have been. Despite Axle using violence against people who hurt me, I feel an undeniable sense of security when I'm wrapped in his arms. His protective presence is unwavering, and I know he'll always be there to keep me safe.

His eyes, full of determination, meet mine, offering a silent promise that reassures me. "Don't cry, baby girl," he says softly as he wipes my falling tears with his thumb. There's a pain in his voice and I want to stop crying, but I can't.

A short while later, the front door slams shut, making me jolt.

"Shhh . . ." Axle says. "It's just Demon."

The van starts and we pull away. "Did you hurt him?" Axle asks menacingly.

Demon lets out a dark chuckle. "Sure did. My knife went through both his hands. He'll think twice before touching another woman against her will. I told him if it happens again, he'll be six feet under."

"Thanks, brother."

"Good times," Demon replies.

TWENTY-ONE
SHE'S MY RIDE OR DIE

Axle

Elena fell asleep in the car, so I carried her to bed and made sure she was asleep before I went to the bathroom to wash the blood off my hands. Adrenaline is still firing through me. I've lost control many times, but never to the point where I wanted to kill someone.

Bomber knocks on the door, his face sterner than normal. "Church, now!"

"Okay," I respond. A weight has lifted with the knowledge that Elena is safe in my bed and that the rapist got what was coming to him. Though I'd be more satisfied if he wasn't breathing. I dry my hands and go downstairs.

I join the men at the table. Demon has a radiant smile on his face. I try to smother a smile at the fact that violence makes him a happy boy.

"Care to explain what the fuck happened?" Reaper asks.

I'm honest. The men need to know. "We got to Elena's just in time before her boss raped her."

There're gasps, then silence around the table. Demon's still smiling, but the rest of the men's faces harden. No one dares to argue the point. Everyone would have done the same if that happened to their girl.

Reaper nods. "That explains it, then. Our contact at the police station called and informed me that a man got stabbed, and two men wearing cuts were seen leaving the scene."

Demon snorts. "They're exaggerating. I only stabbed his hands for touching Elena."

"Nice job," Viper chimes in.

"Thanks," Demon replies, looking pleased with himself. "I would have done more, but there were too many witnesses. I can go back now if you want me to?"

"I'm down for that," I swiftly respond.

"Not now. Will her boss report the two of you to the police?" Bomber asks, glancing at me and then Demon.

"I doubt it," Demon replies. "I warned him if he talks, I'll chop off his fingers one by one and shove them down his throat."

"Jesus Christ," Twitch mutters.

I laugh because I truly believe Demon would do it.

"Is there anything else anyone would like to add?" asks Reaper.

I shake my head. No one says anything, so Reaper bangs the gavel and we all get up to leave.

Cash puts his hand on my arm. "How is she?"

"He would have raped her if we hadn't shown up," I say through gritted teeth, anger flaring. I stretch my neck from side to side, trying to calm myself as the rapid mood change threatens to drown me. "It's shaken her up."

He shakes his head, disgust written all over his face. "Did he get far?"

"I haven't asked. Elena had her clothes on. She was terrified, her hair was a mess around her head, and her shirt was pulled up, showing her bra. She was so drunk"—I swallow thickly—"she wouldn't have been able to put up much of a fight."

He frowns. "I'm glad you got there when you did."

"Me too." But if I hadn't made the bet, I guarantee she wouldn't have been drinking. Elena hardly drinks. This is my fault. "I better get back and check on her," I say.

I rush to Elena, taking the stairs two at a time. I open the bedroom door slowly, not wanting to wake her. The room is dark, but with the light filtering in the window, it's still bright enough to see her.

I take off my cut, then my shirt, and get under the blanket with her. She rolls over toward me and shuffles close. I put my arm around her, pulling her tight against me. I'll do anything to make it right. "I love you, Elena," I whisper. "I promise to make it up to you."

I wake up to sunlight flooding the room and Elena moving in my arms. She stiffens. I lie on my side so that we're facing each other and rub her back, giving her a minute. But then I hear sniffling. I cup her chin and raise her head. Tears streak her face. Her grief pierces my heart. "Do you remember?" I ask.

"Yes," she whispers.

I lean in and kiss her forehead. "You're safe now."

"You came for me . . ." Her voice cracks. "Thank you."

"I'll always protect you." Hell, I'd kill for her . . . I wanted to kill for her. I remember the blood pouring from his face as I lay into him with my fists. That will have to do . . . *for now.*

"Are you hungry?" I ask. "Do you want some food or water . . . or maybe a headache pill?" Lately, I've become very familiar with what a hangover feels like.

"No. I just want you here with me."

"Of course I'll stay with you, baby girl."

She grasps my hand and links our fingers together. She's

staring at my bruised knuckles and the cuts on my hand. "I'm sorry you got hurt."

I briefly close my eyes. "It was worth it." I feel a sense of regret, like I didn't do enough. Her boss should be dead, but at the same time I didn't want to bring too much heat on the club, and Elena needed me.

"What did Demon do to him?" she asks.

"Uh . . . you sure you want to know?" I give her an out because she's not used to violence.

"Yes," she replies firmly.

"Demon stabbed him in the hands for laying a hand on you."

She's quiet, making me think I shouldn't have told her.

"I can't go back to work . . ." she mumbles.

"You certainly won't be." *No fucking way!*

She stares down before making eye contact. "What happened to Cameron?" She shudders. "I'm going to find it hard if I run into him again."

My jaw clenches. I swear if I see that guy again, I'll strangle him. "He's gone and won't be coming back."

She frowns. "What makes you so sure?"

"Because Demon made it pretty clear that we wanted to kill him and that we will if he ever comes back to this town. Hell, I hope he comes back."

Tears fall from her eyes. It kills me seeing her like this.

"Do you think Lucy and all of them knew . . . knew of Cameron's past, but still let him walk me to my room drunk?"

"I have no idea, but I'm sure your boss would have denied everything to anyone who ever asked about his past."

She nods slowly. "I don't want to live with my roommates anymore, in the house where it happened, either."

"You don't have to. I told you to move in here." I don't want to sound like I'm pressuring her, so I add, "At least until

you get back on your feet so that you don't have to pay rent."
But really, I want her to stay with me forever.

"Thank you so much," she whispers. Hurt still lingers in
her voice.

All I want to do is take her pain away. "Whatever you
need. Just say when, and me and one of the men will go pack
up your things and bring them to the clubhouse."

"Soon please. I just . . . I just want that all behind me.
Cameron's friends with my roommates, and I don't want to
associate with any of them."

"Me and Cash will go tomorrow."

She squeezes my hand. "Okay, I need you here holding me
today, though."

"I'm not going anywhere." If she wants me, I'll never
leave her side again.

TWENTY-TWO
I AM HIS AND HE IS MINE

Elena

A MONTH PASSES BY, AND WITH EACH DAY I FEEL STRONGER. My anxiety got worse after the incident, to the point where I was curled up in bed with Axle by my side. His presence calmed me. His unwavering support has been my anchor through it all, and I've slowly pieced myself back together.

I've seen the sincerity of his regret, so I forgave him and chose to move on from our past mistakes, this time without any lies or bets. He hurt me, but he's given me my confidence back, and the whole time I've been with him he's protected me and shown me how much he loves me.

The clubhouse is now my home. The men here are my friends . . . well, most of them. I'm still a little unsure about Bomber and Demon. Grace and Vera have been quieter than usual. I still get the daggers from Grace, and I'm sure it's only a matter of time before she starts being nasty again. I'm not going to let it get to me, and I know I need to work on sticking up for myself.

I'm on Axle's lap outside. We're sitting at the table and he's laughing and talking to the men. I smile at my red flag of a soul mate. The more I'm with him, the more I feel like myself. It's as if I was comatose and he breathed air into my soul. I've changed since I met him, but in a good way. Our love doesn't make sense, but I love who I am when I'm with him, and that's all that matters.

He gives me an adoring smile, then plants a hard kiss on my lips and hugs me tightly. "I fucking love you. You know that, right?"

"Yes," I reply. I smile. He tells me every day.

"We should get married."

I cough. His words have gotten stuck in my throat. "Did you just propose to me?" I ask in utter shock. There's silence around the table.

He smiles wickedly. "Yeah, why not?"

"You don't mean it," I playfully whack him. "You're just joking."

He shakes his head. His playfulness is gone. "You're my ride or die, babe, and you make me a better person. Just being around you calms my restless soul. I know Victor would kick my ass if I let you slip through my fingers."

"Say yes, darl'. You know you want to," Viper chimes in.

"Oh, what the hell—yes!" I beam and his entire face brightens. His lips meet mine. He kisses me longer this time, but with a gentle tenderness. He's got a smart mouth and he's a little crazy, but I can't imagine my life without him. He showed me how to live. I showed him how to love.

IN TRUE AXLE FASHION, WITH HIS RECKLESSNESS AND impulsivity, he demanded we get married within a week. I've managed to organize a wedding in a hall in town. I went with minimal decorations, and a couple of the club members helped to set it up. I purchased my wedding dress online with express delivery. I thought I'd want a big wedding with all the bells and whistles, but I realized that all I want is my friends—who have turned into family—and my sister there. All the rest doesn't matter.

"It's going to be okay tomorrow, babe. Stop stressing," Axle says beside me on the bed.

I scoff. *Easy for him to say.* "I hope my parents don't ruin it for us." The phone call with them was an absolute nightmare. My mom, as per usual, was overly dramatic and had to be taken to the hospital by ambulance. My sister called me to say it was just a panic attack.

"Are they even going to come?" he asks.

"Ava said they would, but as you know, I don't want Dad walking me down the aisle. It doesn't seem right if they don't support us as a couple."

Axle's eyes narrow. "As if I'd let them ruin our wedding. I've talked to the men about keeping an eye on them. You've got nothing to worry about."

I breathe a sigh of relief. He's always protecting me. Thinking of my sister warms my chest. "I'm so excited to see my sister."

"Babe," he says mockingly, "you're supposed to be excited to marry me. Anyone would think you're more excited to see her."

I laugh, then wrap my arms around his shoulders and plant a kiss on his lips. "Of course I'm excited to marry you. It's just that I haven't seen or spoken to her properly in a really long time. She got married and eventually we stopped talking." I miss spending time with her so much.

"Fuck her," he says with a bite in his tone. "You deserve better than that."

"Axle," I warn. "She's a kind, loving person. You'll see! I reckon it's her husband that's created the distance between us. When I see them, there's something off about him. I just don't trust him."

Axle nods. "Always trust your instincts."

My eyes narrow. "And talking about my sister . . ."

He inches back. "Woah, why are you giving me that look?"

"Ava is beautiful. I want none of the MC men trying to hit on her. I know she's married, but I'm sure that wouldn't stop them."

"I can't promise—"

My eyes narrow further into slits.

He chuckles. "Okay, okay. I'll warn them beforehand."

"Promise me?" I don't need drama. My sister would never cheat, but she's a kind person, and I don't want any of the men trying anything. Her husband is overprotective of her, and I don't want any fights.

Axle puts a cross over his heart. "I promise."

I look away, thinking. "I know it's short notice, but I'd still like someone to walk me down the aisle. Do you think if I ask Cash he'll say yes?"

Axle's eyes bulge. "You sure?"

I nod. "It seems right. The whole time, Cash has encouraged us to be together, and he's your best friend. He's always been friendly and welcoming to me, and I'd like it to be someone who believes in us as a couple and who cares about us." It is my wedding . . . my time to be happy.

"Cash would be honored." Axle leans over and kisses my cheek. "Thank you for thinking about me too." There's a tenderness in his words, and I know he means it.

He stands and grabs my hand, pulling me to my feet. "Let's go downstairs and have a few drinks to celebrate with the men. Tomorrow you will be Mrs. Elena Evans."

I smile widely at him. I can't wait for tomorrow. When we reach the top of the stairs, I see all the MC men are around the bar. When their eyes catch us, they cheer and clap. Viper's hollering. Heat rises up my neck and to my cheeks, but I'm smiling. As I step down the stairs, I trip on the first one. My stomach plummets, but two hands come around my waist and pull me upright.

"I've got you, babe," Axle says with a wink. He yells out to the crowd, "She's always falling for me."

The men and I start laughing. I swat at the cheeky devil. We've been on a wild ride. After all the love and deceit, the joy and heartbreak, I still love him. I'm happiest and most confident when I'm with him.

TWENTY-THREE
COMMITMENT

Elena

TODAY IS THE BIG DAY. I'M AN ABSOLUTE MESS. I HAVEN'T SEEN Axle. I need his reassurance right now. Cash and I are outside, waiting for the music to play, to go inside.

"Is there anything I can do to . . . um . . . help you?" Cash asks, his eyes wide. He's keeping his distance from me.

I shake my head. My skin is on fire. I flap my arms, trying to cool down my armpits because I'm sweating up a storm. I hope I don't leave marks on my satin wedding dress. I went with an elegant, white, off-the-shoulder mermaid dress with a short train.

"Do you want me to cancel the wedding?" he asks.

"No!" I reply. My voice is harsh. "I want to get married to Axle. I'm just anxious about walking down the aisle while everyone's looking at me. I'm not good with being the center of attention." I close my eyes. "And what if Axle changes his mind?" I suck in a sharp breath, my heart threatening to burst. "What if he realizes he doesn't want to spend the rest of his life with me? What if—"

"He loves you," Cash says soothingly, his hands on my shoulders. "Everything is going to be o-kay."

I take deep breaths, but my mind tortures me. "What happened to my parents? Are they here? Is my sister here?" I hope my sister's here. I don't want to do today without her.

"Yes, Viper said they're sitting in the front row. Rage is by their side, keeping an eye on your parents so that they behave. Everything is under control."

"Wicked Game" by Chris Isaak begins to play. It's the instrumental version. I thought it was appropriate given our love story. Cash holds his arm out and I link mine with his, then pull him close to me. "Don't let me fall . . ." Because it is highly likely I'll trip over my own feet, especially in these heels.

He chuckles. "I won't let you fall."

I peer up at him to see his soft, reassuring gaze. I smile, grateful I chose him to walk me down the aisle.

One slow step at a time we make our way in and down. I keep my eyes on the incredible man at the end of it. I know everyone is looking at me, so I put all my focus on Axle. He's facing me. He's wearing normal attire—dark jeans, a white shirt with his cut over the top—and I'm fine with that. I don't want to force him to change. I want him to be himself. It's his day too.

I glance at the front row. My sister is smiling widely and dabbing the corner of her eye like she's crying. When we reach Axle, Cash hands me off to him. Axle gazes at me adoringly. My anxiety floats away in his presence and at seeing his love for me. I know deep in my soul that I made the right decision to marry him, and I've never been so certain of something in my life.

Axle slowly raises his hand to my cheek, and I nuzzle into it. "You look beautiful, baby girl."

I blink back tears. We aren't even married yet and I'm barely holding back my emotions. *Don't cry, don't cry.*

His eyes devour every inch of me. He arches his neck and peers around the side to see my ass. "And that dress . . ." He whistles and wipes the sweat off his forehead, giving me his signature grin. He pulls me into him, then his eyes flick to my lips, and before I can utter a single word, his lips are on mine in a slow, tender kiss.

The priest clears his voice, and then I hear, "You're not supposed to kiss her yet." I instantly know the voice from the crowd belongs to Viper.

I pull back, giggling. It's so typical of Axle.

"You taste delicious," he says wickedly. "Are you ready to be Mrs. Evans?"

"I'm so ready to spend the rest of my life with you."

Axle

I PEER AROUND THE CROWD. THE RECEPTION SEEMS TO BE GOING well. I sigh while I look at *my* wife. Fuck, I'm lucky she gave me a second chance and said yes when I asked her to marry me. She's talking to her sister, Ava, at our table. They both laugh, then take a sip of their champagne. I smile at them. Elena looks so happy with Ava.

I thought I was going to hate Ava for how she's treated Elena, but she's sweet and quiet, just like Elena. The two of them have stayed close all night. I look over at Ava's husband. He's a drunk. I have no idea how he managed to score someone like her. The only reason we haven't kicked his ass out is because I don't want to upset Ava, which will then upset Elena, but I've had the men keep a close eye on him.

Viper and Reaper have taken a liking to Ava. I was in shock when Reaper sounded interested. He's never shown interest in any woman since I've met him. I'm just praying to God they listen to me and leave Ava alone. Tonight is my wife's night, and I have to ensure she has the perfect night with no drama.

Elena's parents haven't caused any issues, but even if they tried, we have them under control. They haven't spoken a word to me, which I find hilarious. They haven't hugged Elena or congratulated her, not that I'm surprised. They've just been stone-cold quiet. I think they came just to show their faces, but I'm betting we won't be seeing much of them in the future.

The music suddenly changes to a dirty dancing beat. Reaper is on the microphone. "Everyone, it's time for tossing the bouquet and the garter."

I rub my hands together. My body tingles with anticipation. "The garter first," I yell out. There's a round of chuckles. When Elena looks at me, she smiles. I wink back and give her an indecent grin.

She stands while I move to her. We link hands, and I lean down to give her a brief kiss. As we walk toward the chair in the middle of the dance floor, I say. "Can we get out of here soon? I want you all to myself."

She gives me a knowing smile. "You'll be alright. There's only a few more hours to go."

I snort. "No, I won't be, and this is just going to be a tease."

When we reach the chair, Elena sits. The crowd hums with excitement.

"Over here," Cash calls out. He's holding a blindfold.

"What's that for?" I ask.

"It's to go over your eyes."

I frown. "I don't need that."

"It's a request from your wife."

Well . . . in that case, I don't have a choice. *"Fine!"*

He places the blindfold over my head, covering my eyes. My anticipation heightens.

"Can you see?" he asks.

"Nope!"

"Good," he chuckles.

There's a pause and I'm buzzin'. "Well, can I go to my wife yet or what?"

"Just hold on a sec."

I groan. "What do I have to wait for?" They are teasing me on purpose, I swear. I tap my foot.

"Okay . . . it's time. I'll grab your arm and lead you to her."

My heartbeat quickens. I lick my lips in eagerness. I can't wait to touch her soft, smooth legs.

"Here's Elena," Cash says.

I kneel down, lift her dress, and grab her foot. The crowd cheers. I breathe in . . . Jesus Christ . . . I near gag at the stench. I keep going further, past her calf muscle. I want this to be sexy, so I start to run my tongue up her leg to the garter. Wait . . . her legs are hairy AF! How did the hair grow so fast? She wasn't like that the other day. But I keep going, and when I reach her thigh, I tug the soft material down her leg with my teeth. When I get up, the crowd is in stitches laughing.

I slip off the blindfold to find—to my horror—Viper sitting on the chair with a tablecloth on his lap. He blows me a kiss. I shake my head as my stomach churns. Elena is laughing. She and Viper high-five each other. I turn to the side, gagging again.

Viper gets off the chair and steps over to me. "You loved it, brother."

"You've scarred me for life. I'm going to have nightmares."

Elena comes over, wearing a smug grin.

I raise my brow. "That wasn't very nice, Mrs. Evans."

She laughs. "Oh, *babe*, that was hysterical."

No doubt it's payback for all the times I embarrassed her. At least she's got a sense of humor. I suppose she'd have to to put up with all my shit.

The end.

REAPER

BOOK 2

PROLOGUE – SHE'S NOT MINE

I want her.

Those curves. That smile. I've never been so attracted to a woman. I take a swig of my beer and watch as she talks to her sister, Elena. We are at Elena and Axle's wedding. The men mentioned Elena had a sister, but I have never seen her before today, and I know I won't be forgetting her anytime soon. She leans in, picks up her champagne, and takes a few sips. When she places it on the table, the strap of her dress falls from her shoulder, and all I want to do is taste her.

I readjust myself in my seat.

Viper elbows me. "You like her?" He gives Elena's sister a pointed look.

Bomber leans in from the other side of me, listening to our conversation.

"I do." I want her badly.

"Her name's Ava," says Viper.

I raise a brow, and he grins smugly.

"What?" he says with his hands up. "She's fucking hot, so of course I asked Axle about her."

My jaw clenches. The possessiveness shooting through me surprises me. I don't even know her. I glance at Bomber, and the side of his lip twitches like he's smothering a smirk. The observant bastard misses nothing.

"She's married," Viper chimes in. "Not that it means anything these days."

I lift my hand to my chin. "I wonder how committed."

"Axle didn't say, but he warned me to stay away. He said —and I quote—'I want to have sex with my wife tonight, and I don't want anyone fucking that up for me. So Ava's off limits.'" Viper's voice mocks Axle's.

Ava is still deep in conversation with Elena; then they laugh. The music is too loud, so I can't hear them, but it makes me curious as to what her laugh sounds like.

"Is her husband here?" I ask Viper.

He laughs. "It's the guy sitting next to Elena's mom at the table next to the bride and groom."

I peer at Elena's parents and see a man gulping half of his bottle of beer next to them. His eyes are on Ava.

"She's with the drunk?" I ask, shocked, remembering the man stumbling to the bar earlier.

"Yep. I couldn't believe it either. She's way too good for him."

I stare at the man who has what I want. He's average look-ing, nothing special.

"I saw him earlier, but I thought he was a family member."

I haven't seen him touch or kiss Ava or show any affection that would suggest they're married. If she was mine, I wouldn't be able to keep my hands off her. I'd want the world to know.

"Viper," Candy calls from the dance floor. "Come and dance with me."

His smile widens. "I'm coming." He stands. "Well, fellas, it's my time to shine."

Chuckling, I shake my head.

He fixes his hair like he's a peacock parading its feathers. "What? I've got moves."

"Yeah, okay, Justin Timberlake," I taunt.

He walks to Candy, puts his arm across her back, and dips her backward, lifting a brow and grinning at us. She lets out a squeal and laughs.

Demon's leaning back in his chair, looking at the dance floor. He doesn't look like he's watching people dancing; it's like he sees through them, as if his mind is elsewhere. He taps on the table, and even with his tattoos, bruises and scabs on his knuckles from the other night stand out.

I lean toward him and raise my voice. "You don't have to stay here."

He slowly turns his head with a wicked smile and then stands. He lifts his chin. "I'll see you back at the clubhouse later."

With a sharp nod, I watch as people step away from him, giving him room to move freely to the exit.

I make eye contact with Axle. He leaves a group and walks to us.

"Is Demon leaving already?" He looks at his watch. "It's still early."

"He looked bored, which is usually not good."

He sighs. "Good point."

"Is Ava really married?" I ask, hoping Viper got it wrong.

Axle's eyes widen. "You too?" His shoulders drop. "Just give me one night of wild sex with my wife. I don't want her in my ear saying that her sister had sex with a biker and got divorced over it." His voice is whiney.

Even though it's tempting, I respect Axle too much to do anything about it, but something claws inside of me. "You have my word."

He blows out a gush of air. Elena appears at his side. He looks at her, smiles, and puts his arm around her waist. "You owe me a dance."

She smiles back. "I thought you'd never ask."

He grabs her hand and leads her to the dance floor.

I search for Ava but can't find her. I sit upright in my chair, looking around. "She walked toward the restroom," says Bomber, like he read my mind. We've been friends for a long time. We know each other well.

"Thanks," I reply, my eyes turning to the hallway leading to the bathroom. I fidget in my chair, wanting to get up, but the discussion I had with Axle keeps me seated.

I may never see her again plays in my head. I've never felt a strong pull to a woman before, so I stop fighting myself and then stride toward the restrooms. I won't have sex with her anyway. I'm just curious.

As I get closer, she walks out. Her eyes are on her dress as she tries to pull up its cleavage. Her dress covers most of her boobs, but with big perfect tits like that, I don't know why she is bothering. She looks flawless the way it is.

She huffs when the dress won't cover her further. When she lifts her eyes, they widen when she sees me staring at her, and it's like someone has punched me in the gut.

"You're beautiful."

Freezing, Ava stares at me with wide eyes. She says nothing, but a blush creeps up her neck and to her face. She breaks eye contact as she picks at her dress. When she looks up at me, she smiles and her eyes glisten like she's holding back tears. "Thank you."

In my periphery, her husband approaches us with narrowed eyes, though swaying to the right. The warmth in my chest dissipates, and my body tenses and turns to stone. I glance at Ava, and when her eyes lock onto her husband, she gasps and steps away from me. Her breathing has picked up. Her shoulders have hunched over, and she looks scared.

I fucking hate it. Something isn't right.

When he reaches us, I can smell the alcohol on him. He looks me up and down with his glassy eyes, and I don't miss the tightness in his jaw.

His hand comes out to me. "Beau."

I shake his hand, noticing his firm grip. "Reaper."

He coughs. "Well, that's certainly a name you've got there."

I ignore him and look at Ava. She swallows thickly as her eyes keep darting between me and her husband.

"I'm ready to go, Ava. Your parents are leaving, too."

My eyes widen. No "are you ready to leave?" It seems like an order.

"You can stay with your sister. There are spare rooms available," I tell her.

He answers for her. "Ava's tired." Then he looks at her. "Aren't you?"

"Ah, yes," she replies and gives me a small smile. "But I appreciate the offer."

Beau grabs her arm. She flinches. My hands clench at my side.

"Have a good night," she says before they turn and leave.

It takes everything in me to stay still, to not rip her away from him. My gut churns.

Something isn't right; she fears him.

I close my eyes briefly. "She's not mine," I say to myself. "She's not mine."

ONE
CLIPPED WINGS

One Year Later

Ava

His loud snoring fills the room. I watch him closely as I sit up, then drag the duvet off me. When I turn to the edge of the bed, it causes pain to shoot up my side, making my eyes squeeze shut. When my feet hit the floor, I slowly stand, but the bed creaks. It makes my stomach drop. My eyes flick to him, but he's still asleep. I grab my phone from the night-stand. My feet pad on the floor as I tiptoe out of the room. My heartbeat is surging as I quietly pull the door shut.

Using my phone as a light, I move to the closet in the spare room, then reach up and grab the old beanie. I open it up to pick out the cash I've been saving. I take my jeans and a loose shirt off the hanger and get changed. I put on a black coat and leave the hood up to cover my head.

I grab the backpack with shaky hands and sling it over my shoulder. In the kitchen, I grab my purse and place the money inside.

I peek back once more before I open the front door and step outside.

Fresh air meets my face, making me shiver, but I know it's not just from the cold. I dart down the stairs, then run onto the road, even though every step brings me pain. I run as if someone is chasing me, and even though he's in bed, asleep, it still feels like he's here with me. I hope the fear leaves me, even if it means hiding away from him forever.

A few streets away, I reach an area surrounded by trees and bushes and pull my phone from my pocket and make a call, even though it fills me with shame.

When she answers, loud music and shuffling echoes in the background.

"Ava, is that you?"

My mouth goes dry. *I'm so weak.* I never used to be this person, and here I am, calling my younger sister for help.

"Ava?"

"Hey, Elena," I say through sniffling.

"Who's that calling?" a man asks.

"Shh . . . It's my sister," Elena says.

"What's wrong? Are you okay?" she asks, sounding worried.

For the first time, I say, "No. I'm not."

"What happened?"

My stomach plummets. A car rolls by, so I hide behind a tree, paranoid it could be him. "I need to get out of here," I whisper, my voice coarse.

There's a brief silence before she speaks. "What's he done?"

"Nothing, nothing. I just need somewhere to stay before I

get back on my feet, that's all." I'll quickly burn through that money I saved if I have to pay for accommodation.

"At one in the morning?"

I didn't think this through. She would have a lot of questions. I've had no contact with her since the wedding, and before that we had been distant for years.

She answers, "You can stay here, if you're okay with staying at a clubhouse because we haven't brought our own place yet."

My sister married a biker a year ago, and at any point, I would have said no way, but I will stay anywhere. "That's fine. I promise I won't stay long. It's just until I can get a job."

"Are you guys getting a divorce or something?"

Pausing, I close my eyes. "Something like that."

She sighs. "I'm glad you're getting out of that marriage. It felt like I lost you to him. You stopped calling."

She pays more attention than I thought.

"I'll catch a bus there. Can you tell me the address?"

"Don't be stupid. You have to tell me something."

I exhale through my mouth, knowing no makeup could hide the bruise on my face from yesterday afternoon.

"So am I meeting you at your house, or . . .?"

"No."

"I'm coming." I hear the male voice again.

I have met her husband only briefly, so I'm not sure how he will react.

"Where am I picking you up?"

I think he'll check public transportation for me if he wakes up. "Do you remember the park near my house?" I don't think he'll look for me at the park. I can get there from here without going on the road.

"At this time of night? Are you insane?"

"Please . . ." My voice is strained.

Again, she sighs. "Promise me you'll call if you see anything suspicious."

"I will."

"Okay, we will get there as soon as we can."

Relief floods me, and I make my way to the trail that leads to the park. Without the lights from the street, it's darker, so I turn on my phone's flashlight. Luckily for me, the dirt track has been cleared because the kids use it to ride their bikes through here.

It's eerily quiet as I walk through, and those intrusive thoughts flood my brain. I'm so pitiful that I've had to call my sister for help. I should have gotten out of the marriage sooner. I saw the red flags and talked to Mom about it, but she encouraged me to stay. I should have known better than to converse with her, but who else was I going to talk to? The only people Beau approved of were my parents.

My ankle rolls on unsteady ground, and I cry out in agony when I land hard. My hands burn from protecting my head and body from the fall. I sit up through a hissed breath and reach out for my phone, which slid under a small shrub. I wipe my hand on my coat to get rid of the dirt, and when I peer down, blood is trickling from the wound. I swap my phone to my bleeding hand to check the other, but it's fine.

When I pull my jeans up my calf, I see my ankle is swelling. The swelling is accompanied by a dull ache. My body is sore, but I'm not sure whether it's from the fall or from yesterday. I grasp my bag, bring it to the front of me, and search through it until I find the water bottle. I twist the lid and tip a little on my bleeding hand. It stings, but the dirt and blood run off my hand and onto the ground.

When the bleeding stops, I twist the cap on the bottle and put it back in the bag, then leverage myself up with my other hand. I wipe my damp face with my arm, take a deep breath, and step to walk again. My ankle throbs, so I limp the rest of the way.

My phone vibrates in my hand, and I swipe a little more dirt off the screen before answering it. "Hello?"

"Where are you?" Elena asks.

"I'm nearly there."

"What's with the heavy breathing? Are you walking?"

"I'll be there soon," I reply and hang up. I turn off my phone, take the SIM card out, then snap the card in half and throw it away.

When I reach the clearing, I can see the silhouette of a person swinging on a swing. I have an inkling it's my sister, and I hobble in her direction. The swing stops abruptly.

"Ava," she calls out and runs toward me.

I close my eyes and brace for the impact. Her arms come around me, and she hugs me fiercely, taking all the air out of my lungs. Everything is painful, especially my ribs.

When she pulls back, she asks, "What's going on?"

"Yeah. What is going on?" a deep voice asks. I jump. The familiar panic makes my stomach churn.

Elena touches my shoulder gently. I try not to flinch, but I can't help it. Every part of me is on edge.

"It's okay," she says, her voice soft. "It's only Jake."

I nod, though my heart doesn't slow.

We are in the shadows, so I can't see her clearly. She grasps my sore hand, and I pull it from hers at once. "I fell over."

"Um . . . okay. Well, let's get you cleaned up?"

I follow the two, who are whispering to each other.

He unlocks a van, and as he opens the door, the inside light comes on. When he gets into it, I get a better glimpse of him. He looks the same as he did at their wedding, though his playful mood from that night is nowhere to be seen.

Elena gasps, one hand covering her mouth, and so many

emotions cross her face. Sadness and anger, then sympathy. It burns me to see that in her eyes. This isn't supposed to be how my life turned out. My shoulders drop. I'm so pathetic.

She wipes the corner of her eye with her hand, but she doesn't speak. She stands rigid and stares at me.

Jake clears his throat. "C'mon, Elena, let's get out of here." When I turn to look at him, his eyes widen, then he looks at his wife and frowns.

"Get in," he says to me, underscoring his words with a jerk of his head.

I avoid eye contact with Elena as I pull the backpack off, get into the back of the van, and slide the door shut.

Her soft cries follow the slam of the car door. His hand goes across to her thigh to comfort her. The guilt of making her cry fills me with regret. I hate seeing her sad because of me.

Once we're driving, Jake's eyes flick between the road and the rearview mirror.

"Do you have anything for her?" Elena asks through sniffling. "Like first aid or a clean towel or something."

"Ah, yeah. There should be a metal box in the back there."

"I'm good," I say.

Elena turns to face me, with her eyes slightly narrowed. "You are far from good." A tinge of frustration weaves into her tone.

"I . . . Thank you for picking me up. I promise I won't stay for long. As soon as I get a job, I'll be out of your hair." Being a burden is my worst nightmare come true.

Her voice softens. "You can stay as long as you like."

"Let me run it through Reaper first before you make promises for a long-term stay—" says Jake.

"I have money. Not much, but I've been saving. I'm happy to help clean and cook and whatever I can until I find a place of my own."

"Since you've asked us to pick you up in the middle of the night. I'm going to presume your husband or ex-husband doesn't know you've left. If we're bringing you into the clubhouse, is he going to come looking for you? What should we expect to happen?"

Focusing on my bag, I fidget with the handle. "He doesn't know I left or where I'm going, so there shouldn't be any issues. He might search for me, but he won't know that I'll be with Elena."

"Yeah . . . and what's with the black eye and bruised cheek?" asks Jake.

"When he lost his job, his drinking got worse, so I packed a bag and started saving money because I didn't know how much longer I could handle his nasty remarks and controlling behavior. But yesterday was the first day that he hit me, and I knew it was time to leave because he was out of control and if I didn't get out now"—I lift my hand to my throat—"I don't know how far he would go next time."

Because there would be a next time . . . There is always a next time.

Elena faces me. "I'm so sorry. Why didn't you leave when it got bad? You should have called me; I would have been there for you."

Worthlessness bubbles up inside of me. "I didn't think it would come to this. We had to get through it together. I really tried to make it work." Self-loathing takes its place because maybe I didn't try hard enough.

Closing my eyes, I bring my feet up onto the seat and pull my knees to my chest to hug myself. Distant chatter continues, and exhaustion weighs heavily on me. I'm floating, followed by music and muffled voices, but the pull to sleep is stronger, and it takes over once more.

TWO
BROKEN INSIDE

"Don't wake her."

"Why? What if she has a concussion? It's been twelve hours."

My eyes creep open at Elena's voice. The beat of the drums and guitar riffs are coming from the music downstairs. It takes a moment to get my bearings until the memories of last night hit me.

I scan my surroundings. The room is small and plain, with painted white walls and an old wooden chest at the end of the bed, against the wall. I'm in a gigantic bed with faded blue sheets.

"You saw her. She needs all the rest she can get."

I notice the voice. It's Jake. However, his nickname at the wedding was Axle.

"You can come in," I say, my voice hoarse. There's a light thudding in my head.

The door opens slowly, and Elena's head pops around it, a frown on her face.

"Please don't give me the sympathy look," I tell her while she closes the door.

She blows out a breath. "It's not sympathy." She peers at the ground. "I hate seeing you hurting like this."

She sits on the edge of the bed next to me, her eyes traveling around my face. "You know me. I hate conflict, and I'm not one to wish harm on someone but . . ." She blinks furiously, as if trying not to cry.

She's such a gentle soul, and I have no idea how she ended up here, of all places. I put my hand on hers and squeeze.

". . . I hope he gets hit by a bus or something."

I laugh, then flinch. "Don't make me laugh. My ribs hurt."

"What happened to your ribs?"

"I fell awkwardly when he hit me. I wasn't expecting it, but, god, it's painful."

She frowns. "I never imagined him to be violent, but I thought you could have done better."

When I think back to the last couple of years, even before he lost his job, it feels like one hand was around my throat and the other squeezing my heart. Nothing I did was ever good enough.

"I don't want to talk about it right now . . . Anyway, how did you get a biker as a husband? I never got to ask at the wedding." We didn't get to spend much time together, and when I was coming back from the restroom, Beau saw me talking to a biker. That was it. We had to go home.

She gives me a sad smile. "We met through a dating app, and the rest is history. Now, I wouldn't say I belong here"—her eyes dim a little before she keeps going—"but I belong with him."

"I'm happy you found love."

Three loud knocks come from the door. "Lunch is ready."

Elena looks at it. "I won't be long." She then looks at me. "Did you want to come down, or did you want me to get a plate and bring it up for you?"

I pull the sheet up over my chest. "I can't . . ."

"Don't worry. I'll bring it up for you."

"I'm sorry," I say, and it makes me cringe.

"There's no need to apologize," she whispers.

Usually, everything is my fault. "Old habits, I guess."

Her frown deepens. "I'll go get you something to eat."

"Oh, and"—she cringes and looks to the floor—"the bathroom is to the right at the end of the hallway. I put a towel and some clothes on the chest of drawers there." She points to it.

Swallowing thickly, I nod, too choked up to speak.

As she turns the handle and opens the door, she looks at me over her shoulder. "We spoke to Reaper last night and you can stay, but if you could help cook and clean like you said you would, that would be great." She doesn't wait for an answer. She gives me a small smile and closes the door softly.

As I sit up in bed, pain assaults me from different areas. Everything aches. My mind wanders off to Beau. Was he angry when he didn't find me next to him, or would he even care? I grunt. Of course he would care. He would have no one to take his anger out on.

I pull the sheet off myself, but as soon as I stand, stiffness burns my body. When I take my first step, searing pain shoots up from my ankle and my jaw clenches. I hobble over to get the towel, clothes, and my bag and then limp over to the door. My hand rests on the doorknob, and before I open it, I peer down. My jeans have dirt caked at the knees where I fell over, and my coat has a swipe of blood and dirt on it.

I open the door and peek through the crack to see if anyone is around, then step outside and pull it closed behind me. Every step is agony, and I note to ask Elena for painkillers. As soon as I get in the bathroom, I turn the lock and place the towel and clothes on the towel rack.

Sliding my arms out of the coat, I suck in a breath through my teeth. I take my shirt off and undo the button of my jeans and pull them over my hips before stepping out of them. Inspecting my body, I see my palms are red and one has a scab. The side of my body is a mix of blue-and-purple bruises. A large deep purple one is on my hip and another up the side of my ribs. I touch the tender area.

When I look in the mirror, tears stream down my face. I'm a mess. My left eye is red and purple, and my cheek is more of a swirl of purple and blue.

I don't recognize the person in front of me. Bile rises, and I bend over the toilet in time to vomit. With the back of my hand, I wipe my mouth. I take my underwear off and step into the hot water. I cry in the shower because no one can see my tears, my weakness.

Once I'm out and have finished drying myself, knowing that my sister and I are different sizes, I lift the first piece of clothing in curiosity. She should know I wouldn't be able to get my boobs into her shirts and my ass into any pants she owns. I'm relieved that, instead, it's a burgundy dress, and up against me, it looks loose, so it may even fit. As I'm getting changed, a bang on the door startles me.

"What is taking so long? Hurry up, I need to take a piss!"

My breathing quickens, and my heart thrums as I hastily pull the dress over my head and grab my towel and dirty clothes. I open the door and am met by a handsome man. His face morphs from annoyed to curious as he raises a brow and looks me over from head to toe.

"Excuse me," I mutter. I bow my head, waiting for him to move from the doorway.

He remains still, and when I glance up, he's grinning. "Ava, is it?"

My grip on my clothes tightens as I clear my throat, wondering how he knows my name already. "Yes."

"Oh no you don't," Elena says from nearby. She bumps him aside with her hip, allowing me room to move past.

"I was just getting to know her."

I turn, watching their interaction. Elena shakes her head. "No, no, and no."

He winks at me. "Later, Ava."

She groans and follows me into the room. "There's your plate." She signals to the bed. "Sorry it took so long. I was helping to dish out the food, and those guys just didn't stop eating. I'm surprised they aren't fat, to be honest."

"It's okay. I needed a shower anyway."

She tugs at my dirty clothes. "Here, let me wash them."

I pull back. "I can do it."

She pulls them toward her. "Stop being so stubborn. Let me look after you for at least one day."

My shoulders fall, and I reluctantly pass them to her. The side of her mouth lifts victoriously.

"Did you want me to organize a doctor to come and check up on you?"

I'm quick to answer. "No. It looks worse than it is."

Her brow furrows. "Are you sure?"

"It's okay. They are only bruises. They will heal in no time."

"What about getting a protective order? I can ask the club's attorney about it."

I shake my head. "I'm away from him now. That's all that matters."

"I can get Jake to sort him out for you."

"Elena," I warn, "please stop."

She sighs noisily. "Okay . . . I'll wash these for you. I'll be back."

"Just chuck them out."

"What? Why?" She looks at my clothes. "The dirt will come out."

"I want nothing that reminds me of him. Can we go shopping so I can get some clothes?"

Her eyes dart to my bruises. "I'll organize the clothes. You just relax." She forces a smile.

After she leaves, I get up and flick the lock shut, then go over to the window and pull at it to ensure it's locked as well. After finishing the plate of food, I lie down and roll over onto my side. Still feeling drained, I close my eyes and fall back asleep.

THREE
NEW WORLD

Ava

I sit up abruptly, covered in sweat. I'm panting, trying to catch my breath. The room is dark, but it isn't long until I realize where I am. A blanket of relief covers me. "He's not here," I whisper to myself. I'm on edge and a shadow of who I once was. He's sucked the life right out of me.

The music and voices are loud, reminding me I'm here with more people than just Elena. I will go insane if I stay in this room by myself, dealing with my demons, so I get up and shuffle to the wall before turning on the light. After I blink a few times, my eyes adjust to the brightness. If they are having a party downstairs, it could be the perfect distraction. I grab my makeup bag, unlock the door, and walk over to the bathroom.

After I finish applying my makeup, I lean closer to the mirror. There's no hope of getting rid of the bruises, but I have covered them up somewhat. There's no mistaking my cleavage in this dress. I'm surprised it fits me. I'm lucky it flows out at the bottom. I stare at myself again. This will have to do.

After putting my belongings away, I walk through the hallway. A girl with only a thong on comes running in my direction, so I flatten myself against the wall and look away from her naked body. She's pulling the guy I met this afternoon behind her. He winks at me again as he walks past.

When I reach the top of the stairs, I hesitate. Every ounce of me wants to run back into the bedroom, but I take a deep breath and slowly make my way down. The song playing is "Debonaire" by Dope. I used to love all different music. I'll have to get a new phone to download all my favorite songs, and I'm sure there's new music out I haven't heard yet.

Squeals and high-pitched sounds of laughter make me physically cringe, and when I look over, two women are running away from a man with a different MC cut on. When he catches one, his arm curls around her back, and he pulls her into him and motorboats his face against her boobs. Her head falls back while she laughs.

"Ava!" Elena calls out.

I scan the crowd to see her rushing toward me. My sister is wearing white skinny jeans with a cute blue shirt tied up at the front, exposing her stomach, and it looks as though she's wearing a cut over the top.

When she gets closer, I see that at the top, where a pocket would be, it reads *War Brothers MC*. Underneath it says *Property of Axle*, and it sends shivers up my spine.

"What's this?" I cannot keep the disdain from my voice.

Her brow furrows. "It means that I'm his ol' lady. It's a tradition."

I don't answer, my eyes narrowing a fraction.

She shakes her head. "I can see your mind spinning. It means that I'm off limits to every other man."

"I still don't like it." Not after everything I've been

through. I could wear nothing that suggests I'm the property of a man.

"How are you feeling?"

"A little better after sleep, though I think I could sleep for days."

Her eyes soften and a genuine smile curves on her lips. "That's good."

I look around. "I don't know what I was expecting, but it wasn't this."

MC paraphernalia is plastered everywhere. A flag with their logo hangs on a wall. It's a skull with two guns behind it, with *War Brothers MC* across the top. A motorcycle rests in the wall, and photos of mug shots of the men litter the walls.

Everything is wood and has a masculine style. It has a wooden floor, exposed wooden beams, and wooden furniture, so it has an industrial feel to it. The place is open plan, so I can see what's going on around me.

"It surprised me when I first came here as well." She looks at the bar, then at me. "Do you want a drink?"

I give her a clipped nod and follow her over to where Jake is sitting. When we reach Jake, he puts an arm around her waist. "Ava," he says and tips his beer in greeting.

"Hey, Jake."

Elena sits on the stool next to Jake and pats the spare chair beside her. I take a seat. "Everyone calls each other by their road names, not by their actual names. So Jake's road name is Axle."

"If everyone but you calls him Axle, I'll call him that too."

"Fine by me." She looks at the other guy. "This is Cash. Cash, this is Ava, my sister."

He is tall, wearing a white shirt with his cut over the top, and has short black hair.

"Howdy," he says with a grin as he finishes wiping a glass.

"Nice to meet you, Cash."

"What would you two ladies like to drink?"

"Four shots—all tequilas," I answer, feeling Elena's eyes on me.

He lets out a low whistle. "Big night?"

"Something like that," I mumble, craving the numbness.

As he pours the tequila into four shot glasses, Elena gags. "Ewww. I hate tequila." She peers at me. "Ever since we got drunk off it that time, I haven't been able to touch it."

"Wow, that was a long time ago." I don't remember the taste, but I know it's not pleasant.

Cash places two shots in front of each of us.

"Hmm . . ." Elena looks at the shots like they're poisonous. "It still haunts me."

"I'll have yours, too, if you don't want them."

"No. I'll do it," she grumbles as she picks one up and, with her other hand, blocks her nose. I pick mine up, and we clink glasses and gulp them. The tequila burns the entire way down my throat.

Elena coughs and Axle pats her back. She slides the other shot over to me. "I can't do another." Her face scrunches. "It tastes like what I think nail polish remover would taste like."

Without a second thought, I pick it up and down it, then pick up the other and do the same, not even taking a breath between. It makes my eyes water, and I fight the need to retch, but soon after, a warm sensation fills my stomach. "Two more, please."

Elena gives me a sympathetic smile. "Are you sure?"

I put my hand up. "Yes!" After I slam those drinks down, the stress lifts.

"Why the name War Brothers MC?" I ask.

Her smile slips. "Most of them served in the military. Reaper, Bomber, and Viper were in the military together. When they came back, they wanted that brotherhood again, so they created the War Brothers MC. Bomber's family founded the town, and because Bomber owned this property, the MC decided to set up here, in Crown Village. Jake described it as it gave them a home and a purpose because they got to make friends with other men that went through similar experiences when they were at war."

I respect that, and I raise a brow at her. "So there's more to them that meets the eye?"

"There certainly is," she says as her eyes soften. "Well, I better give you the rundown on everyone here. Jake is the road captain. Cash here," she says and glances at him, "is the treasurer, and as you can see, he's easygoing."

She turns her head to the left and whispers, "The man at the end of the bar with the black hair, that's Bomber." I turn to where she is looking and watch as he slowly brings the glass to his lips and downs his drink, then slams the glass back onto the table.

"He is the sergeant at arms." She leans in closer, making sure only I can hear. "He's very blunt and straight to the point, so don't take it personally."

My eyes widen. "What do you mean by that? I can't handle another man like my husband."

"Oh, no, not like that. I meant he can appear cold, but it's just the way he is. The men here are different to anyone you have met before, but to be clear, none of them hurt women. Well . . . only if they ask for it." Her face flushes pink. "Some women are into that type of stuff."

My head falls back. "Elena. I don't want to know."

"What are you two whispering about?" Axle asks.

Giggling, she looks over her shoulder. "Nothing." She leans in closer again. "So you won't have any issue with Bomber trying to hook up with you, but some others . . ." Before jumping off her chair, she cringes. "I'm going to introduce Ava to everyone," she says to Axle and Cash, then lightly pulls me off my chair.

My head spins from the alcohol, so I grab her arm to stop me from swaying. I'm such a lightweight.

"Make sure you say her name, so they know *exactly who she is*," Axle says.

"I will," Elena replies.

She links her arm with mine, and as we take two steps toward Bomber, a woman steps in front of us and slides in next to him, clutching his arm. When she squeals, I shift to the side to see him grasping her forearm with cold eyes.

"No one touches me," he grates out. It startles me, so I step back and scowl at Elena.

She shakes her head at me. "He won't hurt her, he just"—she looks away before looking back at me and lowering her voice—"he doesn't like them touching him. They keep trying, even though he has made it clear that he won't sleep with them."

"I'm sorry, Bomber, I forgot," the woman says, trying to sound confident, but there's a hitch in her voice. "I can come around later, baby?"

She is so forward. What in the world is this place?

He hisses and lets go of her arm. "No."

It is clear and concise, and no one could have mistaken the edge in his voice. I don't understand why she would try if he didn't even like her touching his arm.

She nods, and when she scrambles out of the way, his eyes land on us. Elena hesitates before giving him a smile. "I wanted to introduce you to my sister, Ava."

His eyes survey my face, and it's a reminder they can see my bruises. He watches me warily and lifts his chin in acknowledgement. I try to smile, though I'm not sure whether it comes across as a grimace.

"Will your husband be giving us any trouble?"

I sharply inhale as my heart beats faster. "I . . . don't think so." He searches my eyes as if trying to find out if I'm telling the truth, and I shift on my feet, my gaze going to the floor. When my eyes reach his again, I reply, "Well, I hope not." He slowly nods at me.

When we turn to leave him, Elena whispers, "I'm sorry. He means well. It's part of his job to ensure the security of the club, so he has to know everything that's going on. He might have more questions to ask you."

My stomach twists, and I don't know whether it's from the alcohol or because I'll be interrogated later.

Elena looks over, searching the room, and points to a chair near the lounge. "The younger one, getting a lap dance with his hat on backward, is Twitch. He's really nice, and he's their computer and all-things-technology expert." He's smiling as he gawks at the woman with the red thong grinding on his crotch.

I look away as I lift my hand to my heated cheek. I'm not used to everyone being so open with their sexuality. "He looks, ah, busy now. Can I meet him later?"

Elena giggles. "Sure." She searches the room once more. "I can't see the prospect around, but his name is Rage."

"Oh, lovely," I reply. Though the alcohol has released some tension, there's still dread from the sound of his name.

Her brow furrows. "It's weird. He's not actually angry in person. I think he gets his name from the fighting competition that the MC hosts. Viper's the one to stay away from. He's the manwhore of the club. Oh, and avoid Demon, too."

"Okay, I'll stay away from them. Demon? The name sounds terrible. What's he look like?" I ask so I can stay far, far away.

"Demon is the enforcer. You can't miss him. He's covered in tattoos and has a mohawk."

At least Beau would never walk into this place with MC men living here.

"Demon's the one that handles club business." She hooks air quotes.

My head tilts to the side. "What do you mean by that?"

"Have you seen the one percent on their cut?"

"Yes, I saw it on Axle's."

"Do you know what it means?"

I answer with a clipped, "no."

"It means they're outlaws. They have their own set of values and laws."

"Okay . . ." I gulp. "But I still don't understand what that has got to do with Demon being a club member."

"So normal people go to jail when convicted of a crime. In the MC, Demon gives out the punishment." She doesn't expand on that, and she doesn't need to.

"Okay, got it. It's a different world here."

"It is," she agrees.

I peek at Bomber again. "Is Demon scarier than Bomber?"

She laughs, and I gawk at her. "It depends on what you think scary is."

"But they won't hurt me?" I ask slower than usual.

She frowns and rubs my shoulder with her other hand. "None of them would hurt you."

"And pretty boy?"

"Pretty boy?" she asks with furrowed brows. "Who's that?" Her eyes widen, and she laughs. "That name suits him. That's Viper, who I was talking about before. Don't be fooled by his panty-dropping smile or smooth talking. He'll try to get into your pants."

"Noted. I saw some woman pulling him along the hallway upstairs."

She rolls her eyes. "That's a normal occurrence for all the men around here. Well, everybody except Jake and Bomber."

After a moment, I laugh inappropriately. "If only Mom and Dad could see us now."

Elena snorts. "It would mortify them. Both of their daughters now being sinners."

"I think I need more alcohol."

She puts my arm around her shoulder, helping me stay upright. "No, you do not. I think it's time for bed."

"What about meeting everyone else?"

"You can do that tomorrow."

"Mmm . . ." I mutter, then yawn, my eyes and body heavy.

Commotion causes our heads to turn to a man with an MC cut on, who is at least six foot five, and a man cowering on the floor below him. "You are no longer welcome here."

The house goes quiet.

The guy on the ground looks terrified, and he furiously nods in response.

"Now, leave." His deep voice echoes in the house. Whoever this man is, he held everyone's attention, and when he spoke, everyone listened.

The other man is shaking. He gets to his feet and runs toward the front of the house.

"I . . . I don't know if I can stay here." My eyes bounce between Bomber and the tall man. When he turns slightly, I can see him side on. He looks somewhat familiar.

"You are safe here with them. They are good men. They're different, but once you get to know them, you will see. Trust me?" Elena asks.

"I trust you."

Four men step forward with a different cut from the others. One of them steps closer to the intimidating man. "I'm sorry, Reaper, that's our new prospect. It won't happen again."

"I don't care who he is. I want him gone, Jude. When our

women say no, they fucking mean it. I have zero tolerance for that bullshit."

"Done." He looks at the men behind him. "It's time to head back to our clubhouse." The men walk out toward the front of the house, but their leader stays behind. "We will set up a meeting soon to talk about the progress and estimated delivery times." The man looks around to everyone and tilts his head forward. "Have a good evening, everyone."

When he leaves, I ask, "Who's that?"

"They were a few members from the Kings of Chaos MC. The last man to leave was their president."

My eyes bounce back to the tall man. "And who is that?"

I'm not yet able to see his full face from where I'm standing.

"Reaper," Elena replies quietly, then pauses. "The president of the War Brothers MC."

He shifts to face our way, and when I see him, it clicks. "Oooh, I saw him at your wedding. I was talking to him there."

I remember how, even in our brief conversation, he made me smile, and it was because he gave me a compliment. My heart squeezes at the thought because it had been so long since I genuinely smiled, and it felt like forever since I had been noticed. Beau and I were together for so long I forgot not all men are the same.

"When Beau and I had sex that night, I was imagining it was Reaper."

She bursts out laughing. "You are drunk."

"Did I say that out loud?"

She giggles again. "Yep." She attempts to help me up the stairs as I lean into her, my arm around her shoulder.

I peek down once more to see Reaper watching me. The intensity startles me and I trip up the last step and land on my ass.

"Are you all right?" Elena's face comes into view, though she's a little blurry.

"Ugh, yeah. I think so."

She grabs my hand and pulls me up. We make it through the hallway, and she opens a bedroom door and helps me through it. I fall on the bed, on my stomach.

"What happened just then with Reaper?" I mumble as my eyes close and exhaustion hits me.

"Even though the women are sweet butts, they are still under the MC's protection."

"Sweet butts," I repeat through a smile. "That's a funny name."

"They do anything the guys need them to, and the MC gives them a roof over their head and food."

One eye cracks open. "So they have to have sex with them?"

"Oh, no," she says with a scrunched-up face. "The women want to. They aren't being forced to do anything, and you can pay your way by helping with cooking and cleaning."

"Thanks, Elena," I mumble. "Thank you for everything."

MY EYES OPEN TO THE TWINGE OF PAIN OF MY FULL BLADDER. Feeling as though it might burst, I sit up in bed. My hand goes to my head as I groan, knowing I shouldn't have had those shots when I rarely drink alcohol. I stand with a hunched back and walk with one arm low so I don't trip over and one arm held out in front so I don't walk into the wall. My body is still sore, but not as much as it was this morning.

I touch a smooth surface, sliding my fingers across the wall until I grasp the door handle and open it. The music is still on, but it isn't as loud as it was before. A faint light shines from the hallway leading downstairs.

After relieving myself, I throw some water on my face. My hands fall on either side of the sink. This is the reason I don't drink, but I welcomed the few hours of distraction. I think Beau has scarred me forever.

When I reach the bedroom, I open the door, though I swear I left it open. I blame the alcohol. When I walk in, it's as dark as it was before, so I reach out again, trying not to run into anything. When my hands meet the bed, I lie down, and a small moan escapes my lips when I breathe in. Whatever that smell is, it smells so good, and I nuzzle into the pillow and sigh.

FOUR
IN HIS ARMS

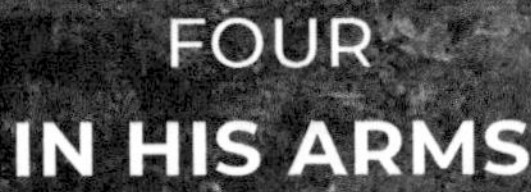

Ava

My body shifts from the heat under me. My hand moves, and my head burrows in, trying to get comfortable, but I'm lying on something hard. There's a distinct, soothing beating sound, *thump, thump, thump.* I open my eyes to a bright light and squint before gazing down. My heart stops. It just stops. I gasp loudly and yank my body off of him and crawl backward. Then I'm falling, and I land on the floor with a thud.

His head turns while his sleepy eyes follow my movements. He blinks a few times as if checking that I'm there, then they widen.

"What are you doing in my bed?" I ask, my voice raised.

He sits up lazily, scratching the back of his head. "You mean, what are *you* doing in *my* bed?" he asks, his voice thick with sleep.

My gaze darts around the room, and the realization makes my stomach sink. "I'm so sorry. I must have mistaken your room for mine last night." A blush burns my cheeks.

"That's the first time I've had a woman apologize for waking up in my bed."

In my head, I'm praying, *Please, God, make me disappear!*

His eyes flick to my cheek, and if it wasn't for his shoulders stiffening ever so slightly, I would have missed that he saw my bruises, but I'm grateful when he says nothing about it.

"Did you know you snore?"

My eyes meet his and narrow. "I do not."

"Yeah, you do. I should know. You slept on top of me for most of the night."

My head falls back with a groan, and I use the edge of the bed to help myself get up. "Well . . ." I say awkwardly. "I'm sorry again." I walk to the door.

"Ava," he says in a deep, husky tone.

I slowly turn to him.

"Did you have a good sleep?" His face is blank, but there's a smugness in his voice.

I nod as my face burns hotter, because last night was the best sleep I've had in a long time, but I won't admit it. Stepping out of his room, I close the door behind me.

"Ava, is that you?"

My body freezes at Elena's voice, and she moves quickly.

Her eyes go wide like saucers. My mouth opens, but I can't speak. She takes my hand and pulls me through the hallway and into a room. Axle is sitting on the edge of the bed, putting his boots on, and looks up at us, watching as we take a seat.

"What happened?" she asks, her voice higher than usual.

I mentally berate myself for even being in this situation. "It's not what you think."

"Well, what was it?"

"I went to the bathroom last night, and I must have accidentally gone into his room instead of mine."

"This ought to be good," Axle says with an ear-to-ear smile. "Whose room did you end up in?"

I gulp and whisper, "Reaper."

Axle laughs, slowly clapping. "Hold up. Hold up." He tilts his head. "He let you sleep in his bed?"

"I didn't have sex with him!" I blurt out. "I'm still married. That's not the type of person I am."

"I know you're not," Elena responds, her voice resonating with understanding. "That's why I was confused when I saw you coming out of his room."

"Hey!" He waves in front of us. "I couldn't care less if you shagged the whole MC."

"Jake!" Elena curses him with narrowed eyes.

He shrugs at her, then gives me his full attention. "Just to be clear, you're telling me you stayed the night in Reaper's bed?"

"Yes," I reply, wondering why he doesn't believe me.

He cocks a brow. "You sure it was Reaper?"

"Seriously?" Elena huffs. "I saw her come out of his room."

"He doesn't let *anyone* sleep or stay in his bed," he says, giving me a pointed look. "He was a sniper in the military. Nothing would get past him. He knew you were there."

I swallow hard, unsure of what to think about that but grateful he let me sleep. Maybe it was how tired I was that I slept so well, or maybe, for once, I unconsciously knew I was safe. The concoction of his scent, warmth, and body was like a sleeping pill I so desperately needed, but I don't need another dangerous man. I've had one. Then why am I attracted to *Reaper?*

THE BRUISES ARE CHANGING COLOR. PARTS ARE A PALE GREEN and yellow. Makeup covers them better now. Even though this morning was one of the most embarrassing moments of my life, today I feel a little different, a little lighter. A new burn of motivation thrums in my veins. Something I haven't felt in a long time.

Elena left a bunch of new clothes in my room, like she said she would. After my shower, I make my way downstairs. The potent smell of alcohol hits me first, and when I look around, Twitch is asleep on the lounge, and the woman with him last night is asleep on the ground next to him. Alcohol cans and bottles litter the floor and nearly every surface I can see.

Footsteps fall behind me. I turn to see a handsome young man. He has a black garbage bag and is picking up the surrounding trash. When he sees me, he gives me an easy smile, so I smile back.

"I'm Ava, Elena's sister."

"The men mentioned you were staying here. I'm Rage."

Elena was right. He does not suit his name.

I peer down at the bag, then gaze around. "Would you like some help?"

His eyes radiate shock. "Hell yeah." His brows pinch together. "I'm starving, though. Can you cook?"

I can't stop the big cheesy smile from taking over my face. "Yes, I can."

He looks to the ceiling and closes his eyes. "Finally," he drawls, "a woman that can cook." He looks back at me. "Can you cook something edible for breakfast for the men?"

My lips mash together as I try not to laugh at "edible." I look to the right and then point to the left. "Is the kitchen that way?" I tilt my head toward the left, guessing it might be through the lounge.

He chuckles and nods. "Yeah, you can't miss it."

I stroll through the house and into the kitchen. Like the

rest of the house, it's dark wood. It contains black stools with worn wooden tops. My hand travels over the counter. It's smooth with a raised surface from the natural wood. The appliances are chrome and state of the art. It has two massive double-door fridges and a coffee machine. I'm in love. There's a buzz of excitement when I see the gigantic oven and cooktop.

"Mornin'," a cheery voice says, making my heart skip a beat. Viper stands a few feet away, making coffee.

I attempt to smile because I want to be polite, but Elena said to stay away from him. "Good morning."

He frowns. "I didn't mean to scare you." He sounds sincere, and it surprises me.

"It's okay."

After the machine finishes adding the coffee to his mug, he adds two teaspoons of sugar. "So what were you smiling at before I bothered you?"

I consider whether to tell him, but I fold. "This." I gesture at my dream kitchen.

He sips and looks at me over the brim of his cup. "The kitchen?"

I sigh. He clearly doesn't get it. "I love cooking. This is a chef's dream."

His lips curve up. "Well, I'm hungry, so go for it."

Excitement returns as I search through the fridges, which are full of food. I pull out the easy things like eggs, sausages, and bacon. Then I move to the oversized pantry, where eight people could easily fit in. My mouth presses into a hard, flat line at the state of the pantry. It's a mess, with pieces of food left on the cupboards. It needs a deep clean. Food containers have been strewn about, so it takes longer than needed, but I grab all the ingredients necessary and put them on the counter. I drum my fingers on the table and turn to Viper.

"Pans?"

"Ahh . . ." He shrugs. "Fuck if I know." He turns to the lounge. "Mercedez, where's the pans?"

There's mumbling, and the one with Twitch stumbles in. Her mascara is smudged underneath her eyes. There are remnants of red lipstick around her lips. She rubs one of her eyes. "What did you say?" she asks in a croaky voice.

"Where are the pans?"

She points. "It's the bottom drawer toward the end."

I lean down and pull the large drawer open and curse at all the kitchen pots and pans carelessly thrown in. There is no order for anything.

"Are you all right?" Viper asks.

"I hate a messy kitchen."

He snorts. "You're going to hate it here, then." He looks at Mercedez and points to the overloaded sink with dirty dishes. "Can you wash up?"

She yawns and moves slowly to the sink.

Another young woman bounces into the kitchen, walks straight to Viper, stands on her toes, gives him a peck on the lips, then turns. "Hi." She smiles, walks to me, and hugs me.

I stand motionless, feeling awkward.

When she pulls back, she says, "I'm Candy. Do you need any help?" I go to answer, but she keeps talking. "I can clean with Mercedez," she offers. She links her hands in front of her. She glances at Viper, then back. "Or I can cook?"

"Can you cook the bacon and sausages, and I'll start on the pancakes?"

"Yes, it's the one thing I can cook," she says, then giggles.

"Did you just say pancakes?"

When I turn, Twitch, Rage, and Viper are standing off to the side with hope in their eyes.

I softly chuckle to myself. "Yes, I did."

Viper rubs his hands together.

"Can you make chocolate chip? My mom used to make them," Rage says longingly.

My heart squeezes. This is why I love cooking. Food makes people happy.

"Sorry, I didn't see any chocolate chips, but I can make both chocolate and vanilla ones."

Viper elbows him. "Stop your whining. I can't even remember the last time we had pancakes."

I move the sausages, bacon, and eggs off to Candy's side and put the hash browns and pancake ingredients on mine, then turn on the gas top.

As I cook, I try to ignore the curious stares and people looking over my shoulder at what I'm cooking until a hand grasps my shoulder. I freeze, then berate myself for acting like that.

When I turn, a woman I haven't met yet is glaring at me. "What do you think you're doing?" she hisses.

My stomach drops. Maybe I should have asked. "I'm . . . helping with breakfast."

Her eyes narrow further as she yanks the spatula out of my hand. "Well, DON'T."

I peek at the stovetop, and I suck in a breath because I don't want to burn the pancakes. Beau hated when I burned the food. I peer back at her, then up at her hand holding the spatula. I snatch it back and pivot. When I flip them over and find the pancakes are a golden color, relief swells in my chest.

"Is this bitch serious?"

I remain with my back to her.

"Do we have a problem here?" I pause at the deep voice resonating around the kitchen, then slowly turn to see Reaper staring between us.

Vera speaks, but Viper talks over her. "Vera is being . . . herself." He pulls a half smile, looking entertained at the current situation.

"Ava is cooking us pancakes," Twitch says, then frowns. "Can't Vera go clean or something? I want my pancakes!"

She doesn't talk back to them, even though her jaw ticks like she wants to.

I already loaded one plate with pancakes, so I extend my arm toward her, encouraging her to grab it. "These are ready. Can you please take them out where everyone is sitting?"

She stares at me before rolling her eyes, grabbing the plate, then walking out of the kitchen. She's followed closely by Viper, Twitch, and Rage.

"Thank you," I say to Reaper, then check on the pancakes.

"The eggs, bacon, and sausages are ready," Candy points out.

"Great." As I open the oven, heat meets my face. With a tea towel, I pull the tray of hash browns out. "These are ready as well."

Elena walks in, smiling at me. "Look at you go." She leans in toward the pancakes and breathes in deeply through her nose, then moans. "I've missed your cooking."

Tears line my eyes, but I blink them away and clear my throat. "Can you help Candy take the food out?"

"I'll be happy to."

I couldn't get the rude woman out of my head, so I bring it up. "There was a woman in here earlier that I hadn't met. She's about my height, chestnut-brown hair. More put together than the other girls."

"I'm guessing you met Vera?"

"That's her. She wasn't happy about me cooking. I thought that's what I was supposed to do. Did I do something wrong?"

She deflates a little. "Sorry, I should have warned you. Most of the sweet butts are manageable, but Vera and Grace are horrible."

"What do you mean by that?"

Her frown deepens, and an unsettling feeling stirs in my stomach. She looks away from me and lets out a heavy sigh. "Nasty women that say nasty things. It's like they never matured past high school."

I monitor her closely. "Are they mean to you?"

Her body stills, and she remains silent.

After I flip over the pancakes, I put my hand on her back. "Is that a yes?"

She turns with a tight smile. "There's a pecking order. I'm an ol' lady, so I am at the top of that. They should respect me. Vera is next because she manages everything in this clubhouse, not that she does a good job of it, may I add. The other sweet butts come after that."

Her voice doesn't sound convincing, and I hate that she's lying, but I keep my mouth shut because I haven't been open and honest with her, either.

"Have I met Grace yet?"

"She's the one that was talking to Bomber last night."

I turn the stovetop off, rest the final pancake on the plate, and put the dirty pouring cup in the sink. Grasping the plate, I step forward and lower my voice. "What was that about when he grabbed her like that?"

She shrugs. "He doesn't like the sweet butts touching him —or really any woman. The other men have no issues having sex with them, but he's different."

With a tight nod, I follow her through the house to the dining area. The room erupts in cheers and whistles as I bring out the rest of the pancakes, and my cheeks heat as I place it on the small table. A thrill courses through me at their gratitude, and their appreciation hits me right in the chest, making me smile. Reaper smiles too.

I grab a plate and put a couple of pancakes on it with some cut-up strawberries and a little cream. Everyone is sitting around a humongous wooden table. Elena has a spare seat next to her, though the man with all the tattoos is sitting on the other side of it. My feet remain glued to the ground as I stare at Demon, but when Elena makes eye contact with me and waves me over, I have no choice but to go take a seat.

When I reach them, Axle smiles at me. "So good," he says through a mouthful of food.

"I'm glad you like it," I say as I place my plate on the table. When I take a seat, I shuffle my chair closer to Elena.

"Like it? I love it! Elena can't cook for shit."

I try not to laugh, but I fail miserably. Elena swats him with her hand. "Hey, I try."

"Yes, babe," he says, smiling lovingly at her.

They are the cutest, and I'm so happy for them.

As I eat my pancakes, I feel Demon's eyes on me. I wipe the corners of my mouth, hoping I don't have food all over my face. I peek up under my lashes, and I was right—he is staring. I find it strange. He wasn't checking me out and it wasn't a hostile glare, but I'm not sure what it was and I don't want to be rude, so I turn my body toward him. "Hi, I'm Ava."

A wicked smile slides over his lips, and he stares at me without responding. My breathing hitches. I shuffle in my seat, suddenly feeling the heat on my cheeks again. His eyes study me, both intense and curious. "So I heard . . ." He tilts his head. "I'd introduce myself but . . ." He lifts his hand to my face but doesn't touch me. "I'll take a guess from your hesitation to sit next to me. You already know who I am."

Swallowing hard, I give him a sharp nod. I've met no one like him before.

He relaxes further into his chair with his crooked smile and pops a strawberry into his mouth, looking at the others around the table.

Elena clears her throat, and when I lift my gaze, she mouths *sorry*.

I focus on finishing my food, but I'm a little confused about my interaction with Demon. At least he didn't ask me about my husband or what I'm going through. In the short period I've been here, I've noticed that they don't pretend to be anyone other than who they are, and even if what they do or say is shocking, it's refreshing because Beau was fake and a different person with me than what he was with others.

"How long are you staying?"

I turn to the left to see Bomber's eyes on me. Everyone's voices stop, and my heart speeds up. I'm taken aback. "I'm not sure yet . . . I was hoping to do up a résumé and start applying for jobs."

"No!" Twitch and Viper say simultaneously.

My eyes go wide.

"She stays with us. We need food," Viper says, looking at Reaper. "Can we make an exception for Ava and pay her? No one else can cook around here." Then he gives the women around the table a cheeky half smile. "No offense, ladies."

His charm impresses me.

Elena tuts. "If you need any help with your resume or looking for jobs, let me know."

Axle shakes his head at me from behind her, and I try to hide the smile on my face. "Thanks, I appreciate it."

"You should have asked Ava before announcing it across the dinner table," Reaper responds, his eyes flicking between us.

Elena's phone rings, distracting me from the rest of their conversation. Axle groans. "Why won't you answer it? It's been ringing all morning."

She bites her lip and glances at me. Tension takes hold of my shoulders. "I don't want to," she replies with a bite in her tone.

Axle's eyes narrow. "If you don't answer it, I will."

She grasps her phone and walks away, so I follow her.

"Hello. Yes, it's Elena. Yes, I heard she's missing."

My stomach drops at her words. We bypass the kitchen and go out the back door.

"I don't know. I haven't seen her."

She paces and groans. "I don't know what you want me to say. I said I haven't seen her. Okay, I'll be in touch with you if I do. Bye."

She turns to see me and jolts back, grasping her chest.

"Who was that?" I ask cautiously.

She lets out a long sigh as she bows her head. "Beau reported you missing." She looks up at me with sympathy in her eyes. "The police were asking about you."

With a lump in my throat, all I can do is nod in acknowledgment.

She reaches out and puts her hand on my arm. "Beau and our parents have called as well. I should have told you, but I didn't want to upset or worry you."

"What did Beau say?" I hate that my fear of him makes my voice unsteady.

"The same as our parents. Asking if I have spoken to or seen you. Mom and Dad sounded worried. Beau also sounded worried. It's scary how convincing he sounds."

I let out a chuckle that has no humor in it. "He used to belittle me and threaten me, but when we went out to dinner or to our parents' house, he was a different person. He's very charming, but with me, he could change like that." I snap my fingers.

"The officer mentioned that if you were to contact them to say you were okay, for whatever reason you left, they don't have to disclose your whereabouts to anyone. I gather that includes Beau."

Her words cut through me like a blade, and I feel no comfort because there's always the "but what if Beau finds out?"

I shake my head abruptly. "I'm not ready."

She gives me a small smile. "I understand. In the meantime, I'll ask Axle to talk to the club's attorney to make sure it's legit."

After helping to clean up after breakfast, Elena and Axle go off by themselves. I'm left alone, a little lost without Elena. Two women don't like me, and the rest seem to have no interest in making new friends.

"Thank you for breakfast," Reaper says from behind me.

I turn to him and grin at his praise. "That's okay. I enjoy cooking, and your kitchen is amazing."

His brows lift high in surprise. "I didn't know a kitchen could make a woman happy."

"Well, it surely can."

"You're an easy woman to please."

"I've always dreamed about working in a beautiful kitchen like yours, with all new state-of-the-art cooking equipment. The black color mixed with the natural wood and the stone countertop is a stunning combination."

"If you like it so much, I can bring the suggestion of you cooking for the MC to church for a vote?"

"I'd be happy to cook for all of you," I reply, hoping I can.

I've been out of work for so long that I have no computer to do a résumé and I can't afford to spend money on it, so cooking while I'm here is my only good option. Luckily for me, I love cooking.

FIGHTING FOR AIR

Ava

I GO BACK INTO MY ROOM, AND IT ISN'T LONG UNTIL MY ANXIETY returns. I wish I was back in Reaper's bed so my mind would stop torturing me with thoughts of Beau finding me and taking me back to hell. I wonder if he would physically hurt me to teach me a lesson or tell me he will never hurt me again but mentally torture me instead, like he has been for years. *Ava, your dress is too short. You look like a prostitute. Have you gained weight? What have you been doing all day? Why do you always forget something when you buy groceries? Are you dumb or do you enjoy pissing me off?*

My nerves coil up so tight I slam my fist against the bed, hating that even though he's not here, he still has control over me, making me scared and vulnerable.

The thought of leaving the MC because Beau causes too much trouble has my stomach churning. Bomber has made it clear that he doesn't want me bringing any drama into the club. It scares me that I may have to leave, but I understand why. They don't owe me anything.

Knock, knock, knock. The door handle wiggles.

"Please, Ava, let me in. You've been in there for a while."

I sniffle, my nose still blocked from crying. "I'm good."

"Then unlock the door."

"I need some time to myself, Elena." My voice breaks a little at the end.

"Okay," she says, defeated. "I'm always here if you need me."

"I know."

Brief silence falls, then she speaks. "You have one day, or I swear I will break the lock."

A sliver of lightness fills my chest at her attempt to be stern with me. "Okay, I promise."

I roll over into the fetal position, pulling the duvet up to my chest. The sadness and stress are overwhelming. I don't have the strength to get out of bed, and I want no one to see me like this. I'm mentally drained, as all the what-ifs and worst-case scenarios keep manifesting, and with each thought, it's like another punch to my already-worsening mental state.

Over the afternoon and night, Elena keeps checking in on me and leaving food, but I can't eat, not with the stress. I try to sleep, but I can't, and I lie there, awake, with my eyes closed.

Needing to go to the bathroom, I pop my head out the door. It must be late because the music has died down again and no one is in the hall, so I drag my feet to the bathroom.

Once I'm done, I open the door but jump backward when I see Reaper leaning against the wall, staring at me.

"At church, the men agreed that you'll cook for us and we'll pay you a wage." His eyes search my face. I'm sure I look as terrible as I feel.

"Thank you," I breathe out. At least I have a job now. "I'll be up early tomorrow to cook for everyone."

"Are you going to tell me why you locked yourself in the room all day?" His voice is tinged with curiosity.

"I don't want Beau to find me." My eyes widen at my honesty.

"What makes you think he will?"

I shrug. "Bad habit of always assuming the worst." Yes, I was paranoid, but if experience taught me anything, it was that Beau always got his way.

"Do you know how to shoot a gun?"

"No."

"I'll teach you tomorrow after breakfast."

"There's no need, really. But thanks."

He raises a brow. "A woman needs to know how to protect herself."

I don't answer because there's truth to what he's saying.

"I can tell you that you're safe living under the roof of my MC, but it's important to learn how to protect yourself in case you ever need to. At some stage your husband will come looking for you, so you should be prepared for anything."

"Why are you letting me stay here then?"

His eyes soften. "If he hit you before, he will rain down hell on you if you return."

The truth makes me flinch.

"Now, get some sleep. I want a bacon and egg burger for breakfast."

My alarm rings, so I grab my phone and turn it off. Today, I woke up with a purpose. Even though it's to cook, it's something I love to do, and at least I can save more money.

After getting changed into jeans and a fitted T-shirt, I grab my wallet, and move down to the kitchen. I gasp when I arrive and see dirty pans in the sink, the overflowing bin, and cups and beer bottles sitting on the kitchen counter. From last time, I should've known that they wouldn't have cleaned up.

When I search the fridges, only a little bacon is left, and ten eggs. In the pantry, I can't find any bread. Dread slithers through me.

"Okay, think," I mumble to myself.

"What about?"

I let out a small scream. "I didn't see you come in."

Rage gives me a half smile and wipes his forehead with his forearm. "Yeah, sorry, I should be more careful around you because . . ." His eyes dart away as he stands awkwardly. "Everything you have been through and all."

Viper comes up behind him, breathing heavily. "You *are* fast."

They are both shirtless, so I gather they have been out exercising. It's impossible not to notice their very fit, very muscled bodies.

When Viper sees me, he flashes one of his cocky smiles. "Hey, darl."

My lips tighten. I don't know how to act around Viper because Elena said to stay away from him.

Rage chuckles and looks to Viper. "I've never seen a woman look at you like that."

Viper playfully whacks his shoulder. "I don't like it." Viper's eyes soften when he glances at me with his hands up in defense. "I don't want to scare you. If you're worried I'll come on to you, then I give you my word that I won't."

I give him an appreciative smile. "Good. Thank you. Now,

I don't want to wake Elena and Axle, so could you take me to do some shopping for breakfast?"

His eyes brighten at the mention of food. "Sure. When did you want to go?"

I bite my bottom lip, hating to sound needy. "Now . . . if that's okay? I didn't want everyone to wait too long to eat."

He looks down at his attire, which is only a pair of shorts. Sweat shimmers across his chest. "I won't be long. I'll go have a shower and get changed."

With Viper's and Rage's muscles and model-like faces, I can see their appeal, but it's the rugged, solid masculine men that are more attractive . . . like Reaper. I shake my head to rid myself of those thoughts.

After Viper leaves, I search the drawers until I find a garbage bag, and then I pick up the bottles and trash. Rage does the same. From the kitchen, we move through the house. By the time we reach the front of the house, we have two full large bags.

Rage's smile spreads. "Thanks for helping."

I smile back. "That's okay. Why doesn't anyone help you?"

"I'm a prospect. It's my job."

"What about the women?"

He chuckles like the question is ridiculous, then cocks a brow. "Because they're lazy. I kept asking them to help at the beginning, but I soon learned that it's easier to do it myself than nag at them." He sounds like a single mother dealing with children.

Footsteps thud, and I look over to see Viper hurrying down the stairs and approaching us. He opens a drawer from a table near the front door and pulls out keys.

I peer back at Rage. "Can you wash up in the kitchen for me so I can start cooking straight away when I get back?"

"Sure. I'll have a shower and get onto it."

When I step outside, I follow Viper down the stairs. I stop, then turn to eye the front of the clubhouse. It reminds me of a small castle with the roof and sandstone cladding. The land around the house is clear, but further along, near where the forest begins, is a fence.

When I turn back, I dash toward Viper. My heart pounds as we walk to a large shed and a few cars and a row of motorcycles. He moves to the truck and gets in. I have to use the side rail to help lever myself up into the truck because it is high.

The truck starts, and we move along the dirt road surrounded by trees and shrubs. *He's a friend of Elena's and Axle's, so I'll be okay*, I repeat in my head. It feels foreign being in a car with another man, even if only to go to the store.

I peer out the window as we drive along further. I'm surprised at how peaceful it is out here. We bypass a large warehouse next. "What's that used for?"

"We hold fighting matches."

"Is that where Rage fights?"

"He sure does. That kid has talent for his age."

"Kid? How old are you?"

He glances at me. "I'm in my late twenties."

I snort. "You are younger than me."

"Not that much older," he says in a flirty tone.

"How do you know how old I am?"

"Axle."

Damn, Axle!

We eventually reach the asphalt road, where he looks right and left before continuing. Ten minutes later, we reach the small town of older and newer buildings. He turns into a parking lot and parks the truck off to the side of a shopping complex. A distant bark echoes from a small old cottage next to the complex. A dilapidated kennel has a rottweiler tied to it. A part of the dog resonates with me.

Viper clears his throat.

I peek back at him, and he shakes his head. "I'm not getting my ass kicked because you wanted to pat a dog and got bitten." He points to the complex. "Now, let's go get food so we can go home. I'm hungry, woman."

I exhale and nod, following him. He pushes the cart while I take the food off the shelves and place it inside. I would usually scan the items for the cheapest available, but I don't bother because if it's cheap, the men may not like it. Plus, my mind keeps drifting back to the dog.

As we go through the aisles, Viper gives a seductive smile to a few women who pass us by. They stop and talk to him, so I take over the cart and keep moving along, not interested in listening to their conversation.

Viper jogs up to me at the checkout and assists with placing the last bags into the trolley. "You're quick. One minute you're there and the next you're gone."

"We have frozen food in the cart. I didn't want it to defrost." That wasn't the only reason, but I decide against mentioning anything else.

"That's $402.05. Will that be cash or card?" the cashier asks.

"Cash," I reply and pull out my purse.

Viper snorts and puts his arm across me, giving the cashier $100 notes. She giggles and says, "Thank you, Viper." He smiles at her as she gives him the change, and she blushes profusely.

I push the cart along to the truck. We place the groceries in the back.

"I'll push the cart back into the bay," I tell him, since it's closer to the dog. The dog watches me and barks once, but as I get closer, its tail is wagging.

"Ava!" Viper yells out with warning in his tone, but it only makes me fasten my pace.

The dog's tail speeds up, *wap, wap, wap*. My heart beats faster as I approach, but when it reaches me, it sniffs my hand, my shoes, and around my legs, then leans into me, so I pat its head. The dog's coat is smooth, but when I glance at my hand, it's dirty.

"Where's your water?"

He licks my hand, lapping up the attention.

There's a red bucket tipped on its side.

Heavy footsteps approach, and I hesitantly turn to see Viper. He runs his hand through his hair. "Ava! What were you thinking?"

I wasn't thinking. I watch the dog, who's frozen, his tail no longer wagging. "I'd step back if I were you." His eyes go wide, and he jumps back, out of reach of the dog.

"Can you get some water? The dog doesn't have any."

He groans. "Only if we go home afterward because your sister and Reaper will skin me alive if you get hurt."

Why would Reaper care? I think to myself. I frown at the dog, and he looks up at me with his big, sad, brown eyes.

"Don't even think about it," Viper clips.

"But he's dirty, and he's got no water. The owners obviously don't care about him."

Viper's jaw drops. "You seriously want to steal a dog right now? Just because I wear this"—he gestures to his MC cut— "it doesn't mean I'm a criminal." He smirks but turns serious. "And anyway . . . it looks like it wants to bite me."

I laugh but stop once I hear a voice.

"What are you doing?" a man asks. I turn to see a man wearing a dirty white tank top and small shorts approaching us.

Viper rushes to step in front of me with no sense of safety for himself. I suck in a breath, but the dog doesn't go for him. Instead, his eyes are trained on his owner. A deep growl resonates from next to us.

"What's going on here?" the man asks.

I step to the side, but Viper moves with me, blocking my view. "We are leaving now," he says.

But I move again. "Hi."

Viper hisses at me.

"We were appreciating the beauty of your dog. My friend here," I say as I glance at Viper, who's giving me the death stare, "was just going to get water to fill his bucket."

The man squints, but the dog's growl gets louder, his curled lip baring his teeth.

"You were getting water for this mutt? Stupid thing—he's always barking. Keeps me awake."

I wince. "If the dog is too much trouble, I can take him off your hands for you."

"For fuck's sake," Viper says under his breath.

The man scratches his chin. "It will cost you. I was going to use it for dogfighting, but I'd have to sedate it just to get near it."

From the moment I saw the dog, I had a gut feeling. My instincts were right. It is meant to be.

"How much?"

Viper shakes his head. "That dog ain't going to the clubhouse until you ask Reaper."

"Sure," I reply with my hand out, waiting for him to give me his phone.

Viper raises his brow, then gets his phone out of his pocket, presses a few buttons, and hands it to me.

A deep voice comes through. "Reaper."

"Hi, Reaper, it's me, Ava."

"What are doing on Viper's phone?"

My eyes widen at the first thing out of his mouth. "He took me to get groceries."

No reply.

"Are you there?"

There's a heavy breath. "Yes."

"Well . . . you know how you wanted to teach me how to protect myself."

Viper cocks his head to the side while Reaper answers. "Yes. Where is this going?"

I swallow the lump in my throat. "I had another idea."

"Hmm . . . and what's that?" Amusement tinges his voice.

"Can I bring a dog back to the clubhouse? Please? I'll look after him," I blurt. "He won't get in the way, and I'll take the dog with me when I leave."

If it were anything else, it would horrify me to beg a man to let me have something, but this dog is different. I've wanted him more than anything else in a long time.

Viper stifles a laugh. "Yeah right. The dog might bite someone, though."

I narrow my eyes, warning him to be quiet.

"And how big is this dog?" Reaper asks.

Viper's lips lift into a blinding smile, so I know he heard. He leans down, closer to the phone. "It's a damn rottweiler. The thing's massive."

Reaper chuckles. "Will it make you feel safe?"

"Yes," I reply sharply.

"On one condition."

"And what's that?" I reluctantly ask.

"Only if you learn how to use a gun."

My heart beats faster. "Yes, that won't be a problem." My voice heightens in excitement.

"Okay, well, I'll see you when you get back."

"Thank you, thank you," I reply and hand the phone to Viper, then smile up at the man. "I'll take him."

SIX

BUILDING RELATIONSHIPS

We are sitting on the lounge when Elena says, "I can't believe you got a dog."

"His name is Conan."

"That is not a dog's name."

Lifting my chin, I say, "It is so." I lean down, patting Conan, who's lying by my feet. "I thought you loved animals."

She shuffles closer to Axle. "Not ones that are going to eat me."

"He seems fine with women. It's men he's wary of, but he has showed no sign of aggression to anyone since I brought him here. He's just been following me around, but I get the impression if he senses aggression or a threat, it might be a different story."

"Remind me never to yell, and it's not a dog, either," Axle says. "It's a small horse."

I peer back to Conan. "Don't you listen to them," I coo.

"It's one dog. Did he really need all that stuff? I saw the truck when you arrived. It was packed."

I arch a brow in disbelief. "He's a big dog, and it's not like the MC had anything for him."

Axle snorts. "You bought the dog clothes!"

Without a beat, I correct Axle. "His name is Conan." I can't help but smirk. "You never know—it might get cold."

"Poor dog," he replies under his breath.

"It's good to see you smile."

I purse my lips at Elena's comment. Then Conan looks up at me, so I pat him. "I always wanted a dog. I wanted the company . . . and the affection, but Beau said no."

"Why didn't you just get one anyway?" Axle asks.

If only it were that easy. I shake my head. "You don't understand."

"What don't we understand?" Elena asks.

I peek up at her but pause, unsure whether I want to bring it up. "Well, first, I didn't have access to the bank account. He only gave me cash to pay for groceries. I didn't work, so I had no money. When his drinking got worse, I spent less on groceries and put some money aside in case I needed it."

I looked down at Conan. "We only had one car, and I could only drive it when Beau said I could, and I don't know for sure, but I'm pretty sure he had a GPS tracker on the car. He seemed to always know where I was and where I went. I tried not to think too much about it, to ignore his controlling behaviors, but I reached my limit. I asked for a dog once. He said no, and when he said no, it meant no, and if I got the dog, he would have yelled at me and would have given the dog away." *Or killed it.*

"I hope he comes looking for you," Axle says. "I want to punch him for you."

"Are you ready?" a deep voice asks, which makes me

recoil. I glance up to see it's Reaper. Conan stands and turns, his eyes trained on him.

"He's a good guard dog."

It makes me smile. "He is."

"Are you ready to use a gun?"

My hands fidget in front of me. I know I promised, but I'm still dreading it.

"Axle taught me," Elena says. "Trust me, you will be fine."

Conan and I follow Reaper through the house. I can feel the others staring as we walk through, and when I glance up, Vera and Grace are watching me through narrowed eyes. As we pass the kitchen, I bend and grab the bag of dog food and continue until we're outside.

"Wait a moment," I call out to Reaper as I walk over to Conan's bowl and fill it.

Reaper's patiently waiting as I hurry back to him. He's wearing black jeans that cover his tree-trunk legs and a fitted black shirt that stretches over his chest, with his cut over the top. His height, solid build, and deep voice epitomize a masculine man.

When I reach him, we walk along a gravel road. I have to rush to catch up to his long strides.

"Thanks for letting me have the dog here."

"Viper said you went straight up to the dog. What made you think it wouldn't bite you?"

I think back. "His tail was wagging, and he had a doggy smile."

Reaper shakes his head. "You trust too easily with appearances. Not everyone wants to be your friend."

I frown. "I'm not naive."

He releases a throaty chuckle. "I never said you were, but you shouldn't have put yourself in a dangerous situation like that."

He's probably right, but in that circumstance, I made the right choice.

We walk for ten minutes until three thick wooden planks with white-and-red bull's-eyes on them are ahead of us. He pulls a small gun from his holster. "The gun is not loaded, but safety is paramount." He holds the gun and points his index finger along it. "You don't point the gun at anyone unless you plan to shoot it. Otherwise, keep it aimed at the ground. Your finger should be straight against the frame of the gun."

I swallow thickly, as if trying to swallow my nerves, but it doesn't work.

"When you grip the gun, your hand needs to be high and your grip needs to be firm."

"I don't think I can do this."

"Yes, you can. Today we'll focus on grip and stance, and when you're comfortable, you can practice firing the gun at the target."

"Okay," I say through a long exhale. "I can do that."

He hands me the gun and puts his hand over mine. His touch sends a subtle shiver up my spine. "You need to grip the gun tighter." I do, and he bends and taps my thigh. "Spread your legs shoulder-width apart and bend your knees slightly." Embarrassment and *something else* I haven't felt in a long time flood me, making my skin heat, but I try my best to ignore it and follow his instructions. His eyes scan my stance, then he stands next to me. "Now, face your target and lean forward, with arms straight out."

When my arms come out, I feel his criticizing eyes on me.

"Perfect."

His praise hits me in the chest, but I bite back a grin.

"Now, put your finger on the trigger and remember the gun isn't loaded."

I release a shaky breath and move my index finger to the trigger.

"Pull back slowly. Do you feel that wall?"

"Yes."

"Watch the front sight and squeeze the trigger back."

A light crack snaps when I pull my finger back, and the gun moves.

I drop my arms, and with one hand, I pass it back to him. "I really don't like it, and I'm shaking, so I don't think I'll be good at hitting any target."

He gives me a reassuring smile. "I know it's daunting, but you did well. It takes time and practice to get used to it."

I learned something different, and I appreciate he's trying to help me.

We walk in the direction of the clubhouse. "How did you sleep last night?"

My shoulders drop. "Not good. I'm tired today."

"I didn't sleep well, either."

My eyes dart to the ground. We had a better night's sleep when we were in the same bed *together*.

"What are you going to get up to now?"

"I think I'm going to introduce Conan to his toys."

He gives me a small smile, though it looks like he's trying not to laugh at me.

"What?" I ask defensively, with a hint of amusement.

"Nothing." He's quick to respond. "I've got to talk to Viper first. I'll be back." He walks toward the people sitting on the seats.

When I reach the house, Conan is inside his new doghouse. It was worth every cent to see him happy. He gets up to greet me.

"Hold on," I tell him, then go inside and head to the cupboard where I store his things and pull out a squeaky, soft chicken toy and a tennis ball and make my way out the back.

As soon as I open the door, Conan's tail rises and wags.

His awkward jump of excitement makes me laugh. He pounces up on me next, making me step back.

"Wow! Conan," I say as I budge him with my arm, "get down before you push me over."

He drops, though his tail is in full force. I place the toy on the roof of his dog kennel and bend, showing him the ball. "Look what I have." He sniffs it and licks my hand. "Are you ready?" I pull my arm back and fling the ball as far as I can. His eyes follow the ball and he sprints after it.

I skim the clubhouse and see Reaper watching me as Vera, Candy, and Viper talk around him. He gives Viper a chin lift, then walks toward me. Vera's eyes narrow.

Conan comes running back and drops the ball at my feet. When I pick it up, it's wet and thick with slobber. I grimace. "Conan, gross!"

A throaty chuckle comes from beside me as I throw the ball again. Reaper looks amused, though I feel Vera's hostility boring holes into my back.

"Are you with Vera?" He inches back with a quizzical look on his face. I nudge my head in her direction. "She does not look happy."

He turns back, and Vera's eyes soften. Then she goes back to talking to Viper and Candy.

"There's nothing between us, and there never will be. I've told her many times."

I give him a tight smile, thinking she has not gotten the hint, and if she didn't hate me before, she does now.

Once everyone goes inside and Conan is exhausted, I walk inside to Axle, who's sitting by himself in the lounge. "Where's Elena?"

He turns his head from the TV. "She said she was going to the bathroom."

Knowing I need to wash my hands after spending time

with Conan, I walk in the bathroom but pause when I hear Grace's voice.

"And you call yourself an ol' lady." Laughter erupts.

When I peek around, I see it's Grace standing in front of Elena. Her back is against the wall and her head is bowed. It makes the hairs on the back of my neck stand. I notice the signs. The taunting and ridicule are something I know all too well, and the sudden onslaught of anger burns through me.

I rush to them. "Leave her alone."

All heads turn to me. Elena's eyes go wide while Grace laughs. "What are you going to do about it?"

My hands clench by my sides.

Grace steps close to me, her eyes studying me, and she smiles. "You don't scare me. You're pathetic, having a cry because your husband hurt you." She huffs. "Most of us women have gone through so much worse. You two are weak. You both don't belong here."

Elena steps around her and strides over to me. "Don't worry about her," she whispers. "She's not worth it." She pulls me by my hand, and we walk away from her.

"Is she always like that toward you?"

Elena smiles but knits her brows at me. "When none of the men are around."

"Tell Axle."

"It will only make it worse."

"How will it? Axle will put them in their place."

"Vera is with Reaper, and Vera and Grace are best friends, so I've always been reluctant. I didn't want to put Axle in a difficult position."

My stomach plummets. "Reaper *is* with her . . . He told me he wasn't." I can't hide the disappointment in my voice, but it explains why she was not happy.

"They aren't a couple, but they have sex." Her face scrunches. "I think she wants to be his ol' lady."

"Why would Reaper let me sleep in his bed, then?"

A smile tugs on the side of her lips. "He's not into her."

"What about Grace? What's her deal?"

"She used to sleep with Axle before he met me. So, in her head, I took her man."

I huff as my anger sizzles. "If either of them starts on you again, come and tell me. I'll always be by your side when you need me."

She smiles and playfully barges into my shoulder. "It's okay. I'll be fine. I ignore them."

She turns when I stop. "I'm serious. I haven't felt anger like that in a long time. I won't let anyone bully my little sister."

"Okay, okay." She chuckles. "I'm not so little anymore."

I smile back. "You will always be my little sister."

The men walk past us and into a room with a door I've paid little attention to. The wooden door displays a carving of the War Brothers MC logo. When Axle reaches us, he leans over and presses a kiss to Elena's cheek. "We've got church."

Now, I know little about MC clubs, but I know what church means. "I'm guessing club business?" I ask Elena.

"Yep."

"I'd better get a start on lunch, then."

Her hand comes out toward me. "I'd wait. Sometimes after church, they leave to do whatever they do."

"You don't know?"

"No . . ." She pauses. "And I don't think I want to."

Viper said he wasn't a criminal, but they are bikers, so he probably lied.

I step closer to the window and gaze at the cloudless sky, so I turn to Elena. "Is there a path or somewhere we can go for a walk? It's nice weather, and I don't want to sit around all day. I'm sure Conan will love it, too."

She looks away, as if in thought. A hand comes to her chin.

"There is, actually. The MC has a small cabin up the mountain. There's a road that leads there. At a guess, I would say it would be an hour's walk."

"Great. I'll go get my shoes on, and I'll meet you back here."

She nods. "I'll wait for Axle to see what they're doing. My trainers are by the front door anyway."

I move up the stairs and through the hallway and open my bedroom door to see my bag open. My heart hammers. I dart over to it and fumble through it, pulling out clothes and toiletries and my birth certificate. When I reach my wallet, I pull it out and unzip it and count the notes.

A rush of relief hits me when all the money is there. The lack of sleep is taking a toll on me. Maybe I left it open and I don't remember doing it. I put all the items back in, bend down, then slide the bag under the bed. I grab my shoes, sit on the bed, and put them on, tying my shoelaces as I go.

When I reach the top of the stairs, I can see the men coming out of the room they were in. As I step down, my pace slows as I sense the tension in the room. There are no laughs or smiles. All have stern looks on their faces.

"Be safe," Elena says to Axle, then wraps her arms around his neck.

His arms come around her waist. "You have nothing to worry about, babe."

She gives him a chaste kiss on the lips, then drops her arms.

"We won't be long. We should be back later tonight. Rage and Twitch will stay with you two. If you have any problems, I'm a phone call away."

He kisses her once more. Her body slouches as she watches him leave.

When I reach the bottom, I walk toward her. "Are you okay?"

She sighs. "Every time he leaves, I feel sick to my stomach, and I don't get any relief until he returns."

"I'm sorry," I reply, not sure of what to say because I don't know what they are doing and how dangerous it might be. "How about we go for that walk so we can get away from the other women?"

She pauses. "Okay, you get Conan and I'll let Twitch know."

I walk through the house and out the back door. My body stiffens when I can't see Conan. Maybe I should have put him on a leash. "Conan," I yell and walk farther out, searching around the table and chairs, then around the bonfire. "Conan!" I shake my head at my stupidity. He most likely doesn't recognize his name yet.

Loud motorcycles pierce the air, making me jolt. Through it, I can faintly hear barking. He must be out the front. The loud rumbling seems to get farther away as I walk through the house, and when I push the door open, I can see the last few motorcycles tear down the road, kicking up a cloud of dirt in the air as they go.

Conan is standing next to Elena, watching the motorcycles.

She turns. "I was just coming to get you to tell you Conan is here."

"It's fine."

Conan turns at the sound of my voice and walks over to me with his long tongue hanging out of his mouth.

"Are you ready to go for a walk?" I ask enthusiastically.

His tail wags faster, and I bend down to pat his head.

"Twitch gave me a walkie-talkie," she says as she clips it onto her belt. "The service here can be unpredictable."

We follow the dirt road, but instead of going straight ahead, we veer left. The road has a rocky surface and ditches.

High shrubs grow on both sides, and plants grow along the hump between the tire tracks.

A ringing filters through the air. Elena stops, puts her hand in her pocket, and brings her phone up to her face. She groans when she sees who's calling but answers it anyway. "Hi, Mom."

I swallow thickly. Mom's muffled voice booms through the phone, but I can't make out what she's saying.

"I still haven't heard from her, either," Elena says as she looks at me. "No, I'm not lying. I'm sure she's safe." She pauses. "Okay, I'll let you know if she calls. Bye."

I glance at Conan, who is ahead of us, sniffing around a tree.

"We spoke to the club's attorney. She said the police were telling the truth. You can call them and say you're safe, and you don't have to tell them where you are."

My chest constricts. "I don't think I can do that yet."

"It will call off the search party, and Mom and Dad will know that you're okay."

"Beau won't stop looking for me." Tears threaten to fall. "I can't go back to him." My voice is strained.

"Even if he finds you, he can't force you to go anywhere."

I shake my head. "You don't know what he's capable of. He will say and do anything to get his way. He must be in control of the situation and of me."

I search for Conan because he's no longer in front of us. "Conan!" I call out. Off to the left, I see his tail. He comes out from the bushes and jogs on the path again. The hill gets steeper, making my breathing heavier.

"What did you mean by being in control?"

"Everything. He controlled the money. I never got a say about sex. It was always when and what he wanted, regardless of whether I wanted it or not." A shiver creeps down my spine at the memories. "I was told it was my duty to please him, and if I didn't, he would go elsewhere." My vision blurs with fresh tears. "I wanted to become a chef, but he wanted me to stay home and be a housewife because he wanted kids."

I wipe my eyes with my hands and chuckle. "We kept trying for kids, but it never happened for us. When we went to the doctor and had tests, I was diagnosed with endometriosis."

Elena's arms come around me, squeezing me tightly. "I'm so sorry you had to go through that," she says in a consoling voice.

I hug her back. "I'm glad I came here."

She pulls back and gives me a small smile. "Me too. I love you."

"I love you, too."

A whine wails from beside us, so I bend down and pat Conan's head. "I love you, too."

Forty minutes later, we reach the cabin. It's small and solely made of wood. It has only a couple of windows, and it's surrounded by trees, so it blends well into the environment. We are both panting.

Elena has her arms above her head. "I'm so unfit," she says through loud breaths.

My hand goes to the sharp ache on my side. "I have a stitch."

Elena laughs. "This was your idea."

"A stupid one at that." I wipe my sweaty forehead with my arm. "I don't know if I can walk back."

She pulls the walkie-talkie out from her waistband and holds down a button. "Twitch."

"Yo," he answers.

"Can you pick us up? We don't want to walk back."

He laughs. "It's downhill."

"Please," I say loudly, hoping that he would hear.

"Give me fifteen minutes."

SEVEN

CHALLENGING TIMES

Ava

"THAT DOG STINKS!" TWITCH SAYS AS WE GET OUT OF THE TRUCK.

I sigh. "Yes, he does. The tap is at the back of the house, isn't it?"

"It sure is," he replies with a screwed-up face, watching my dog jump out of the truck.

"I purchased some doggy shampoo, so I might give him a wash."

"Do you want some help?" Elena asks.

My eyes scan over Conan's body. "Yes, please. I hope he'll let us wash him."

Elena's eyes widen. "He better not bite me!"

My heart is beating faster, hoping Conan won't be a problem. We walk out the back and toward the tap.

"Can you connect the hose, and I'll get the shampoo?"

Elena gives Conan a wry glance. "Okay."

I dash through the house and into the kitchen. My shoulders drop at the mess already. My fingers itch to clean it up. *If*

Beau saw our kitchen in this state . . . I cringe, then shake my head. Beau isn't here. I open the cupboards underneath the sink and grab the shampoo and comb. After walking over to the fridge, I pull the door open and get out some ham. I walk back to hear Elena laughing. She is trying to wet Conan, but he keeps chasing the stream of water from the hose, trying to bite it.

Elena looks at me. "Your dog thinks it's a game."

I smile at Conan as he bolts one way, chasing the water, and when Elena dashes the hose the other way, he follows it, barking.

"Conan, I have some food for you."

He pauses and looks at me, back to the water, then back to the ham in my hand before running to me.

Elena giggles. "The food is obviously more important."

When Conan gets to me, he jumps. "No. Sit."

"He probably doesn't know what sit means."

"Sit." I press down on his back near his tail, and he sits. His eyes never move from the food.

"Good boy." I pass him his well-deserved piece of ham, and he gently takes it from my hand and practically swallows it.

"Did he even chew that?" Elena asks.

I laugh. "No, he's a pig!" I pull out another piece of ham. "Try with the water now."

I hand the ham to him as Elena directs the water over his back. It trails down his body and drips from his belly.

"Pass me the hose and I'll do his chest."

She does, and he sits there with his doggy smile while we take turns making sure we get his coat wet. He stands, and before we can step back, he shakes himself. I close my eyes as he flicks the water all over us. We both burst out laughing.

"It's shampoo time." Conan backs away, so I quickly pull

out another piece of ham. He steps toward me. "At least he's food motivated."

Elena cocks a brow. "Aren't most men?"

I smile back at her. "True!" I give the ham to Conan, then lean down, grab the shampoo, drizzle the bright yellow liquid all over his back, and put the container on the ground. We both lean down and rub it into his coarse coat.

"Look at the color of the suds," Elena points out. It's a light brown, showing just how dirty he is.

I frown. "He's probably never been washed. Make sure you get his legs."

"I am. Check out his tail." It's wagging rapidly. "He is loving this. He's nothing but a big softie."

I put more of the thick liquid into my hand, lather it into his tail. "He sure is."

We use the hose again to wash away the suds. I hear chatter, and when I glance over my shoulder, Vera and Grace are walking by us. "Stop the water," I whisper to Elena. Her brows knit together but then her smile goes wide. And we both leap back in time for Conan to shake the water from him. Some of the water flicks onto me but nothing compared to before.

"That's disgusting," Grace hisses. "Now I'm going to smell like a dog."

The comeback is on the tip of my tongue. My eyes meet Elena's, and from the laughter dancing in her eyes, I think she's thinking the same as me. But I swallow the words.

"Stupid mutt," Vera says. She steps toward me but stops when Conan growls. "If it bites me, I'll shoot it myself."

My heart drops to my feet. My first thought is, *It's just a threat*, but her icy glare tells me otherwise. That burning anger returns, and it courses through my veins. I stand taller, pulling my shoulders back, and now it's me who's baring my teeth. "Don't you dare threaten to hurt my dog . . . or my sister."

A savage undertone lines my voice because I mean every word.

Their eyes widen. Grace steps back, but Vera studies me. "Whatever." She rolls her eyes and walks away. Grace follows.

"Well . . ." Elena says awkwardly, "you either warned her away or you just poked the bear."

"I'd say I just poked the bear."

She sighs. "I think so, too. Well, I'm going inside to have a shower."

I peer at my damp clothes. "Me too."

After my shower, I make us sandwiches and watch Elena. Her eyes keep going back to her phone.

"Is everything okay?" I ask before her phone rings.

"Hello." Her shoulders drop. "I wanted to check you were okay. It took a while for you to call me back." Elena's face falls, then she gnaws on her lip before saying, "I was worried, that's all. When will you be back?" She nods. "See you then. Love you, bye."

"They will be back either late tonight or tomorrow."

Elena goes to bed early. I hate seeing the worry in her eyes. The sweet butts are getting drunk, so I go to bed too, but I can't sleep. I pull my phone from under the pillow. I squint at the bright light and 2:05 a.m. and let out a small groan.

The best night's sleep I had was in Reaper's bed. *He's not here . . . Maybe if I get up early, I can sneak back to my bed.* I scold myself. Knowing my luck, he will walk in and catch me. I can't be sneaking into the president's bedroom, no matter how tempting it is.

"Ava," my name is called out from outside my room.

It's morning, and I haven't slept.

"Yes," I reply to what sounds like Twitch's voice.

"Can you come out here?"

Flutters of anxiousness flood my stomach. I yank the duvet off and unlock the door to see Twitch standing there. His usual casual demeanor is replaced with worry.

"Can you come into the office?"

"Okay," I reply and follow him. "Is everything okay?"

"I'm not sure," he replies, then walks into a room with computers. "Is that your husband?"

Dread feels like a heavy weight on my shoulders. I scan the computer screen Twitch is staring at, and the sight of Beau has me in a chokehold. I can't breathe.

He's found me.

My eyes can't leave the screen. It's the person in my nightmares. I can't speak, so I nod. Beau stands by his car, which is parked off to the side from the gated entrance.

"I want to talk to Ava, my wife," Beau says through the speaker by the gate.

His voice immobilizes me. He sounds concerned, but there's an undertone of anger in it. I know how fake he is in front of people.

Twitch looks at me. "Did you want me to tell him you're not here?"

I blink a few times. "Yes." My heart beats out of control.

Twitch sits in the chair in front of the computer and microphone. "I don't know who you're talking about." Amusement weaves into his voice.

Beau doesn't flinch but keeps his anger under control. "I was told she's here."

I'm quick to respond to Twitch. "No one knows I'm here." Elena would never have told him. Axle wants to punch him, and the other men didn't want to get involved.

Bomber. He didn't want me to bring my drama here. Maybe he thought Beau could take me away so they don't have to deal with it. I swallow down the vomit threatening to come up.

"Sorry, mate. They made you drive out here for no reason. She isn't here."

"I want to speak to Elena, then."

"Yeah, that's not happening. She's still sleeping."

My mind races with uncertainty. Maybe I should leave this place? What if Bomber contacts Beau again? It's the clubhouse of the MC men. Elena isn't one of them. I doubt her feelings hold much weight.

"Axle, Elena's husband, and the rest of the MC will be home at any moment, so I think it would be better if you left." A bite of warning punctuates Twitch's voice.

Beau doesn't reply. He walks to his car and starts it. I watch as he leaves. I can only imagine how hard it was for him to rein in his anger. I know that won't be the last I'll see of him.

Twitch swings his swivel chair around to look at me. "Who knows you're here?"

"Bomber must have told him."

Twitch laughs, making my brows furrow. "Bomber is loyal to Reaper and to the club. There's no way. Have you spoken to any family or friends?"

I shake my head. "Elena spoke to our parents, but she said she never told them or anyone else, so I don't know who it was." A heavy breath falls from my mouth. "Can you let me know if Beau comes back?"

Twitch nods. "But I don't think you will have anything to worry about. That guy won't have the balls to return."

I hope he's right. After walking out of the room, I wondered what my next move should be. I need a distraction, so I move to the kitchen and pull out the ingredients from the pantry and the fridge to make two large batches of baked omelets for the men.

My hand shakes as I grab a large dish. "Hey," someone says from behind me and I jerk, dropping it. The dish lands on the floorboards, followed by a ringing clang.

Elena curses under her breath while I apologize. "I'm so sorry."

She moves toward me, but I unconsciously step back. My arms wrap around myself. I'm on edge, and Elena frowns and slowly picks up the dish. "You have nothing to apologize for. It was an accident."

"Beau found me." The three words I was hoping I would never have to say make my eyes water.

She gasps and steps toward me, like she wants to comfort me, but stops. "Are you okay? Did you have to talk to him?"

"The gates are locked. He spoke to Twitch via the intercom, but Twitch told him I wasn't here and told him to leave."

"Okay, but how would he know?" she asks and puts her hand over her heart. "I promise you. I never said a word to anyone."

"I believe you. It must've been someone who lives here. No one else knows."

A phone rings. Elena pulls her phone out of her pocket and her shoulders slump. "It's Mom. No doubt Beau called her. I'll tell her it's a lie."

My head thumps from stress and the lack of sleep, but I go back to mixing the ingredients of the omelets, then put one in the oven.

Elena walks over and sits on a stool, her elbows leaning on the counter. "Mom doesn't believe me. She thinks you're here."

I pause before pushing the dish all the way in. I grab the

other dish and put it on the lower shelf. I shut the oven door, then turn to look at her.

Elena's hands come up. "I can't believe she believes him over me . . . Even though I am lying . . . still."

"I'm not surprised." I fold the tea towels and put them to the side. "He is persuasive."

"Maybe someone saw you shopping that day with Viper."

"I don't know anyone in this area but you and Axle, but I guess someone could have."

She shakes her head. "Axle should be home soon, so I'll talk to him about what we should do next. I don't want Mom and Dad turning up."

"I need some air. Can you check the omelets and take them out when they are golden brown on top?"

"I can do that."

"Golden brown, not black," I clarify.

She huffs. "Yes, I hear you. Don't worry, we will get all of this Beau stuff sorted."

I'm not as confident as she is. I walk toward the back of the house, open the back door, and step outside. My eyes close at the warmth from the sun, and I try to take deep breaths to calm down.

A whine draws my attention, and when I look down, Conan's glancing at me, nudging my leg. I pat his head and lean down until I'm sitting on the ground. I don't care that the small rocks dig into my skin or that the ground is hard. The weight of helplessness takes over. My hands cover my face as the tears fall.

Conan nudges me again with his gigantic head, then wetness travels up my cheek. I pull my hands away from my eyes to see Conan lean in and lick my face again. My chest warms as I cuddle him.

Rumbling motorcycles approach. Conan pulls away and barks, rushing toward the front of the house. I wipe my eyes with my hands and stand. Sniffling, I try to pull myself together. The last thing I want is for someone to see me crying.

I wander to the table and sit on the wooden bench. I wipe my eyes and cheeks again. The sound of the motorcycles gets louder. I listen closely as one motorcycle after another turns off. My throat tightens. Twitch will tell them everything. My mouth goes dry and my anxiety spikes. I should pack before I get made to leave. Save myself the embarrassment.

Making my way inside, I rush through the house and up the stairs before anyone can see me. Once in my room, I pick up my bag and open it wide. I grasp my clothes folded neatly on the bed, then place them in the bag. The men's voices get louder, and my heart beats faster.

I tense. Heavy footsteps stop in front of my room. The door is open, so I know he can see me, but I'm frozen. He gets closer until his presence looms behind me. My eyes squeeze shut, and I flinch when his arms wrap around me. His hands rest on mine, and he pulls my hands away from the bag ever so gently and pulls me into him.

With his warmth behind me, his calming presence and the caring nature of his hug break something inside of me. I sag into him and the tears come fast. He pulls me into him tighter as I sob. My body trembles, and I can no longer hold myself up. His arm comes underneath my thighs, and he picks me up with ease. He lays me on the bed and pulls the duvet over me.

He leans down, brushing the hair out of my eyes. The gesture makes me cry again, and his frown deepens. When he sits on the bed, it dips beside me. "We will keep you safe. There's no reason for you to run."

I take in the gorgeous man next to me. "Can you stay with me? I don't want to be alone."

He takes his boots off, shuts the door, and walks back. He

pulls his phone out of his pocket and it lights up. He types on it and then places it on the nightstand, pulls his gun out and sets it next to his phone. His belt and holster are next, then he sits on the duvet before lying down next to me and pulling me into his chest.

"I called my contact who is a police officer in the local district." His voice rumbles. "I told him to inform the department in charge of missing persons you will come in today to tell them you are okay and to explain why you left."

I shake my head at him. "I can't do that."

He shuffles back and lifts my chin to meet his eyes. "Tell me why."

I glance away, breaking eye contact.

He waits a moment for me to answer, then sighs. "Can you go there to show them you are okay?"

He didn't get angry or push for me to tell him, which I appreciate, but it's confusing, and my silence was almost loud.

"Being away from him seems too good to be true." My heart sinks. "I'm a coward, but . . ." My lip trembles. "I can't shake the feeling that I'm going to be forced to go back to him, and if I go back, telling the cops about what he has done will make it worse." Memories of Beau saying sorry when he saw the bruises from when he had hit me flood back, but it wasn't long after he threatened me not to tell anyone.

Reaper shuffles closer again and pulls me back into his chest. "You are courageous. He is the coward." His voice hardens at the end.

Instead of telling me to get out when I brought issues to their clubhouse, he is here, holding me. I burrow further into his chest like he's my safety blanket.

Even at the beginning of my relationship with Beau, he never showed affection or held me when I was upset. I wasted so much time on him.

When I was with him, all I wanted to do was scream. Scream for someone to help me. Scream at Beau for making me feel worthless. But I was worried about the consequences. I need to do something now. "Okay. I'll go to the police station."

He kisses the top of my head. It makes the weight of hopelessness lift slightly.

Two light knocks sound from the door, followed by Elena's and Axle's voices.

"I told you she is fine. Reaper is with her."

"She's *my* sister. I need to hear it from her."

"You stubborn woman!"

Reaper chuckles and sits up. "I'll let her talk to you. If you need me, I'll be downstairs and ready for whenever you want to go."

I shake my head and sit up, then reach over and take his hand in mine. "Please stay." His eyebrows pinch, making his forehead wrinkle. He wraps his arm around my waist, pulling me into him. "If you need me to stay, I won't leave until you ask me to."

"Come in, Elena."

She bursts through the door, her eyes bulging.

"I'm sorry, Reaper," Axle says while staring with narrowed eyes at his wife. "I tried, but when it comes to her sister, there's no talking to her."

I give Elena a small smile to reassure her that everything's okay.

"It's not a problem," Reaper replies to Axle.

Elena's eyes move to my and Reaper's hands, but then they wander to my bag and the few scattered clothes around it on my bed. She frowns. "You were going to leave?" She sounds hurt.

Axle frowns at me too. So many emotions course through

me at once, but Reaper squeezes my hand as if he can sense my feelings.

"I didn't want to cause any trouble here," I reply honestly.

"I told you we will sort it out."

"Someone from the MC contacted Beau, so I thought I wasn't welcome anymore."

"I'll find out who it was," Reaper assures me.

"We had a meeting," Axles says. "All the men agreed to you staying here. We were all aware of the implications."

It makes no sense, then. Why would someone call the police on me?

"Did you want me to go to the police station with you?" Elena asks.

I glance at Reaper. "It's okay. Reaper said he will take me."

EIGHT

STAY WITH ME

Reaper

AFTER ALL THE SHIT WE WENT THROUGH OVERSEAS IN THE military, me, Bomber, and Viper came back home and forged friendships with men who also worked in the military. Creating the MC was like finding a home. Ava makes me feel the same.

As soon as I heard her husband was here, I ran to her as fast as my feet could take me because she differed from any other woman I had met before. She's the only woman I've wanted a future with.

For the first time in my life, I ignored my instincts, the pull I had to Ava at the wedding and the connection we shared. I could sense her discomfort at how scared she was of her husband, but I still let her go. What type of man allows that to happen? I could have saved her from the domestic violence.

Whatever it takes, I'll protect her from him . . . but it's not just him I need to protect her from—it's from myself and the

MC as well. A group of men swearing and partying. It's not her scene.

We manage an illegal fighting ring and grow and distribute marijuana for a living. We are the opposite of what she needs, but I'm selfish and I can't let her go. A part of me hopes she can see past all that.

Axle said she was here, but I had to see her for myself. When I saw Ava packing her bag, the sudden assault of emotions crippled me. After everything she has been through, I didn't want to scare her. I could barely stop my hands from shaking when I gently pulled her away from her bag. Having her in my arms eased some of my tension.

"I'm nearly ready," Ava says with confidence.

My warrior.

"Make sure you have your ID."

She leans over, drags her bag across the bed, then rustles through it until she pulls out her driver's license.

"I'm going to the bathroom to wash my face, and then I'll be ready." She moves to Elena and wraps her arms around her.

When Elena opens her eyes, they glisten. She pulls back. "Please don't leave again."

"I won't," Ava replies softly. She gives Axle a small smile and leaves the room.

Elena's hands rise, covering her face, and she cries.

"Babe," Axle says, bringing his arms around her. "She's okay."

Her hands fall and so do the tears coursing down her face. "I should have checked on her. What if Reaper didn't get back when he did?"

The thought has me closing my eyes. When I open them, Elena is staring at me.

"Thank you so much."

"I won't let anything happen to her." My tone comes out harder than I intended.

She searches my eyes for a moment, then nods as if she realizes Ava means more than being Axle's wife's sister. Ever since I saw Ava, I had this pull and a loss of control that is a concern. Bad things can happen when a leader doesn't have his head on straight.

"I want her husband dead," I blurt. The dark inner part of me rejoices. I want to remove him from this earth so that Ava doesn't have to worry about him again.

Axle mashes his lips together like he's trying not to laugh. Elena's mouth goes into a straight line while horror flashes in her eyes.

"Will she hate me if I kill him?"

Elena goes quiet, lost in thought, so I wait for her answer. "She's gone through enough already. I don't want her to blame herself or feel any worse than she already does."

Disappointment slices through me. "I won't, but if he tries to hurt her in any way . . ." I shake my head. "I won't have the willpower to stop myself."

I glance at my gun. My hands itch to touch it at the thought. Having been a sniper at war, I'm used to eliminating the target, protecting my brothers. Stopping that urge will be difficult, but I'll try . . . for her.

Ava walks toward the bed and grabs a smaller bag, then places her wallet and driver's license inside of it. "Okay, let's go."

"Are you sure you don't want me to come?" Elena asks uncertainly.

"It's okay," Ava says.

I stand and put my belt on, pick up and place my gun in the holster, and grab my phone. I put my hand out, gesturing for Ava to walk out first, and then I follow her through the hallway.

"Hold on," I say as I open my door and step inside my room. I walk out to Ava. "Here." I hand her the phone. "This is yours. My phone number is already in your contacts." She stares at it. "It's a burner phone, so it can't be linked back to you."

She slowly takes it out of my hand and brings it to her face as she goes through it.

I pull out my phone and tap on my contact at the police.

"Hello," Parker answers.

"It's Reaper. We are on our way."

"I will let the investigator know. He will interview her."

I hang up, and she's staring at me.

"Thank you for the phone." Her voice is unsteady, still full of emotion.

She's an excellent cook, kind and caring and sexy as fuck. What the hell is wrong with her husband? We move down the stairs and through the house, but she halts where the keys are. "Did you want to go in the truck or on my motorcycle?"

A touch of a smile crosses her face. "I've always wanted to ride on a motorcycle."

I was hoping she would say that. After I grab my keys, we walk out the front door and head for the shed. Rage moves toward us, holding a case of beer. "Can you tell the women to get dinner ready because Ava won't be making it tonight?"

His chin lifts. "My pleasure," he says in a smug tone.

His hard work as a prospect doesn't go unnoticed. He will make a good MC club member.

In the shed, I grab Elena's helmet from the table and her leather jacket, then walk over to my motorcycle. I glance back to see Ava walking leisurely over to me, her eyes darting between me and the motorcycle.

"We can take the truck?"

She shakes her head. "No. I want to go on the motorcycle."

I open the jacket for her. "Whose is this?" she asks.

I cock a brow. "Does it matter?"

Her lips pinch. "Yes, it does."

"It's your sister's."

She nods, as if confirming that she will wear it. She slips her arms in it, and I pass her the helmet.

"It's your sister's too," I say before she questions it.

She slips it on over her head and tightens the straps. I climb on my motorcycle and stare at her. She somehow looks better than I imagined she would look like dressed in leather.

"Hop on."

She hesitates before placing her hand on my shoulder and climbing on. I lean down and point to the foot peg.

"Put your feet on the pegs and wrap your arms around my midsection." Her arms come around me loosely. "Tighter."

"What?" she asks.

I'm not sure if she doesn't understand or if she's frightened. I pull both her arms around me tighter and gently tug her calves toward me so she's flush against my back, and she lets out a small laugh. "I can't have you falling off."

Her grip around me tightens further, making me grin. I make no apologies for how turned on I am right now.

The motorcycle roars to life when I put the key in the ignition. I pull forward slowly, trying not to scare her. We go onto the dirt road, slightly bumpy from the rocks, but when we reach the asphalt, I speed up. She laughs. I fucking love it.

"Faster," she says from behind me, so I speed up. She squeals louder.

When I reach the main street of the town, I slow down and my mood plummets. When I reach the police station, I park in an empty spot out the front, then climb off and hold my hand out to her. She stares at it for a couple of seconds, then places her hand in mine. I help guide her off the motorcycle. She pulls the helmet off, and it's made her auburn hair fuzzy.

"You suit the helmet and leather jacket."

Considering what she's about to do, I see she still has a small smile on her face.

"Thank you," she replies.

It's a win in my books.

I put the helmets in the saddlebags. "Did you know you are the only woman who has been on my motorcycle?"

Her smile spreads.

It's true, and it's my way of telling her she's different from any other woman.

I glance at the police station, then back at her. All I want to do is haul her ass back on my motorcycle and get back to the clubhouse. She's been through enough already. But I had to make sure the police won't turn up at the clubhouse because they think we kidnapped her or something over-dramatic.

I stare into the distance. Is this guilt I'm feeling? I shake my head. She's not even mine, and I'm going soft already.

With my hand, I gesture toward the police station. "I've got you. You only have to answer a few questions."

I see her swallow, and that damned guilty feeling gets worse. We walk to the entrance and I open the door for her. She stands off to the side as I approach the front desk.

"I'm Reaper, and I'm after Parker."

No need for pleasantries. I don't like them, and they don't like me. The MC has an arrangement with Parker—money for information.

The woman at the desk gawks at my cut as she picks up the phone. "Parker, you have a visitor." She puts the phone down. "He will be with you in a moment."

I glance at Ava, and she hasn't moved. She's nibbling on her lip.

"Hey, Reaper," Parker says through a cheery smile as he walks to me.

I give him a sharp nod and turn to Ava. "Are you ready?"

"I am," she replies and steps toward us.

"Hi, Ava. I'm Parker. If you follow me, I'll lead you to the investigator who will do your interview."

I step forward, but Parker shakes his head. "You can't go in with her."

I scoff. "I am if she wants me to."

Parker chuckles nervously. "It's a conflict of interest. She needs to be alone, or they may think you are interfering or that your presence will influence her answers, especially since her husband has made a complaint that she is being held against her will at *your* clubhouse."

Ava gasps.

"He has no proof she's even there."

Parker breaks eye contact. "Yes, he does. He sent in photos of her there, and I can tell you now, it certainly looks like your clubhouse from when I was there last."

The thought of my men betraying my orders twists my gut.

"Ava, if you follow me." Parker looks at me and lowers his voice. "I'll meet you outside to have a chat."

I gaze at Ava. "Is that okay with you?"

Parker isn't calling the shots. She is. They've seen she's alive. Every cell in my body is screaming to return home and demand answers.

She shrugs. "I guess. I want this over and done with."

"If you don't want to answer any more questions, make sure you tell them that. If you need me, phone me. I'll be outside by my motorcycle, waiting."

"Okay," she answers and follows Parker.

As I'm walking outside, every muscle is tense. I pace by my motorcycle. How quickly a day can go to shit! My mind is scattered. I want to be in that interview room with her, and I also want to know what the hell is going on within my MC. The door opens, and Parker strides toward me.

"Do you know who has been giving her husband this information?" I snap.

I trust my men with my life, so I'm struggling to even consider that one of them has done this.

His eyes bug out, then he turns, looking from left to right, as if checking no one heard. "Keep your voice down," he mutters.

I crack my neck from side to side. "Tell me who it was."

My ice-cold voice lets out a warning. If he doesn't tell me, there's going to be consequences. One of my brothers wouldn't dare go against me . . . or the club . . . after every-thing we have been through . . . it makes no sense.

"Her husband forwarded the email to us. It came from your generic War Brothers MC email address."

I yank my phone from my pocket and call Twitch.

"Hey," he answers.

"Someone has accessed the computer room and emailed Ava's husband. I need to know who it was."

I glance back at Parker. "When was the email sent?"

"Yesterday."

It happened when we were away. That lowers the poten-tial candidates.

"They accessed it yesterday." I need to find out who the traitor is because I find it difficult to believe it was Twitch or Rage. Video surveillance covers the outside of the room near the doorway.

"Ah, yeah sure. I'll get onto it now," he responds.

"I want it by the time I get home."

I clench my phone as I give my attention back to Parker. "How would anyone track her husband's email address?"

"Him and her parents have put up posters and have had her disappearance splashed all over the media in her town."

This time, I pull up Bomber's name on my phone and bring it to my ear. As soon as he answers it, I say, "I need you in the computer room with Twitch."

"I'm going there now."

"Someone accessed the computer yesterday and contacted Ava's husband, putting her at risk, so check the emails first to tell you the exact time the email was sent and cross reference it with the video surveillance to see who was on the computer at that time. I need you to go through it *with Twitch*."

"On it."

Ava walks out toward us from the entrance. I search her face, but her expression is passive so I can't tell how it went. I lean down, pull out her helmet, and hold it out in front of me with an outstretched hand. When she reaches us, she takes it from me.

"I have to go back to work," Parker says. "If I hear anything else, I will call you."

I gaze at Ava, who slips on her helmet. "We have to go home. I'll take you for a longer ride around town another time." My jaw clenches.

That's if she stays.

NINE
TRIGGERED

Ava

After Reaper helps me off the motorcycle, I notice the stress in his shoulders and the darkness in his eyes. Tension radiates off him. I've spent years analyzing Beau's behavior to tailor my own, so I have become an expert in noticing the minor details. I keep my distance but follow him.

The men cleaning their motorcycles raise their heads and smile. When they see Reaper's face, their smiles fade—they sense it too. Upon opening the front door and walking inside, Reaper marches in the direction of the computer room, making me frown.

I go through the house in search of Elena but find Cash behind the bar serving beers to Axle, Viper, and Demon.

I walk over to the side of Axle. "Hey, do you know where Elena is?"

Axle turns his head toward me and smiles. "Hey. I'm not too sure. She was here a moment ago." He scans the room. "How did it go at the station?"

The thought of the conversation I had with the officer makes me cringe. "I told him what I've been through and he suggested filing for a protective order."

Viper grunts. "Sorry, darl, but a piece of paper won't stop him."

I open my bag and grab my phone, which is cool to touch, and place it in front of Axle on the bar. "Can you put your number in it?"

He peers down. "Sure." Smirking, he picks my phone up and types. He stretches his hand out to pass it, but before I take it, Viper's hand comes out and snatches it. When he finishes, he passes it back with a mischievous look in his eyes.

I glance at my phone to see Axle, Reaper, and "Sexiest Man Alive" in my contacts. I roll my eyes, and Viper laughs.

Giggles tinkle from behind me, so I turn to see Vera and Grace walking through the house. I stiffen. A few moments later, Elena comes from the same direction. Her face is pale.

I rush to her. "What's wrong?"

Even though I'm looking at Elena, I can sense Vera and Grace approaching us.

"Did you have a pleasant trip to the police station?" Vera asks.

The smugness in her voice makes me grind my teeth. I turn, making sure that I'm in front of Elena so they can't see her anymore. "Why do you care? And, anyway, what did you say to Elena?"

That burn of anger keeps rising.

Vera looks at Grace, and they giggle again. My glare sharpens. My heartbeat is in my ears, my breathing deep and constant.

Vera leans in closer to me. "So I gather your husband got my email."

Anger tears through me. My blood's on fire and my hands are shaking.

Axle is suddenly by my side, but Viper cuts in first. "I wouldn't upset Ava. It's only going to piss Reaper off."

Vera's head swings to him, then she looks back at me, glowering with so much hatred. "You fucking bitch," she yells and lunges at me, but Axle steps between us. She looks over his shoulder. "He's mine!"

A loud laugh roars from Demon. "And you guys call me insane?" he asks, looking around at everyone. "She's a fucking headcase!"

Viper laughs, slapping his back. "No one can match your crazy."

Axle rises to his full height and gets in Vera's face. "Back down," he warns.

She steps back. Grace whispers in her ear.

When Axle looks back at us, I scowl at him. I have no patience left. "How did you not know Vera and Grace have been tormenting Elena?"

My voice is a mix of frustration and sadness. I observe Elena, frowning, hating that they have upset her. We are more alike than I realized—too nice, not wanting to cause trouble. *It needs to stop!*

"What are you talking about?" he asks.

When I glance back at him, worry is etched on his face.

"Those two," I say, pointing to Vera and Grace. Fear flashes across Grace's face. Elena's eyes dart between Axle and me. "She shouldn't have to deal with them being nasty to her in a place she calls home."

Axle's face drops. The room is silent, the tension heavy.

"Vera and Grace, pack your bags and get out of my clubhouse."

I jolt from the roar of Reaper's voice. When I peer over, it's Reaper, with Bomber standing on his right and Twitch on his left.

"I will have no one who is disrespectful or disloyal living here and especially"—Reaper's eyes cut to Vera—"someone who betrays the club."

Vera's eyes bug out, and Grace cries. I have no sympathy for them because I know I won't be missing their callous behavior.

"Ava is here for a whole of two minutes. She's not a sweet butt or an ol' lady," Vera says.

"*You* betrayed *my* orders. End of discussion," Reaper snaps at Vera. "Bomber and Demon, help them pack their bags and make them wait out the front for their ride." His dark glare remains on the women. "I never want to see your faces *ever* again."

Bomber and Demon move to them.

Demon flashes a smile at me. "I thought you were going to punch her."

His voice is full of amusement, but it has the opposite effect on me. It makes me nauseous. I was angry, but from what I've been through, I could never . . . even if I hate her. An urge to run creeps inside of me. The arguing, the yelling, and the crying are all too much, but I try to breathe through it.

Bomber and Demon escort the women up the stairs.

Axle takes Elena's hand in his. He looks at her with adoration. "I'm sorry, babe. Can we go upstairs and talk?" She nods, and they are next to go.

I can't take it anymore, and I bolt toward the back of the house.

As I leave, I hear Reaper yell, "Church in thirty minutes!"

I burst out of the back door. It bangs on the wall as I scan the area for Conan. The banging sounds must have woken him, as he's on his feet within seconds, his ears upright. His body is still until he sees me, then his tail wags.

I plop myself on the ground next to him and hug him. Tears fall from my eyes. His head nudges into me. My breathing eventually slows, and some of the tension releases.

The backdoor opens, making me stiffen, and then Reaper's towering over me. He bends over with outstretched hands, and with no hesitation, I place my hands in his. He helps me onto my feet.

He gently cradles my face in one of his hands and softly wipes one tear from my cheek. His tenderness calms me, but his hands soon fall by his sides as he steps back, giving me room. "I looked over the video surveillance with Twitch and Bomber. That's when I found out it was Vera who emailed."

"She told me she did it and seemed quite pleased with herself."

"You're not going to take off again, are you?" His voice is teasing, but his eyes don't lie.

I never thought I would feel anything for anyone after what I experienced with Beau. There is no way I can trust again, especially a man in a one-percent MC, but being with him feels right. I shouldn't judge what he does, because he's treated me better than any man.

"I'm not going anywhere," I reassure him.

The warmth in his eyes and his slow, sexy smile melt away my worrying thoughts. Being with him makes the happiness seep back in. I step toward him and wrap my arms around his solid body. His arms slide around my back and squeeze. Something about him eases the tightness in my chest. His body shifts, and he chuckles. I peer up at him and follow his line of sight to Conan, who is nudging Reaper's leg for pats.

"It looks like you have a new friend."

One of his hands falls from my back, and he leans down and rubs Conan behind the ear. "Luckily, because it seems you two come as a packaged deal."

"What's your real name?" I ask curiously.

"Bain White."

I give him a small smile. He didn't even hesitate to tell me. "I like the name Bain." It's unique but masculine. It suits him.

Amusement ghosts in his eyes. "Well, that's good, because I wasn't planning on changing it."

His head jerks down. "What is that?" Conan bolts off, and Reaper steps toward him. "Conan!" his deep voice booms.

Confused, I notice the wet patch on Reaper's jeans. It takes everything in me not to laugh while Reaper curses. "Maybe your relationship with Conan is a work in progress?" I'm struggling to keep the laughter out of my voice.

He shakes his head. "Now I've got to go have a shower, get changed *again,* and get ready for church."

I glance at his wet jeans again and burst out in a fit of laughter.

His face softens. "I'm glad you find it amusing."

I clear my throat. "Sorry, but it is pretty funny . . . For dinner, I was thinking of cooking a baked meal. Do the men eat vegetables?"

"The men will eat anything," he says as his hand goes to his stomach and a smile stretches across his face. "But it will thrill them to have a home-cooked dinner."

AFTER SPENDING OVER AN HOUR IN THE PANTRY, I SMILE AT THE food as I locate the ingredients, which are neatly organized on the shelves. I gaze at the bin beside me, which is overflowing with out-of-date food, and pull the drawstring together. The bag doesn't budge when I pull it out of the bin. I grunt and pull the bag higher, trying to wiggle it out.

A deep chuckle snaps my attention to Reaper, who's watching me. "Would you like help?" he offers.

Offended, I scowl at him. At home, I never asked for help. I did everything myself.

"I can handle the trash."

He shakes his head, then looks around at the pantry. "I don't think I've ever saw it this—"

"Clean, practical." I look at the bin again and scrunch up my nose. "You're lucky you and the other men didn't get food poisoning or end up dead. Some of that food was out of date by two years!"

His swoon-worthy smile disarms me. "We're lucky you're here, then."

On the spot, I dissolve and smile stupidly back at him.

He steps toward the bin. His biceps bulge as he easily takes the full trash bag out of the bin, and I sigh as he walks away.

My phone vibrates in my pocket, and I pull it out to see a private number calling. Hardly anyone knows this number, but my curiosity gets the better of me, so I answer it.

"Hello."

"Hi, Ava. It's Kirsty. I'm an attorney who represents the War Brothers MC. I thought I'd call and introduce myself."

"I appreciate it. Thank you, but I don't have money to pay you."

"I'm on a retainer with the MC, so unless Reaper asks you for payment, there's no bill on my side. I have been told some of your story, but I would like to discuss it in more detail in case you decide to proceed with a protective order or file for divorce. I wanted to confirm that your sister will be available if needed to corroborate your story and confirm that she saw your bruises."

Remembering that night and how upset Elena was, I cringe. "Yes, that's correct."

"I could not find further police reports of abuse. Was this an isolated incident, or has it happened before, and is it the first time you have reported it?"

"It was the first time he was physical, but he has punched the wall and broken furniture around the house," I reply weakly, knowing that if I left earlier, it may not have gotten that bad.

"Was there any other abuse, like emotional, financial, sexual?"

My breath hitches, making me cough. "All of them." I'm uncomfortable talking about this with a stranger.

"Did you tell anyone during that time? Friends, family, a counselor—or go to the hospital or doctors."

"My mom, but I can't imagine she would support me." I lean against the shelving. Besides my sister, it would be my word against Beau's. "The protective order would be a waste of time, wouldn't it?"

"Domestic violence cases are complicated and complex. I would do my very best."

"Thank you." I struggle to keep my voice even.

After the call ends, I take a moment to get myself together before I walk out. When I do, Viper is sitting on a stool at the island.

"Here she is," he says with his usual flirtatious grin. "Bomber's outside watching the pig on the spit for me. Rage and I are going to the store to get alcohol. If you need anything else for dinner, can you shoot through a message with what you need?"

"Definitely potatoes, pumpkin," I mumble to myself.

He clears his throat. "So you'll send me the list?"

I blink a few times, realizing I didn't answer him. "Yes, sorry, I will. Should I cook cauliflower and broccoli, or will it end up in the bin?"

"Cook some. Me and Rage will eat it."

I pull up a new message on my phone and type in *potatoes, pumpkin, broccoli,* and *cauliflower.*

"Hey, Ava?"

"Mmm . . ." I reply as I slowly bring my eyes up to gaze at him.

"Stop saying sorry."

"Sorry." I flinch and he chuckles, shaking his head. "I can't help it." It's ingrained in me, and I know it will take a long time to get rid of those habits.

"What alcohol do you want?"

"I'm not a big drinker, but the wine at the wedding was nice. I don't know the names of them."

"It's all right. I'll check with Elena or Axle." He yells, "Twitch, do you need anything at the store?"

Heavy footsteps get closer until Twitch comes into view. He rubs his eyebrow. "No . . . I should be fine." He was replying to Viper, but his eyes were on the pantry. He takes two more steps, then freezes. He slowly pivots, his cold eyes landing on me. "What did you do?"

Guilt strikes me, and I question myself. I shouldn't have touched their food.

"It looks better if you ask me," Viper says, as Twitch moves past me and into the pantry.

Silence.

I wait nervously, racking my brain for what I've done, but I've only chucked out expired food, and everything is organized and easily accessible.

As he walks out, I watch him closely, trying to gauge his mood as he talks to Viper. "Who's going?"

"Me and Rage are getting alcohol and whatever else Ava needs."

"I'll come and shop for the food then, and you two can get the alcohol."

Viper raises his chin. "We're leaving now. Are you ready?"

"Yep," he replies and steps over to him.

The thought of upsetting Twitch makes me feel terrible. "Did I do something wrong?"

He turns, then his face falls. He steps toward me and puts his arm around my shoulder, smiling at me. "Nah, girl." He bends down and whispers, "But next time, give me a heads-up before you do a cleanup."

"I can do that," I reply, still unsure whether I did something wrong.

THE MUSIC IS LOUDER ONCE I STEP OUTSIDE. EVEN WHILE holding the tray with a tea towel, I can still feel the heat from it. After walking over to the tables, I put the large tray down. Elena, Rage, and Axle pass by me with the other trays of food as I walk back inside.

As I grab the two jugs of gravy, Elena comes up behind me. "Is there anything else you want me to take?"

"Plates, forks, and knives." When I reach the back door, I stop and let Axle and Rage walk through first. "Oh, and napkins, salt, and pepper." I take another step, then halt. "Can you get all of the sauces too?"

Rage picks up the apple sauce and takes the lid off, then brings it to his nose and takes a deep breath. "That smells good," he murmurs, putting his finger in it.

"Rage," I warn.

He stops and looks at me with innocent eyes.

"Don't even think about it."

His shoulders drop. "What do you have this with anyway?"

"It goes on the pork."

He looks back at the jar. "I might give it a go."

I smile and continue back outside with the gravy.

AFTER DINNER, ELENA AND I ARE STANDING BY THE HOUSE, chatting.

"Did you want another glass of wine?" Elena asks.

I lift the flute to my mouth and finish the remaining mouthful. "Yes, please."

She fills it three quarters of the way, then fills her own.

"Is everything okay with you and Axle now?"

"Yes, and you were right. I should have told him earlier, but I'm the only ol' lady here and I didn't want to cause any trouble."

"Well, they are gone now. I do admit I was glad to see them go."

She turns her head, looking around outside, and sighs. "And those are no doubt the new ones taking their place."

I follow her line of sight to two new women holding cards around a table with Viper, Cash, Twitch, and the other two sweet butts. The men cheer, then one woman seductively lifts her bandeau, exposing her breasts, and throws it at Twitch's face. The men cheer again.

"Are they playing strip poker?"

"Yes. The men love it, obviously."

"The other two sweet butts who live here seem okay."

"They are. They've always been nice to me. I think they are here for a good time, rather than to claim a particular man as their own. Where's Conan? I haven't seen him since dinner."

Giggling, I point to his kennel, where he's fast asleep. "Everyone was giving him food. I think he's in a food coma."

Elena rubs her belly. "I know how he feels."

"Babe!" We turn to see Axle standing by the bonfire, waving us over. "Come sit down over here."

The fire is huge, and the closer we get to Axle, the warmer it gets. When we reach him, Elena walks into his arms and they kiss. I turn away to give them privacy and see Reaper and Demon sitting on the sandstone blocks around the fire. Demon leans back, blowing rings of smoke from his cigar. Reaper gives me a smile, so I wander over and sit on the other side of him.

"Are you having a good night?"

"I am," I reply, feeling the buzz of the wine.

"Dinner was . . ." Demon forms a chef's kiss with his fingers.

I get ready to reply, but loud motorcycles thunder up the road. Conan barks twice, then gets up out of his kennel and moves toward the side of the house.

I jump to my feet. "Conan." He stops and glances back at me. "Come here." He looks forward again and barks twice, as if he's not happy with my instructions, then makes his way over and stands beside me. "Good boy!" I pat the top of his head.

"Did you want any more wine?" Elena asks.

I raise my hand to her. "No more for me," I say through a yawn. "I'm ready for bed."

Axle puts his arms around Elena and kisses the top of her head. "We're going to bed too," he says with a cheeky wink. Elena giggles.

A familiar group of men and one woman walk beside the clubhouse and toward us. "Hey!" the president of the Kings of Chaos MC yells out to the people playing poker.

Viper glances and waves back. "Hey, man. Go grab a beer, and you can play next round."

"You three should go to bed now."

I peer back at Reaper because the lightness in his voice has gone. He looks at Axle and gestures his head toward me.

Axle steps closer. "I'll walk you up to your room."

More motorcycles echo in the air.

When the group gets closer, Conan barks, and it's deeper than it was before. It wasn't an "I'm going to rip your throat out" bark, but it was a warning.

"Demon, tie the dog up to its kennel."

Reaper's gaze hardens at me, Axle, and Elena. "I need you three gone *now*," Reaper commands.

His cold voice makes my breath seize. I snap back to my previous home, with Beau screaming at me. Tears line my eyes, and my throat tightens, forcing me to run past Axle and my sister. I faintly hear "Ava . . . Fuck!" but I can't look back. All I can do is run. My heart is slamming against my chest as I move through the house. When I reach the stairs, I grab the railing and race up as the walls feel like they're caving in.

As soon as I reach my room, I take two steps in, slam the door, and lock it. I hop into bed and cuddle the pillow as I try to catch my breath, though the tears fall hard and fast.

"Ava, are you all right?" asks Elena. The doorknob jiggles. "Let me in."

"I'm good," I croak out.

She sighs. "No, you're not. Please—"

"I am. Reaper's stern voice just . . . I don't know—triggered me, I guess."

My stomach drops from the way I acted in front of everyone. Angrily, I wipe the tears from my eyes. Beau's presence still lingers. It took one trigger for me to be back in that house, back with Beau, and, suddenly, my world came crashing down.

I sniffle and wipe my eyes again. "I'm tired. Tomorrow, we can talk."

There's a brief silence.

"Love you," Elena says, sadness tainting her voice.

She wants to help, but I don't want to talk to her about it. She doesn't understand what I'm going through, and I don't want pity.

"Love you, too," I reply.

I lie there with my mind going one hundred miles an hour. My jaw clenches as I wonder how long I will suffer. Every day without him, I'm feeling better, but now it's like I've taken two steps back. I thought if I moved and started fresh that I would be free of him and I could be me again.

The legalities are not on my mind. He can keep the house and everything in it. All I want is my life back and to smile again. I don't want to cower when he's around and suffer in silence while putting on a fake smile for everyone else.

I grab my phone from beside me and glance at it. *Great.* I've been lying here for three hours. I roll onto my other side and shuffle my body around, trying to get comfortable, though it's not working. I stare at the door and sit up, swivel around, and walk over to unlock it. I want to go to his room . . . his bed . . . to be in his arms. That's my happy place. My hand pauses on the handle. Maybe I shouldn't. He's probably angry at me from earlier.

My shoulders fall as I let out a heavy sigh. I walk back over to my bed and lie back down. Reaper's been good to me. The last thing I want to do is annoy him, especially in his room, in his personal space. I cringe. He's probably embarrassed too. Ugh! Tomorrow's going to be awful.

Footsteps thump, then two loud knocks on my door.

"Elena! I said I'm fine."

"It's Reaper."

My heart picks up pace. "It's open," I reply softly.

As soon as the door opens, I speak. "I'm so sorry for embarrassing you like that," I blurt, knowing why he's there.

Light from the moon and the bonfire casts onto him

through the window. His eyes drift over my face, and without words, he sits beside me. I stiffen. He frowns.

"I shouldn't have spoken to you that way. I'll do better."

I blink a few times in disbelief. "You're not angry?"

His brows pinch as he stares at me, then they widen and he leans back. "I'm not like your husband." He sounds offended. "Do you think I would hurt you?"

"No, no . . ." I reply quickly. "I know you're not like him. I thought I embarrassed you, so I wanted to apologize."

He pauses, and his face softens. "You could never embarrass me."

The relief is profound. I didn't realize how much it means to me for him to say that. I sit up and shuffle next to him. I wrap my arms around his middle and hug him tight as his arms go around me, pulling me to him.

"Motorcycle clubs follow different rules than society." His voice rumbles, but I don't move and stay where I am, my head on his chest. "I trust my men . . . When I told them you are off limits, I knew they would follow my orders. The men who just arrived"—he pauses, his body stiffening—"are from an MC we work with. They see you without a property cut, and to them, you are available."

I raise my eyes to him. "So that's why when they arrived you asked me to leave?"

He nods sharply. "And if they touched you." He shakes his head. "I can't afford to lose control . . . Not in front of you and not in front of another MC."

He would have protected me . . . because of Elena. "Okay."

His head tilts. "Just okay?"

"Yes, I'm so tired, but I can't sleep in here . . ." I never thought being in the arms of a biker would be where I felt safe.

His face softens, and the side of his mouth twitches, like

he's smothering a smile. "Did you want to sleep in my room?"

"Maybe I'll get a better sleep." I try to keep the relief out of my voice because I need a good night's sleep, and I don't want to be alone.

He stands and flashes me a smile while holding out his hand. I get up and place my palm in his, and head for his room. When we enter, it isn't pitch black, so I can see the bed. The bedroom is cool, the light breeze of the fan blowing on my skin. I stare at the bed longingly. The weight of tiredness hits me.

As I peek to the side, Reaper's hands grasp the bottom of his shirt, and as he brings it over his head, I blush like a teenager. My heart races as I gawk at his impressive body. My eyes follow his broad shoulders to his bulging biceps. Even his forearms are impressive. And, suddenly, I'm hit with insecurity. I'll never be skinny like the sweet butts or Elena. I got the curves and big boobs from Mom's side, whereas Elena got Dad's petite frame.

I pull the cover back and climb onto the bed. As I lie down, my body sinks into the mattress and I pull the duvet over me. I roll over to give him privacy as he gets changed but listen closely to the sound of him pulling off his jeans. The belt buckle clings as it lands on the floor. A part of me wants to turn around and see him in all his glory because I'm sure it is perfect, like the rest of him.

The shower is running, so I shuffle in bed, trying to get comfortable. I'd like to say the reason I sleep better in here is because of his bed, but I know that's not true. I close my eyes and wait for him to return.

It isn't long until the bed dips beside me, though he doesn't touch me. I take a deep breath of his cologne. The scent is unique, like roasted marshmallows with a hint of citrus and vanilla. It makes a moan slip out of my mouth. I'd usually be embarrassed, but I'm not.

"Your cologne is by far the best thing I've ever smelled," I say as I shuffle closer to him.

He opens an arm out wide, and I snuggle further into him, loving every second of being in his muscular arms.

"Goodnight, beautiful."

I can hear the smile in his voice.

TEN
SHENANIGANS

Ava

When I wake, I find myself in the same position as last night, except my leg is over his. I try my best to lift my leg slowly, not wanting to wake him, but it doesn't work. His breathing speeds up and he turns his head, his eyelids heavy.

"How was your sleep?" he asks in a deep, sleepy voice.

I sigh with relief. "Much better."

"Me too," he replies.

"I'd better get up and start breakfast," I say as I sit up in bed and scoot over, putting my legs over the edge of the bed.

"Don't worry about it. We have plenty left over from last night."

I stand and turn to him. "It's my job."

"I'll pay you your leave entitlements."

I crack a grin. "Well, in that case, I'll go down and clean. I can only imagine the sight of it from last night." It makes me cringe.

"You love it!"

My chin lifts. "There's nothing wrong with having a clean kitchen."

He looks at me with warmth in his eyes. "It's been great having you here."

Happiness ricochets right through me. "Did you want me to help with anything else today?"

"Hmm . . ." His eyes flare in recognition. "I do, actually."

I stare at him, waiting for an answer. "I want you to rest and—"

"I don't think so . . . and what else?"

"Can you check out the window to see if the clothes are still on the line?"

I step over to the window. "They sure are."

"They don't even cook anymore, and they still can't get the clothes off the line." Annoyance coats his voice.

"Don't worry, I'll get them."

He smiles. "No, it's fine, I will."

I proceed to the door but pause and turn to face him. "I'll do your washing for you from now on." I walk out. Other women touching his clothes is not something I like.

After getting the leftovers ready for breakfast and finishing cleaning up the kitchen, I walk outside to greet Conan, who's sitting by his kennel. In my hand is the leftover food scraped off people's plates. When he sees me, his tail wags. He stands and stretches before walking over to me, then sniffs the air as the food catches his attention.

"Sit!" I say firmly. When he does, I place the plate in front of him. He stares at it with bulging eyes and drool coming from his mouth. "Eat!" He stands and goes for it—well, rather, shovels it in.

The back door opens, and Reaper walks out. When he sees me, he smirks and shakes his head. "You're going to make that dog obese."

Offended, I drop my jaw. "He was too skinny before!"

Reaper's eyes lock onto Conan's stomach. "I'd say he's caught up."

I stare at Conan's belly. *Oh, damn. He has a point.* Conan will have to be taken for a walk again. I frown, thinking about how much of a bad idea that was before.

"What's wrong?" Reaper asks when he sees the distress on my face from the thought of having to exercise.

"Twitch had to come get me, Elena, and Conan last time we went for a walk."

His head tilts to the side in bafflement. "Why?"

"Me and Elena couldn't walk home." I cringe at how lazy and unfit we sound.

His laugh is loud. "You two couldn't or didn't want to?"

"Oh, no we couldn't! Conan loved it, though."

"Viper and Rage go running most mornings. Why don't you ask them if they will take him?"

I shift uncomfortably.

"Conan will be fine," he answers like he can tell I'm not sure about the idea.

"I know. I feel like an overprotective mother."

He steps over to me, puts an arm around my waist, and places a tender kiss on the top of my head. The small display of affection makes my pulse spike. Being with him is easy. He's not overbearing. I'd love to spend more time with him.

"The fights in the warehouse are on tonight."

My head snaps up to him. "Who's fighting?"

"Rage."

"No!" I reply sharply.

He leans back with an odd expression on his face. "What do you mean, no?"

"I've grown fond of the men here. Them getting hurt"—I rub my eyes—"stresses me out!"

His hand moves up and down in a soothing motion. "No

one is making Rage do anything he doesn't want to do. He enjoys it."

"He's too young. I thought Demon would be into something like that."

"I won't allow him to compete."

"Why?" I thought he would be a perfect competitor from what Elena has hinted at.

"We make money from running and organizing the fights, so including a prospect allows for a level playing field with the other competitors from around the area and others who travel from around the state. Viper and Bomber have specialist hand-to-hand combat skills, and anyone who knows about our MC will have heard about Demon's reputation. No one would be stupid enough to compete against them, and if there's no competition, there's no money."

I nod slowly, now understanding the thought process behind it. "You're running it as a business."

"Yes. Now, we're going for a ride to the Kings of Chaos clubhouse this afternoon. Do you need anything while I'm out?"

A tick of nervous energy zaps me. It seems every time that MC is around, there's conflict or tension, but I try to forget about it because I've only seen them twice. "No, I'm good, but I might see if Elena is free. I wouldn't mind going to get some more clothes."

"Take Rage or Twitch with you."

My eyes dart away.

"Hey," he whispers and tucks a strand of hair behind my ear. The tender touch makes me look at him. "It's for your and Elena's safety."

"Okay." Even though it's weird having a bodyguard around with us.

"Sometimes my voice comes out harder than I intend it to,

but if I upset you, I need for you to communicate that with me. Honesty is important to me."

"It's important to me too." I could never communicate how I felt because I didn't want to make the situation any worse than what it was with Beau. "It wasn't just your tone." My hands fidget in front of me. "If it sounds like you're giving me a command, I struggle with it. I know you're not Beau and that you have my safety at the forefront of your mind, but it's hard to rewire years of feelings, so bear with me."

He kisses the top of my head again. "I should have known. I'll do better." He steps away and walks over to the clothesline.

I shake my head, feeling confused about "I'll do better." I don't know if he will understand how much relief that gives me. I watch on, grateful that I've found him. Reaper is the man all women want. Good-looking, loyal, supportive, and kind. He looks like a savage beast of a man but treats a woman like a queen and with the utmost respect. I never thought men like him existed, and it blows my mind that he's interested in me.

He takes his shirt off the line, then he turns to face me, and when his eyes pierce mine, a slow grin appears. My stomach is in knots as he prowls toward me with a shirt in hand. My breathing quickens when he reaches me, and I can't take my eyes off his lips. I stand on my toes and wrap my arms around his neck as he bends down, pressing his lips to mine. They are soft but firm, and I close my eyes and let myself enjoy him.

Reaper's arms are around my waist, pulling me tighter against his hard body. Parting my lips, I deepen the kiss, tilting my head to give him better access. His silky tongue dances with mine. I moan as heat spreads through my body, but he slows the kiss, then smiles against my lips.

I pull back, my breath ragged, but I can't resist the urge to press one last kiss on his lips before I bring my heels to the ground and reluctantly drop my arms from his neck. "Have a safe ride." I smile as my head spins.

His chest buzzes with laughter. "I could get used to that." His smile falls, and he looks at Conan, who's running away. "Conan!"

I peer down to see another wet patch on Reaper's leg.

There's deep laughter, and I peer over to see Viper with his head back in hysterics. "Hey, Pres, no disrespect, but I think Conan's trying to mark his territory."

Reaper's eyes narrow to slits. "And what's that meant to mean?"

Viper lights up, clearly enjoying this. "You're his bitch!"

I burst out laughing, while Viper dashes back inside.

Reaper chuckles lightly, but I hear "fucking prick" under his breath.

"Tsk-tsk. You need to get your men under control," I taunt.

"That's an impossible task. I'll put the money we owe you in your room. Did you want me to put it anywhere in particular?"

"At the front of my bag will be fine."

"I'll do that now." He cuts Conan with a glare and says, "And go change my jeans." He peers back. "I'll see you later, beautiful."

Licking my lips, I check him out as he saunters away, thinking all I want is to have his lips on mine again.

After I fill up Conan's water, I go inside and see Elena at the fridge, pulling out a bottle of water.

She closes the fridge door, and when she sees me, she asks, "Did Conan pee on Reaper's jeans again?"

I giggle and nod twice. "I shouldn't laugh, but I can't help it."

"That's so funny. I wonder why he does it, and only to Reaper."

"I have an idea."

Her eyes widen. "Tell me!"

"I have a feeling Conan's showing his unhappiness with Reaper and I getting close."

"If that's the case, the men are going to *love* tormenting Reaper. Conan's food motivated, so maybe Reaper can buy him a steak to win him over."

"That's not a bad idea! It might work. On that, can we go to the store today? Reaper paid me, so I wouldn't mind getting some clothes, but after that, I'm hoping to save more money."

Her smile fades. "You're saving up to leave already?" She peers down, rubbing her arm. "I was enjoying having you around."

"No. Actually, the opposite. I was going to ask Reaper if I could stay for a while so I could pay for a chef course in community college because, if I get in, I don't think I'd be able to afford the course and pay for accommodation and everything else."

She claps, her face instantly brightening with a wide smile. "Oh, that's amazing news! I remember you saying you wanted to cook professionally. You're going to kill it, and you can practice all your new skills and recipes on us."

"I was worried about leaving Beau. I never thought any of this could be a possibility, and, honestly, I'm so grateful for everything you and the MC have done for me."

Motorcycles whir, then speed up as the sound of their exhausts gets more distant.

"What's going on with you and Reaper?"

I inch back, surprised by her question. "I don't know. He's great, but . . ."

"What's wrong?"

I slump down on the stool and confess. "I'm not skinny like all the other women here, and I come with baggage. I'm not even sure if I'll ever recover from what I've been through. Why would he want that? Why would anyone want that?"

She slips her arm around my waist. "You need to stop putting yourself down. Everyone has baggage. You're an incredible person. You have a big heart, and everyone adores you."

I smile weakly. "Thanks, but you're my sister, so you're biased."

"Stop it!" she warns. "I've never seen Reaper care about a woman before. Axle said that Reaper's loyal and has always been there to support every man in the clubhouse. Axle said he will treat you the same. He hasn't rushed you into anything, has he?"

"Now that I think about it, he let me make the first move when it came to kissing and sleeping in his bed."

She nods as if happy with my answer, but her eyes go wide, and she points at me and scowls. "And don't you dare talk about your body like that again! I think it's unfair you got all the boobs and ass." She looks down at her breasts, then back at me. "I think you got both of ours." We both laugh at that. "Reaper's got the best of both worlds."

My insecurity lessens. "I didn't think of it like that."

She points to under her eye. "Look!"

I lean in further, not sure of what I'm supposed to be examining. "I don't see anything."

"My first fine line. The wrinkles have begun."

She sounds devastated, but I see no line.

I snort. "You're still in your twenties. Don't be ridiculous."

She rolls her eyes. "How can you not see the line there?"

"At least *I* don't have to worry about wrinkles."

She quirks a brow. "Hmm, and why is that?"

"Fat don't crack, baby!" I say with a wink.

She smothers a laugh before her face falls back into seriousness. "You're not fat!"

A phone rings, and I know it's Elena's because it's a Cardi B song. She brings it to her face, grimaces, but doesn't answer it. She just lets it ring. She peeks at me from under her eyelashes, then back down at her phone.

"It's our parents, isn't it?"

She smiles sadly. "Don't worry, I won't answer."

I let out a long sigh. "It's okay, I'll talk to them."

Her brows rise high. "Are you sure? You don't have to."

My hand comes out as I wait. She hesitates before putting her phone in my hand. I answer it. "Hey, it's me, Ava."

"Ohhh . . ." I have to pull the phone away from my ear at Mom's squeal. "Ava, finally. What happened? Why didn't you call us?" Her voice is filled with concern.

Guilt leaves as quickly as it came. "I told you things weren't good between me and Beau."

There's a momentary silence.

"But it's a marriage. You don't leave when it gets tough." The clip in her tone makes me choke. I have to pat my chest to get my bearings. *Did she really just say that?*

"He hit me. That isn't what a loving marriage is about."

"He told us he accidentally pushed you and you fell. He feels terrible. Look, you just need to give it some time. You two will work it out."

"He said that, did he?" I ask, spitting venom. That distinct burn fires through me. "He lost control and hurt me," I say, louder this time. "I was black and blue. How can you defend a man that abuses his wife? I'm your daughter! In what world am I the villain and he's the victim?"

She breathes heavily through the phone. "You know I love you, but you're saying he hit you, and he's saying he accidentally pushed you. Then you leave without a word. Is it possible that you misconstrued the situation, thinking the accident was deliberate?"

My heartbeat is frantic, and my breathing is out of control. I'm desperately trying to reign in my emotions. "Why aren't you listening to me? He is lying to you. I refuse to live like that anymore. He controlled every aspect of my life and made me miserable. I want the parts of me he stole. I want to be happy again."

"Beau has been over here every day, seeing if we have spoken to you. He was crying, Ava. If he doesn't reconcile with you, he's thought about killing himself. He's sorry, and he loves you."

I laugh, but it's cold and flat.

"There's nothing funny about this!" Her tone is curt.

"They were crocodile tears, and I don't believe him. It's the ultimate manipulation, threatening to kill himself, so that I'll return. He shows you what he wants you to see. You haven't met the other side of him. He didn't love me. He liked to control me. He's mentally ill, Mom. He needs help."

I'm baring my soul to her, but I wonder if it's a waste of time.

"How do you have empathy for him and not for me?" My voice is uneven as I struggle not to cry. "Would he have to beat me so bad that I'm hospitalized or dead for you to understand how dangerous he is?"

She sniffles and a muffled voice chimes in, "Ava, it's Dad. Your mom's very upset about everything."

"She's upset?" I ask in a high-pitched tone. I'm the one tormented in a domestic violence relationship for years, so how are my mom and Beau more upset than me?

"She has been beside herself since you left. We put up posters and were calling around town. We were so worried."

"I'm sorry for worrying you, but do you understand that this is the reason I never called? You two are encouraging me to go back to an abuser. You would rather me be unhappy or end up dead so no one in the church finds out your daughter left her husband."

"How could you say that?" he asks, sounding offended.

"Beau will not change! I want to feel safe, and I want to be loved. Why won't you support that?"

"You're going from a person who you said abused you to staying with a motorcycle gang? You must see how that is hard for us to comprehend. One day you're smiling with Beau, and the next we find out you're having an affair with a biker."

"Excuse me? What makes you think that?"

"A woman who was living in the MC ended up connecting with Beau, and she said you were with the president of the MC called Reaper. *Reaper . . . really, Ava?*"

I think back to Vera. She's a pain! But I'm not embarrassed at being close to Reaper, either.

"Of course he told you," I reply sarcastically. "Well, Dad, you know it's bad when I have to go to an MC clubhouse for safety and that man *Reaper*," I mock in the same tone he used, "has treated me better than Beau ever did."

He lets out a long sigh. "We miss you. When are you coming home? You can stay with us."

Holding the bridge of my nose, I take two breaths before answering. "You live in the same town as him, and you welcome him into your home. There's no way I am going anywhere near him. I'm getting a divorce."

Dad sighs again. "Your mother won't be happy about that."

"I'm the one who has gone through hell. If you want to talk to me, I guess you two will have to come to the clubhouse and then you can see *both* of your daughters."

There's a pause.

"We love the both of you . . . I'll try to get your mother there."

Good luck with that, I think.

"I love you."

My hand rubs down my face. "I love you, too, Dad. Bye."

I hang up and pass Elena's phone back to her. Her smile is wide and she claps slowly. "Well, you sure told them!"

Anger, disappointment, and annoyance clashes inside of me. "I shouldn't have to explain why I don't want to stay married to an abusive husband. Going against their beliefs is one thing, but Beau has been going over there every day, trying to make our parents believe me and him can overcome it. I'm getting treated as if I'm blowing all of this out of proportion."

Elena sits up straighter, then blinks rapidly as if she's trying to process what she's hearing. "Are you serious?"

"Beau plays the part of the victim so well I could vomit."

"He needs to get over it and move on with his life." She cringes. "God help the next woman he ends up with."

A shiver travels through my body, and I glance at the goose bumps on my arms. "No one should go through what I had to go through. I don't want it to ruin our day. Did you want to go shopping now?" I ask as Twitch passes us, going into the kitchen.

"I'm ready," Elena replies.

I walk over to see Twitch and find him in the pantry. I can hear him unwrapping something. He's hunched over, stuffing something in his mouth. I peer around him. He's holding a big box with anchovies written on the side. I step back, not wanting to interrupt his feast, but he stands straight and slowly, then turns around while chewing, and it takes every-thing in me not to laugh. He has chocolate on the side of his face near his lip.

He swallows his food. "Don't tell anyone where my stash is, since you chucked out my last box!"

My mouth gapes open. "I knew something was wrong with you that day. You should have told me. I chucked everything that was out of date."

"What was *in the box* was perfectly fine."

Elena walks in, and her eyes bulge. "YOU better share that, or I'll tell everyone you've been holding out on us."

His gaze sharpens, and he shakes his head at her, then glances at me. "Your sister's not being very nice, making threats like that."

"You're not very nice!" Elena says to him. "Do you know where Rage is? We want to go shopping."

"He'll be getting ready for tonight. I'll take you." He wraps up the top of his precious chocolate and puts it back in the cardboard box marked as anchovies. He pulls out the rice and puts the box at the back of the shelf. He places the rice in front of it.

I bite my bottom lip as I smother a laugh at the effort he is going through to hide chocolate from everyone.

"I'll meet you two at the truck." He shoots a wary glance at Elena.

Elena and I go to our rooms.

I pull out my bag and unzip the front section. As I pull out the notes, I gasp. This is way too much. I take one hundred dollars out of it and place the rest back, making a mental note to give it back to him. I open the top of the bag, take out my wallet, and place the money inside it. I get up and close the door behind me. I hurry along in case they are waiting for me.

When I open the back door, there's no sign of Elena, so I take a seat in the truck and close the door.

"If you were so worried about your chocolate, why don't you store it in your room or somewhere private?"

When Twitch glances over his shoulder from the front seat, he's smirking at me. "Because I have no self-control."

"So you sneak into the cupboard and hope not to get caught?"

His hand goes to his chin. "I guess I do, but did you know anchovies are one of the most hated foods in America?"

"No, I did not know that."

"See!" He gives me a playful glare. "It was a *perfect* plan!"

"You know you'll have to find another hiding space. Elena will tell Axle."

He lets out a long groan. He turns the ignition at the same time that I see Elena approaching the vehicle. When she gets closer, the truck jolts forward and stops. I'm grinning, knowing what Twitch is doing. Elena stamps over, but the truck accelerates, making me giggle.

"Twitch!" Elena yells.

The doors lock as she walks over to us again.

"Twitch! Open the door," she warns, with a hint of amusement in her voice.

I lean forward in my seat to get a better view of their bickering.

His window slides down. "Yes, Elena, how can I help you?" Smug and oh so cheeky!

"Let me in the truck."

"Hmm . . . it depends."

"On what?" she asks with suspicion in her voice.

"If you're going to tell Axle or anyone else where my chocolate is."

There's silence.

"Okay, fine . . . I won't."

"You won't what?"

"I won't tell Axle or anyone else where your stash is."

The doors unlock.

"Well, hurry up, then. I don't have all day."

THE SHOPPING WAS UNEVENTFUL. TWITCH WAS IN SURVEILLANCE mode, scanning every store we went to.

As we drive back into the driveway, my eyes skim the clubhouse. The men's motorcycles aren't there, so they still aren't home yet.

"How long do the men usually stay at the other MC for?"

"Not too long. Why?" Elena asks, then smirks. "Are you worried?"

"No . . ." I answer and see Twitch watching me in the rearview mirror. "Maybe . . ." I answer truthfully. "The way Reaper's mood changed when that MC was here was unsettling."

The truck comes to a stop out the front. We get out and move to the back to get the bags.

"I can't believe you're going to be living here . . . with me!" Elena squeals and jumps up and down.

"Let's take it one day at a time."

A part of me is scared—disturbed, even—that I would think of being with someone else so fast. But by being with Reaper, I'm feeling like the old me again. Or better yet . . . the new me.

"Well, if Reaper didn't bag you, someone else would have. We weren't letting you go anywhere."

My mouth falls open at the compliment—or the insinuation of a suggested kidnapping. "I know you're joking, but when talking to a woman, maybe . . . think about your choice of words."

He gives me a lopsided grin. "It's a good thing. You're a catch!" He playfully elbows me as he takes about eight bags in two hands.

There's the distinct sound of motorcycles, and it's like music to my ears.

"They're . . . back!" Elena says in an upbeat voice.

We get the rest of the bags out, and Twitch parks the truck while we wait for the men. They come in single file, and it's the first time I notice their custom bandanas covering the bottom half of their face. They all have similar skulls, but each has their own personalized edition.

As the men park, I squint to get a better look. Reaper has the grim reaper, Viper has a snake intertwined through the skull, Bomber has fire around the skull, and Demon has a scary skull with horns, which I assume is a demon. I have to take a few steps to my right to see Cash. His bandana has a skull surrounded by dollar signs.

Reaper walks toward us, his hair flipped in different directions from the helmet.

I giggle to myself. "Can you bend over and—"

A loud laugh interrupts me. Then I see Axle with his arm around Elena.

"It's always the quiet ones you have to be careful of." He gives Elena a pointed look, and her jaw drops, eyes bulging.

She whacks his chest and goes bright red. "I have *never* asked you to bend over!"

"It's okay, baby," he purrs. "You don't have to lie to them. No judgment here."

Elena looks like she's about to die from embarrassment. She smacks him twice more. "Stop lying!"

He laughs. I cringe. I don't want to hear about what goes on in their bedroom.

"You couldn't help yourself, could you?" I ask Axle.

Amusement swirls in his eyes. "Don't be like that . . . I'm your favorite brother-in-law."

"You're my *only* brother-in-law," I deadpan.

"You've been spending too much time with Viper. He's rubbing off on you," Reaper says.

Viper strides forward beside Axle. "I heard my name."

They keep walking, but I tug Reaper's arm to get him to stop. When he does, I stand on my toes. He tips his head forward, and I run my hand through his hair, trying to tame it. It's like silk between my fingers.

"There," I say. "Much better."

His genuine smile hits me right in the chest, but it's the flash of heat in his eyes that makes me blink a few times to check it was real. As we walk inside, he asks, "How are you coping with the swearing and all the shit-stirring between the men?"

I shrug. "I'm not a fan of the swearing, but it doesn't bother me, and I try my best to ignore anything sex related that comes out of their mouths."

"It's only friendly banter. The men can't help themselves."

Axle and Viper come straight to mind.

"I noticed."

"The fight's on later, but we'll be leaving soon to check the warehouse is ready."

I frown, thinking about Rage fighting, but I try to hide it by changing the subject. "Did you want dinner?"

"Most of us won't be here. I'll give you money to order pizza. I pay them extra to come out our way. Leave the boxes in the fridge, and some of us will eat it when we get home."

I shake my head, narrowing my eyes at him. "On that, you gave me way too much money. So I'll use it to get the pizzas."

He snorts. "Like hell you will. It's your money. You earned it."

"You overpaid me!" My mouth presses into a hard, flat line as I exhale through my nose. "I want to earn my way and be independent. It's important to me."

"I understand—"

"But?" I ask, beating him to it. He's not taking me seriously. The humor in his eyes only proves me right.

"I'm not having you pay for dinner. The MC paid you what you earned, and I put in the rest."

My eyes widen. "That makes it worse!" I screech. "I'm getting the money now and giving it back to you."

As I turn, he grasps my wrist. "I have heaps of money, and I want to help you."

With a shake of my head, I tell him, "You've done too much already, and I can't take money off a man." I peer at the ground. "Not again." I have to earn my own way and anyway, I'm not *that* person who takes and takes and takes.

His hands move to my cheeks, tilting my head up. His eyes are intense as they gaze into mine. Up close, the gold flecks sparkle in his hazel eyes. "I. Want. You!"

I gasp, surprised by his forwardness. "Why?" He could have anyone.

"I was in the military. I always trusted my instincts, and they never let me down, so I'm not going to stop now. From the moment I saw you, I knew you were different. Tell me, did you feel anything for me when we first met?"

I hesitate. He says nothing, just waits for me to talk. "Yes, I did."

"And now, how do you feel?"

I swallow thickly as my heart hammers. "Those feelings are stronger now."

He slowly nods. "I'm not going to rush you, but I'm hundred percent in this. I don't give a shit about money, but I care about you, so whatever's mine is yours. I've got your card linked up to my account. I've already organized and picked it up."

I open my mouth, but nothing comes out, so I shut it.

"Don't overanalyze it. The money is there for you whenever you need it. All I want is to see you happy."

His hand goes to the back pocket of his jeans, and he pulls out his wallet, opens it up, slides out the black-and-gold card, and hands it to me. I stare at it, and sure enough, my name is on it. I blink in disbelief. He leans down, placing a soft kiss on my lips as his hand touches my hip.

When he pulls away, he smirks. "I've got to get going." He peers down. "I've put the card in your pocket."

Emotion chokes up my throat. I'm worried that if I talk, I'll cry. It's not about the money; it's his trust and faith in me . . . in us. I've been trying to deny my feelings because I thought it was too soon, but he's the reason I've been able to keep my head above water since I've been here.

As he walks away, I clear my throat. "Reaper." He turns. "Can we go for that motorcycle ride you promised me?"

The corner of his mouth curves, flashing white teeth. His smile instantly calms me, making the remaining negative energy fall away.

"We can go tomorrow."

Rage walks in wearing shorts and no shirt. I keep my eyes above his shoulders. Viper's hands go to Rage's shoulders, and he shakes him. "You psyched up for your fight?"

Rage laughs and steps away from him. "Get off me."

"I want some," Viper says, rubbing his fingers together, making the money gesture and swaying his hips. "Money, money, money."

"You need help! That's what you need."

Viper kisses the air, and Rage shakes his head and laughs again.

Viper claps and yells out, "Come on, let's go win us some money, boys!"

Cheers roar, then they walk out the front door. When the last person walks through and the door slams shut, I run straight to Reaper's room. My heart pumps quickly as I hurry up the stairs. When I get into his room, I dart over to the bed, jump onto it, and land on my back. I cackle to myself. I forgot how good it feels to smile . . . to be seen . . . to feel appreciated. Their motorcycles start up, and they take off. I pull my phone from my pocket and look up the local pizza spot, place an order, then set my phone beside me. I snuggle further into his pillow and close my eyes with a smile.

My eyes flutter open at the faint sound of a door opening and closing, so I know Reaper's home. The bed dips beside me, and he shuffles over behind me until his body is flush against mine, making me smile. His arm comes around me, holding me, and he places a soft kiss on my shoulder.

"Mm . . ." I mumble, still sleepy, but then remember where he's been. "Is Rage okay?"

"He's fine, and he won. Sorry for waking you. Go back to sleep."

And I do just that.

Ava

At lunch time, Reaper and I leave to go on our first date. As we walk into the restaurant, the hum of voices hushes when we step inside. I feel everyone's eyes on us. I survey the room, and I'm correct. This is a beach town, and everyone is dressed casually, like they have just walked in from the shore. I straighten my boho dress.

"I'll be back," I say to Reaper, pointing to the restroom sign. I walk in, hoping that by the time I return everyone will be back to their conversations. While I wash my hands, I glance at my face and smile stupidly at the state of my hair from the motorcycle ride. I pat down my hair.

A couple of months ago, if someone told me that my new favorite hobby would be on the back of a motorcycle, that my best friend would be a dog, that I would be close to my sister again, and that I would be dating a sexy biker, I would have laughed in their face and told them they were crazy. Yet here I am.

I hook my bag strap over my shoulder and walk out. I have to walk slowly because of the two men, who came from the men's restroom, staggering in front of me. They are very intoxicated. When they take a seat, I can see better, so I scan for Reaper. When I see him, I move toward him until a leg comes out in front of me, making me stop.

"Aren't you something?" the man slurs.

They look young—maybe midtwenties. The speaker's glassy eyes slowly travel up and down my body.

I stiffen at first, but then a burn of annoyance makes me glare at him. "Can you move your foot . . . please?" I try to be polite, but there's a distinct edge in my tone.

He chuckles and looks at his friend. "She's got manners too."

"Have we got a problem here?" Reaper growls.

The place quietens, and I feel eyes on us. Both drunk men gawk at Reaper with wide eyes, then sink into their seats. The man with his leg out moves it, allowing me access.

"No, no problem," they repeat, shaking their heads.

Reaper's gaze warms when he glances at me. His eyes study my face as if to see whether I'm in any distress.

"Were they harassing you?" He's eerily calm, but I sense it's a front.

The men peer up at me with big doe eyes, like they're silently praying I say no.

"They were rude," I say to Reaper, then glance back at them. "But they were just going to apologize. Weren't you?"

"Yes, yes. Sorry, ma'am," one says, then the other.

"We are very sorry." The man looks up at Reaper. "We didn't know she was yours."

I glower at them with a twisted scowl. That saying does not sit right with me. I'm not property, but . . . I am his, and he is mine.

Reaper's eyes are on me, and he's watching me closely, so

I stand straighter. "Well, I am," I say boldly. "So watch what you say when you're speaking to a lady. You just don't know who her partner is."

"Yes, ma'am," they say in unison.

I give them a sharp nod, feeling empowered by the interaction, and when I step over to Reaper, he gazes at me with a devastating smile on his face. As we move to our table, the two men leave. When Reaper and I take a seat, his eyes roam the top half of my body. When his eyes return to mine, the heat of his gaze makes my insides coil.

"That dress . . ." he says, shaking his head with the hint of a smirk. "You look unbelievably sexy."

I glance down at the dress and smile. I wore it because I wanted to look as good as I feel. My eyes scan the restaurant. I'm glad *most* people aren't paying attention to us anymore. He passes me a menu, and I skim it. Once I've made my decision, I look around.

"It's nice here."

It has an industrial, rustic look. To the far right are exposed bricks. The chairs are simple black steel, but the tabletop is a mix of different shades of wood.

A young female server comes to our table. She smiles at me, but when her eyes land on Reaper, they widen before she pastes a fake smile on her face. "Hello, my name is Cassie. I'll be your server for today. Would you like a drink?"

"A water," I reply.

"Beer."

She gives us a sharp nod. "Have you decided on your lunch, or would you like more time?"

I peek at Reaper. "Are you ready to order?"

"Yes." He looks at the server. "I'll have the pork ribs."

"Chicken burger for me. Thanks."

She writes it down on her pad, giving us a polite smile. "Great. I'll go get your drinks for you."

He looks at me with a raised brow.

"What?"

"I thought you would have ordered something fancy."

I fight to keep a straight face. "Sometimes you can't beat the classics. So . . . tell me something about yourself." I inwardly cringe at how lame that sounds.

He leans back in his seat. "What do you want to know?"

"Why the nickname Reaper?"

He scratches the back of his neck. "You sure you want the answer to that? It might change the way you see me."

My stomach drops, but I want to know. "Please tell me."

He shifts in his chair, looking uncomfortable, making my stomach drop further. "During our tours, they called me Reaper because the grim reaper is death. They gave me targets to take out, and I was very good at my job."

"Is that all?"

His lips partially open as he tilts his head. "What did you think it meant?"

Before looking at him, I look away. "I don't know what I expected, to be honest."

"My turn," he says with a devious smirk. "What's your plans over the next two years?"

I've never been asked that question before, but then I never thought I'd do or be anything other than a housewife. "I am going to apply for a chef course at a community college."

"You know there's a college about fifteen minutes from here."

"Yes. That's the one I was looking at applying to. I was going to speak to you about staying at the MC while remaining the cook there so I can afford to pay for college."

He studies me. "The MC *is your* home."

Joy fills my heart at his words . . . home. "I admit, it feels like home."

"Your home is also in my bed . . . with me." His expression is dark but sexy.

I clench my thighs together and laugh it off. "Yes, your bed is very comfortable."

He clears his throat and raises a brow. "And what about me?"

"You're *okay*, I guess," I reply coyly.

His face falls. "Okay?" He raises his brows, sounding offended. "*Just* okay?"

"I'm only there for the comfortable bed," I joke, amused at his reaction.

He leans forward and squeezes my thigh under the table, making me jolt. With a smile, he answers, "I think you're a little liar."

I smile widely back at him as the server appears at our table, putting the drinks in front of us.

"Can I order a rare steak to go as well? The biggest that you've got," I ask.

"I'm sorry," she asks, looking confused. "Can you repeat that?"

"I want to take a steak home for the dog."

She giggles as she writes it down on her notepad. "I'm sure we can organize that for you."

Reaper shakes his head. "You want to hope Viper and Rage will take your dog for a run because if you feed him the way you're going, he may struggle to walk."

I like the way he doesn't mention the cost but mentions the health of my dog, when I'm sure he doesn't even like him. Just puts up with him because of me.

"The steak is for you to give to Conan."

He blinks in disbelief. "Why would I do that?"

"Me and Elena were talking about it. Conan is food motivated. It could be a peace offering."

He snorts. "I guess anything is worth a try to stop him pissing on my leg."

I burst out laughing, holding my stomach as I remember the wet patches on his leg and Conan sprinting away. Once I have controlled myself, I say, "Next question! Have you been married or had a longtime girlfriend?"

"No," he responds swiftly.

"Why?" When I look around, a group of ladies is watching us—well . . . watching him. "You have plenty of admirers. I'm sure it would be easy for you to get a woman."

He shrugs. "It was never a priority. I was overseas all the time, and I saw men who struggled to be apart from their wives and children. I didn't think it would be fair, and I didn't want the distraction, either."

"But you've been home for a while now. Haven't you been in any relationships?"

His deep frown twists my gut. "We were all messed up for a while when we came back, and then I put all my time and energy into the club to make it what it is today. I'm president, and the men rely on me and trust that I make the best decisions for the club, and I wanted nothing to interfere with that."

A lump in my throat makes it hard to keep my cool. "And how do you feel now?"

Reaper's hand comes out, reaching across the table and putting it on mine, and it settles some of the unease. "Seeing Axle and Elena together opened my eyes that it is possible to have a partner while still managing club responsibilities. Then I saw you at the wedding, and I had never wanted someone else so bad."

"So it was love at first sight," I tease.

"No doubt about it, beautiful."

Our lunch arrives, and during the meal we are engrossed in conversation, but every time I glance at the women's table, at least one is blatantly staring at Reaper. I get it—he's sexy and hard not to gawk at, but I'm uncomfortable.

After our meal, the server passes me the steak in a container and gives us the bill before picking up our plates and cutlery.

I open my purse, but Reaper pulls cash out of his wallet and places the money down next to the receipt. "I'll pay for mine." I reach for the receipt to see the cost, but he takes the receipt and cash and slides it over to his side.

"You don't pay when you're with me."

My mouth opens, but from the confident look on his face, I don't think I'll win this battle, so I slam my mouth shut. When we stand, he slides his hand in mine.

The ladies are loud when they talk.

"He's fine," one says.

"I'd let him do unimaginable things to me," another says, and they all cackle.

Reaper shifts to stand in front of me. Cupping my face in his hands and tilting my head up, he leans down and gives me a firm kiss. I gasp, and his tongue delves in, claiming me.

The women start cheering. One woman yells, "Go get it, girl!" making me pull back and laugh as those insecurities fall away.

AFTER OUR MOTORCYCLE RIDE AROUND THE COAST, WE RETURN home. He parks in the shed, and when I get off the motorcycle, I hand the helmet to Reaper. I wait for him, and we walk inside together. When we walk through the house, it's silent until everyone claps and someone wolf whistles.

My hands cover my mouth. Have I forgotten something? Is it Reaper's birthday?

Viper steps forward. "Is it official? Are Mommy and Daddy finally together?"

I laugh at my crazy family, then step over to Reaper. He bends down as I lean up on my toes, and he brings his lips to mine in a sweet, soft kiss. Everyone cheers again. The look of devotion in his eyes has me wanting to kiss him again, but I resist—*for now*.

Elena runs over to me with the biggest smile on her face and gives me a hug. "I'm so happy for you . . . and for me," she laughs. "I've got you back!"

She's the biggest sweetheart.

I wipe my eye. "I love you."

She pulls back. "Aww . . . are you crying?" She hugs me again, tighter this time. "I love you, too."

We have a small celebration with drinks, but Reaper and I leave early. Reaper walks into his room, but I pause by the door as I watch a woman follow Bomber into his. She has a short, fitted dress on, and I find it odd because I've never seen him with anyone before. After Bomber's door closes, I walk into Reaper's room and close the door behind me.

"I just saw a woman walk into Bomber's room," I mention as I get into bed and pull the duvet over me. Reaper gives me a quizzical look, so I keep going. "Elena said he's never with the sweet butts."

Reaper's mouth goes into a straight line, like he's trying not to laugh, but his eyes give him away. "What are you trying to say?"

"I thought he was celibate." I had no other explanation.

He barks out a chuckle, making his chest shake. "*No*, he's not celibate, far from it."

I shrug. "I don't know. He got angry when Grace touched him."

"You're correct. He doesn't sleep with sweet butts. The woman you saw going into his room is an escort."

My face scrunches. "Why would he pay for it when he can get it for free?"

"No attachments."

I frown, taking a moment to think before I respond. "He never wants to find a partner?"

"No."

"But why?"

He raises a brow and the corner of his lip curves. "Why do you want to know?"

"Surely, he doesn't really want to be alone forever, does he?" I'd like to think that finding that special someone could make him happy.

"It's his choice. He doesn't want to get involved, and for him, it's a transaction. He gets what he wants and there are no emotions, no commitment, just sex."

I raise my chin and shake my head.

He chuckles. "You see things differently. The socictal norms. Nothing about us is normal. Don't try to understand the men in this MC because you most likely never will. Accept them for who they are."

"I do, but . . . Bomber seems so . . . I thought a woman could improve his mood."

Reaper's arm comes around me, pulling me into him. "Bomber is directly responsible for the club's security and safety. There's a story about why he is the way he is, but I can't share it with you. I can say that it contributed to why he takes his job seriously."

"It's bad, isn't it?" I ask.

"Our experiences shape who we are today. Every member of the MC has a story, and, yes, most of us have gone through a traumatic experience. Some people meet the devil and come back to earth still swinging."

I couldn't agree more. "I've met the devil." My shoulders slump. "His name is Beau."

"If he's the devil, I'd die to be cast to him, to show him exactly what hell is." Reaper's voice crackles with anger, a reminder of his darker side, the soldier who needs to protect everyone he cares about.

I sit up. "You know about my past. Can you tell me more about yours?"

Something flashes across his face, but I wasn't sure what it was. "What do you want to know?"

Excitement buzzes inside of me at getting to know Reaper. "I have so many, but let's start simple. Do you have any siblings?"

He slowly nods. "A sister."

"What about your parents? Do you still talk to them?"

"I don't know where they are. My last memory of them was when me and my sister were taken away from them and placed into foster care."

"I'm sorry," I reply, feeling bad for them.

He shrugs. "No need to be sorry. It was a long time ago, and we turned out fine."

"Do you talk to your foster parents?"

"No, but they weren't bad people. They did their best. Sherrie and Larry took on five foster kids of different ages. Sherrie worked two jobs and got money from the government for looking after us, and her partner, Larry, stayed home."

I pull my hair over my shoulder and rake my fingers through it as I think about what else to ask. "What made you want to join the army?"

He let out an exasperated sigh. "Everything."

"What do you mean by that?"

"Larry watched the news every night, and most of the time I watched it with him. Every day, they talked about violence, war, and terrorists, and as I got older, I wanted to help and do something about it."

I lean up and place a soft kiss on his cheek. "You're a good person."

His face goes blank, and a shiver racks my body. It was as if I saw his soul leave his eyes. "Don't get me confused and put me on a pedestal. I killed who they ordered me to kill. I never asked questions about who they were or what they had done."

A coldness solidifies his voice, and it makes me frown. I didn't mean to upset him. "You have a past, but my feelings about you won't change."

He looks away, and that familiar fire returns to my stomach. When I sit up, his eyes return. "Why don't you believe me?" I'm annoyed and saddened. "You risked your life to go to war for your country."

He sits up with his back against the headboard. His pained expression nearly levels me. "I've killed a woman before."

I pause, but he would not kill for no reason. "Why?"

He hangs his head, then rubs down his face, and the Reaper I know is back. I crawl over and straddle his legs. I grasp his face, feeling the prickles of his beard on my fingers. I lift his head to make him look at me. The torment in his eyes is palpable. I blink a few times, holding back tears; it hurts me to see him in pain, but I know it's my turn to be strong. "Please, share with me what happened."

His eyes close briefly before he speaks. "With all my training, nothing could have prepared me for war. Every day was death and destruction. But I'll never forget killing that young woman. She wore a coat that looked too big for her, and I thought she had a bomb under it." His voice cracks as sadness falls from his lips and regret fills his eyes.

Reaper's face blurs. "Why did she have a bomb strapped to her?"

"I'm not sure if she had one, but I heard stories of women

wearing them by choice but also because they could have been forced to. They used woman and children against us, knowing full well that we value their lives."

My chest constricts but I need to know more. I want him to share this burden with me, knowing how much better I felt when I told Elena about what I had gone through.

"What happened?"

He goes quiet, lost in thought, so I wait patiently for his response. "We were given information that a target was in an area close by. So we traveled there, and the men were going through each home, one by one, searching for him. When they came out of one home and were about to walk into another, the woman had come from the back of the house to the side and was moving toward them. She had a large coat on and . . ." He shakes his head and swallows. "I couldn't see a bomb, but I had seconds to react, so I shot her."

I kneel, wrap my arms around his shoulders and hold him tightly, his chest against mine as his arms snake around my back. The tears fall, and my emotions strangle me. I inch back and peer into Reaper's tortured eyes, and all I want to do is take his pain from him. Leaning forward, I kiss a tear falling down his cheek.

"Did you find out if she had a bomb on her?" I ask in a small voice.

He shakes his head. "We had a mission to complete."

"You had to make a tough decision, but it doesn't make you a bad person. Thank you for sharing your story with me."

I needed it as much as he needed to talk to someone. Seeing his vulnerability and hearing his struggles only makes me love him more.

I focus on his lips, then on his eyes.

I love him.

My body pulses with the need to kiss him. My hands seem

to move on their own accord, and I wrap my arms around his neck and pull his lips to mine. For a second, he pauses as if in shock but then relaxes and kisses me harder.

He coaxes my lips open, allowing his tongue access, then expertly massages it against mine. There's a hurricane of emotions inside me. He's the one for me. My arms tighten around his neck, increasing the passion of the kiss, causing my lips to plump under the assault. My body heats, but there's also an ache between my thighs that no kiss will fix, so I pull away, leaving him open-mouthed.

Lifting one leg over him, I crawl to the edge of the bed and step down. I grasp the edge of my dress and lift it over my head, then drop it on the floor by my feet. As his eyes admire my body, I've never felt so sexy, so I unclasp my bra and slide my arms out. A small moan escapes my lips in relief, and my nipples pebble from the cool air.

"I've been fantasizing over your body for a long time now, and every inch of you is perfect."

With the hunger in his eyes and his deep, hungry voice, I believe him. Tension coils from his body, like he wants to get up and touch me but he's forcing himself to stay seated.

My underwear is next, and I pull them down my ass and thighs, step out of them and to the bed, and crawl toward him.

"You're in control, baby."

My pulse thrashes against my skin. "Shirt off!"

He leans forward from the headboard, lifts his shirt over his head, then throws it to the side.

My teeth dig into my lower lip as my greedy eyes gaze at every ridge on his body. When my eyes reach his groin, his cock is straining against his jeans, so I reach for his belt and work on his button, my fingers fumbling, a mix of nerves and desire.

He takes over, pulling his zipper down, then brings his

jeans and briefs under his ass and down his legs, kicking them off when they get to his feet.

He's relinquishing all control, and I'm sure it's not easy for a man like him. I know I need it, but I will also take full advantage of it.

"No touching me until I say."

His jaw clenches, and his head falls back onto the headboard with a light thump. I wrap my hand around the base of his cock. His head whips up as he hisses through his teeth, and it makes me feel powerful. I grip him firmly and stroke his thick length again and again.

I shift closer and place my hand on his shoulder for leverage. I tremble as I lift one leg over him to straddle him. He lifts his hands. "No touching," I say in a seductive voice, and he swears under his breath. My hand reaches between us, grabbing his shaft again, then I shift back so he's exactly where I want him to be. Inching down, I arch my back so he's at my opening.

He stretches me as I ever so slowly inch down further, but I hover there and grind on him, working only the tip, letting him feel how wet I am. The groan that comes from deep within his chest does crazy things to my insides, and I grind again, being careful not to go down any farther.

"Fuuuuck, Ava . . . You're torturing me! I need to touch you. Please let me touch you."

Reaper, an alpha male begging to touch me, only makes the ache between my thighs worse. "Okay," I whisper and welcome his touch. Without missing a beat, one hand tangles in my hair, and he crashes his lips to mine while the other is on my breast, kneading it. I moan when his thumb rubs against my nipple, but it's swallowed up by the kiss. Tongues collide as my body burns with need.

His lips leave mine and he places open-mouthed kisses on my throat and linger on my pulse point. His hand moves to my other breast, and he bends down, taking it into his mouth, making my head fall back as he swirls his tongue around my nipple.

The need is too strong, so I lower myself, inch by inch, down his cock, as deep as I can until it is buried to the hilt.

"Condom," he says through a ragged breath.

I raise myself and grind down. There's a mix of pleasure and anguish on his face. "I don't think I can get pregnant."

"Good. I want to feel you around me. Ride me, beautiful."

My insides lock onto him in bliss as I feel his hand on my hip, his mouth on my other breast, inducing a faint moan. As I arise, my arms tighten around his neck and I grind down, getting into a rhythm. A sheen of sweat covers my body, strands of hair sticking to my forehead.

My rhythm gets faster as the pressure keeps building, my body desperate for release. Reaper's thumb meets my clit, and I gasp at the sensation. He applies pressure and rubs circles. With a low cry, I break apart as my body clenches and shudders around him. Distantly, I hear him say my name as I struggle to catch my breath at the pleasure coming in waves. He lets out a guttural groan, and I collapse, my body leaning against his.

Once the haze fades, I realize something. "That's the first orgasm I've ever had with a partner."

TWELVE

KING REAPER

Reaper

I FEEL LIKE A KING.

I can't believe it was her first orgasm. I'm getting a hard-on just thinking about it. I'm thrilled she's back in my bed, where she belongs. The warmth of her body, the soft sound of her breathing, soothes something inside me. I relish the fact that she's finally *mine*.

Last night was incredible. She's lying on her side away from me, but when I lift the blanket, I can see the sexy curves of her hips and ass. I smile to myself. I'm a lucky son of a bitch. All I want to do is sink back into her.

My phone rings. I roll over and see the private investigator's number up on my screen. My stomach twists at the familiar feeling that something's wrong.

"Reaper speaking."

"Hi. I'm calling to update you. I've been staking out Beau's house for days, and he hasn't come home."

Dread washes over me. "Do you think he's planning something?"

"It's a possibility," he replies before a long pause. "I have covered cases like this before, and they don't end well."

I glance back at Ava, who's sleeping so soundly, and shake my head. "He dares comes near her, and he'll regret it."

"Once the victim has left a domestic violence relationship, that's when it's the most dangerous for them. I know she's safe with you, but keep that in mind because you don't know what state of mind that guy is in."

"I appreciate it. Can you stay there and do your best to search for him by any means necessary to find out where he is or where he's gone?"

"I'll keep you updated."

I white-knuckle the blanket. The beautiful woman in my bed has found her feet and is smiling again. The last thing I want to do is ruin that because of that oxygen thief.

Looking at my phone, I go through the contacts and call the club's attorney.

"Hi, Reaper,"

"What happens if Ava wants a divorce, but no one can locate Beau?"

"The judge will most likely rule in Ava's favor."

Rubbing my chin, I peer off. Well . . . that could work for everyone because that asshole will never hurt her again. Being in the military, I know how fragile life is, but being with Ava has shown me a whole new meaning. I've lost brothers, but I won't come back from losing her.

"Thanks. Bye."

Ava rolls over toward me with heavy eyes, her long auburn hair draping over her shoulder. "Good morning," she says in a husky voice.

"Good morning, beautiful."

She smiles but averts her eyes.

"What do I have to do or say to make you believe that you're beautiful?"

Her nose scrunches, but it gives me an idea.

"Are you ticklish?" I ask with a raised brow.

Her eyes narrow warily. "I am . . . Isn't everyone?"

She can't even lie, knowing it's to her detriment.

I jump up and roll her onto her back. She squeals in surprise. I grab her tiny hands and raise them above her head. Her bright-green eyes and mouth are wide, and it makes me give her a wicked smile while leaning over her. "Now say 'I'm beautiful.'"

Her head rocks from side to side. My free hand rises. She bucks as I slowly trail my fingers down her arm. Her breathing quickens as I get closer, then I gently dig my fingers into her side and her underarm. Her laugh is like music to my ears as she wiggles and bucks from side to side, still laughing.

"Okay, okay," she says through heavy breaths. She looks me in the eyes, looking so serious, and says, "Reaper, you're beautiful."

My hands go straight to her sensitive spots again, and she cackles in laughter while trying to get out of my hold. "My woman has a smart mouth on her!"

"Okay, fine!" she says louder. "I'm beautiful."

I smile from ear to ear. "That's more like it."

Her chest is heaving, and I can't help but admire her perfect tits. My head moves to her boob, and my tongue rolls around the tight pink nub. A small gasp escapes from her mouth. I take her mouth in mine and devour her. I'll never tire of this.

Breakfast was amazing as always, but afterward, when Ava, Elena, and the sweet butts go to clean up, I call for a meeting in church.

I'm at the head of the table and observe the men. Viper as VP is on one side and Bomber as sergeant at arms is on the other. The other men follow around the table.

"It's time to decide Rage's fate, whether we will patch him in. All hands raise in agreement," I say as I raise my hand.

Around the table, everyone raises theirs with no hesitation. Rage has felt a part of this family since he arrived, but we have a process, and every prospect has to earn their right to wear the club's patches.

"Ava is my ol' lady, and I'll be getting her a property cut." I peer down at the table. "Cash, can you organize this?"

He nods his head sharply.

Axle chuckles, making me look at him. "Have you got something to say?"

"Elena told me Ava didn't like that she was wearing one, especially the term 'property of.'"

I frown. I didn't even think about that. "Ava's husband has gone missing. We need to be on high alert. Ava and Elena are not allowed to leave the compound."

"Why is Elena not allowed to leave?" Axle asks.

"I think he'll come for Ava, and I don't want to give him any leverage. It won't be forever, and we can review this at a later stage, but until I find out about Beau's whereabouts, I want the women to remain here under our protection."

"That's a good plan. Thanks, Pres," Axle replies. "Before Beau went into hiding, Elena told me he was sending her and her parents messages, threatening to kill himself if he doesn't see Ava."

"Did she tell him to get it over and done with already? Saves us the hassle."

Everyone's eyes fall on Demon, and from the amusement

on the men's faces, I'd say he said out loud what everyone else was thinking.

"Twitch, do whatever you have to. I need to find him."

Twitch gives me a salute.

"I need everyone to be vigilant. On a different note, everything is ready for the marijuana deliveries, but I'll be staying with Rage and Twitch, just in case Beau tries anything. Viper will be in charge." Viper's smug smile shows he will love that. "The Kings of Chaos MC will meet you by the road, at the end of our property, when a time has been confirmed."

Bomber leans closer. "Did you get a sense that something was different last time we went to their clubhouse?"

I think back to that day. My mind was on Ava. "I didn't notice anything. Why? Did you?"

Viper chimes in. "They were quieter than normal."

Bomber and Viper have the strongest instincts and intuition I have seen, and that is why they have the positions they do.

"The Kings of Chaos president couldn't even make eye contact when you were talking," Bomber says.

"I'm calling tomorrow off," I bark.

The room is silent. Everyone's staring at us.

Viper's hand goes to my shoulder. "We've got this, Pres. Delivery is due. We can't afford to piss anyone off. We'll get it done with no issues. You have our word."

My stomach twists knowing he's right and that I can't watch their back makes me anxious. "If anyone gets even the hint of suspicion about anything related to the Kings of Chaos, inform Viper immediately."

As we walk out of church, I move straight to the bar, open the fridge, and take a cold beer out. I twist the lid off and gulp down the refreshing liquid. It relieves none of the tension in my body. Ava stands by the dishwasher. When I make eye contact with her, she frowns at me.

She closes the dishwasher door and walks over to me. She takes the beer from my hand, and turns, putting it on the bar, then stands on her toes, draping her hands around the back of my neck. The hint of a smile crosses my lips, my arms going around her. Everything seems better when I'm holding her.

"Beau's gone missing. I've got a private investigator looking into him. We'll find him," I reassure her.

"I'm sorry," she says, then sighs. "I'm sorry, *again*. Beau is a nightmare that won't go away."

He sure is, but I pull her tighter.

"Never apologize for him. Do you know where he could be?"

"I wouldn't know. He never spent time with his family, and the only friends he spoke about were his colleagues, but he never saw them after he got fired. He mostly stayed at home."

In her eyes, I can see that she's scared. "I'll be here for you, to protect you, so try not to worry."

"I know . . . and I'd be happy to never hear his name again." She peers off before looking at me again with a seductive grin, and all my problems vanish.

The only thing left is her. She pulls away but puts her delicate hand in mine, lacing our fingers and stepping forward. Tugging on my hand, she gestures for me to follow her. Over her shoulder, she gives me a suggestive eyebrow raise, and that's all it takes to get my dick hard.

We hurry through the clubhouse and up the stairs. I stop until she turns around and looks at me, then I pick her up. She shrieks, her legs wrapping around my waist.

"Put me down. I'm too heavy."

I laugh at her ridiculous comment. When I get to *our* bedroom door, I open it, step inside, then kick it shut with my foot. I move to the bed and gently pull her arms from my neck and push her onto the bed. She bounces slightly on the mattress.

"You're my fantasy." I lean down over her, with one hand supporting my weight, while the other cups her tit through her bra. I enjoy her little gasp.

"These are the best tits I've seen in my life, and this . . ." My hands move to her side and travel down her body to her thigh. "Perfect curves, round ass, and creamy skin. I'll never get enough of you."

Heat flares in her eyes. "Kiss me." Her voice is a breathy plea.

My mouth collides with hers. She tastes sweet, but her tongue is desperate and wild, which increases the ache deep in my groin. There's a tug on my belt, but I pause and inch back, in case she changes her mind.

"Reaper," she pleads, "get your pants off. Now!"

The sassy comment is the approval I needed, so I lever myself off her body and make work of my jeans as she undoes hers. After I kick them off my feet, I slide my arms out of my cut, placing it on the ground, followed by my shirt. I watch on, enthralled, when she takes her bra off and throws it to the side. She then spreads her legs wide, welcoming me.

An animalistic growl sounds low in my throat. My eyes travel up her body. While appreciating every curve, I stroke myself. Ava's tongue pokes out of her mouth, sweeping across her bottom lip as she watches me, like she's starving. I step toward the bed and slowly moved up her body, watching her chest rise and fall.

I slide my hand from her smooth belly to her breasts, and she shivers from my touch. Her skin is warm and soft. Her hand moves between us, and she grips my cock, gliding it between her folds and onto her clit. My eyes roll back.

Thank fuck for no condoms—but only with her have I never worn one.

Gripping her hips, I position myself at her entrance, then press inside inch by aching inch. Our gazes lock, and the intimate connection is intense. I lean down and my mouth finds hers again, my tongue sinking inside her mouth. When her legs wrap around me, I rock my hips, thrusting in and out, slowly at first. There's a pinch of pain in my back from her nails sinking in.

Breaking the kiss, I look down. Her eyelashes flutter as she writhes underneath me.

"Harder," she begs, digging her heels into my ass.

I slam my hips against hers, releasing a cry of pleasure from her throat. Sweat drips from my skin as her muscles tighten around me. Her moans get louder as my pace gets faster. My dick pulses with the need to come.

Reaching between us, I rub her clit. She jerks when I press harder. Ava's teetering on the edge, but I didn't wait for her to come. Instead, I keep pounding into her, and she explodes like a goddess, screaming my name. I thrust two more times and follow her over the edge.

I JOLT AWAKE. MY EYES SHOOT OPEN AS I GASP FOR AIR. I RUB MY eyes. The room is dark. Ava stirs in my arms. "Shhh," I whisper, and she snuggles in, falling back asleep.

The nightmare I just had, of Beau taking her, was one of the worst I've had. It used to be the flashbacks of war that haunted me every night. The screams of men, the explosions, the gunshots. It never ended until Ava spent the night in my bed and silenced those demons. But now that there's a potential threat to her life, those nightmares have changed to losing her.

Most of the men have PTSD, but that's the consequences

we bear from going to war. I'll never regret going because of my brothers I have saved and protected and the targets I've eliminated to protect our country, like I'll never regret protecting Ava.

I lean in closer to her, breathing in her sweet vanilla scent, listening to her breathing. She's with me, and she's safe. This powerful pull urges me to go into sniper mode and hunt Beau down, but I can't bring myself to leave her side.

THIRTEEN

THE PERFECT STORM

Ava

"WE'VE GOT TO MAKE A DELIVERY TONIGHT WITH THE KINGS OF Chaos," Reaper says from beside me. He's sitting up, leaning against the headboard.

I pull my hair over my shoulder as I keep braiding it, wondering whether I should talk to him about it. "Are you allowed to tell me what that means?"

"You can ask me anything. We grow and distribute marijuana."

Relieved, I blink a few times. I can live with that. "Where do you grow it?"

"Further up the mountain, past the cabin."

His honesty is always refreshing.

"Why do you need the other MC? Don't you have enough men?"

"They have chapters around the country, so they are one of our biggest customers. Their MC provides additional protection until we unload, then they distribute it between themselves."

Everything makes sense now.

"I'm going to miss you."

"No!" He stares at me with a weird look on his face. "I'm staying here with you."

I'm torn. I selfishly want him to stay, but he wants to go.

He leans down and kisses my forehead. "We have done this many times before. The men will be fine without me."

The dark circles under his eyes say otherwise.

"Have you slept?"

The touch of a smile graces his lips. "Don't you worry about me."

I frown. "I'm not *that* girl. I don't want to force you to choose between me and your men."

"*You're* not making me choose. I want to stay here with you."

He sounds sincere, but I still feel like he's being forced to choose.

"Well, I'll go with you on the ride. Then you won't—"

"Not a chance in hell."

"Why?"

He shakes his head. "I want you *away* from the danger."

"You don't need to babysit me. No one has seen Beau, and it's not like he has any close friends. He wouldn't be able to go against anyone in your club, so if Rage and Twitch are staying, then I'll be fine."

He cracks his neck to the side. Any time Beau's name is brought up in conversation, a tension radiates from Reaper's body, and I don't blame him.

"Twitch and the private investigator have been spending every day looking for him, so until I know his exact location, I'm not leaving your side."

I attempt to smile because I am grateful, but the guilt still eats at me. "It means a lot that you have organized all of that. I have noticed there's always at least one man in the computer room, watching the cameras." I wish I could help. My face brightens. "I'll have to make something extra good for the men for dinner to say thank you."

"Believe me, they appreciate every meal you cook for them. It's not that I don't think the men can do the delivery without me. I'm struggling with letting go of control because this will be the first time I don't have their back."

My lips curve into a cheeky grin. "You don't struggle to let go of control when it comes to me."

He swiftly moves and leans over me, pushing me down onto my back. His lips are so close to mine I can breathe in the air he breathes out. "You're different," he says, then kisses me.

I LIFT THE CUP OF COFFEE TO MY LIPS AND HAVE A SIP OF THE HOT drink as I watch Reaper pace in the kitchen. It's unsettling.

Elena is sitting next to me with her elbows on the kitchen counter and her head in her hands. She mindlessly stares at the wall. They are quiet, but I can see the worry in their eyes. I was asleep when the men left late last night. Conan barks again.

"What's wrong with Conan lately?" Elena asks. "He's been barking more, and he's getting worse. It's at all hours too."

I've noticed, but I don't believe he barks at nothing. "Maybe he's been seeing more wildlife than normal."

A phone rings, interrupting our conversation. Reaper swiftly grasps his phone from the counter.

"Reaper," he answers on the second ring. I can hear the

hum of a voice but not what is being said. "What do you mean Jude isn't there? No, he didn't tell me." Reaper nods. "Okay, okay." His body relaxes, so I gather everyone and everything is okay. "I knew you would be fine without me, but I don't enjoy being left here. How long until you will be back?" He looks to Elena, who's leaning forward toward him, watching his every move.

"Can you put Axle on for me?" Elena sits up taller, her eyes widen, and her hand comes out for the phone.

"You should appreciate your wife." There's a pause. "Because I'm here, and the whole time, she's been worrying about you." Elena smirks at Reaper. "Here, I'll put her on." He hands the phone to Elena.

"Babe! Please tell me you will be home soon." She sighs. "Good." She breathes out a gush of air. "Can you please take Reaper with you next time?"

Reaper gives Elena a puzzled expression. There's laughter through the phone.

Elena looks Reaper dead in the eyes when she says, "He's been stressing out, which has made me stress more!" There's laughter again while Reaper shakes his head. "Okay, babe. Love you. Bye." She hands the phone back to Reaper.

He takes it and crosses his arms. "I haven't been stressed."

I glance at Elena, and we both quirk an eyebrow at him.

These two stress heads can sit and watch the clock together. "I'm going outside to play with Conan."

As I move through the back of the clubhouse and out the back door, I scan the yard for Conan, but I can't see him.

"Conan," I yell as I search again. Barking is coming from the front, so I trail around the side and make my way to the front to see him standing like a statue with his ears erect. He barks again.

"Hey," I call out, and his head whips to me. Instantly, his ears drop, his tail wags, and he runs over. When he reaches me, I pat him. "We need to have a serious conversation. You have to calm the barking down. People are starting to whine."

His head tilts, though I'm sure he has no idea what I'm talking about.

Motorcycles rev in the distance. My first thought is, *Wow, the men were quick.*

Conan barks and bolts toward the gate. I groan at having to walk down the driveway. "Conan!" I don't know what's gotten him so on edge lately.

I squint at the men. I don't recognize them. Considering the Kings of Chaos are out of town as well, it's most likely people I don't know. Conan isn't fond of strangers, so I run to him, then pull on his collar.

"C'mon, out the back. Let's go."

As the motorcycles get closer, my heart becomes frantic.

"Out the back now!" My voice is louder and stern. Conan looks up at me, and I point to the backyard. He follows as we make our way to the house.

As the motorcycles get to the gate, I glance back once more. I swear the men are from the Kings of Chaos.

I take Conan through the house because I'm not sure whether the men were going to come inside or out the back. Rage meets us at the front door, then smiles at Conan, patting him on the head. "Hello, boofhead." He glances at me, then over my shoulder. "Are the men here already?"

"No, but I swear it's the Kings of Chaos."

He gives me a weird look as Elena rushes toward us. "It's not Axle," I tell her, knowing who she is keenly waiting for. She stops and glances at me with a deflated look before turning and walking away.

Rage turns swiftly and walks toward the computer room, so I follow in curiosity. When we enter, Twitch and Reaper are looking at the screen that shows the front of the house, but it's zoomed in toward the gate.

"I didn't expect them here," Reaper says, and an unsettled feeling takes root in my stomach.

Twitch looks up at Reaper from his seat. "Do you want me to let them in?"

He pauses. "Not yet."

"What's Jude doing with them?" Rage asks.

"I don't know, but let's find out."

Twitch nods and presses the intercom. "Hey, Jude, what are you doing here?"

Jude chuckles. "I decided to come up and have a beer."

Reaper leans down and presses the intercom button. "Viper mentioned you weren't with your men during delivery."

"That's what I came here to discuss."

All eyes are on Reaper as we wait for his decision, but he turns to Rage. "Call the men now. It's only a precaution but tell them to be on alert. Jude is here with two men I don't know, and that prospect is with him, the one I told him to get rid of."

Rage pulls out his phone and walks out of the room.

"Have you got your gun on you?" Reaper asks Twitch.

His question makes my stomach sink. Twitch pulls a gun from under the computer table.

"Are you going to let us in? I'm desperate for a cold beer," Jude says.

Reaper shakes his head.

"Maybe another time," Twitch replies.

One man we don't know gets something out of his backpack, and as he walks toward the gate, the others reverse. "What are they doing?"

An explosion makes me take a few steps back. There are also distant screams, which I presume are from the sweet butts. I release a shaky breath as I get my bearings. Conan's barking, but I've got hold of his collar.

Reaper swiftly moves to me. "Go upstairs and grab my spare gun. It's in the top drawer of my cabinet."

The monitor shows a plume of smoke, and the men walk through the entrance with their guns drawn.

Reaper squeezes my shoulder, and I blink a few times. "Did you hear me?"

My heart is in my throat, but I nod. "I've shown you how to use it, and there are already bullets in it. Take Conan with you and find Elena."

The mention of Elena's name changes me from a state of shock to focus. She's depending on me, and I need to keep myself together.

Rage runs in the room. Reaper looks at him. "Go get the keys to the truck and go with them. We will force them away from the driveway to give you safe passage."

Rage leaves immediately.

"No!" I yell. Reaper can shoot well, but it didn't matter. There were four men and only two if Rage plays bodyguard. "You need Rage with you. We will be fine."

My eyes flick back to the screen, and the men are getting closer to the house.

Rage returns and stands by the door, waiting for me.

"There's no time. I need you to go now! Rage, give her your gun and get the sweet butts upstairs first."

Cracks of gunshots hit the clubhouse, making me scream. Conan is barking, going ballistic. I turn to my name being yelled. It's Rage.

"Go," Reaper yells at us. I give Reaper one more look over my shoulder. He must see my hesitation because he points to the exit. "Please, I need you safe."

I reluctantly turn and follow Rage.

Elena is at the bottom of the stairs. Tears stream down her cheeks as she talks on the phone, her hand shaking. "Who is here?"

When we reach her, we all stand against the wall. Rage takes the phone from her hand and brings it to his ear. "Axle, we need you now! Jude is here, shooting at us." He hangs up and gives Elena her phone, takes Conan's collar from me, and peers at Elena. "You need to take Conan while Ava takes my gun." Elena swallows hard, then grasps Conan's collar. Conan pulls forward, like he wants to run after the men shooting at us, but Elena holds her ground, pulling back on his collar.

"Hold these," he says and places the car keys in my hand. He reaches down, pulls out his gun, and passes it to me.

I stare at the cold metal object in my hand. I never wanted to use this.

"Stay here. If anyone comes through the back door, shoot them!" Rage runs through the house.

The gunshots are loud cracks, one after another, but then I hear the shattering of glass. With all the commotion, from the screaming to the bullets and to Conan barking, all I can think about is Reaper.

Rage returns to us, the sweet butts behind him. They are crying, their hands covering their faces.

"Upstairs," he yells to them. They quickly dart up, following his instructions.

My heart constricts more and more with every gunshot. *I can't lose Reaper.*

I turn to Elena. "We are getting out of here now."

She looks at me questioningly. "But Rage said . . ."

"The men need all the help they can get. Now come on before he gets back!"

I shove the keys in my pocket, then place both hands on the gun. Elena grabs my shirt, and we all move swiftly through the house. "Get farther back."

We reach the back door. I open it an inch and peek out. When I see no one, I push it open farther and slowly walk outside, scanning every inch of the backyard.

"It's clear."

My heart pounds. Rage will be here any moment, so when Elena and Conan meet me, I rush to the side of the clubhouse. I draw my gun as I check again, but like Reaper said, he would be forcing them away from us. The gunshots sound farther away than they did before.

I turn to Elena and pull the keys out of my pocket. "The truck is there. Run with me!" I press the fob and the lights of the truck flash, then we sprint toward it. "Get in!" I open the back door for Conan.

He jumps up with no hesitation. I shut the door and jump in the front seat, place the gun in the center console, then put the key in the ignition.

Elena puts her seatbelt on. She stares ahead with big eyes. I put the car in drive and take off. When we leave down the driveway, I look in the rearview mirror to see Rage with his arms up in the air. I frown, but I'm convinced I made the right decision. I floor the gas pedal, and more dirt kicks up behind us.

Elena's phone rings. She pulls it out of her pocket. I glance to see Axle's name on the screen. She brings it to her ear. "Hey, I'm with Ava. We drove away. How long are you going to be?" With frantic breaths, she pauses, listening to his response. "Yes, we are okay. Thirty minutes? Please hurry. They need you. Be safe. I love you, too."

We travel the dirt road, driving past the warehouse. "Thirty minutes seems so long."

I don't get to hear her answer because a car comes from the right, crashing into us with a *thwack* and the tearing of metal on metal.

FOURTEEN

I'D DIE FOR YOU

Ava

I slowly blink a few times. My body is heavy. I'm hunched over in my seat. My head's throbbing, with a warm trickle of liquid oozing down my face. I touch my head and peek down at my hand to see bright-red blood.

My head turns. "Elena."

My voice comes out, but it's barely audible. She's leaning off to the side closest to me with her hair covering her face. "Elena," I say, panicked. I grab her shoulder and shake it. She doesn't answer and my heart skyrockets. Tears burn my eyes. A whine in the backseat makes me think Conan is alive . . . for now.

I undo my seatbelt. When I turn to Elena's side, I lean over to check her pulse and hear a car door shut. I turn my head and suddenly I can't breathe. I frantically search for the gun or Elena's phone. I scan under my legs, then over to Elena's. The gun is by her foot.

As I lean down my door opens. Beau stands next to me,

staring with wild eyes. "Get out of the car," he says in a feral snarl.

I don't answer straight away, considering my options. Rage or Reaper could be here any moment now. Conan's growl rumbles from the back, making me wonder if he can move.

"NO!" I scream back at Beau.

His eyes widen, his stare hardening. He reaches for me, but I shove him away. He keeps trying, but so do I. I shove, slap, then I turn my leg and try to kick him away while Conan barks. Beau's arm goes to his waist and he pulls out a gun. I gasp.

I slowly put my hands up in surrender. "Okay . . . I'm getting out."

I turn and put both feet on the ground, my legs shaking as I stand. My head spins, but I keep myself upright.

Conan's deep, constant barks make Beau turn and aim his gun at the back seat. I leap, taking two steps over to stand in front of the back door, in front of Conan.

Beau glares. "You'd protect a dog but make an idiot out of me?"

His breathing is heavy, his eyes showcasing dark circles.

"Ava," I hear softly from the front seat.

"Take me," I blurt out to Beau, not wanting to draw any attention to Elena. "You came here for me. Now what?"

His head cocks an inch to the side. "We're going for a drive." He grabs the top of my arm, his grip painful. I don't fight. I want Elena and Conan safe. "Where are we driving to?" I ask loudly, hoping Elena can hear.

He mumbles to himself as we walk to his car but then stops, and as soon as I see that hostile look in his eyes, I know what's coming because I'd seen it once before.

I feel a stinging pain between my eyes, and the force of the blow makes me fall. My head throbs as I taste copper in my mouth. Everything is off center. I can't see straight. He grips my arm and then I'm being pulled to my feet, toward the car, though I keep stumbling.

He pushes my head down and I fall into a familiar seat. My eyesight slowly levels out while the driver's side door shuts. The car starts, but it makes a winding sound. His hands slam on the steering wheel, making me jolt. He tries it again, and it turns over and starts, though it backfires and the engine is louder than normal. A familiar beep signals the lock on the doors. As he reverses slowly, metal screeches as the vehicles pull away from each other.

I'm on the edge of my seat, my eyes scanning Elena. The side windshield has shattered, and there are patches of blood on her arm.

Her head turns our way and she blinks, but she looks disoriented. Her mouth moves, but I can't understand what she's saying because the motor is loud. Worry slices through me. I hurt Beau's pride, so he may still stop to hurt her. He doesn't, though; he keeps driving, and at least knowing Beau won't hurt them provides a small bit of relief. I hope the men get to them in time.

My heart is heavy because I never told Reaper I love him. In a short period, he's shown me more about life and love than anybody I've met. He's become my sanctuary. Being with him has allowed me to finally feel safe, secure, and at peace with who I am and what I want in a partner. The thought of never seeing him again fills me with terror. We needed more time. I turn my head to look out the window as I try to hide my tears.

"What are you crying about?" The disgust in his voice is unmistakable. "Your dog, your sister, or that criminal? I should be the one upset." He takes one hand off the steering wheel and points to his chest. "Me, not you! Me!" he screams.

His eyes return to the road, but his hands clench the

steering wheel. "Where are we going? You know the other men from the MC will be back soon. So just leave me here, and you will have enough time to escape."

He veers off to the side onto an overgrown dirt road. "If I can't have you, then no one can."

I look down at my hands tightly folded together. I loosen them and focus on my escape. I subtly move my legs to the side to see if there's a weapon or anything by my feet, but there's nothing. Then to the center console—nothing. I remember there being only registration papers in the glove compartment.

The car rocks as it travels over the rough ground.

"I gave you everything."

My eyes dart back to him. I bite back my reply because I know it wouldn't help me, but I can feel that burn of anger. I shove it down. "I know you did," I reply in the fake loving voice I know all too well.

"Then, why did you leave me? You had everything. You didn't work. I stayed with you, even though you couldn't get pregnant."

I flinch at the pregnancy taunt. It always wounded me when he mentioned it.

I clear my throat and sit up straighter in my seat. "I panicked."

His face scrunches as he glances at me, then his gaze returns to the road. "It was your fault! If you didn't carry on the way you did sometimes, maybe I wouldn't have gotten angry."

My jaw clenches, my knuckles white, as I hold my emotions in. I wait and try to breathe out some of the tension. "I'm sorry." I'm proud of how calm my voice sounds.

"It's too late now!"

I knew this when I looked into his cold, dead eyes. He came here to kill me. I try focusing again. If his gun is back in his holster, I could try to go for it. But he's much too strong for me to overpower him.

The steep mountain forces me to slide farther back into my seat. The car jolts forward, once, twice, then stops. Hope releases some of the pressure from my chest as I watch him turn the ignition over from the corner of my eye, but nothing happens.

"FUCK!" Beau screams and slams his hands on the steering wheel, startling me.

Now that the car is off, there's the sound of another car in the distance, and I pray that it's Reaper. Beau whips his head to see out the back window of the car. The beep signals the car's unlocked.

He pulls out his gun and aims it at me. He slowly opens his door and gets out. He rushes around the front of the car and to my side. I grip the door handle. There's tension on the other side of the door as he pulls it, but I lean back, gripping the door with everything I have. He bangs on the window, but the sound of the car is getting closer. If I can just hold on . . .

Glass shatters over my skin. My ears ring as he yanks the door open. I'm being pulled out to my feet. I search around my body, expecting to have been shot, but there are no wounds, only a couple of small specks of blood from the glass.

He tugs my arm hard again as the familiar MC van stops, with Reaper in the driver's seat, his eyes trained on us.

"Get out slowly!" Beau yells. "I'll kill her if you do anything stupid!"

The door opens and Reaper gets out. His muscles tense as he walks toward us. My eyes scan every inch of him. I can't see any injuries.

"Not any closer!" Beau warns as he shoves the cold gun

hard into my temple, making my eyes close briefly as he forces my head to move an inch to the side.

Reaper is still, but a vein is popping out in his neck.

"I know you've got a gun. Slowly, put it on the ground." Reaper's hand goes to his holster, but Beau yells. "I said slowly!" Reaper follows his command and grabs his gun. "Now, throw it away."

Reaper obeys. My mouth goes dry and my anxiety skyrockets. Reaper raises both hands in surrender and takes two steps closer to us.

"I said don't move," Beau booms, but motorcycles echo in the air, distracting Beau as he peers behind Reaper.

Reaper launches himself at Beau, but not before another piercing sound rings out. Blood drains from my face, leaving it cold. Within seconds, Reaper disarms Beau and headbutts him, making him fall. Reaper stands over him, aiming Beau's own gun at him. Then another gunshot cracks in the air, blending with loud motorcycles and a scream.

Beau's arm bleeds.

Reaper puts the gun in his holster and steps toward me. His eyes scan my face and body, then he pulls me into his chest. The tears come quickly as I melt into him. My arms are around him and I'm clinging to him like he might disappear.

"I've got you. You're safe now." He tenderly kisses the top of my head.

My arms only hold him tighter. His scent, and his warmth, engulfs me. Being in his arms is my happy place, my home.

"I thought I'd never see you again."

His lips curve up into a sexy smile. There's a cold sensation on my shoulder but then a thought comes to mind, so I pull back.

"Did you see Elena and Conan?" I ask, struggling to draw air into my lungs. "Are they okay? Are they alive?"

"Pres, is everything all right?" Viper says from beside us, gun in hand.

"We have a doctor and a vet on the way to the clubhouse. They should be there soon. Axle and Rage pulled them both from the car, mostly superficial injuries, but Conan might have a broken leg," Bomber answers me.

A weight lifts from my chest. "Thank you."

When I peer down at my shoulder, it's still cool, but it's wet and red. I gasp. *It's blood!* I lift my shirt a little to see under it, but there's no wound.

"You've been shot!" Bomber says.

Horror widens my eyes when I look up at Reaper, blood oozing from between his heart and shoulder, soaking his shirt.

Panic shoots through me as Viper says, "I'll call the doc."

Reaper takes his shirt off, but I snatch it from him and apply pressure to the wound.

"You shouldn't have done that," I say to him as guilt takes a hold of my throat. Tears fall.

"I've been through worse." His hand clasps the side of my face, and I lean into it. "As long as you're okay."

"Fucking lowlife scum!"

I turn to see Demon bend down and punch Beau in the face.

He stands and smiles his evil smile. "That's more like it!" Then he looks to Reaper with a raised brow. "I thought you were a perfect shot."

"I am, but I didn't want him to bleed out . . ."

My eyes bounce between the two, confused.

Demon's grin spreads and excitement flashes in his eyes. He looks back at Beau. "Oh, we're going to have some fun with you."

His voice is unnerving. I think I know what he means, but that thought goes to the back of my head. All I care about is

Reaper right now. I feel a coolness in my hand, so I glance up to see blood soaking through Reaper's shirt.

"Reaper needs the doc now!" I cry out.

"I'll get Rage to bring the other van back so him and Demon can pick up this piece of shit," Viper says as he tilts his head in Beau's direction.

Reaper sways and takes a step forward but falls. A scream tears from my mouth, but Bomber and Viper are on either side of him, holding him upright. They move briskly to the van, and I follow them.

Bomber opens the back door. "Ava, you go in first."

I step up and move to the back. Then Bomber and Viper lifts Reaper inside and places him on the ground in front of me. Bomber takes his shirt off and applies pressure to Reaper's wound as Viper rushes out of the van, slams the door shut, hurries to the driver's side, and gets in. The van starts and I hear Viper on the phone, but I'm too focused on Reaper's face draining of all color.

I sit on the ground and gently lift Reaper's head, shuffle forward, and put his head on my lap. One of my tears falls on his cheek and runs down his face. I gently wipe it, feeling the prickles of hair on my finger. "I love you. I love you so much." I lean down closer to him. "Please wake up," I whisper. "We haven't had enough time together. I want my happy ever after with you."

There's a touch on my back, and I look up to see Bomber. "He's strong."

The sadness that cuts into his tone only makes my tears fall faster. It's a reminder that everyone loves Reaper and that we are all struggling to see him like this.

I gaze at Bomber's hand, where the blood has seeped through the shirt. I gasp. "But that is so much blood."

Bomber doesn't reply. He's not one to lie and say everything will be okay when it may not be. Time goes by slowly while we travel back to the house. Every minute feels like an hour. My skin is hot and I'm flustered. The van jolts and skids on the driveway, and the back door flies open. I squint from the sun beaming into the van.

A woman and Twitch are behind the door, and I watch helplessly as Bomber and Twitch carry Reaper out. I get up and walk on shaky legs through the van.

"Ava!" Elena yells. As I step out of the van, she rushes over to me with one arm bandaged. We embrace each other. "I don't know what I'd do without you," she sobs.

My arms tighten around her as the tears fall again, making my eyes burn. I might be okay, but Reaper's not. I pat her back and try to pull away. "I'm sorry, I have to be with Reaper."

She lets go of me and hastily wipes her tears. We dash inside the clubhouse together.

"Where are they?" I ask as I desperately scan the house, but I see only the sweet butts standing by the bottom of the stairs.

"Ava!" Candy yells. They turn their heads, then rush to me. "I'm so glad you're okay."

I try to muster up some energy to give her a polite smile. Mercedez pats my back, and I see their eyes are red from crying. "Are all of you okay?" I look them over for injuries.

Candy's eyes widen, then she gives me a genuine smile. "We are. Thank you for asking." Then she peers up the stairs. "They set everything up in Reaper's room, ready for him for when he arrives. The men are up there."

I sniffle and try to hold myself together. "Thanks, girls." The adrenaline courses through me as I silently pray, *Please be alive.*

Elena and I dart up the stairs. As I walk through the hallway, I see Axle walking to us with his arms open, so I run to him. "Have you heard anything?"

My voice was raw and hoarse from crying. I know little time has passed, but my anxiety is making me feel physically sick. I want to see him, touch him, and tell him I'm here. He needs to fight . . . fight to come back to me.

Axle frowns. "Not yet. It might take a while. The bullet didn't go all the way through, so doc has to get it out and stop the bleeding, but that's only if there're no complications."

My legs collapse from underneath me, but Axle catches me. His arms hold me tight but his words shred my heart, and a sob tears from my throat from the agony assaulting me.

"It's my fault." I struggle to keep my voice even.

"No. It's Beau's," he reassures me. "He shot Reaper."

"Because of me!" My voice carries through the hallway.

He pulls back to make eye contact. "We were well aware of the risks of you staying here. Reaper protects people he cares about, at any cost. Even if it puts him in the firing line, it's who he is."

I know that, but the guilt still has a firm grip around my neck. My feet find the floor, and I stand upright and step out of his hold. I move toward Reaper's door. Bomber and Cash are leaning against the wall with their heads bowed, and Viper is sitting on the floor.

He looks up at me. "Don't blame yourself. None of us do."

Unfortunately, his kind words don't make a difference. Because I do blame myself. There's an eerie silence as we wait. The minutes blend, and I don't know how much time has passed.

Demon and Rage meet us. When I see that their hair is wet and they have showered, I stare at my red-stained hands and another sob rips out of my mouth. My tortured soul is in pure agony.

"Go have a shower. If anything happens, I'll come and get you," Elena says softly from beside me.

I need a shower, but I can't leave him, not even for a minute. "No." I glance at Bomber and Viper, who also haven't had showers.

The door opens and I step toward it, holding my breath. Viper stands, and we all wait for the doctor to speak.

She scans us. When her eyes land on me, she says, "I've stopped the bleeding and cleaned the wound. Because of the location of where the bullet is lodged, I'm unable to remove it."

Worry widens my eyes. "So you're leaving the bullet inside of him?" I ask, dumbfounded.

Her shoulders fall an inch. "Yes, I don't have all the surgical equipment here, and even if I did, removing the bullet can cause additional health issues and damage. In my medical opinion, it's not worth the risk."

I turn to Bomber. "Do we need to get a second opinion?"

She snorts, but I don't know her, and I want the best for Reaper.

Bomber's lip twitches as he looks at her and back at me. "Ava, meet Milly . . . Reaper's sister." He looks at her. "Milly, this is Reaper's woman, Ava."

My stomach sinks at how rude I was. I turn to apologize, but a smile has brightened up her face.

She leans in like she wants to hug me but stops when she looks at my clothes and hands. "It's a shame my brother didn't introduce us under better circumstances, but I can't tell you how happy I am that he's found someone."

The sincerity in her voice has me holding back tears, but I blink them back.

"We will need to talk later," she whispers to me, then looks around to everyone again. "He should wake up within the next few hours."

"Can I see him?" I blurt out. There's this desperate need to check for myself that he's alive.

Her hand comes out onto my arm. "Go have a shower. He's okay," she says slowly. "Then you can spend as much time as you want with him."

I suck in a sharp breath. Every part of me silently screaming *no*. An arm comes around my shoulders, and I look to see Elena.

"Come on, I'll get your clothes ready, and you can come straight back."

Milly gives me a reassuring smile. "He's going to be out of it for a while. You're not missing out on anything."

"O-kay," I answer reluctantly and walk toward the bathroom.

After I scrub my hands and arms of Reaper's blood and finish my quick shower, I get changed into the clothes Elena left and run into Reaper's room. The men are all stationed around him, except Bomber and Viper, who I assume have left to have showers too. As I step toward the end of the bed, I see Reaper still sleeping.

"Has he woken up yet?" I ask no one in particular.

"Not yet," Twitch answers. "I think he's been waiting for you."

At first I smile, but then my eyes narrow. "Where have you been?" All the men were here, except him. I want an explanation.

Axle chuckles. "She's onto you," he says to Twitch.

"I was here," he responds quickly. "Helping Milly during the operation."

"Yeah, because you want to bang her. You've got a death wish, I'm sure of it."

The men are laughing when Milly walks into the room.

"Shut the fuck up, Axle," Twitch grits between his teeth as the men laugh harder.

I shake my head at them and move to Reaper's side. I

crawl over to him on the bed. Bomber walks into the room, his eyes going straight to Reaper, then me.

"Everyone downstairs. Give Ava some time alone with Reaper. Milly, come and get us once he wakes up."

When it's only Bomber remaining, I say, "Thank you." He turns and gives me a small nod before he leaves.

Milly sits next to me on the bed. "Before you lie down, let me look at you. I'm not having Reaper wake up and then curse at me for not looking after his ol' lady."

A touch of a smile graces my lips because I can imagine him doing that. I shift in the bed to face her.

Her eyes travel around my face. Her hand comes to my nose and she feels it, making me flinch. "It's not broken." Her hands go to my arm, and she brings it toward her as her eyes study it. "Superficial cuts. Are you injured anywhere else?"

"No."

She raises her arm toward Reaper. "I won't stop you any longer. You can lie with him now."

I shuffle over and lie beside him. I briefly close my eyes, appreciating the warmth of Reaper's skin against mine. His face is still a little pale, but it is better than what it was.

I feel his sister's eyes on us. "He's the best person I know," she says, and when I peer at her, she's wiping the corner of her eye. "I told you before, but I'm so grateful he's found someone to love."

"Do you two have a close relationship?"

She smiles sincerely and stares off as if remembering the past. "I couldn't have wished for a better brother. Even when he was at war, he always sent me as much money as he could to help me pay for university. I got a scholarship, but I wouldn't have been able to afford it without Reaper. He has always had my back, no matter what."

I smile as my eyes drift back to Reaper, then to Milly.

"That sounds like him. Always doing everything he can for everyone around him."

"Keep going with the compliments," a gravelly voice says next to me.

Milly laughs as I shriek, "You're awake!"

The guilt hits me as I lean over, making sure I put no weight on him and press my lips to his. When I lean back, I say, "I'm so sorry you got shot." But then frustration washes over me. "Why did you do that? Put yourself in harm's way. I was so worried that I didn't get the chance to tell you I love you, and I do, Bain White. I love you so much." I press my lips to his again. I feel his smile against my lips, accompanied by a deep throaty chuckle.

"I love you, too, beautiful."

FIFTEEN
MC FAMILY

Six Weeks Later

Reaper

I lift my shirt and inspect the dark pink scar from the gunshot wound. It's still tender, but I've healed well. I'd do it again if it meant protecting Ava. To see how easily she fits in and genuinely looks after and cares for the men only makes me love her more.

As I pull the shirt over my chest, my phone rings. It's the attorney, but that can wait. I'm sure she's calling to update us on how the divorce is going. It's unfortunate that the process will take a lot longer since they cannot locate Beau. I chuckle to myself, knowing that they will never find him.

I've been waiting for Ava to ask me what happened to him, but she hasn't. Deep down, she probably knows but doesn't want to acknowledge it. I put my arms through my cut, walk over to the bathroom, and spray on the cologne Ava loves. When I walk out, I put my phone in my pocket, stride through the hallway, and step down the stairs but stop at the bottom when I see Cash and Bomber. I stare at Cash first. "Is everything sorted?"

Cash gives a clipped nod. "Sure is, Pres."

My heart races. I'm nervous about how Ava's going to react.

"Is Milly here yet?"

"I think she just pulled up."

"Get the word out to everyone. Do not let Ava go out the front."

He smirks. "I'll do it now."

When he leaves, my attention goes to Bomber. "What did you think about the meeting this morning with Graham?" Graham is the founder of Kings of Chaos.

"He had no issues with us shooting Jude. Did you know the prospect was Jude's nephew?"

"No, I didn't, but that Jude and him were stealing weed and dealing it on the side . . ." I shake my head and let out a low whistle. "I think he got let off too easy."

"I agree, but what are your thoughts about the future?" he asks, rubbing the side of his head with his hand. "Did you want to keep doing business with them?"

"We don't have a choice. We have to until we find another buyer."

Bomber takes a deep breath, a hint of a smile curving the edge of his lip. "Your woman can cook."

"Yes, she can," I reply with a smile. "You know . . . she thought you were celibate."

Bomber's mouth opens in disbelief.

"Don't worry, I set her straight," I taunt. "But she was worried that you would be lonely."

He stills. "Did you tell her about Zara?"

I playfully barge him with my shoulder, trying to lighten the mood. "Not my story to tell."

He subtly nods. His eyes peer off.

I wish I'd never brought it up. He really must have loved her to never want a relationship with a woman again. I never understood it, but now that I have Ava, I do because I could never see myself with anyone else. Even if something happens, I'd never be able to move on.

"Let's go get some breakfast."

As we walk through the house, it's quieter than usual, but then voices come from outside. I go to touch the back door handle, but I step back, letting Bomber go ahead while I go to the fridge and pull out the steak. I shake my head. I'm the alpha male here. I shouldn't have to give the dog a gourmet dinner for it to damn well like me.

I step toward the back door and open it. When I step outside, I see the men sitting at the tables and stuffing their mouths full of food. "Pancakes again?" I ask, then point to them. "My woman spoils all of you too much!"

Rage grins at me and Axle smiles with a mouthful of food, giving me the thumbs up.

I open the plastic covering the steak and reluctantly place it in Conan's bowl. He trots over and sits in front of it, drool oozing from his mouth. A part of me feels like making him wait for ages, but I don't.

"Eat," I tell him. When he does, I look at his leg in the plaster cast. "Well, at least you can't piss on me now."

As I walk over to Ava, I chuckle to myself. When I come up behind her, I bend down and kiss her cheek. "Hello, beautiful."

She blushes but flashes me one of her blinding smiles. "I'll get you a plate. How many pancakes do you want?"

"No, thanks. I'm saving myself for lunch," I reply. Really, my stomach is doing somersaults, worried about how she's going to respond. My hands rise to her shoulders and I massage them, enjoying the contented sigh that falls from her mouth.

Elena elbows Axle, who's beside her. "You don't rub my shoulders."

"Babe," he draws the word out while drilling displeased eyes into me. "Stop making me look bad," he says in a mocking tone.

I laugh as he turns back to his wife. "I'll rub your shoulders tonight. How about that?"

She smiles back. "You better!"

"A rub for a rub." He raises his eyebrow suggestively. Elena swats his chest as Ava's face screws up.

I lean down. "Don't listen to him," I whisper into her ear.

Her head falls back as she relaxes into the massage.

I love making Ava feel good. She's mine, and I will worship her every day for the rest of my life.

Ava

"Turn it up," I yell.

The volume of "Jump Around" by House of Pain gets so deafening I can feel the music. I sing, bopping to the lyrics, stirring the potato salad to go with the barbecue lunch. Viper slides into the kitchen like he's Tom Cruise in *Risky Business*, and he jumps around with me to the lyrics. Axle walks in, shaking his head at us but then breaks out dancing while raising his hands in the air. My heart is full as I laugh hysterically at them.

When the song finishes, Viper, Axle, and the sweet butts come in to help take the food outside onto the tables.

"Ava," Reaper calls, gesturing for me to go to him. I feel everyone's eyes on me as I make my way to him. Reaper searches the crowd but stops when he sees Rage. "You too. Come on, get up here."

The men cheer. Rage's eyes widen. He hesitates but then slowly makes his way over to us.

"Everyone, quiet," Reaper says to the men. "Today, we celebrate . . . our new patched-in member, Rage!" Cash passes Reaper Rage's new cut, and Reaper hands it to a frozen Rage, who looks shocked. But then the corner of his mouth curves into a smile showing all of his teeth.

I cheer and clap along with everyone. Rage puts his hands through the holes and pulls the vest up. It suits him.

Reaper shakes Rage's hand. "Welcome to the family." Reaper looks back at everyone. "But that's not it. We have two more things to celebrate."

I try to remember what else we're celebrating today. No one has mentioned anything. Cash passes another cut to Reaper, then Reaper turns to face me.

I look to the side of me, but no one is there. Reaper holds the vest out toward me. I stare at it until recognition flares in my eyes. It's mine.

"Now, don't get mad at me," he says in a charming voice.

There are no negative feelings toward the vest, not anymore. It means so much more than what I first thought the day I saw Elena's cut. It's the MC's tradition, and I want to be a part of that.

"I love you," he says with emotion in his voice. "And I want everyone to know that you're mine."

"I love you, too."

He holds the vest up to me as I slide my arms in both holes. Everyone cheers again, and I get a little teary but blink those pesky tears away. I examine the cut, my fingers traveling over the *Property of Reaper* patch.

I glance up at him. "Thank you." I rise on my toes to kiss him on the lips.

Elena rushes to me and hugs me, then leans back and points to both our vests. "Now we're matching," she says through a smile but then raises her hand. "I've got a surprise for you. I'll be back." She runs off.

Milly steps up next, puts her arms around me, and squeezes tight, then pulls back. "In biker terms, welcome to the White family."

"Thank you," I reply, my voice struggling to stay even.

Elena comes back with Conan, who is hobbling around with his plastered back leg. "Hey, Conan." His tail wags, and when he reaches me, I see a collar around his neck. It's leather, and on it is a patch that says *Property of Ava*. Next to it is the *War Brother's MC* logo. "This is amazing. Thank you!" I tell Elena.

Reaper steps to my side. "I've got a surprise for you too."

"Another one?" I ask in shock. Everyone laughs around us.

He puts his hand in mine, lacing our fingers together, pulling me along the side of the house, with everyone following us. When we get out the front of the clubhouse, there's a white SUV. "This is yours so you can drive to your course during the week."

I stand, speechless, my jaw on the ground. I glance up at him. "It's mine?"

He gives me a nod, then I abruptly leap into Reaper's arms. "It's beautiful. Oh my gosh."

"You got into your course?" Elena yells. "You never told me!"

I pull myself away from Reaper. "I opened the acceptance letter this morning."

Her hands fly to her mouth. Tears fall down her face, making my stomach drop. I step over to her. "Why are you crying?"

"Because you've come so far. I'm beyond proud of you, sis."

I blink furiously. "Stop crying! You'll make me cry. But know that I couldn't be where I am without you." My life isn't the same without her in it.

I peer back at Reaper. "If I only got accepted this morning, how did you organize the car so quickly?"

"I knew you would get in. We stored the car at Milly's house in the meantime."

I stare at the love of my life.

Being with him, I learned how to smile again. I no longer feel caged, because he's set me free.

The end.

BOMBER

BOOK 3

Sometimes love needs to struggle in the darkness to transform into something beautiful.

BEST
FRIENDS

ONE
EIGHTEENTH BIRTHDAY PARTY

Zara

Age: Eighteen

"Happy birthdayyyyy to you."

I peer over my bowl of cornflakes to see Misty with a wide grin and a gleam in her eyes.

"Happy birthday to you," she sings as she walks closer to me, her hands behind her back. "Happy birthday to my best friend and sister, Zara"—she takes a deep breath—"happy birthday to youuuu." As she's opera singing the last few notes, Misty passes me a pink envelope.

I smile at her. "You didn't have to get me anything."

She hisses. "Yes, I did!"

I jump off my chair and wrap my arms around her, squeezing her tightly. "Thank you."

She pulls back and stares at the envelope. "Come on, open it."

"Okay, okay." I slide my fingers underneath the flap of the envelope to rip it open, then glide the card out.

The front has a love heart, and inside it says "You will always be the sister of my soul and the friend of my heart."

"Aww." I grin, feeling touched. I open the card and two small rectangular pieces of paper land on the table. I put down the card and pick them up to see Sun Dance festival tickets.

I lift my eyes to hers. "How did you get these? I thought they were sold out?"

"I have my sources," she replies.

Which basically means Knox and Kane's mom, Audrey Crown, pulled strings to get them for us. Her family founded Crown Village—where we live—and owns every successful business in it. Her reach has no bounds.

Crown Village is a coastal town packed with amenities: beaches, a lake, restaurants, a resort, a casino, and a park. It has a small population and a tight-knit community for the people who reside here, but it's also a holiday attraction for the rich and famous.

"The guys are taking us in the limo, and since the festival is at the amusement park, I thought we could go on a couple of rides before DJ Mesah comes on."

I clap my hands in excitement—Mesah is our favorite DJ.

"Mesah's playing at noon, so we'll at least get to see her set and some of the DJs after her. We'll be home in time for your party . . . where we can have some drinks."

My eyes dart to the entryway of the kitchen, checking no one had heard. "I wouldn't be saying that out loud if I were you."

We're lucky if Mom allows us to have a glass of champagne *in her presence*, let alone whatever strong alcohol Misty has conned Kane into getting.

"But aren't you still sick?" I heard her retching this morning. She hasn't been able to get rid of whatever illness she has.

"I told you something I've been eating hasn't been sitting

well with me." She shrugs. "I don't know. My body hates me. Anyway . . . enough about that. I think you may have forgotten something." Her eyes latch back onto the envelope.

Lifting the envelope, I feel there's still something inside. I tip it upside down to see a silver necklace drop into my hand. It has a charm on it, half a heart that says *Friends*. Misty's hand goes to her neck, and she pulls a similar chain from outside of her top to show me that her part says *Best*.

"I know it's lame, but I saw it and I had to have it."

I roll my eyes as I pass the necklace to her and lift my long hair. "Can you put it on?"

She drapes the necklace around my neck, and I feel the cold metal against my skin.

"There," she says.

I let my hair fall down my back and gently tug on the necklace, feeling it's secure.

Iris walks in. "Happy eighteenth," she says in a sing-song voice.

"Thank you!" I reply.

Iris, who's in her fifties and from the Philippines, has been working for us since Misty and I were little. She helps around the house three days a week with cleaning, laundry, cooking, and looking after us. She's petite, with an exotic appearance— black hair, olive skin, and dark-brown oval eyes.

"What cake would you like for tonight?" Iris asks.

I salivate as I think about it.

Misty snorts. "I thought you would have made the cake by now."

Iris narrows her eyes, but her lip twitches like she's smothering a smile. "I can't, and it's because of you, that's why!"

Misty's mouth falls open. Her hand goes to her chest. "Who! Me?"

"Yes, you! You little pig!"

Misty's cackle is loud. She turns to me, then makes a point of snorting even louder.

Iris laughs. "You can't help yourself. I wasn't baking two cakes because you couldn't keep your hands off of it."

"It's not my fault!" she complains.

Iris's brows lift high on her forehead. "Then whose fault is it?"

"Yours!"

Mom walks through the kitchen as I'm giggling, listening to them bicker.

"Happy birthday, sweetheart," Mom says before walking to me and placing a tender kiss on my forehead.

I smile at her.

"Your father said to say happy birthday. Something came up at work this morning, but he said he'll come home when he can."

I bob my head in acknowledgment. Then my attention drifts back to Misty and Iris.

"How is it my fault?" Iris asks.

"You're a damn good cook. I've had really bad cravings lately. I just can't resist your food."

Iris laughs and places her hand on Misty's head, then messes up her hair.

"Hey!" Misty whines as she attempts to flatten it.

"Can I have a chocolate cake, but with a layer of chocolate cream and fresh strawberries?" I ask Iris.

"That sounds yummy!" Misty chimes in.

"I'll go get the ingredients this morning," Iris replies. She turns to Mom. "Do you need anything else for tonight?"

"Audrey's organized catering for the party, so we should be fine. But thank you." Mom turns to me. "You'll have to wait to get your birthday present from us when your dad gets home."

Knox and Kane barge into the kitchen like it's their own

home. Our parents were really tight and our families were inseparable. But then, things changed when their parents split. However, it didn't mess up our bond with the boys—or the connection between Misty and Kane or me and Knox. We're all still as close as ever!

My eyes wander up and down Knox's body. He's wearing a fitted black shirt that shows off his chest and broad shoulders, ripped black jeans, and black boots. Knox is that total package of deliciousness. It's not just his face and build that draw me to him but also that bad-boy swagger he wears so well. That moody behavior he has toward everyone except me.

Knox's eyes lock onto mine. He strides over until he is flush against my back and folds his arms around me. He bows his head and nuzzles my neck, making goose bumps travel along my arms.

"Happy birthday," he says in my ear.

My chest warms. "Thank you."

"Happy birthday!" Kane yells, his larger-than-life personality on show.

The Hart brothers look similar with their signature whiskey-colored eyes, but their personalities differ. Kane is all smiles and mischief; Knox is broody and intense. While Kane is easygoing, Knox is distant and quiet.

Even their clothing sense is different. Knox is mostly in black and might wear something white for contrast, whereas Kane is usually dressed in bright fashionable T-shirts with matching-color, branded sneakers.

Knox's arms slip away from me. I turn to see him pull a small jewelry case from his back pocket. When he places it in my hand, I touch the soft velvet material of the lid before opening it to see a large blue emerald-cut crystal surrounded by tiny diamonds. I clutch my chest as I suck in a breath through my teeth.

I feel a hand on my shoulder. I glance to the side and see Misty. She whistles.

My hands tremble. I open my mouth to speak, but I can't. A deep chuckle comes from Kane. Knox gently takes the case from my hands, and I watch as he pulls the ring out and then slides it onto the fourth finger on my right hand.

I thought someone would purchase a ring for my birthday. Misty wasn't very subtle in going to the jewelry store, trying on different rings, and measuring my size while we were there.

"Mom told me the band is platinum and the big crystal is a sapphire. The crystals around it are diamonds . . ." He rubs the back of his neck, suddenly shy. "It's a family heirloom."

A range of emotions strike me at once—happiness, appreciation—but I also worry that I'll lose it. It looks expensive. I rise onto my toes and give him a chaste kiss on the lips.

"Where's my diamond-and-sapphire ring?" Misty taunts Kane before elbowing him in the ribs.

He coughs, then caresses his side where she elbowed him. "Maybe you can get a ring next year."

Mom and Iris hover around me, so I turn and hold my ring out to them, feeling giddy and spoiled.

"Oh my . . ." Mom says. She looks at Knox before looking back at the ring. "It's absolutely stunning."

Iris tugs on my hand, pulling it closer to her. "For heaven's sake, child, don't lose it."

I bring my hand back to my side and lean into Knox. "Thank you."

He kisses my temple. "You're welcome, precious."

"How about we go get changed?" Misty suggests.

On the way to our bedrooms, Misty halts and turns to me with a deep frown. "You don't have to wear the necklace I got you. It looks so lame compared to the ring Knox gave you."

My heart aches for her. I lift my hand and hold the necklace charm in my palm, as if I'm protecting it from Misty's cruel words.

"Please don't say that. I love it."

Misty is an extrovert, but there are moments like this when I can see her insecurities.

Although my family is well-off, our wealth pales in comparison to what Audrey Knox, and Kane's mother, inherited from her family. I gather Misty paid for the necklace herself.

My dad is an accountant at Crown-Hart Casino, which was owned by Knox and Kane's parents, but their dad, David, got it and the house in the divorce. Although Audrey kept all the assets she inherited from her family and their holiday houses, David got the casino on the condition that Knox and Kane would be a part of the business and inherit it once David passes, though I get the feeling Knox isn't interested in it.

Misty gives me a small smile before she enters her bedroom.

After I get changed into shorts and a shirt, the sound of someone clearing their throat makes me hastily turn. Mom is standing awkwardly by my bed.

"You scared me." After I get over my shock, I ask, "What's wrong?"

Mom looks at the floor before staring at me. "Do we have to have *the talk*?"

My eyebrows furrow. "What talk?"

"*The* talk. Now that you're eighteen."

My stomach drops. "Mom, no! The talk is not needed."

"Should I take you to the doctor to put you on the pill?"

"Mom!" I cringe and my cheeks burn from embarrassment.

"Well, I'm here if you ever want to talk about it or go to the doctor."

I attempt to smile at her in thanks and wait for her to leave the room. I wait ten more minutes to ensure that I'm not bright red before I walk downstairs.

An hour later, the limousine arrives. We travel through the suburban part of town, toward the amusement park on the main strip of road close to Crown Beach.

Excitement shoots through me—I love the amusement park. We're always guaranteed a good time, and Misty and I both see it as our happy place. It's where Knox and I and Misty and Kane had our first double date. The restaurant, with its ocean view, is where our families have celebrated special occasions over the years.

We walk to the available ticket booth. When the worker sees us, his eyes widen.

"I'm Zara. This is Misty," I glance between the guys. "This is Knox and Kane. Their mother is Audrey Crown. We're here to get the VIP passes."

The employee blinks a few times, then pushes his glasses up his nose. He looks at Knox and shuffles back in his seat like he's scared of him. His colleague, who has finished serving a family at the next window, looks over and says, "Billy, the Crowns own the amusement park. Just give them the VIP passes."

The guy turns away, picks up the passes, and places them on the counter. He clears his throat. "Have a good day."

As we walk through the clown-face entryway, I'm greeted by a variety of carnival music and laughter. In the distance is the top of the red-and-white Ferris wheel, and to my right is a large roller coaster.

As we walk toward the food shops, the scent of coffee wafts to me first, followed by the smell of something oily and deep fried. Then I smell popcorn and candy floss, which makes my stomach rumble.

"I want ice cream. You want some?" Misty asks, her eyes darting between the three of us.

"Yes, please," I answer.

"Kane, come help me carry them back." He moans under his breath but follows her to the ice cream stand.

Misty and Kane stroll back to us and hand us our ice cream.

"Can you hold mine for a second?" Misty asks me with a wicked glimmer in her eye.

She hands me her ice cream cone and glances at Kane. When he brings the ice cream up to lick it, her hand bolts out and she smashes it into his face.

Misty, Knox, and I burst out in laughter as Kane stands and blinks a few times with his mouth open wide. Chocolate ice cream is everywhere—all over his face, even in his eyes. It drips off his face onto his shirt.

The shock evaporates, and a slow, evil grin paints Kane's face. Within seconds, he hurls himself at Misty, who screams. He rubs his head on her neck, spreading the ice cream into her hair.

It isn't long before Misty's in the bathroom cleaning herself up while cursing Kane.

I put my hand under the tap and then run my fingers through her hair to try to get the stickiness out. "You're not going to get all of this out now."

She whines loudly, still trying to rub her shirt with water. "I give up. I want to go on the rides before DJ Mesah starts."

When we return to the guys, Misty checks her watch. "Okay, we have time to go on two rides. What to choose, what to choose?"

She wiggles her eyebrows at us, exaggerating the hard choice, but we know what she'll choose. "Bumper cars to make the guys happy." She gives me a pointed look. "And our favorite, the carousel?"

Kane groans. "What is with you two and the carousel? It's a kids' ride."

Misty has been dragging me on the carousel since we were young kids. It's our thing.

Misty snorts at Kane. "Funny, because you're the biggest kid here."

He rolls his eyes. "What about the sledgehammer or big dipper roller coaster?"

Both being thrill rides, I'm not surprised he chose them.

"No. Fair is fair. Bumper cars for all of us and then the carousel because it's Zara's birthday. Better watch yourself on the bumper cars, Kane," she taunts.

Kane flashes her a roguish smile. "Bring it on."

We climb into our bumper cars. My gaze cuts to the others and I grin at them in excitement. I grip the steering wheel as I focus in front of me. When the green light flashes, Misty and Kane ram each other. Misty cackles.

As I'm watching them, I see Knox aiming for me. I turn and go as fast as I can to get away from him while a woman and child in one car bump into him, which turns him away from me. I smile back at him in victory.

After our time finishes, we get out of the bumper cars. Knox takes my hand, and we take the steps down to the ground, where we make our way past the small kids' roller coaster and the spinning teacups.

The next is the carousel, with its gold crest and range of horses and carts. Kane and Knox wait outside as Misty and I show our VIP pass to the man operating the ride. We step up to the platform and weave between the seats until she finds a horse rearing up on its back legs. I get onto one that looks as though it's galloping. Misty swings her leg over and hops on. She holds on with one hand, peers over her shoulder, and smiles at me.

Soon after we finish the ride, we walk to the large event.

We show our tickets to the ticket collector. Once inside, the noise is earsplitting.

"I want to get up to the front," Misty calls out. Kane nods, grabs her hand, and pushes through the crowd. Misty clutches my wrist and pulls me along, while Knox steps to my side and helps me get through the bustle.

As we get closer, my heartbeat speeds up.

"Hello, everyone," DJ Mesah says into the microphone.

People cheer, and we keep shuffling. We cannot stop bumping into the mountains of people crammed inside, though there's a genuinely happy vibe in the crowd.

"I'd like to thank all of you for coming, and I hope you enjoy the set."

Misty and I cheer. We end up in the center about five people back from the barricade near the stage.

The music starts, and people lift their phones, videoing. The intro of the song starts slowly as the lights around the stage flash. When the beat kicks in, green lasers flicker through the crowd. The atmosphere of joy and excitement sends a chill down my spine.

The tempo increases, and then the beat drops. The chorus makes the crowd erupt in yells and cheers. Misty and I jump to the beat, our arms up. The guys are flush against us, protecting us from the rowdy people.

Half an hour in, Misty freezes. When I look at her, her hands are covering her mouth and she has paled significantly.

"Do you want to go?" I yell over the music.

Her eyes stretch wide and she frantically nods.

I turn to the guys and tap them on the arms. "We need to go now. Misty looks sick," I say loudly over the music.

Knox's and Kane's eyes flash with understanding. Knox walks ahead, creating room for us to move through the crowd. Once we make it through, Misty runs to the bathroom stalls.

My eyes flicker between Knox and Kane. "Can one of you call the limousine to pick us up? We'd better go home so Misty can get some rest before tonight."

MY HEART RACES AS I LOOK IN THE MIRROR. I HATE BEING THE center of attention. I wipe my sweaty hands on my dress.

"Zara. Marie. Pratt," Mom says. "For the love of all that is holy, do not wipe anything on that dress."

I flinch, then straighten my back. "Sorry, Mom."

When I saw this dress, I wanted it, but now I feel a sliver of guilt that it might have cost too much. I was so giddy when I saw it that I didn't even look at the price tag. It's a gold floor-length gown with a sweetheart neckline and sequins around the top half. I went with natural makeup and kept my hair simple by straightening it.

Misty steps into my bedroom and wolf whistles.

I stifle a laugh and swat at her. "You look pretty too."

Rarely does Misty grace us in a dress. She's wearing a floor-length green mermaid dress with a V neckline that makes her blue eyes pop. Her long blond hair is half up in waves.

"How are you feeling? You don't have to celebrate tonight. I understand if you want to go back to bed and rest."

"Actually, I'm feeling a little better," she replies.

"My girls are beautiful tonight," Mom says, her voice cracking at the end.

Misty and I may not share the same blood, but she is my sister. Our parents adopted Misty because they didn't think they could conceive, but Mom fell pregnant soon after adopting Misty as a newborn, which is why we are so close in age.

"Don't get too excited. Look at these bad boys," Misty says as she lifts her dress, revealing socks and black-and-white Vans.

Giggling at her, I shake my head and sneak a peek at Mom. She's glaring at Misty, but then her shoulders drop an inch, as if she's defeated. She knows as well as anyone that when Misty has made her mind up, nothing can change it.

Mom sighs. "Can you at least keep the dress down so no one can see your shoes?"

Misty looks up as if considering her response. "I can do that," she says with a smirk.

"The guests are arriving."

I turn to see Iris by the bedroom door. She rarely works this late but offered to stay back and help. My birthday wouldn't be the same without her here. She's like family.

Iris's eyes dart between me and Misty, and she fans her face like she's trying not to cry.

"Not you too?" I say. My family's overly emotional today.

She holds up her palm to me. "I need a minute."

Knox and Kane's mom, Audrey, walks in past Iris. She claps. "Family photos. I have the photographer ready downstairs."

Audrey's wearing a long, elegant dark-blue dress and a necklace with large round diamonds, which glisten in the light.

The uninterested look on Misty's face makes me laugh.

"Do we have to do photos too?" she whines.

"Misty . . ." Mom warns. "Before I know it, you two will be out of the house, living your own lives. It won't kill you to smile for a couple of photos."

Audrey steps closer to me. "Stunning." She peers down at the ring on my finger, and her lips curve higher.

I smile back in appreciation.

Audrey glances at Misty, who pulls up her dress to show

off her shoes to try get a rise out of Audrey. It works—Audrey's face twists in disgust.

Audrey and I have always had a strong bond, but there's been some tension between Audrey and Misty. They're polite, but they're not exactly best friends. Audrey doesn't approve of Misty's behavior and rebellious attitude. And because of that, she's not thrilled about her son Kane dating Misty.

"Thank you. Are Knox and Kane here yet?" Anticipation at seeing Knox dressed up thrums through my veins.

"Yes, they are. Photos first!" Audrey warns. She knows me and Misty well.

Mom steps over to Audrey. "I can't thank you enough for helping to make this a special day for Zara."

"Helen, stop! I am your daughter's godmother. Organizing this was easy." Audrey shoos Mom away and swings her head toward us. "Girls, downstairs."

We walk out of my bedroom and down the stairs to see Dad waiting for us at the bottom. When he sees us, a smile envelops his face. He spreads his arms wide, and when I reach the bottom stair, I step into them.

"Happy birthday," he says when he pulls back out of the hug. "The both of you look beautiful."

"Thanks, Dad," Misty replies.

I peer around at the subtle mix of gold, black, and white decorations. The photo booth is adorned with *18* in gold balloons.

Iris walks past before Mom and Audrey arrive. Audrey steps in front of us and points to the man holding a camera. "The photographer will be taking photos all night, but we should do a formal family one before Helen gets into the wine."

Dad laughs.

Mom scoffs. "That's pretty rich coming from you."

Audrey's head falls back as she laughs. "I've got us some lovely bottles of champagne."

"Can we get this over and done with? You alcoholics can get back to chatting about your wine afterward."

I nod with Misty.

Audrey walks further into the center of the house. She points to a backdrop under the chandelier, where all the photography lights are set up. We follow her lead.

"Zara first, by herself, then Misty, Zara, and the family."

I step into the middle of the equipment and follow the instructions, smiling and trying my best not to blink every time the bright light flashes.

After the family photos are finished, I pose for one photo with Audrey.

"Iris," I call out. She's talking to a server and looks up when she hears me call. "Please come and take a photo with me."

Iris's eyes widen. She says something to the server and makes her way to me. "I'd love to have my photo taken with you." She's beaming.

I wrap my arm around her and smile into the camera.

When we finish, I see Misty standing with Kane and Knox. I start walking toward them, but I hear Mom calling my name.

"Come and see your birthday present." She tilts her head toward the front of the house.

My stomach flutters. "Where is it?"

"Your present is outside."

My heart thumps in my chest, and all I can think is, *Please be a car, please be a car . . .*

Dashing toward the front door, I pass Audrey's security guard, and Mom giggles behind me. I pull the door open wide, my eyes scanning the driveway. Dad is next to a small white Mercedes Benz. I squeal and rush to it. It beeps and flashes when I reach it, and I turn to Dad, who is holding out the key.

I jump into his arms. "Thank you." I step to Mom and hug her.

"I hope you like it." Mom beams.

It's a hatchback, and it has a big Mercedes Benz logo in chrome on the grill.

"I love it!"

They smile at my eagerness, though Mom takes the car key from Dad. "You can have the key tomorrow. Now it's time to celebrate."

TWO
SHE'S MY WORLD

Knox

Age: Eighteen

"Oh, baby, I can't wait to rip this dress off of you."

I groan. I don't want to hear that. I look at Kane and Misty. "Get a room, would you?"

They smile at me. "You don't have to tell me twice," Kane says, grabbing Misty's hand and striding away.

I shake my head. My sarcasm was lost on them. I search the room, checking that Zara hasn't walked in and seen them bolt upstairs. I hate knowing something she doesn't. Kane told me they're sleeping together, but Misty is yet to tell Zara. I don't understand what the delay is.

Scanning the room again, I see Dad, who has stepped through the front door. My mom is off to the side, talking to her bodyguard. When she sees Dad, her lips tighten and she shifts, turning her back to him.

At least Dad has tried to be friendly in their divorce. Mom's been a bitch toward him, and it annoys me because

Dad let it slip that Mom was the one having the affair. It should be Dad who's angry with her, not the other way round. If I were to guess . . . it's the guard who's by her side all the time.

Zara became my air through my parents' divorce. As my mom's son, I enjoy advantages like chauffeured limousines, unrestricted access to money, luxurious mansions, and lavish holidays. But I would gladly trade it all for a genuinely happy family life. Kane and I have always felt like members of the Pratt family, thanks to Zara's parents, Helen and John, who treat us as if we were their own kin.

Dad sees John and walks toward him. When they meet, they shake hands. I go to them.

"Hey, Dad, did you see Zara?"

He smiles. "Hey, yes. I met her outside."

"Everyone's arriving, so Zara's outside with her mom, greeting everyone. That was my opportunity to let them do their thing and get myself a whiskey," John says. He holds up a glass of honey-colored liquid.

"All I can say is good luck, son," Dad says to me.

I cock my head. "Good luck with what?"

His eyes mock me. "Zara's getting more gorgeous every day. You're going to have your work cut out for you."

I stare at him, emotionless, waiting for him to explain.

"It means you're going to have competition."

Possessiveness spreads through my chest. "I don't fucking think so."

"Knox!" Dad scolds me.

"Well, you better treat her right," John chimes in.

"Of course."

I thought I was stating the obvious. The lot of them will castrate me if I hurt her. Anyway, they have nothing to worry about.

I'm not naïve. I see the way women look at me. I'm confident that between my looks and my family's wealth, I wouldn't have to say much to take a woman home with me, but that's just it. I care for no one except Zara. She's my entire world.

A server comes around, offering us some posh food that looks like garbage. I don't know how my mom eats it.

"Where's the sausage rolls or something edible at least?"

Dad laughs. "There will be no sausage rolls tonight, son."

"It's an eighteenth birthday party, not a wedding," I point out.

"Did Zara like the ring?" Dad asks.

I think back to the look of happiness on Zara's face when she saw it. "She sure did."

Dad sighs with a smile. "I knew she would."

The crowd goes quiet. I turn my head toward the entrance. I freeze and swallow hard. Zara always looks good—a classic beauty with creamy skin, a petite build, chocolate-brown eyes, and long black hair. Tonight, she looks older than her age.

When her eyes land on me, her genuine smile hits me right in the chest. She rushes over, so I meet her halfway. She hugs me, with one hand around my back and the other on my chest. I peek at the sparkling ring on her finger.

"You look handsome," she says.

I pull at the collar of the button-up shirt and lean down and lower my voice. "I feel ridiculous." *In this stupid suit Mom made me wear.*

"Well, you don't look it."

My eyes make their leisurely way up her body. "You look incredible." Desire floods me when I look at her lips and feel the need to kiss her.

She blushes. I lean closer and fold my arms around her back. I take a deep breath through my nose. "You smell amazing."

"I'm happy you like the new perfume. It was a present from Iris."

I lean down, nuzzle her neck, and pretend to bite her. She squeals and giggles.

"Have you seen Misty? I want to talk to her about my car. I don't know how she kept it a secret from me. She's terrible at keeping secrets."

I cringe and try my best to keep my face passive. "I'm sure she's around here somewhere."

Her smile fades.

"Don't worry about it." I grab her hand and we walk through the house. There're a few stares, probably because I'm leading the birthday girl away from the party, but I need a moment alone with her.

I slide the back door open. After she walks through it with me, I pull her to me, with one hand behind her back, the other tipping her chin up. My breath quickens at being so close to her.

Leaning down, I bring my forehead to hers. "I love you," I whisper. I might be only eighteen, but I know what love feels like because I couldn't imagine it feeling any better than it does now.

She lets out a gasp, but before she can respond, I bend down and bring my lips to hers, where they belong. Zara's lips are soft, and the kiss is tender at first. My mouth parts hers, my tongue sliding in as a low noise escapes my throat. Our tongues move together, teasing and searching. My body feels overloaded with senses, from her taste to the feel of her small frame against mine. Her arms snake around the back of my neck and she stands on her toes, eagerly deepening the kiss.

Fire burns through me, eager, intense, and full of passion. I pull her closer. Her hands tangle in my hair and she lets out a soft, seductive noise that makes my dick harden. I pull back.

One ragged breath . . . two ragged breaths. I kiss her jaw, then her forehead. I loosen her arms from around my neck and step back.

Someone calls Zara's name from inside the house. My head falls back, my eyes closing.

She frowns and touches her now-plump lips, and it takes everything in me not to take her mouth in mine again.

I let out an exaggerated groan. "We'd better go."

She pauses, so I pull her to my side and place one more lingering kiss on her head. I subtly readjust myself as I open the door.

Zara pauses and peers up at me. "Knox."

"Yes, precious."

"I love you too."

I smile at her, warmth flooding my chest.

We reluctantly walk inside. I stay back and lean against the wall. Zara makes her way around the crowd, thanking family and friends for coming.

Misty walks down the stairs, patting her hair. When she reaches the bottom and sees Zara, she dashes to her. I look up, knowing it won't be long until I see my brother walking down the same stairs. A minute later, he does.

When he sees me, I shake my head at him.

"What?"

"It's Zara's birthday. You couldn't wait?"

"It was your suggestion!"

"I was being sarcastic. The last thing I want is to see Zara upset."

His eyes narrow a fraction. "Why would she get upset?"

"It's a big day for her is all that I'm saying. If she finds out that you two are sleeping together, and she hears it from anyone but Misty, it could upset her, and I wanted her to have a good day."

He groans. "You've made your point. I couldn't resist Misty tonight. Her in that dress." He clicks his tongue.

"I don't want to hear about it. When is Misty going to tell Zara? I hate keeping shit from her."

He pats my back. "Soon, I promise."

"Good!"

Misty and Zara make their way to us.

"We have two hours before cutting the cake, so let's have a few drinks before they notice," Misty points out.

My eyes dart to Zara. "You don't have to drink if you don't want to," I reassure her.

She drops her eyes to the floor and then looks back up. "I want to." She peers back at Misty. "Are you sure you should drink when you're already sick?"

Misty waves her off. "I'm fine. I swear." Then she clasps her hands in excitement. "Taking a ride on the wild side, are we, sister?"

Zara's smile matches hers. "I guess so."

"I can't wait for you to try my favorite whiskey," Misty says.

"You won't regret it, I promise." Misty pauses in thought for a second. "Until tomorrow . . . you will definitely regret it tomorrow."

BEST
FR_ENDS

THREE
TURNING POINT

Zara

Age: Eighteen

MISTY GROANS AS SHE TRUDGES INTO MY BEDROOM, LOOKING LIKE death. She plops down on the bed beside me.

"Did you have a little too much alcohol last night?" I ask, trying to keep the amusement out of my voice.

She rubs her temples as she closes her eyes. She and Kane had much more than Knox and I did.

"Hmm, don't remind me. My head's about to explode."

I snicker. Always so dramatic.

A thought comes to mind as my eyebrows furrow. "Where did you go last night? You weren't with Mom and Dad when they gave me my birthday present."

That question is a little silly. Misty didn't have to be there.

She stares blankly, taking a moment to respond. "I must have been stuck talking to someone from the family. You know what they're like."

I frown. I didn't see her anywhere in the main room.

"Sorry, I shouldn't have left you."

I force a fake smile. "It's fine."

Misty looks toward the bedroom door. "Do you want to watch a movie in the living room?"

"Sure."

We've binge-watched Netflix for two hours when Knox and Kane walk in. Kane stares at Misty, and when I look at her, she's still pale. Her arms are crossed and she's glaring at Kane.

"Aren't you a ray of sunshine this morning?" Kane says, then chuckles.

"It's your fault I'm this sick. You're a bad influence. Why aren't you hungover?" Misty grumbles.

He sits on the other side of her. "Because I'm not a lightweight!"

She shoves him. "I'm not a lightweight!"

Knox sits on the other side of me and gives me a genuine smile.

"Yeah, you are! What are we watching?" Kane asks.

"Some superhero series," Misty responds.

"Boring!" Kane exclaims.

Misty huffs. "Who cares about the storyline? I'm here to watch those fine men in their tight outfits."

"Of course you are," Kane deadpans. "Me and Knox have put our board shorts on. How about we all go for a swim?"

"Sounds good," I reply.

Kane's face brightens. "We'll meet you at the pool."

I rush up the stairs, but I can't help but look back when I reach the top. Misty's holding on to the rail to help herself up.

From my wardrobe, I pull out the drawer that contains my swimsuits. My fingers travel along the silky material. As I'm looking at them, I admire my ring. It shimmers in the light with the movement of my hand. I can't get over how beautiful it is.

After getting into my swimsuit, I go downstairs and to the kitchen for water, as my mouth is dry from last night. I chug a whole bottle before heading to the linen closet for towels, then make my way to the pool.

When I open the gate, I see Misty lying on a huge inflatable swan in the water, with massive sunglasses covering her eyes. Knox is sitting on the edge of the pool, bopping to the music pumping through the speakers.

My eyes scan his body. I got lucky with him. He has an athletically lean body with a defined chest, broad shoulders, and wavy, messy bed hair. I can see all his muscles with perfect clarity, even from here.

In my peripheral vision, Kane comes flying out and runs toward the pool. He jumps in, folding his body as he hits the water hard, and splashes a wave onto Misty and Knox. Once Kane resurfaces, he laughs at Misty, who is furiously wiping droplets from her sunglasses.

"Real mature," she quips.

He grins at her, showing all his teeth. Kane acts like the youngest, but he's the oldest at nineteen. Misty and Knox are eighteen, and now, so am I.

As if he senses my gaze, Knox looks up and gives me a sexy smile that's reserved only for me. I smile back. If I get to see that smile every day, I'll die a happy woman.

THE NEXT DAY, I WAKE UP TO THE ABRUPT SOUND OF THE ALARM on my phone. Clasping the phone in my hand, I blink from the bright light. We're going to be late for school! Misty threw up again yesterday evening, so we had an early night.

I stumble to my wardrobe and change into skinny jeans and a casual beige shirt. I brush my teeth before I go to see

Misty. My feet pad against the floor on my way to her bedroom. When I open the door, she's curled up in a ball. She brings the comforter down from over her face. Her blond hair is a tangled mess. She has dark circles under her eyes and looks pale.

I rush over and sit on the bed beside her. "I thought you said you were feeling better?"

She shakes her head. I give her a pointed look. "Well . . . if it's not the food and it's not the alcohol, you're going to have to see a doctor."

Her lips curve into a deep frown. "I know."

"Are you going to let me ask Iris to call the family doctor?"

"No, no. I'll do it."

"Do you want me to go get you some breakfast?"

She sits up in bed, massaging her temples. "No. I'll just vomit it up."

Glancing at my watch, I say, "I've got to go."

But I don't want to leave her. Despite my internal struggle, I know Mom won't let me stay home when I'm fine.

"I hope you feel better soon," I say as I walk to the doorway. I turn over my shoulder and blow her a kiss, and I'm rewarded with a chuckle.

I make my way downstairs and go to the kitchen.

Iris smiles. "Good morning. What can I get you for breakfast this morning?"

"Hello, sorry, no time," I reply and lean over the counter and grab an apple from the fruit bowl.

"Where's Misty?"

I cringe. "She still isn't feeling well."

Iris's eyes widen, then something flashes across her face, but it disappears.

"Is Mom home?" I ask.

"She will be out today. Pilates, then lunch at the resort,

and I think she mentioned shopping as well. I would say you'll most likely beat her home. Your father mentioned he was going to be home late from work tonight as well."

"Thanks." I sling the bag over my shoulder and dash out the door.

The limousine is waiting in the driveway. I open the door and slide along the leather seat next to Knox.

"Cutting it fine today. Where's Misty?" Kane asks across from me.

I pull my bag onto my lap and lean over to pull the door shut. "She's still sick."

My stomach churns. I feel terrible leaving her there. Iris will be at home for a few more hours to help her if she needs it, though it does nothing to ease the guilt.

"I'm surprised she hasn't gotten me sick yet," says Kane.

Shrugging, I think the same thing about myself.

The limousine drops me and Knox off at school, then takes Kane to work at the casino. It makes more sense to drop Kane off first, given the casino is closer to their home, but he enjoys seeing Misty every day before school.

The day goes by slowly, and school isn't the same without Misty. I peer down at my phone at all the messages I've sent throughout the day.

Misty

How are you feeling?

Are you okay?

Why aren't you replying?

Knox is in a few of my classes and I have acquaintances, but Misty is my only close friend. I feel lonely and spend the day scolding myself for leaving her alone when she's sick.

At the end of the school day, I call her, but it goes straight to voicemail. Knox and I walk to the limousine.

"Misty's still not answering!" I say with frustration.

"She could have forgotten to charge her phone," he replies.

I press on Kane's name in my contacts and bring the phone to my ear. It rings three times.

"Hey."

"Have you heard from Misty yet?" I ask.

I'm met with silence. Then Kane says, "I haven't. I'd say she's sleeping it off."

She would not be sleeping *all* day.

"Okay, thanks. Bye."

When I get into the limousine, Knox asks, "What's wrong?"

"I feel like crap that I left Misty home alone when she's been so sick lately."

He puts his hand over mine, his thumb rubbing soothing motions on my hand. "Did you end up finding out what's wrong with her?"

"I'm hoping she went to the doctor today. It's unlike her not to reply."

"Try not to stress. The doctor probably gave her some strong meds and she's sleeping."

My foot is tapping the floor when the limousine turns and parks in my driveway.

I lean over and peck Knox on the lips. "I've got to go," I blurt out and shuffle over, opening the door. When my feet land on the ground, I turn to him. "I'll see you tomorrow."

He gives me a small wave.

When I get inside, I throw my bag on the floor, kick off my shoes, and dash through the living room and up the stairs.

When I make it to Misty's bedroom door, my breathing is heavy.

Knock, knock, knock.

No answer.

I'm stuck, unsure of what to do. *Should I knock again, or is she asleep?* I don't want to wake her, but selfishly, I want to know how she's feeling.

My shoulders fall. I should let her sleep longer, but after two hours, I'm checking on her. I drag my feet to my bedroom and put on the TV, hastily flicking through the channels. Time drags on . . . every fifteen minutes feels like one hour. By the time two hours have passed, I stand. *That's it!*

When I reach her door, I bang louder this time. "Time to get up!" I grasp the handle. "You have slept for way too long!" I announce.

I feel silly when she's not in her bed. Strange.

As I scan her bedroom, I can't see her bag or phone. *She might have left to go to the doctor,* I think to myself. But she's been gone for hours now, and she hasn't replied to my texts or my phone call.

I huff. She will hear it from me when I find her. I walk out and search every room before I take my phone out of my jeans and call Kane.

He answers, though there's a lot of background noise.

"Is Misty with you?" I ask him.

"Nope! She sent me a message about coming to see me, but I checked with Mom and she never did. I messaged Misty back, but she never replied. Me and Knox are out for dinner with Dad."

"Well, she's not at home," I reply.

"Is her car there?" Kane asks.

I didn't look, but I presumed it would be in the garage. I move to the stairs, and when I get to the bottom step, I lean toward the wall and flip the light switch.

"No," I reply. "Her car's gone."

"She's out, then."

"No, Kane. She's been gone for hours."

"Can you call Misty's phone?" he asks someone on his end.

I bite my lip, waiting impatiently.

"It went straight to voicemail," Knox says in the background.

My heartbeat quickens as a feeling of dread settles in my stomach. "Something isn't right. She's never ignored my messages all day."

"Maybe she went to the shops," Kane suggests.

"She's sick. You should have seen her this morning. She couldn't get out of bed. So she wouldn't have gone anywhere." I try to keep my voice even, but my chest is tightening and my throat is closing, making it difficult to breathe.

"Don't get ahead of yourself. She's obviously left to go somewhere in her car. If she hasn't shown up by seven, we'll help you search for her, but it's still early. Don't stress—she'll turn up."

He was wrong.

FOUR
THE HEAVY BURDEN OF GUILT

Six weeks later

Knox

Age: Eighteen

Zara's house has been inundated with people. Her parents Helen and John, me, and my mom sit in the dining area, waiting for the psychiatrist to come out after talking to Zara.

I rub my eyes, which burn from staying awake for so long. Zara woke up screaming again, and it takes a while to settle her down to go back to sleep. Then I stay wide awake worrying about her.

I don't know what's going on in the investigation into Misty's disappearance. Mom's been communicating with the police and a private investigator, but no one can find her. I zone in and out of conversations, feeling as though I'm an unwilling participant in this nightmare.

"Knox, how did it go with you and Kane with the posters?" Helen asks.

The posters she gave us has a recent photo of Misty under "Missing person." Below the photo is a detailed description of her looks, height and weight, and the car she drives. It also has the police phone number and a mention of the million-dollar reward my mom has offered in relation to anyone providing details that can locate Misty.

"They are posted in the front window of nearly every business in Crown Village, and Kane and I put them up all over the amusement park." Someone must have seen something.

"Thank you," Helen responds softly. "Did Kane go home?"

"Ah . . . yeah," I answer.

Kane was drinking from his flask while we were handing out and putting up posters. I hate seeing him in pain and watching him self-destruct.

I look around. "Zara asked where Iris went. She noticed she hasn't been around. When will she be back?"

Helen's mouth opens, but Mom speaks. "She finished up with the Pratts. Said she wants to spend more time with her family."

My stomach sinks. I don't want to tell Zara.

"Why didn't Iris say goodbye? Why would she do that to Zara when's she's already hurting?"

Annoyance clings to me. What the hell is wrong with everyone? Misty disappears, Iris leaves without so much as a bye, and I've noticed Mom gradually pulling away. I thought she would be here every day with me to support the Pratts, but she randomly turns up to see them, and it's like her offering a reward is doing "her part."

Helen looks to Mom for an answer, which is weird. "I'm

not too sure. Maybe Iris wanted to give the family some space," Mom answers.

I clench my fist repeatedly as I breathe deeply, trying to calm down, because sometimes everything gets so overwhelming I can't breathe. My life used to be easy, then Misty went missing and everything turned to shit. There's this lingering anger and bitterness toward everyone who has brought pain to Zara.

"Have you given any thought to enlisting yet?" Mom asks, causing my body to freeze.

I glare at her. It's not the right time to talk about this. I considered it before Misty's disappearance because I was never interested in the casino or managing any other business. That's what Kane wants to do, not me. I want to do something I'm proud of, but I'm not leaving Zara and her family now. They need me.

John frowns but Helen's eyes are wide. "When are you going to do that?" Helen asks.

I shake my head. "I'm not going anywhere." Zara needs me . . . my brother needs me.

"Knox has always wanted to join," Mom adds.

My mouth tightens and my eyes dart to the stairs, checking that Zara isn't around. I've never spoken to Zara about my thoughts of joining the military because it means I would be away from her for long periods over many years. Now I definitely can't go, and I don't want Helen and John thinking I'll desert them and Zara during this. I'm not like everybody else.

"I know you feel like you have to stay for Zara, but you can follow your career in the military if that's what you want. Misty will be back soon, you'll see," Helen says.

I hope she's right, but I would never have thought Misty would leave.

Everyone stops talking as the doctor enters the room. He looks at us and shakes his head. He's frowning. "It's my professional opinion that Zara should seek ongoing treatment. She's experiencing a nervous breakdown, considering all you described." He looks at Zara's parents, then me. "The stress of her sister's disappearance has caused anxiety and depression, which has made her isolate herself here at her home.

"She's not eating or sleeping well or looking after herself. I took a blood test to see, but she may need IV fluid if she isn't drinking any water. I have prescribed her anxiety and antidepressant tablets for the morning and an antipsychotic to help her calm down at night. However, I think it's best Zara goes to a facility where she can get twenty-four-hour care."

The blood drains from my face. John is nodding, whereas Helen has tears in her eyes again.

"Is the stress why Zara has also been losing so much hair?" Helen asks.

I flinch. I noticed that too.

"Yes," the doctor replies.

Mom puts her hand on Helen's arm. "That medical treatment center I was telling you about has the best resources money can buy, and I want that for Zara. I told you I'd pay for it, so you don't have to worry about a thing."

"It's a bit soon to be discussing that, don't you think?" Irritation infuses my tone. "I'm here. I can make sure she takes her tablets."

I look between Helen and John. "Let me help her, please," I beg. No offense to them, but they are struggling as well. I can look after Zara. "What if Misty comes back? Zara won't leave, not now."

I don't mention that she hates when I have to leave her too, even for short periods, but I believe I can be there for her, be what she needs.

Helen bobs her head and peers at me. "It does seem too early, but it's something we can look at if she gets worse."

"These are the prescriptions." The doctor leans over with a piece of paper in his hand. Helen takes it from him. "There are instructions on how much she is to take of each tablet and for how long. You'll see that there is a gradual increase with each medication. If Zara gets worse or has any severe side effects, please call me."

"Thanks," Mom says to the Pratts' family doctor. "I'll pay for any and all of Zara's expenses."

"We can't allow you to do that," John replies sharply.

Mom lifts her chin. "You can, and you will. Let me pay Zara's medical bills. You just focus on your family."

There's no fight in Zara's parents. They look as exhausted as I feel.

After the doctor leaves, Helen turns to my mom and asks, "Has there been any update from the private investigator?"

"None. I have spoken to the local police that are managing the case and who we have in our pockets. One said that because she is over eighteen, Misty legally doesn't have to return home. So unless there's proof that there was an involuntary disappearance, there's not a lot else they can do."

I slam my fist on the table. "That's bullshit!"

Helen jumps, so I soften my tone. "Sorry."

I didn't mean to snap, but we've done more investigation than the police and that so-called investigator have done. It's us who have called businesses and people, put up posters, offered rewards. What have they done? Interviewed people . . . and what? Checked Misty's phone records and laptop to tell us what we already know—that no signs led up to her disappearance?

I stare at Mom. "You tell that private investigator to do better. It's not good enough. I can only imagine how much you're paying him. Six weeks later and there's still no sign of her?"

When I see movement in the corner of my eye, I glance to my left to see Zara. All conversation stops. She pauses at the bottom of the stairs. She's lost a lot of weight in a short time. It's scary.

"Come sit, precious," I say as I wave her over.

I want to include her in conversations around Misty's disappearance. It's important she talks about it.

She hesitantly wanders over. I shuffle the chair back so she can sit on my lap. I wrap my arms around her frail body and pull her to my chest.

"We were just talking about putting more pressure on the private investigator because there needs to be something that leads us to Misty."

"You should consider the fact that she ran away," says Mom, making Zara stiffen in my arms. "She was a free-spirited young woman who liked to break the rules."

"I don't think so, Audrey," Helen replies. "She didn't take any money out of her bank account."

"But your camera shows Misty leaving in her car. She took her wallet with her. She could have been saving up, or maybe she met someone else." Mom shrugs casually, like she didn't just insult Misty.

Zara abruptly stands. "No! She loved Kane. She would never cheat on him."

I sigh and watch Zara storm away and back up the stairs. "I'll go to her," I tell Helen, who has a deep frown on her face.

"Thank you," she whispers.

I rush up the stairs and to Zara's room to see her lying on her stomach with her arms under the pillow on which her head rests.

"Don't listen to my mom," I say as I sit next to her. "She doesn't know Misty like you do."

"There's so many unanswered questions that I'm starting to think I didn't know her at all . . ."

Her voice is without emotion. Her mood changes every day from crying to anger to numbness.

I tuck her hair behind her ear. "You don't believe Misty would have run away, do you?"

"I don't know what to believe anymore. Are you staying tonight?"

"Ah, yeah. Sure."

I can't shake this overwhelming guilt. When I'm with Zara, I feel bad for leaving my brother alone. And when I'm with him, I worry about leaving Zara. I can't be in two places at once.

I think Zara wants me with her because she's worried that I'll abandon her like Misty did, which is why I don't want to go to the military. I don't want her to leave either. We can get through this . . . *together*.

BEST
FR_ENDS

FIVE
MENTAL TORTURE

One year later

Zara

Age: Nineteen

A BUZZ ECHOES THROUGHOUT THE SMALL ROOM.

"Ow!" I whine as the tattoo gun marks the top of my thigh.

Even though I've had some whiskey, it still burns.

"What are you getting again?" Kane slurs before he takes another gulp from his flask.

Today is the first anniversary of Misty's disappearance, so Kane and I have gotten drunk. I'm getting a tattoo to mark the occasion. It's the word *Misty* written in calligraphy, with two small doves raising their wings to fly. Knox watches with his arms crossed over his chest, the same, usual worried look in his eyes.

Once we're home, Knox helps me up the stairs and insists that I wrap up my tattoo with a bandage so it doesn't get wet before I have a shower. Afterwards, I collapse on the bed and shut my eyes.

When I wake up, I need to go to the bathroom. Knox is asleep next to me, with one arm stretched out touching me. He looks so peaceful in his sleep. In contrast to when he's awake and worry lines mark his forehead—all because of me. Sometimes, I feel like my pain is bleeding all over him.

Knox has been staying on and off at my house ever since Misty disappeared. At nineteen, he should be out partying and enjoying life. There's a tightness in my chest about him spending all his time with me. Maybe he'd be better off without me? Maybe death would be preferable to enduring all this pain? I struggle to stop those dark thoughts from polluting my mind.

During the year since Misty disappeared, I've hated the pitying looks from everyone. It makes it so much worse. People ask how I'm doing, but I sense they're being polite—they don't want to know. I put up a facade, telling them I'm fine while my heart is screaming in pain.

I'm struggling to live without Misty. How do I go from one day having this perfect life to drowning in my personal hell the next? No matter how hard I try, I can't claw my way out. Misty's disappearance has created a wound so deep that the pain won't go away.

There are still times when something happens and I go to call her to tell her, and it's those few seconds of peace I revel in—when I think she's with us, when it hasn't registered yet that she's gone. Every time I travel outside of the house, I search for her in the crowds.

My heart aches from missing her, and my mind tortures me with the memories. Her ghost haunts this house. It's not much of a life I'm living, but knowing that Knox—this beautiful human next to me—has walked alongside me on this dark path makes the struggle to hold on worthwhile.

I slowly get up, trying not to wake him. When his hand falls away from my skin, his eyebrows furrow and he reaches out for me. But then he drifts back to sleep, and I tiptoe to my bathroom and close the door.

I don't look at myself in the mirror because I know what will stare back at me in the reflection. After using the toilet and washing my hands, I open the bottom drawer of the bathroom cabinet and move my makeup bag until I see the shiny silver object. Long before I got the tattoo, I had the thought of cutting myself. I haven't been able to stop thinking about it.

I lift the bottom of my nightgown before taking the cling film off my tattoo. I grab a clean washcloth and wet it under the running tap to pat the smeared ink.

Picking up the icy blade, I take a deep breath. A hiss escapes my mouth as the razor pierces my skin. My eyes water as I drag it across. There is now one cut under my tattoo, marking one year.

Weirdly, I feel temporary relief afterward. The tattoo and cut also remind me that the past was real, that she was real.

I'm so deep in thought that I don't hear the door open. When I see Knox's anguish as he sees what I've done, my high is depleted. He walks away and my body is cold. I let out a heavy breath.

He comes back with supplies from the first aid kit. His touch is delicate as he washes and cleans the wound. I watch him in awe as he treats me with care while he covers it with a dressing.

He kisses the bandage and everything lights up. As he stands, I take him in. His gray sweatpants hang low on his hips, accentuating the V of his six-pack abs. I lick my lips as my gaze continues to travel up his fine body to those whiskey-colored eyes.

He grabs my chin in his hand, his eyes boring into mine. "You bleed, I bleed."

The intensity and devotion in his voice makes me shudder. Overwhelmed with emotion, I can't speak, so I nod. He takes my hand and pulls me back to the bed. We lie back down on the crumpled white bedsheets, his arm around me. I rest my head on his chest and I'm immersed by his warmth. Everything fades as I listen to the steady rhythm of his heartbeat.

SIX
SACRIFICE

Knox

Age: Nineteen

It's been the longest year of my life. No one has found Misty. Not even the police or the private detectives have any leads. My mom offered a million-dollar reward for any information that leads to finding her. There have been calls, but all have led to dead ends.

This nightmare taunts and follows me everywhere I go. I'm stretched so thin, trying my best to be there for Zara and Kane. There's pain wherever I go, and I can't fix anything or help anyone because I can't bring Misty back if I don't know where she's gone.

For so long, I've been through every conversation and every moment leading to her disappearance that would give me any inkling of where she might've gone. Kane has turned into an alcoholic and workaholic, and Zara is mostly in a zombie-like state. She might be with me, but her mind is elsewhere.

I flinch at a loud crash upstairs. Zara! I jump off the sofa and run up the stairs and into her room. The pain and anger on Zara's face physically hurts my chest. An overturned chair lies by the wall, under damaged plaster and the smashed TV.

Her shoulders rise and fall. I slowly step toward her and reach out, but she lashes out and pushes at my chest. I let her. She pushes and slaps repeatedly, but at least she's feeling something and she's showing emotion.

I see Helen by the door, watching her daughter.

"Zara, stop! No more!" Helen wails as tears stream down her face.

"Don't worry, Helen. I'll look after her."

She gives me the smallest nod. Helen has lost a lot of weight. She looks so fragile now. John needs to stop working so much and come home and be here for his family. I think, like my brother, avoidance and keeping busy is their way of dealing with their pain . . . or not dealing with it.

When Helen leaves, Zara screams, "Why isn't Misty home yet?"

A sob comes from outside. Helen must have heard her. I step toward Zara, put my arms around her stiff body, and pull her to my chest. I lean down and whisper in her ear, "It's okay. Let it out."

Instead, her body goes limp. I gently pick her up, as if she were glass that could shatter, and place her on the bed.

She peers up at me with tormented eyes. "Please hold me," she croaks.

As I lie down next to her, she rolls over onto her side. I pull her into me. Tears roll down her cheeks. A catatonic stare has replaced the flash of anger.

Misty's disappearance has created a tsunami effect that's severely affected my family. My mom has moved away. I thought she, more than anyone, would've been here for Helen, but she went to live at one of our holiday houses in the mountains. She said she's giving everyone room and time to grieve. I think she's a coward, so Kane and I have little to do with her anymore except the occasional phone call. We live with our dad full time now.

Once Zara's breathing levels out, I slowly move my arm off her and shuffle to the edge of the bed and stand. I look back at her once more before I drag my feet to her bedroom door and, as quietly as I can, pull it closed behind me.

Dread creeps up from the pit of my stomach as I walk down the stairs. I've separately spoken with each of Zara's parents about Zara's depression. My thoughts go back to my discussion with John.

His eyes were dark underneath, his hair was messy compared to its normal slicked-back look, and his tie hung haphazardly off to one side.

"I'm losing my family, and I don't know what else to do." His body slumped further into the seat at the dining table.

"I want to comfort Helen, I do, but I don't know how when I'm struggling so much myself."

A deep ache took root in my chest. "I know," I replied. "I'm struggling to be there for both Zara and Kane."

He gave me a sad smile. "Audrey suggested Zara is too reliant on you, and I would have to agree with her. It worries me. The treatment facility she showed us sounds promising. It offers a range of health practitioners to help her, and it has world-class therapeutic interventions. I think it could really help Zara cope and give Helen some peace in knowing she is dealing with what she's experiencing."

Zara would be better off moving away and getting the psychological help she needs. I stupidly thought if I loved her and was there for her, she would snap out of her comatose state and live again. But after I saw her cut herself, I knew I wouldn't be enough.

My breathing quickens as I make my way down the stairs

to search for Helen. As I walk through the house, I hear the TV, so I go to the living room.

Helen is sitting in her usual easy chair, with Misty's blanket over her. Her sad eyes peer over the edge of the blanket, and she attempts to give me a smile.

I sit on the sofa. Tension takes over every muscle in my body.

"She cut herself with a razor blade last night." My voice is tortured and raw.

Helen gasps. "My baby is in pain. She needs professional help."

I let out a shaky breath. "I can't lose her," I try to explain, knowing it sounds selfish.

"You will never lose her. She needs to find herself. I don't want her to go either, but the mental health treatment center Audrey proposed sounds like the perfect place for her. I wonder every day if today's going to be the day where her grief is too much and she . . ." Her voice is riddled with pain.

I know how she feels because I've had those thoughts as well. Every time I have to leave her house, I'm a total wreck, worrying if Zara will be okay by herself. Her grief is so heavy it cripples her. I've tried my best to be the person she needs.

But I feel like a fraud. If I were helping her, shouldn't I witness a change in her? I see a spark now and again, like a firefly—a speck of light in the darkness—but then it's gone as quickly as it comes.

"The psychiatrist thinks she's codependent on you and it's hindering her recovery. You have been there for her. I know you love her, Knox, and I can never thank you for being there for her. However, I think we both know she won't willingly leave you. You are going to have to end your relationship with Zara." She pauses. "Do it for her."

Everything I've ever tried to do is for her. I cover my face briefly. The pain of knowing she would be better off without me is like a red-hot poker in my heart, and my chest is on fire, burning me from the inside out.

I look up at her, defeated. "When?"

"The sooner, the better. Audrey has already spoken to the manager at the center. They have a spot available for her."

I can't reply. She wants me to end our relationship today. I'm not ready . . . but then again, I never will be.

"Your mom mentioned your interest in joining the military. If that's what you want to do, you should pursue it. Don't put your life on hold. Zara will get better, and I believe Misty will return."

I realize Mom was right. It's not like I'm helping Zara or Kane by being here. Now's the time to enlist, while Zara can improve. Maybe later we can get back together. Lots of men in the military have wives and kids. Maybe it could work for us too.

Since Misty's disappearance, our relationship didn't stand a chance. Instead, Zara and I are prisoners of war, caught in the crossfire. I'll never forgive myself for hurting her when I break up with her. But she needs help. And even though I've tried, I realize now I'm not enough. Even if it is for Zara's well-being, I'll still hate myself for ending it.

BEST
FRIENDS

GHOST INSIDE MY HEAD

Nine years later
Present

Zara

Age: Twenty-eight

Misty is sitting on the saddle of a unicorn in front of me, laughing as her long blond hair wisps in the breeze. The carousel rotates to the sound of carnival music. It's nighttime, and it's lit up in a galaxy of colors and glass mirrors.

All I see are her beautiful blue eyes shining at me with that infectious smile. I smile back at her because it's impossible not to.

She looks at me with warmth in her eyes. "I miss you," she says, but the music is so loud I can barely hear her.

My brows furrow in confusion, and just when I'm about to reply, the carousel stops and I'm jolted forward.

I peer at where Misty was sitting, but she's no longer there.

"Misty," I call out, but all I hear is silence. Stepping around the unicorns, horses, and carts, I search for her face, but I can't find her anywhere.

My body jerks and I wake up, blinking, trying to see where I am. My eyes adjust to the darkness. The harsh reality hits me: I've been dreaming. I sit up in bed, my shoulders sag, and I lift my legs to my chest as I hug myself while tears stream down my face.

I clasp the chain around my neck and hold on to it. It makes me feel close to her. The best friend charm Misty gave me when we were young is now one of my most cherished possessions.

It won't be long until it's the tenth anniversary of the day she went missing. Every day she's gone hurts, but every year feels like a slice of pain through my heart. She's like a ghost inside my head, and I don't know whether it's a blessing or a curse because I see her face and hear her voice in my dreams.

I don't always dream of Misty. Sometimes I dream of Knox, the boy who consumed my mind, body, and soul. I believe at the time he loved me, as he always showed me how much I meant to him.

One day, he decided to join the military. I gather he didn't want me anymore, and as much as it hurt, I understood. I wasn't the same girl after Misty left, but it did not stop the excruciating pain of his absence. My soul yearns for him, every second of every day.

Occasionally, he doesn't seem so absent, like I could reach out and touch him. It's times like that I worry I might be losing my mind. I believe both were my soul mates, Misty as my sister and best friend, and Knox as my boyfriend. I know I won't find that with anyone else again.

I look at the window beside my bed. I lean forward and move the curtains aside to look at the night sky. It's a full moon and the stars are bright. I wonder what Misty and Knox are doing right now. Do they think of me like I think of them?

When they left, they cut pieces out of my soul. Those pieces have left gaping holes that have never healed. It makes me question whether I meant as much to them as they did to me, since it was so easy for them to leave. Sometimes I feel like I'm stuck inside my own head, with each thought and memory piercing my heart like shards of glass.

AN ALARM WAKES ME FROM MY SLEEP. IT'S TIME TO GO TO WORK at the women's shelter. When I get out of the shower, I look in the mirror. It's as if it's someone else's reflection. Cold brown eyes with dark circles beneath, which contrast with my skin, stare back at me.

I apply makeup before making my way to the kitchen. I shuffle to the fridge and grab an energy drink before I sit at the counter. The can hisses when I open it, and I take a sip, willing the cold, sweet liquid to give me the buzz I need to get through the day.

My phone rings, vibrating in my pocket. I pull the phone out to see a private number calling.

My body tenses as I answer. "Hello."

"Hi, Zara. It's Mae. Just giving you the heads-up. We had nine new people last night."

"Nine," I repeat. The center is well and truly at full capacity.

"Yes, one woman arrived with five children. The youngest is an infant, so the baby will sleep with her. The other is a young mother with two young children."

"What condition are they in?"

"Mostly scared. They're having breakfast now. After they

finish, I'll talk to the women about the resources we have available for them."

"Great," I reply. A beeping indicates another call, so I pull my phone away from my ear to see my mom calling. "I have to go. I have someone trying to call me."

"Okay. Bye."

"Hi, Mom."

"Hi, hon, how are you doing?"

"Good." I cringe at my lie, but Mom doesn't need to worry about me. "How's your trip going?"

"We're home. Hawaii was breathtaking. We loved it so much I think we'll book to go back."

I smile at her enthusiasm. My dad retired two years ago, so my parents have been traveling, making the most of their free time. "Where are you planning to go next?"

"We're staying home for a couple of months."

"Oh, okay."

I have an idea why, but I don't want to talk about it.

She sighs heavily. "I'm holding a vigil for Misty to remind the public about her disappearance, and I'd like for you to be there."

I cough, then gasp for air. I clear my throat because it feels like I'm choking.

"Are you all right?" Mom asks, concerned.

I pat my chest. "I don't know what to say, Mom," I answer honestly. "Misty's anniversary is painful enough, don't you think?" Tears begin to fall.

"Why am I the only one who sees the benefit in this? I'm hurting too, but what if Misty's picture and a reminder of the reward sparks someone's memory?"

"Who else doesn't agree?" I ask curiously.

"Everyone. You know what your father is like. He doesn't like to talk about it. Audrey mentioned that Kane wasn't happy about it. The only person who thought it was a good idea was Iris."

I pause, waiting for Knox's name to be mentioned, but she doesn't say it. I consider whether I should ask her. He was in the military for years, then moved back to our hometown. Now he's in a motorcycle club. He and Mom cross paths occasionally.

I bite my lip but give in. The urge to find out more about him is too tempting. "Have you spoken to Knox?"

"No, not yet. You should give him or Kane a call. Every time I bump into them, they ask me about you."

My heart races at the thought of communicating with Knox. "I don't think that's a good idea." Kane, maybe . . . but there's too much uncertainty with Knox. I couldn't bear to hear he's moved on with someone else.

Mom sighs again. "Please tell me you're coming. Iris is excited to see you."

My chest lightens at the thought of seeing Iris. I miss her. Just another person on the list of people who broke my heart when they left. "When did you see Iris?"

"I didn't. I called her."

"Where are you holding the vigil?" I ask in a tight voice.

"I've spoken to Audrey and Alec about having it at the amusement park."

I suck in a sharp breath. She spoke to Knox's mom and his cousin. I gather she needed their approval to have it at their family's amusement park. The thought of going back there makes my soul crumble and bleed in pain.

"It's on Misty's anniversary date, the—"

I cut her off. "Yes, I'm well aware of the date." I don't mean to sound rude, but that day I could never forget. It's burned inside my brain. "I'm not sure if work will allow me to take it off."

Guilt strikes me first, then shame. We are always busy, but

my boss would allow it. We have people who volunteer, and Mae can take on some of my responsibilities.

"I need you here." Mom's voice is soft, with an undertone of pleading and sadness.

I close my eyes briefly. No matter how much pain I'm going to be in, I can't leave Mom to go through that without me. We should show a united front. It's been around nine years since I've been home. It's about time I faced the past. I'm surrounded by courageous women at the shelter every day.

"I'll make it work. I'll be there."

"Oh, thank God! I'd love for you to come tomorrow."

"That is really short notice." The pitch of my voice rises.

"You never go anywhere. Wouldn't you have leave available? I don't want you to stay one day and leave the next. You haven't been home since you left for the treatment center."

That annoying guilty feeling strikes again. I haven't been home in a long time for good reasons, because that house is full of memories and those memories are a painful reminder of everything I no longer have.

"I can only ask my boss. I'll get back to you when I get a response."

"Hmm . . . maybe you should give me her number? I'll tell her how important it is that you take some leave."

My eyes widen. "No, Mom. I'm not a child anymore."

"You're still my baby!"

"I'll try my absolute best."

"I'm happy to hear that. Ask for at least a week off and let me know when you will be coming so I can make sure your bed has fresh sheets."

I cringe at the thought of being there for one week. "Yes, I will. Bye."

I phone my boss, who gives me today and the rest of the

week off. She understands my circumstances, as I've told her about my past.

Anxiety creeps up on me once my bags are packed, and my heart pounds faster in my chest. My fingers tingle with nervousness. I climb into the car and start the ignition. The engine purrs to life.

I write a quick message to Mom, telling her I'm on my way. Afterward, I flick through my contacts. I can't bring myself to contact Knox, so I find Kane's contact instead. My finger hovers over the call button. I take a second before pressing it.

Kane answers on the second ring. "Oh, look, it's the friend who never called me back."

Wincing, I say, "I'm sorry."

There's nothing else I can say. After I finished up at the treatment center, I stayed in the same city so that I could still attend my appointments with my counselor and specialists. Once that was over, I remained in the city for good, having stopped taking everyone's calls except for Mom and Dad. I shut everyone out. As selfish as it was, I couldn't go back—and I didn't want to. It wouldn't be the same without Misty and Knox.

"Tsk, tsk," Kane counters, lightening the mood.

"Well, I'm on my way to Crown Village now."

"Really?" he asks, raising his voice.

"Yes. Mom wants me there."

"So they're going ahead with the vigil? It's fucking bull-shit. What's the use? Misty's not going to wait ten years to suddenly reappear. If she wanted to return, she would have a long time ago."

I gape at his anger, but I also don't know what to say to him. "I'm leaving now, so I'll get home around seven tonight. Did you want to get together tomorrow?"

"What about Dad's for dinner? Chinese food, like we used to do."

My heart clenches. I've missed all of them so much. "Sounds good," I reply, blinking back tears.

"How long are you staying for?"

"A week. I might stay longer if Mom needs me."

"Six o'clock at Dad's tomorrow. Don't forget because I know where you live." He chuckles at his own joke. "I can't wait to tell Knox!"

Beep, beep, beep . . .

I look at my phone. He hung up on me! Unease ripples through my body. It's been so long. I wonder what Knox looks like. Does he have a partner? Mom never mentioned he had kids. My chest burns with envy at the thought.

AROUND NINE HOURS LATER, I ARRIVE AT MY PARENTS' HOUSE and park in the driveway. I sit in my car, frozen in place. The house hasn't changed in the eight years I've been gone. It wasn't a home anymore after she left. It was more like a prison.

A knock on my window startles me. Mom is smiling at me. I step out into her outstretched arms. She has a fluffy pink nightgown on. When I pull back, tears pool in the corners of my eyes.

She pulls me back in for another tight embrace before letting me go. "Thank you for coming. I wouldn't be able to do it without you."

I give her a sad smile.

She peers over at my car. "Your car is still going, I see."

"And going strong!"

"Zara!" I hear Dad call out. I glance over to see him

walking toward us. Mom steps back as Dad gives me a bear hug. "It's good to see you home." I pull back and smile, though from his expression, I'd say that I wasn't very convincing. "You two go ahead. I'll get your bags."

"Are you sure?"

"Yes, I'm not that old."

I follow Mom, but when I take one step inside the house, I close my eyes for a second, gathering the courage to move forward. Mom's footsteps stop, and when I open my eyes, we gaze at each other. Not a word is said because she knows why I'm struggling.

After I regain my composure, I follow her upstairs until I reach my old bedroom. My eyes fixate on my door because I can't bring myself to look at Misty's bedroom. When I open my door, I scan the room. It looks the same as it did when I was living here, but the memories hit me like a slap in the face. All the good ones of Misty seem to be tainted with the pain I felt from her absence.

"How have you lived here without her?" I ask. "All the memories . . ." I shake my head. "I don't know how you've done it."

She glances at me before she stares out the window. "I miss her every day."

"What do you think happened?"

Her shoulders fall. "I've asked myself the same question, and I can never come up with an answer."

"I don't believe she ran away. She was sick. She lost weight. She loved us, and she was happy."

Mom steps toward me, putting a hand on my shoulder. "In my heart I believe she will come back to us."

"You still believe she will come back after ten years?" I ask, my voice brittle.

"I won't accept any other possibility."

Dad walks in and places my suitcase beside my bed. "Did

you pack for a month?" he gasps, struggling to speak, as he shoots my luggage a dirty look.

I bite back a smirk. "Are you okay, Dad?"

He stands taller, rolling back his shoulders. "Yes, I am. We got you your favorite sushi downstairs."

I grin in appreciation.

"We'll let you get settled in," Mom says.

When they leave, I browse the bookshelf to see a photo of Knox, Kane, Misty, and me standing by the pool with our arms around each other, laughing. I sigh at those good times we shared. My fingertips brush the soft material of the satin quilt. My body trembles as I remember how Knox's scent used to linger in the sheets, how he used to hold me. As much as I hate to admit it, *I miss that feeling.*

EIGHT
CRAVING A TASTE

Bomber

I'm sitting at the table out in the backyard when my phone rings. My brother's name stares back at me.

"Yes, Kane?"

"Fuckin' hell . . . where do I even start?"

"Just say it."

I don't want to listen to him carry on. There's no need for bullshit. He needs to be clear from the beginning.

"Zara's coming back home tonight, and she's staying for a whoooollle week."

My body turns to stone. My phone falls onto the table, but I remain paralyzed. I take a moment before I slowly pick up my phone.

"Bro, you there? Knox!"

"I'm here."

"Has Mom called you about the vigil?" he asks.

"I had a few missed calls . . ." I've never been able to forgive her for leaving us.

He lets out a heavy sigh, causing me to frown.

"It's for Misty, isn't it?" I ask.

"Mmm," he answers solemnly.

"I'll be there."

"I'll keep you updated. And Knox?"

"Yeah?"

"We're having dinner tomorrow at Dad's. Six o'clock. And Zara's coming."

My dead black heart beats for the first time in a long time. "I wouldn't miss it."

"I bet," he says with a hint of sarcasm.

"See you then!"

"Is that a smile?"

I look up to see Viper walking toward me with a grin.

"You smiled!" he says, but my eyes narrow. He takes a seat beside me and playfully elbows me. "It's okay," he whispers. "It can be our little secret."

I push him. "Fuck off!"

He laughs. "Ohhh and defensive!" He blinks a few times, then his eyes widen. "It's that chick, isn't it?" He clicks his fingers. "What's her name . . ." He points at me. "Zara!"

I give him a clipped nod. "She's back in Crown Village."

He rubs his hands theatrically, true to form. "When can I meet her? I've been wanting to ever since you told me and Reaper about her."

I curse under my breath. "Look, I don't think you will." She probably won't even want to talk to me.

"You should have gone and seen her years ago when we got back from the military."

"I have seen her," I point out, though I know what he's talking about.

"No, like in person, instead of stalking her."

My lip twitches, though I try my best not to smile. "It's not stalking. I go a few times a year to check up on her. I like to know that she's doing okay."

I have resisted the urge to go to her and talk to her. But she's set up a new life, one without me in it. She doesn't come home because of her grief, and I could never ask her to stay in a place that strongly affects her. She seems a lot better than she was, and her well-being will always be more important than my own.

"Ah, yoo-hoo?"

I blink twice, Viper coming back into view. "Sorry, I was out of it."

"Women do that to ya."

I raise an eyebrow. "And how would you know? Have you even been in a relationship before?" I ask. Axle walks toward us.

Viper snorts. "I'm not stupid!"

Axle sits beside me with a wide smile, looking at Viper. "I strongly disagree."

Viper points to his patch. "I'm smart. See this patch? VP, motherfucker."

"That's because you love sucking Reaper's dick," Axle says, flicking his balled fist to his mouth in a jerking-off motion.

Viper's grin spreads. "You're a bastard!"

Axle laughs and slaps the table.

My lips mash together as I try not to laugh at these idiots.

Axle's jaw drops.

"What?" I ask.

He stands and leans over, touching my forehead with his hand. "Are you feeling okay? Do you need to go to the hospital?"

I shove his hands off of me.

"He's smiling because he finally gets to see his girl," Viper says.

My eyes narrow at Viper's big mouth. Though I would give anything to call her mine.

"What girl?" Axle asks. He clears his throat, giving me a pointed look. "What girl?"

The only one.

All those years watching her from afar, now I can see her, touch her, and—if she can forgive me—be with her again.

AFTER SPARRING WITH VIPER, AXLE, AND RAGE, I'M FRESHLY showered and lying on my bed, thinking about Zara. I lived and breathed her. Who I was pales compared to what I have become. There's no going back because I can't erase the past, but every day away from her felt like I was dying a little each day.

I've missed the feel of Zara's silky hair cascading through my fingers, the scent of her perfume, and the taste of her lips. Everything about her. Each time I saw her, a pang of regret stung my chest, followed by self-loathing. I shouldn't regret putting her well-being above my own feelings, but every day without her has been a struggle.

After she left, my life revolved around the military, and now the MC. I have meaningless sex with escorts to fill the void.

Time may have moved on, but I haven't moved on from her. I can't, and I've never wanted to. Every time I left Zara to come back home to the MC, I consumed myself with work. Being the sergeant at arms is easy because without Zara in my life, I have no heart or any real moral compass. I enjoy hurting others—it's a reprieve from my pain. That's what Demon and I have in common: fucked-up pasts. Demon is the enforcer, my right-hand man that protects patch members and the club.

The smell of cooked food wafts into my room. Reaper's ol' lady, Ava, can cook! I was unsure about her at the beginning, but despite how much pain she's been through with her ex-husband, she still is friendly to everyone. She reminds me of Zara.

I jump off the bed and grab my phone and wallet from the side table. I shove my wallet in my back pocket and swiftly head down the stairs to the kitchen. I inhale deeply, which makes my stomach growl.

I walk past the living room to see Elena, Axle, Viper, Candy, and Twitch watching TV. The echo of loud cracks gives me the impression the other men are outside practicing their shooting.

As I step into the kitchen, I lightly knock on the cupboard, aware of how jumpy Ava can get. But over time, she seems to have gotten more comfortable here. But I still don't want to trigger her.

She looks up at me and smiles.

"Do you know when dinner will be ready?"

"At least an hour. There's a big turkey in the oven."

I give her a chin lift, proceed through the house, and grab the keys to the van. I hope Zara likes the present I'm going to buy for her.

AFTER DINNER, THERE ARE CONVERSATIONS AROUND THE TABLE. I lean in closer to Reaper. "I need to speak to you at some point."

He slowly nods. "I've been meaning to try these new cigars I got. How about we go out the back and talk?"

I rarely have a serious one-on-one conversation with Reaper because my life is the club, so I gather he knows what I've got to say is important to me.

"I'll meet you out there."

My chair squeaks against the wooden floor when I stand. I pick up my plate and go to the kitchen. Elena and the sweet butts are in there cleaning. I use my fork to scrape off a large portion of my food into the container for the dog.

Elena's eyes drop to my plate. "You didn't eat much."

I pause. Despite the awkward silence, I don't tell her why. She plasters on a smile, reaches for my plate, and takes it from me.

I move to the back door and open it, but I'm met with resistance. I shove it harder. The door opens wide. Conan, Ava's dog, stands there. Judging by the drool hanging from his mouth, he must be able to smell the food. The door shuts behind me, and as I'm walking to the table outside, I look over my shoulder. Conan is sitting outside the door, patiently waiting for Ava to feed him.

Shortly after, the back door opens and Reaper walks through, stops at Conan, and shakes his head. "Rottweilers shouldn't be that fat. Is he getting bigger or what?" Reaper asks as he strolls toward me with a box in his hand.

My eyes skim over Conan's gut. "He has put on more weight."

"I keep telling Ava to stop feeding him so much."

I wait until he sits beside me. "I don't think it's just Ava."

His brows furrow. "What do you mean?"

"Everyone feeds the dog, and most people also give him snacks throughout the day. I know because I've sat here and watched."

I like this spot outside. Trees surround us, the air is fresh, and it's quiet. It's relaxing. I hate being confined indoors.

"Are Viper and Rage still taking the dog for runs?"

"Yes, but the dog gets fed all day and at night."

The back door opens again. Ava comes out with a massive container of scraps and places them in Conan's bowl.

"Sit," she says in what is supposed to be a commanding voice, but she's too softly spoken for it to sound like that. "Eat."

"Beautiful, your dog's getting too fat. I think you need to stop feeding him so much."

Ava lifts her gaze to us. She smiles. "No, I think we need to get another dog."

"Another one?" Reaper pipes up. "One is more than enough."

She quirks a brow, then walks back inside.

"She's getting another dog, isn't she?" I ask, my voice tinged with amusement.

"I fucking hope not." He pulls out a cigar and uses a cutter to slice the cap off. After lighting it, he hands it to me.

I bring it to my mouth and draw in, savoring the taste, before blowing out the smoke.

"Zara's back in Crown Village. Her parents are holding a vigil for her sister's ten-year anniversary."

"Has it really been ten years?" he asks, surprised. "I remember you telling us about her."

"Mom had the police on our payroll. She also paid for a private investigator. I will never understand how Misty just vanished."

"But that's it. People don't vanish. So what happened?"

"Misty was home because she was sick. The Pratts' camera shows her leaving the house in her car, but she never returned. She told my brother she would meet him at our mom's house, but she never showed up."

"How was she acting?"

"No difference in behavior apart from being sick. She was the happiest I think I'd ever seen her."

He glances away as if thinking, before looking back at me. "What about social media or bank accounts?"

I draw in the smoke from the cigar and blow it out slowly through my mouth. "No social media accounts were accessed. They went through her laptop but found nothing to suggest she was leaving. No bank accounts were ever accessed, and they never found the car."

Reaper scratches his jaw. "Do you think she left?"

"I'd known her for most of her life, and not once would I have suspected she would leave, but it's either that or a kidnapping. She wasn't a child. She was a grown teenager. We lived in Crown Village. Someone would have seen it. My mom offered a million-dollar reward for any information that would lead to finding Misty. They would have come forward by now."

"You mentioned a vigil? We'll be there for you, no questions asked."

My chest loosens. "Thanks."

"Will they need any help to set up?"

"My brother didn't say much. It's at the amusement park."

He gives me a blank stare. "That's an odd place for a vigil."

"It was Misty's favorite place, so it's more sentimental."

He puts his hand on my shoulder. "Anything you need, brother, just let us know."

The next day, I lie in bed. I didn't sleep well last night. I've been in a daze, going through the motions. I can't get Zara out of my head. All I can think about is she probably hates me, but I hate myself more for lying to her about the real reason I broke up with her. I've lived with regret ever since.

I didn't want to break up with her, but I had pressure from her family to do the right thing by her. I was the only one keeping her here. It came down to her safety and well-being.

Even though I was selfish and wanted to keep her, I knew if something ever happened to her, I'd never forgive myself.

BEST
FR—ENDS

NINE
BURNING WITH DESIRE

Zara

I smile a genuine smile. Going out for breakfast and shopping with Mom was enjoyable. I was happy to get out of the house. Apart from what felt like running into every person in Crown Village, it was great to spend time with Mom. I've missed her quirky comments that make me laugh. It hurt a little when Mom was talking about the vigil with others in the town, but everyone was sympathetic and respectful.

Since moving away, I've grown used to living in the city and keeping to myself, but I love Crown Village's small-town vibe, especially when everyone gathers as a community. I guess I wish it was for a different reason. Rubbing my forehead, I wince. I have a terrible headache that hasn't gone away all day, probably because of seeing the Harts in an hour.

I look in the mirror at the third outfit I've put on. The first was my favorite tight black dress, but I didn't want to look like I was trying to impress Knox. Second was jeans and a casual shirt, but secretly, I wanted to look good to show him what he's been missing all this time. I think the casual black maxi dress is the winner. It still shows off my curves, but it doesn't look like I'm trying too hard.

I lift my best-friends necklace over the top of the dress. My hand goes to the ring Knox gave me. I pull it higher up my finger. "Should I?"

"Should you what?" Mom asks, making me jump. "Oh, sorry, sweetie, I didn't mean to scare you," she says as she walks toward me.

I give her a sad smile. "Should I take the ring off?" I don't want to give him mixed signals, even though I've missed him.

Her eyebrows squish together and she purses her lips. "Why would you do that? Do you want to take it off?"

"No. He might want the ring back, though. It is a family heirloom."

Mom frowns. "No, he won't. That family will still adore you as much as they did back then. That won't change."

I massage my chest as my heart aches.

Mom sits on the bed. "Are you okay?"

I shake my head. "What's Knox like now?" I ask in a small voice.

She looks away, as if thinking about her answer. Her eyes return to me. "He's the same . . . but different . . . He goes by the name Bomber now."

"That doesn't tell me much, Mom. And how did he get that nickname?"

"I don't know how he got it." She pauses. "Knox looks the same but older. His personality . . ." Her hand goes to her chin. "Well, he's harder now. He has more life experience, and he's come back from war, so I understand, but I guess you'll see what I mean when you spend time with him. I've heard a few rumors about their MC, but I could never imagine the Knox I knew to be violent, so I guess that's what they are—

rumors. But then again, he is the sergeant at arms of the club."

I pinch my lips together. "Violent in what way? Sergeant at arms. What does that mean?"

Mom sighs. "Don't listen to me. I think it would be best to talk to him to make up your own mind about him."

I grab my phone from the bed and put it in my bag.

"Have fun," she says with a smile.

I walk the few steps to her, bend down, and peck her cheek. "See you when I get home."

My stomach flutters as I go down the stairs. I step through the front door to see a limousine waiting outside. When he sees me, the driver gets out and stands near the back door. One of the Harts must have organized it.

As I walk to the chauffeur, he greets me with a nod.

"I'm fine, thank you. I'll drive there myself."

"Please, miss, let me drive you, David insisted." He must see my hesitancy because he opens the door for me, giving me a reassuring smile.

I can't say no to David. He was like my second dad.

I sit in the leather seat and place my bag on my lap. The chauffeur closes the door. I glance down and pick at the couple of dots of white cotton on my black dress. As the car accelerates, anxiety causes my heart to skyrocket. I blow out a series of quick breaths to gain control.

Do I look okay? Will he be happy to see me or will he not care? God, I don't think I'm going to cope well if he isn't happy to see me. We had a past together, even if he broke up with me, so that should count for something.

I peer out the window to avoid my escalating thoughts. I grew up in a suburban part of Crown Village, whereas Knox's parents lived closer to the beach. As we descend down the hill, the view of the water is breathtaking. It's windy, so the water looks choppy as the waves crash against the shore.

When we arrive, I could vomit. I look up at the cream-colored house. It hasn't changed a bit since my childhood. I'm regretting my decision to come here. I should have met some place, there're no memories attached.

"Ma'am."

The chauffer's voice lifts me out of my daze. He puts out his hand, and I grab it as I get out of the car on shaky legs. After I step onto the grass, he shuts the door behind me. I turn to the chauffeur. He gives me a small smile, even though he just cut off my exit.

I can do this. It's just dinner. I stand taller with some fake courage, walk to the intercom, and press the button and wait. It beeps, and the click of the door unlocking sounds.

"Zara, come on in." David's cheery voice greets me.

I rush to the front door, and when I'm about to open it, it opens wide, and I'm met by David with outstretched arms.

I'm petrified. I can only stare at him. My heart is beating so fast in my chest it feels like it's going to explode.

He hasn't changed much. His hair is a little grayer now and his beard is longer, but aside from that, he's still the same handsome man I remember. The same whiskey-colored eyes Knox has gaze at me.

A smile that shows all his teeth spreads across his face. "Where's my hug?" he asks as his eyes sparkle with warmth.

I breathe out a harsh breath as tension eases out of my shoulders. I stand there for a second, searching his eyes. There's no resentment or malice from me leaving and never returning, just love. I step to him and wrap my arms around him.

He chuckles and takes me into his embrace while patting my back to soothe me. I can't stop the tears from cascading.

He pulls back, and I reluctantly let go.

"Well, I missed you too," he declares as he kisses my cheek. "Just as beautiful as I remember."

Someone's clearing their throat, and I turn to see Kane waiting for me. "Are you going to cry for me too?" he asks, his voice laced with mischief.

I chuckle at him, wiping away the tears with my hand.

"It's because I'm special, isn't it, sweetheart?" David challenges with a devilish grin.

My eyes skim over Kane. He's tall, like David and Knox, but he's grown up so much. He steps forward, pulling me into him. It's obvious he's put on a lot more muscle since I saw him last.

We break apart, and he looks at me. "It's so good to see you again. You look"—his eyes roam over my face—"well . . ."

I assume he means I look better than the last time he saw me. It's good to see him. I playfully squeeze his bicep. "Look at you, all muscly now."

Flexing, he grins smugly. His fitted shirt stretches across his chest and arms, showing every muscle. He hasn't lost his sense of humor.

My body goes rigid when I lay eyes on Knox. I didn't think he could look hotter, but he has aged ridiculously well. His hair is a few inches longer, as well as his beard. I give him the once-over. He's wearing black jeans and a white shirt that shows off his defined muscles. He looks rugged . . . more masculine.

Knox's gaze travels from my feet to my legs to my breasts, then pauses on my face. I shift on my feet, feeling uncomfortable under his intense gaze.

"Can you two not give each other the sex eyes while I'm right here?" Kane declares.

I snap out of my daydream as Knox curses under his breath.

Knox gives me a small smile, and it warms my soul. "Zara," he says in a deep voice. No hug . . . no nothing.

The warmth I felt from seeing his smile and David and Kane vanishes. All that's left is a cold sensation. I frown.

"Knox," I reply curtly.

The nerve of him. All this time and all those years we spent together, and I don't even get a hug? Did I mean nothing to him?

I will not let him put a damper on my night with David and Kane. "You don't have to be here," I tell him, even though it pains me to say it.

Squinting, Knox tilts his head. "I want to be here."

His voice is firm and confident, but I honestly don't know what to think. I'm annoyed. I shouldn't let him get to me.

"Well . . ." David says, cutting through the awkwardness. He looks at me. "I'm going to order Chinese. Is honey chicken still your favorite?"

"Yes, thank you."

He glances at Kane. "Don't you have a phone call to make?"

My stomach drops. They're going to leave me alone with Knox.

I give Kane my best don't-you-dare-leave-me eyes, but his smile kicks up an extra notch. "Why, yes. Yes, I do."

I shake my head at the liar.

They walk away from us, but David looks over his shoulder. "Play nice."

"After you," Knox says, putting his arm out for me to walk first.

I gaze into his eyes before continuing. This is weird, and I'm suddenly overheating. As I walk through the house and into the living room, I fan my face because I'm flustered.

Nothing has changed. David has the same furniture they had when I was here last. I move toward a familiar family photo on the wall.

I chuckle. "Oh, I remember this photo. You and Kane are so young here."

The photo is of the four of them. David and Audrey in the background and Knox and Kane in the front. The photo is professionally taken. Kane is missing teeth, so he must be around six years old, and his goofy smile makes me laugh. Knox looks so innocent here.

I turn to look back at Knox, who's raking his hand through his thick black hair, wearing a thoughtful expression.

"Do you see much of your mom anymore? Is she still at your old holiday house?"

He shrugs nonchalantly. "I don't have much to do with her. Kane talks to her more than me."

"So you don't see her?" I ask again.

"Once a year, if that. She doesn't like to leave her house."

I raise my eyebrows at the animosity in his voice.

It's strange. Audrey used to be busy and managed so many things in our town, the town her family founded. Then she moved away and stopped having anything to do with anyone.

"What?" he asks.

"So much has changed. I think it's going to take a while to get my head around it all."

He moves to the sofa and sits, so I walk over and sit beside him. He inhales deeply. "You still wear the same perfume."

My face burns. *He remembers.*

"Yes, I do. Mom said you're in a motorcycle gang now." I lean toward him. "Tell me about it."

His eyes narrow. "It's not a gang. It's a motorcycle club."

I cringe, hoping I didn't disrespect him. *Club, not gang, got it.*

"Sorry."

He doesn't speak straight away, so I wait for him.

"A couple of us served together in the military. We wanted

to make a safe place for men who were lost after returning home. I own land here in Crown Village, so we didn't have to fork out money to buy a place. We set up here, and I've been here ever since."

Even though he seems distant, it hurts me to think he was struggling when he returned home.

"You never came to see me."

With as much as I tried, I couldn't take away the disappointment in my voice. It still stings.

A sad smile curves his lips. "You were happier without me."

I raise my hand to my bleeding heart because he just cut me wide open. "How do you know that?"

"I checked up on you."

I scrunch my nose. "I never saw you. When did you do that?"

His face falls, and he looks away before his eyes fixate on me. "When I came back from the military and joined the MC, I checked on you a few times a year."

My eyes bulge. "And not once did you think to come and say hi?" Irritation coats my voice. "What's wrong with you? I thought we would at least be friends after everything we've been through."

There were so many times I would have done anything to have him back with me . . . to hear his voice . . . to feel him.

His lips press together into a straight line, like he wants to talk but doesn't.

"Tell me why!" I demand.

"You were better off without me. You looked healthier, happier. I wasn't going to ruin that."

My mouth opens, but Kane walks toward us, so I remain silent. This is a private conversation between me and Knox.

"So what have you been up to?" I ask Kane as he sits across from us in the easy chair. I sense Knox shuffling closer to me until our bodies touch. I gasp while trying to focus on Kane, but I'm struggling.

His eyes light up. "I still work with Dad at the casino." It's obvious he loves working there.

Knox rests his hand on his leg, though it's so close to mine.

Focus!

"And what happens when David retires?"

Kane smiles widely. "I'll take over management responsibilities and become CEO. I heard from your mom and"—he gives Knox a look with a raised brow—"someone else, that you work in a women's shelter. How's that going?" A tinge of sadness laces his question, even though he smiles when he says it.

I look away as I try to think about using the right words. "It's upsetting but rewarding at the same time."

"After everything you went through, how could you work in a shelter helping people in difficult circumstances all the time? I honestly thought you would do something completely different, like be a teacher or something."

I clear my throat and rub my hand up and down my leg. Knox puts one of his hands over mine. That there is the Knox I remember. My eyes close briefly, but I lift his hand off. I look at him and shake my head. He's had plenty of time to comfort me over the years—hell, to even say hi—and not once did he.

I look back to Kane, whose eyes are darting between me and Knox. "Should I leave and let you two get it on?"

My eyes bulge, and I shake my head rapidly. "No. Stay." Kane raises a brow. "Helping other people helped me, I guess. I found peace in giving women and children a safe place to stay and helping them to get back on their feet."

Kane gulps. Misty's disappearance is the only thing I've ever seen upset Kane, and rightfully so. The torment in his eyes is profound.

"Dinner is on its way," David announces. I watch him as he makes his way to us. He sits on the other easy chair next to Kane. "Wait until you try the Chinese food. They've been here for a year, and the shop is literally up the road. Anyway, what are we talking about?"

A moment of silence swells.

"My job at the women's shelter," I reply, since Kane's mind seems to be elsewhere.

"And how's that going?"

"It's rewarding."

"I always knew you were special. What you do"—he shakes his head, his eyes thoughtful—"is incredible. You should be proud of yourself." He looks at Kane, then at Knox for a little while longer. "Because I know we are."

I raise my head and blink furiously, trying not to cry. "Thank you," I respond, emotion clear in my voice.

"Hell . . . don't cry, precious," says David in a consoling tone.

Ouch! I cringe at the nickname Knox used to call me.

"Don't worry about it. I guess seeing everyone has made me a little emotional."

"How long has it been . . . eight years?"

"Yes, it has been." I glance at Knox.

He is repeatedly flexing his fingers and making fists. He gets up abruptly and walks away. His sudden movement makes David frown. As Knox leaves the room, I track his movements until I can no longer see him. When David turns back, he shuffles forward on the edge of his chair, leaning in toward me with sadness in his eyes.

"Can you do me a favor?"

Oh god. Dread washes over me. "Suuuure."

"Promise me you'll spend some time with Knox while you're home."

My breathing quickens. I nod again, feeling choked up.

My feelings for Knox are a hurricane, swirling around. I don't know what I'm going to feel next.

"I see the way he looks at you. He's never gotten over your relationship ending."

Rubbing my throat, I try to find my words, but it's as if my throat is tightening. "But he broke up with me," I croak.

David sighs heavily and slouches. I glance at Kane to see him shaking his head at his father.

"It's been hard without Knox . . . without all of you," I tell David.

The front door buzzer makes me jump in my seat.

"That must be the Chinese. Why don't you sit in the dining room. And Kane? Why don't you tell Knox that food is here?"

"Certainly," Kane responds.

David leaves the room.

"What was that about?"

Kane's brows lift. "What was what about?"

I narrow my eyes at him. "When you shook your head."

He shrugs. "I'm going to go find Knox."

I reach out to stop Kane. I stand instead. "No, I'll go find him."

I walk through the living room, then survey the hallway.

Knox is leaning against the wall. Where he's standing, he most likely heard our conversation.

"Food is here."

He doesn't even look my way. I walk until I'm standing in front of him, but he still doesn't lay eyes on me. I hesitantly raise my hands and place them on either side of his face. Feeling his rough beard against my hands, I bring his head down to make eye contact. His whiskey-colored eyes search mine. The haunted look in his sends a shiver down my spine.

So many questions filter through my mind. *Why did you leave me? Why didn't you speak to me? Do you still love me?* But the only question I can ask is "What's wrong?" because I hate seeing him so torn.

"I've missed you." His voice is a whisper, but the longing crushes my soul. I suck in a sharp breath. My hands tremble against his face. He tilts his head. "But you know what?" he asks, his voice deep and raspy.

The heat in his eyes makes me drop my hands and step back until my back is against the wall. He follows me, his eyes never leaving mine. He raises his arms on either side of my face, caging me in. I swallow hard as desire swirls inside of me.

His eyes drop to my lips, then he leans in close. I feel his breath against my ear. "I think you've missed me too."

My heart hammers. Need strikes me. When he pulls away from me, I wrap my arms around his neck. I pull him close, and when my lips collide with his, a wave of ecstasy washes over me.

This is no slow kiss; this is years of hunger. His hands drop to my waist, and as he pulls me closer, his fingers dig into my side. My arms tighten around his neck. His tongue sweeps over mine, a throaty moan escaping him. My body feels overloaded with senses, from his taste to the sensation of his hard body against mine. One kiss is bleeding into another as he claims my mouth again and again.

He pulls his head back, breaking the kiss, but then lowers his head. His lips meet my neck, and his open-mouthed kisses blaze a trail to my collarbone. Shivers erupt over my body. His lips meet mine once more. But now he's hungrier and kisses me harder, with a vicious desperation and passion I've never experienced before. I claw at him to get closer. He nips at my lip. My eyes spring open, but the pain's gone in an instant as his tongue travels over it soothingly.

"Dinner's here."

David's voice snaps me out of the moment. Panting, I

stand dazed. My eyes dart away, and I rush out toward the dining room.

As I sit, Kane smiles at me like the Cheshire cat. He knows something went down.

David walks in with two full bags and places them in the middle of the dining table. He opens one bag, takes out containers, and lines them up in the center, then leaves toward the kitchen. Knox sits next to me, but I refuse to look at him, so my eyes skim the table. There's no alcohol—dammit! I try my best to ignore Knox . . . but it's hard when my skin burns from where his lips traveled across it.

"Have a little moment together, did we?" Kane asks, amused.

My eyes flash open, but I mask my feelings before glancing at him and shaking my head.

Kane raises a brow at me in disbelief as David returns with beers and a bottle of wine. Relief takes over my anxiety. When he puts the wine on the table, I stand. I lean over and take a glass of wine from him, giving him a tight smile.

David chuckles. "You should have asked for a drink earlier if you were thirsty. I would have gotten you something."

I awkwardly smile back.

"So, tell me, how was rehab?" asks David.

"I was relieved once I confided in the counsellors and my peers. It made me realize that I wasn't alone in going through a traumatic experience and that what happened wasn't my fault."

With a lively conversation and a couple of glasses of wine, time whizzes by. David and Kane tell stories about their antics and make me laugh. The mood is light. I glance at the time—9:00 p.m.

"I'd better get going," I tell them and grab my bag from the floor.

"I'll take you home," Knox says.

"No need," I counter. "Is the chauffeur still here? He can take me back."

"Please let me take you." Knox's tone is gentler. He's almost begging. "So I know you got home safe."

My eyes soften at his request, and I nod.

"I'll be right back," he says and leaves the room.

Kane, David, and I stand and walk toward the front door. I give them a hug, but when I pull away from David, he pauses and whispers in my ear. "Please see Knox. I'd do anything to see my boy smile again."

He pulls back before I can respond. I give David a tight smile. Knox spending time with me isn't going to make him happy. Though I don't have the heart to tell David that.

We step outside.

"Goodbye," I say.

Knox walks through the entrance, then closes the front door. I shiver from the wind. Knox is holding a sweatshirt in his outstretched hand, and in his other is a helmet.

"Here," he says. "You'll get even colder on my motorcycle."

My eyes widen. Excitement and nervousness rush through me, but I look down at what I'm wearing. "I can't get on the motorcycle in a dress."

His lips mash together like he's concealing a smirk. David's words come back to me. *I'd do anything to see my boy smile again.*

I take the sweatshirt and raise a brow when I inspect it: *War Brothers MC* is written across the back, with a skull-and-guns logo. I pull it over my head anyway. I chuckle when I peek down. It comes to my knees. "I look silly."

"No, you don't."

I gaze up at him to see his eyes drifting up my body, and when his eyes meet mine, they're dark with lust.

I swallow hard and follow him to a black Harley Davidson. It's a beauty. He hands me a helmet. When I pull it over my head, it's a tight fit, and suddenly, I'm hit with jealousy. This is a woman's helmet. How many others have worn it? I know I'm not being fair. I have no reason to be upset.

"Can I have your bag?" he asks.

I pass it to him and he puts it in the saddlebag at the side of his motorcycle. He takes out a helmet and puts it on. He steps toward the motorcycle and swings his leg over it and gets on. He oozes sex appeal and confidence. My hands now fidget in front of me. I can't stop staring.

"Pull your dress up a little and hop on," he says, his voice muffled by his helmet.

I grumble as I do so and bring my leg over the motorcycle. I shuffle into the seat but feel the warmth of his back when I move in close.

"Hold on to me. Lean when I do and keep your feet off the exhaust."

"Okay, I will."

I cling to him, letting go of all thoughts and immersing myself in the present, finding solace and pleasure in the ride.

BEST
FRIENDS

TEN
AN EMPTY ROOM

I'M GRINNING FROM EAR TO EAR. THAT WAS AN EXHILARATING ride.

"Did you enjoy it?" he asks, his voice hinting that he already knows the answer.

"Yes, I did."

After pulling the helmet off my head, I attempt to pat my hair down. I put out my hand to pass him the spare helmet, but he shakes his head.

"The helmet is yours. I bought it for you."

I stiffen, mouth agape. "You bought the helmet for me?" I clarify.

"Yes, it's yours."

I touch my throat as I gaze at him. "And how did you know I was going to get on the motorcycle?"

The corner of his mouth curves. "I just hoped you would."

The smile. Maybe . . . just maybe . . . there was truth to what David was saying. He looks sexy on that motorcycle, but I shake my head to get rid of the thoughts. I'm not having my heart broken a second time. With that thought, I turn to leave. The high from riding the motorcycle dissipates with every step.

Heavy footsteps sound behind me. Knox grabs my wrist, but I turn and yank my hand away as if he's burned me.

"What's wrong?" he asks with knitted brows.

"I can't do this . . . with you and me . . . not again."

My head's a mess. I need a break to think clearly. His eyes swirl with a mixture of emotions as he turns and strides back to his motorcycle without so much as a backward glance. I watch as he speeds off. I stand with the helmet in my hand, feeling confused at the way we were acting tonight, both hot and cold.

I sneak inside in a daze, hoping my parents won't hear me come in. I curse myself for what happened tonight. After he had already ripped out my bleeding heart, I cringe at the thought that I threw myself at him . . . but I can't stop the way my body reacts to him. His presence consumes me, wreaking havoc on my senses, making my mind go blank whenever he's around.

Slowly, I drag myself up the stairs, thinking about him. I huff in annoyance. David suggested that Knox still cares for me, but if he did, then why did he let me go?

In bed, I lift the neck of the sweatshirt to my nose and inhale. It smells like him. His cologne, his hard, muscular body against mine, and those sinful whiskey-colored eyes all taunt me in my sleep.

THE NEXT MORNING, I WAKE UP DYING OF THIRST FROM THE alcohol I consumed with David and Kane. I swing my legs over the edge of the bed and pad downstairs to the kitchen to get water. On my way back to my bedroom, I grab what I think is the door handle to my room and open it. The sight that greets me makes me freeze on the spot.

I'm not in my bedroom; I'm in Misty's.

A gut-wrenching scream rips out of my throat. I wrap my arms around myself, holding my chest tight, tears coursing down my face.

Dad bursts into the room, with Mom behind him.

"Call Knox," Mom yells. She stands in front of me and puts her arms around me, pulling me into her. My tears wet her top as I cry. I sob at losing my sister, who I never got to say goodbye to.

My parents talk, but I can't understand what they're saying. All I hear is white noise. Mom ushers me to the bed and I sit.

I glance at Misty's wardrobe and notice most of her clothes are gone.

My chin trembles. "Where are all of her clothes?" I ask, distraught.

"Oh, Zara . . . I'm sorry. I gave some of her clothes away to the local charity."

All the air leaves my lungs. "You gave them away? How could you?"

She looks away from me, and I watch the tears fall from her eyes.

Dad steps toward us, his frown deepening when he sees Mom. "Keep in mind, we were broken for a long time. It wasn't until the last few years that we've done little things like give Misty's clothes away. Looking back, we should have put some aside for you, but you never came home, and we knew if Misty were to return, they are material possessions, which we can replace immediately."

I nod at him but glance away. My jaw clenches. To an

extent, I understand what he's saying, but my heart doesn't care. It still aches for her. I wanted everything to remain where it was, and it pains me to see anything missing.

Mom and Dad step out of the room. I'm grateful, because there's tension between us. The front door slams and heavy footsteps trudge up the stairs. I look up to see Knox walk into the room, taking cautious steps toward me.

"I can't stay here. I thought I could, but . . ." I pause. "Get me out of here," I tell Knox, my voice cracking.

He moves closer to me, his eyes full of sympathy. "Get changed and go get me your bags. We'll leave right away."

Relief surges through me. I return to my room and mindlessly pack everything in my suitcase before doing up the zipper. He grabs the handle and I follow him down the stairs. He says a brief goodbye to my parents and looks back at me.

"I'll be in the truck, waiting," he says and leaves out the front door.

My parents' faces are etched with sadness. Tears still line Mom's red eyes. Even though I think what they did was wrong, I hug my mom, peck her on the cheek, and remind her that I love her, no matter what.

My eyes flick between them. "Thank you for allowing me to stay . . . I just can't stay any longer."

Mom raises her hand and rubs my shoulder. "We understand. I was enjoying you being home. What about your birthday? We can go out for lunch."

Guilt assaults me for leaving them, but I shake my head at Mom.

"You know I don't celebrate it. I'm still going to visit you. What time did you want me at the vigil?"

She sighs. "You should celebrate today. It's still your birthday."

I briefly shake my head at her and wait for her to answer.

"It starts at 7:00 p.m., but I'd appreciate it if you could

come early in case members of the community want to talk to us."

I nod, knowing it's only two days away. "I'll be there, but I'll talk to you before then."

THE JOURNEY WITH KNOX IS SILENT. WE TRAVEL THROUGH Crown Village, then toward the national park. When we meet a dirt road, I turn to him. "Do you have your own house out here?"

He briefly glances at me. "No."

I shift in the seat. "Where will I be staying?"

"With me."

An unsettling feeling twists my gut. "So I don't have my own room?"

"No."

I rub the side of my face. I was in such a rush to leave; I should have followed him in my car or got a hotel.

When we reach a gate, Knox puts in a code and it slowly opens. We travel up the gravel driveway until we reach what I presume is the clubhouse. I'm pleasantly surprised. I was expecting some rundown shack, but it's far from it. It's a modern two-story farmhouse in a mix of wood and stone.

He pulls into a shed and parks beside a van, but it's the line of motorcycles that draws my eyes in. Knox turns off the truck, gets out, and goes toward the back of the truck. I open the door and jump down. Knox meets me at my side with my luggage in his hand.

I follow him past the motorcycles, where there's a man leaning over, working on one. When he sees me, he stands and beams a bright smile.

"Axle, not now." Knox clips out to him before the man

speaks. He's handsome, with brown hair and a short beard. He mockingly zips his mouth shut, but when Knox turns his back, the man whispers, "Hello," when I walk past him.

Because of his friendly and playful attitude, I can't help but smile at him.

I hurry to catch up with Knox, and when we walk inside, a tall, solid man meets us by the front door.

"I need to organize a church meeting," Knox says to him.

The large man's eyes lock on me. He scans my face and puts out his hand. "The name's Reaper."

Odd name. I'm guessing it's an MC thing. I place my hand in his. "Zara."

"I know who you are."

My head turns in Knox's direction, and I lift an eyebrow. I'm curious what exactly he has told him.

His eyes return to Knox. "We can have church now if you want?"

Knox's eyes flick to me and then back to Reaper. "Yeah . . . now."

Reaper pushes the door open. "Axle, church!"

"Coming!" the friendly man calls out.

"Help me find the men. Ava and Elena are inside if you want to introduce them to Zara."

"This way," Knox says to me, and I follow him through the house. "Church," he barks when we pass by the living area. His tone makes me jump.

I sense everyone's eyes on me. I'm used to dealing with a range of people within the community, so I smile and give everyone a small wave. A good-looking man struts toward us with a grin, but Knox stands between us. "Viper. Don't start your shit! It's time for church."

Another strange name.

His friend laughs, his eyes full of mischief. He's got a

manicured beard and short hair on the sides of his head, with longer hair on top.

"Why are you going to church?" I ask them. It didn't do much for me. The one thing I prayed for—I begged for—was to bring Misty home, and that never happened.

Viper bursts out laughing. "It's not that type of church." Knox turns his body toward me, giving me an odd stare.

"Is there another type?" I ask them.

"Club meetings, darl," Viper replies.

Knox's head jerks to Viper, his eyes cold.

Viper steps back with raised hands. "Woah! Warning received."

Warning?

"Ava," Reaper calls out as he walks toward us. When I look at him, he's waving at a woman in the kitchen. She puts down the tea towel and walks out. She's attractive, with long red hair, and a curvy body.

"This is Zara, Bomber's . . ."

"Ol' lady," Knox answers.

Interesting. I'm not sure what that means.

The woman's eyes widen and she gives me a smile. She looks up at the men. "You all go to church," she says, brushing them away with her hand. "Us women will be fine." I don't know what I was expecting, but it wasn't her.

"I'll meet you in there," Knox says. "I'll put Zara's suitcase in my room first."

Knox turns to me. "I won't be long." He studies me, and I give him a sharp nod to reassure him I'll be okay.

As Knox leaves, the woman steps toward me. "My name's Ava. Are you hungry? Would you like some breakfast?"

I cringe. My stomach is still queasy from this morning. I won't be eating for a while. "No, I'm okay."

She stares at me. "Are you sure? It won't be a problem. I'd be happy to get you something."

"I haven't had the best morning, so I'm not hungry, but I appreciate the offer."

She frowns. "You remind me of me when I first came here. It's overwhelming, but most people were kind and welcoming."

I don't miss the *most*, part.

"Would you like a drink, then?"

I could do with a stiff drink. "I don't drink very often, but it's my birthday, so I'll say yes to alcohol."

Her hand covers her mouth. "It's your birthday? What are your plans?"

I shake my head. "Nothing, and please don't go out of your way for me." But I can see the thrill of excitement all over her face.

"But I must. Let me bake you a cake?"

"No, thanks. I don't celebrate my birthday."

"Are you making a cake?" I hear another woman say.

I shift my attention to her; she is petite, with long blond hair. When she notices me, her eyes widen, then narrow. She looks at her friend.

Ava gives her a smile. "This is Zara, Bomber's ol' lady," Ava says.

The woman's face instantly softens. "Hi, I'm Elena"—she tilts her head at her friend—"Ava's sister and Axle's ol' lady."

She's with the friendly man outside . . . Okay, got it. I look from one to the other. "What does ol' lady mean?"

Elena giggles. "Wife or partner."

I flinch. "I am not Knox's ol' lady." We are not together.

Elena looks at her sister, and Ava frowns. There's an awkward, lingering silence.

"Where can I get that drink?" I ask.

"So sorry, I'll get that for you now. Come to the bar," says Ava.

I follow the two women, who whisper between themselves.

"I needed drinks early in my stay too," Ava says in passing as she goes behind the wooden bar. I sit on the stool next to Elena. "What will it be?"

I think of Misty and her favorite drink. "A shot of whiskey, please."

"Coming right up." Ava pulls out a shot glass, and I watch as she fills it.

"Is that Crown Village whiskey?" I ask her, glancing at the familiar white-and-black label.

After pouring the liquor, Ava lifts the bottle upright and tilts her head, looking at the label. "It is. You must know your whiskey."

"No, I know Crown Village whiskey. It was my sister's favorite, and it's owned by Knox's cousin, Lawson."

Ava passes me the shot. As I pick it up, it spills down the glass and onto the bar. I lift it to my mouth and toss the shot down, feeling the burn. After I swallow, I wince.

"Was?" Elena asks. "Does your sister have a new favorite one now?"

Elena's question makes me flinch. "No . . . umm." I rub my throat again, feeling it tighten. "My sister went missing ten years ago," I clarify. "That's why I'm staying here. It was too much at my parents' house where we grew up."

They gasp. "I'm so sorry," Ava says with genuine sadness in her tone.

"We had no idea," Elena says. "I had heard about it, but I never knew it was someone close to Bomber. God, I opened my big mouth. I wish Axle would have told me."

"Knox is a quiet person. I doubt he wanted anyone to know."

Elena looks deep in thought, then her lips curve. She points at me. "You're the reason he smiled. I heard Axle and

Viper talking about it. They mentioned a woman, but now I know it's you."

"Uh, okay."

There goes that smile being mentioned again.

"Can I ask you a question?" Elena asks.

"Okay," I answer reluctantly, unsure where this question will lead.

"Bomber is so umm"—she looks up, then cringes as if considering her choice of words—"reserved, and if you don't mind me saying . . . a little cold. How do you deal with that?"

"I haven't spoken to him in over eight years, so there's not much I can tell you. I have spent little time with him too, but everything about him seems amplified."

Elena leans in closer. "Please, keep going. We know nothing about him."

I clasp my knees tightly together. I don't even know where to start.

"Another shot?" Ava asks.

"Two please."

She gets to work pouring them for me. "I think I had five or six shots my second night here." She places the shots in front of me and leans in. "Just make sure if you have to go to the bathroom, you go back into the right room," she says with a wince.

That makes me smile. "Where did you end up going?"

"I accidentally ended up in Reaper's bedroom. But it worked out for the best, I guess."

Elena raises her brow. "But was it an accident?" Her voice was filled with amusement and suspicion.

Ava's mouth opens wide, her hand on her heart. "It certainly was."

"I don't know about that," Elena says in a mocking tone.

"Knox has already told me I'm sleeping in his room. Is there a spare room?" I ask them.

"Yes, there is for guests," Ava answers.

"Bomber doesn't seem like the type to negotiate," Elena chimes in.

I down one drink and place the glass on the bar, then the next. The burn is ferocious. I swallow a few times to ensure I don't bring it back up.

"He never argued with me," I point out, thinking back to when we were younger. "He had a soft spot for me and was fiercely loyal and caring." *Which only increased after Misty's disappearance.*

"Bomber is protective of the club. If he called you his ol' lady, he's going to be even more protective of you, so I can't see him letting you sleep anywhere but with him. There's plenty of single men here, and without a property patch, anyone can hook up with you."

My stomach drops. "I didn't realize. I guess I am staying with him, then."

I have mixed feelings about that.

"So what do you do?" Ava asks.

"I work in a women and children's shelter."

Ava inhales sharply. A flash of terror widens her eyes. Elena peers at her and frowns.

My eyes dart between the two of them. "Is everything okay?"

Ava's body slouches, tears lining her eyes. I stand and lean over, putting my hand on her arm. "What's wrong?"

"I got out of a DV relationship last year. It was a nightmare."

I gently squeeze her arm, giving her a sad smile. "I can contact my boss and see what resources are available here for you at Crown Village."

"Thank you, but no need. I'm feeling better and I'm healing. It's been a slow process."

"Before I leave, make sure you take my number down, in case you change your mind."

Ava smiles. "There needs to be more people like you in the world. Even though I'm enjoying my chef course, I'd love to do something meaningful like that."

My heart clenches. "From what I recall, there's no shelter here, but there might be one in the surrounding towns. You could call them, see if they need any help."

She stands straighter. "Excellent idea. I'm going to do that."

"Count me in," Elena says.

The women are friendly.

"I'm sure they need all the help they can get."

My gaze goes to the living room.

"Who are the other women, sitting on the couches?"

"Sweet butts," Elena answers. "They cook and help out for a roof over their head and food and . . ." She drops her gaze to the ground, then looks back up at me. "I'd say they are mostly here for the sex, though."

Ouch! Another blade to the heart.

They must see the look on my face because Elena is quick to say, "You have nothing to worry about. Bomber never slept with any of them."

My shoulders fall as the tension dissipates.

Ava asks, "The vigil is in two days, isn't it? Reaper mentioned it."

"That's right."

"Would you like some company, or we can help somehow?"

I smile at their kindness. They don't even know me. "Thank you so much. My mom would appreciate the help. Can I have two more shots, please?"

Ava grabs the two shot glasses and brings them down to the bar, filling them once more.

I'm gulping the last one when I hear a door open, followed by footsteps. I sense his presence. The familiar prick of awareness travels up my arms and makes me shudder. I turn so suddenly to look for him that the chair wobbles. I gasp as two muscular arms come around to steady me.

Knox checks me to ensure I'm okay. I say nothing.

"What happened to her?" Knox asks Ava and Elena, concerned. His voice is tinged with anger.

The women go quiet, and I turn more carefully this time. "I needed a drink."

His posture is rigid. "Can you come upstairs so we can talk?"

"I can do that." I scoot off the chair. My head spins.

His arm comes around my back, and he pulls me to his side. We walk slowly toward the stairs as he helps support my weight.

"Lovely women you've got here."

He doesn't reply. He is solely focused on helping me walk, and he glances at my face every so often. We slowly make our way up the stairs and down the hallway into what I presume is his bedroom, where my suitcase has been placed by the bed.

The room is white, except for one black wall where his enormous bed is against.

Aside from a chest of drawers and a wardrobe, there's nothing in here. Very clinical, with no personal touches other than a large painting above his bed. It has a creamy, textured background. The center of the artwork is an image of a butterfly. It looks so real, as though it could fly out of the painting. Its wings are a stunning shade of blue.

My eyes fall back to his bed and its black comforter and two pillows. I can't help but wonder how many women have stayed here. How many women have had him inside of them? I let out a weighted sigh and step to his bed to sit.

When I look at him, his eyebrows are set in a V. "What's wrong?" he asks.

"Everything's all right." I haven't seen him in years. What he did during that time is none of my business. "Is there something you wanted to talk about?"

"I've spoken to the men, and you can stay here."

"Thank you."

I was unaware he had to ask them. I presumed I could stay, but my body slumps in relief.

He sits beside me and the bed dips. "Happy birthday."

"Thank you. I think Ava wants to organize something. Please reassure her that I don't want to celebrate it."

"I can do that."

I lean down, take my sandals off, then scoot back on the bed to lie down. His pillow smells like him. I clear my throat as emotions threaten to drown me. I feel his eyes on me. I peek up to see him watching me.

Knox takes out his gun, which surprises me, though I guess I should have known he would be armed being in an MC. He places it on the nightstand. His belt and holster are next. He lies beside me, on his side.

"What's sergeant at arms mean?" I ask.

"I'm responsible for the safety and security of the club."

"Okay . . . well, why is your nickname Bomber?"

"Everyone has road names. I was in the military with Reaper and Viper. My specialty was disarming live explosives."

Shock and disbelief widen my eyes. I bite down, my jaw clenching. "After everything we've all been through . . ." I shake my head in disappointment. "You'd risk your life? Make us go through that pain all over again?" My voice cracks as tears fall. I roll over onto my side, turning my back to him.

He shuffles in closer until I feel his body flush against

mine, and his arm comes over me. His warmth consumes me. I allow him to hold me, even though he is the one who upset me.

"Every person in my life who I was close to was suffering. I joined the military because I wanted to do something worthwhile, so I could be proud of something in my life because I felt like I was a failure from not being able to help you or Kane.

"When I came home during my vacation, I spied on you and saw you doing better . . . much better without me. Kane wasn't drinking as much either. He put all his energy into helping Dad with the casino. I thought it wouldn't matter as much if I did specialize in something dangerous. I wasn't going to have much of an impact if I died compared to someone else with a big family or a wife and children."

I turn in his arms and a sob breaks through. Tears flood my face. "How could you?" Pain echoes in my voice. "I wouldn't survive losing you too . . ."

He leans over and places a lingering tender kiss on my temple. "Shh . . . I'm still here with you."

After my tears dry, I speak. "It's been hard without you and Misty."

He squeezes me tighter. "It's been hard without you too."

His voice throbs with emotion.

"I still listen to Misty's voicemail. I taped it. What I would give to hear her laugh again or listen to her being feisty with Kane."

There's a brief silence before he speaks.

"I tried . . . My mom had a private investigator. Kane and I called every place we could think of that Misty visited."

I release my breath. "I know . . . everyone tried."

He nuzzles his nose into my hair and into my neck. My eyes get heavy, and I drift off.

I wake up, blinking in a dark room, to see my phone ringing. Knox's arm is still firmly around me. I stretch over to the side table, grasp the device, look at the screen, and bring it to my ear.

"Hello."

"Hey, I was calling to check up on you. How are you feeling?"

"I'm okay. Sorry, Mom, I didn't mean to upset you. I wish I could have stayed with you and Dad, but it all became too much."

"We understand. There's no need for an apology. How have you settled in there?"

"The club said I could stay for as long as I need to. I've met some women here, and they've been warm and welcoming. They offered to help at the vigil as well."

She sniffles through the phone. "That's so very kind of them, and it's a relief that you are okay with staying there. I wasn't sure how you would do, but they sound like a good bunch of people."

"They are. What time did you want me at the vigil again?"

"I'd like you to be there an hour early to ensure everything is prepared."

I pause. "I'll meet you there at six, then."

"Great. Well, I'll let you go. If you need anything, I'm a phone call away."

"Thanks, Mom. Bye."

"How's your mom?" Knox asks, his voice thick with sleep.

"I think she was worried about me." I grab his arm and place it on him so I can sit up and shuffle my back against the wall.

He abruptly sits up, then puts his legs over the bed, turning his back to me.

It stings, but it's for the best. There's so much going on, I can't handle any more.

Someone knocks on the door.

"Dinner is ready," Ava says.

My stomach grumbles.

"Thank you," I call out.

I move toward Knox, put my feet over the edge of the bed, and stand. "Are you coming down?"

He stands beside me, his face emotionless. He puts his arm out, signaling for me to walk out. We move down the hallway and then the stairs. Knox is close behind me. All the members of the MC and the women are sitting at a gigantic wooden table, with Reaper at the head of it.

As I move toward them, Knox is by my side. "Sit beside Elena."

There are two spare seats between Ava and Elena, so I stride to them. Knox pulls out my chair and I sit, and he sits beside me. I glance at Ava, then Elena, and they smile back at me.

After looking at my empty plate, I look at the tacos, large plates with ground beef, and bowls with slices of tomato, lettuce, and avocado on the table. Smaller bowls hold shredded cheese and sour cream. Everyone is helping themselves, so I stand, lean over, and pick up two taco shells, then sit after filling them.

I feel Knox's eyes on me every so often. When I finish, I grab a napkin and wipe my face, then glance at Knox. He stares back but says nothing.

"Would you like me to introduce Zara to everyone?" Reaper asks Knox.

Knox's eyes don't leave mine. "Are you okay with that?"

"Yes. I'd like to meet your friends."

Reaper's gaze returns to the table. "Excuse me." His deep, loud voice carries over the table, and all conversations stop. "I'd like to introduce Zara to everyone."

I lean forward to see everyone's faces. "Well, you know Ava and Elena. Then beside Elena is Axle, who is the road captain." Axle gives me one of his playful smiles.

"Beside Axle is Demon, the enforcer, then Cash, the treasurer."

Demon is covered in tattoos that peek out of his shirt, with both arms and his neck covered.

"Hey," Cash replies. He has short black hair and is leaning back in his seat in a laid-back manner.

"Then it's Rage, a patched member." The youngest man gives me a sincere smile.

"Twitch is head of IT security." The man has wavy brown hair, an ear piercing, and a sprinkle of stubble. He gives me a small wave.

"And Viper is our VP." Viper tips his head, then winks at me.

When I glance back at Bomber, he's glowering at Viper.

I look around the table once more. "Thank you for allowing me to stay in your home"—my eyes land on Ava—"and for your hospitality."

She blushes. "You're welcome."

After dinner, the conversation flows effortlessly. I listen intently to the people around me. Ava and Elena stand and grab other people's plates, piling them on top of theirs, and walk toward the kitchen.

They come back and Elena grabs mine.

"Would you like any help?" I offer.

"No, you stay seated. It's your birthday."

I watch as they and the other women collect everyone's plates and leftover food.

They then bring out bowls and spoons. I wonder if I can fit

in the dessert, but I guess it depends on what it is. Ava walks out with a big smile and a gigantic cake on a tray with one pink candle. As she walks to me, my chest warms and I blink back tears.

The cake is white, with icing swirls around the top edges and multicolored sprinkles on top. I lean to the side, allowing space so that Ava can place the cake in front of me. "You didn't have to do this."

"I wanted to," she says through a smile.

After the women sit, Ava sings happy birthday, and everyone joins in. I stare at the cake, and once everyone finishes singing, I blow out the candle, then close my eyes.

I wish to find out what happened to Misty.

BEST
FRIENDS

ELEVEN
EMOTIONAL ROLLER COASTER

Zara

AFTER DESSERT, I DECIDE TO HAVE AN EARLY NIGHT. KNOX LEADS, and I follow him into his room. There's an awkward tension between us. I kneel, open the zipper of my suitcase, and flip the lid open. I move my clothes aside until I uncover my silk summer pajamas, which are a set of singlet and shorts. I cringe, wishing I had packed something that covers more skin.

I stand and turn to him. "Where can I get changed?"

His face is emotionless. "In here." He turns his back to me, giving me privacy.

I grab my dress, lift it over my head, and throw it on my suitcase, followed by my bra. Then I slip on the singlet and step into the small shorts.

"I'm finished."

He turns, and his eyes drag the length of my body. When I look down, my nipples are erect against the silk material. I cross my arms. His gaze lowers and lingers. When I look down, I see that he's staring at the scars on my thigh. He frowns, so I hastily step to the bed, fold the comforter down, and shuffle under the covers.

The nine marks underneath my tattoo represent so much. They're a reminder of each year I've been robbed of seeing my best friend.

Knox walks toward a wardrobe, opens it, and grabs another War Brothers MC sweatshirt off the coat hanger before throwing it on the end of the bed. "If you're going to wear *only* that"—his eyes dart to my chest—"you're not leaving this room without my sweatshirt on."

I press my lips in a firm line, trying not to smile at his overprotectiveness.

He lifts a brow. "Are you going to answer me?"

"Yes, I'll wear the sweatshirt when I leave the room."

His shoulders fall an inch. He puts his gun into another holster on the side table. He lifts the fitted shirt over his head, and I bite down on my lip. My eyes wander over his muscles, but when I notice the scars that litter his body, my heart feels heavy that he was injured. I look away, not wanting to draw attention to them or make him feel uncomfortable—though, even with the scars, he's gorgeous. They align with his now hardened personality. He radiates masculinity, and all I want to do is go over every mark on him. We wear scars of painful pasts, but it's the internal ones nobody sees that hurt the most.

He steps to the other side of the bed and gets in beside me. I'm lucky the bed is large enough so that we have space between us. As much as I want him, my heart can't handle being cracked open again.

I roll over onto my side to look at him. "Can you ask if Kane will meet us earlier at the amusement park?"

"What time?"

"About five. Because I haven't been back in so long, it

would be nice to spend some time together with just us. I thought going on the rides and eating the food we used to would be a positive way to spend the afternoon because the vigil will be . . ."

Something passes between us. He nods, like he understands without me having to explain how hard the vigil will be.

"Kane will like that." He pauses. "He may joke around and not show it, but he's very much still in pain."

A heavy weight engulfs my body. "Since I've been gone, have you found out anything else about her case?"

"No." A bite seeps through his tone.

"Do you think she left or . . ." I can't bring myself to say the other option.

He looks away, deep in thought. "I can't answer that because, when looking at the facts, nothing makes sense."

I was in denial for a long time. I wasn't interested in the facts because I was in too much pain, and all I cared about was when and if she was going to return.

"Do you remember what happened to her real birth parents?"

"The police interviewed them. They didn't know where she was living, and they had a strong alibi. Everyone else was interviewed and cleared."

What else . . . What am I missing?

"What about her phone?"

"The police wouldn't share the information, but Mom has police officers on her payroll, and she said they told her it showed up nothing."

Frustration builds up inside of me. "What about Iris? Have you seen her around? Mom said she's going to be at the vigil."

He shakes his head. "No."

Even with everything, there's a sliver of hope inside of me

to find something out about Misty's disappearance while I'm home.

"I want to have a chat with Iris—since she was the last one to see Misty. Hopefully, Mom can give me Iris's phone number."

"I'm going to be looking into Misty's case as well," says Knox with a determined look in his eyes.

We are desperate for answers . . . clinging to finding even a snippet of information that we don't already know.

"Can I ask you a question?"

"Yeah, okay . . ." he replies slowly.

"What are your scars from?" There's no judgment, just sadness.

"It's shrapnel wounds from a bomb that exploded."

I nod and swallow thickly. I turn and roll over before I do something stupid like touch him or kiss him. "Good night," I say as I shuffle toward the edge of the bed.

A SLOW, SLEEPY SMILE SPREADS ACROSS MY FACE AS KNOX PLAYS with my hair. I press my lips together, trying not to moan. I sit up next to him and let my eyes travel down his body. Even though my lids are heavy with sleep, my gaze remains on his scars. I reach out and touch his muscular shoulder. His skin's warm as I trace a round, silky scar.

His eyes are closed, and his breaths quicken as my fingers travel from the scar on his shoulder and make their way over the hard planes of his chest. His body shudders as I move down to the top of his abs, where I trace a jagged scar.

My fingernails dig in as they graze over each ab until they reach a light trail of hair that starts from his belly button. I follow it further down to his boxer shorts. When my fingers creep in at the top, stretching the material, he grabs my wrist and stares at me intently.

"Are you sure you want this?"

I blink a few times, then whip my hand away and shuffle backward until my back meets the headboard. "I'm sorry."

Even in my sleepy state, I crave him. His deep frown slices my heart. My cheeks heat as my stomach sinks.

"I'm sorry," I repeat.

He bows his head, then stands and opens the wardrobe. He grabs a pair of dark-blue denim jeans and a white shirt and walks out of the room. I'm left sitting there, rubbing my chest where it aches. I hate seeing the anguish on his face, the tension in his body. I'm doing exactly what I used to do. I'm hurting him *again* just by being here.

I'm being pulled in two directions, one part lust, the other wariness. I want him to hold me . . . The other part of me is terrified that I'm opening myself up to heartbreak, and I can't go back to that dark place . . . not again. There's a light knock on the door, so I hastily wipe my eyes, then pull the comforter up to my shoulders. "Come in."

No one comes in, but I hear a soft voice. "I don't want to intrude. I wanted to let you know breakfast is ready."

A small smile touches my lips. "Thank you, Ava."

"It's pancakes." Her voice brightens, like she's trying to convince me with food to come down.

I sigh, knowing Knox will have a meltdown if I wear my pajamas. I shuffle toward the edge, then stand and slide into Knox's sweatshirt. I go to the door and open it. Ava smiles at me and claps twice.

"Where are you going?" Knox's voice carries through the hallway, startling Ava and me.

I turn to him and narrow my eyes. He never used to be this abrupt.

"I'm going downstairs for breakfast."

"I'll come down with you."

Shifting back to Ava, I say, "Sorry."

She tries to smile at me, but it looks forced. "It's okay. Breakfast is outside this morning."

When she leaves, I stare at Knox, and my eyes trail over him. His fitted white shirt shows off his broad shoulders and defined chest. I lick my dry lips. As he breezes past me, I'm hit with his cologne. A fresh, clean, masculine cedarwood scent. When he comes out of his room, he has his leather motorcycle vest on.

My hands move on their own accord to his vest, and I feel the leather texture between my fingers. "What's this called?"

"A cut."

My fingers rise to the top patch. "One percent, what does that mean?"

"Outlaws."

I drop my hand as a breath rushes from my mouth. He doesn't want to talk to me but doesn't want me out of his sight either.

"I'm going to breakfast," I say curtly.

He says nothing but follows me. I go down the stairs. The music is pumping, and when I hear the vocals of the song, I know it's Linkin Park.

I trail through the house. As I open the back door, people are seated around a large table. Cash and Demon are leaning against the back of the house, smoking.

Viper yells out the lyrics of the chorus, while a very large rottweiler howls.

"Even the dog is telling you to shut up," Reaper says.

There's an array of deep chuckles.

Viper stops singing and laughs. "He's singing *with* me." He bends down and grabs either side of the dog's face. "Aren't you?"

Ava turns to Reaper. "Honey, we have been through this. His name is Conan."

The dog sneezes on Viper. "Really, Conan?" He wipes his face.

I laugh at them, then all eyes land on us, so I give everyone a warm smile. When I get to the table, Ava stands. "You stay seated and finish your breakfast," I tell her while looking from her eyes to her plate.

She has one and a half pancakes left. Her lips press together, like she wants to disagree with me but doesn't say it. She's too kind.

Rage stands. "Here, you can take my seat."

"Thanks, Rage," Knox answers before I can.

Rage lifts his legs over the wooden seats.

"Oh, look at you, Mr. Gentleman," Axle says in a mocking tone.

Rage gives him the finger. Axle laughs.

Elena clears her throat. She waits, then shakes Axle's shoulder. He looks at her. "What?"

She gives Knox a pointed look, then peers back at him.

He shrugs, his head tilting. "What? Speak, woman!"

Elena lets out a long groan. "Can you move so Bomber can sit next to Zara and they can have their breakfast?"

"Ohhh," he glances at us, then stands and moves aside.

Once we reach the table, I sit, but before Knox can, Axle grasps his arm. "I kept the seat nice and warm for you," he says with a cheeky wink at the end.

Knox shakes his head at him.

"Be happy, man. Your woman is here," Axle says with a smile.

An awkward tension fills the air. Elena whacks her forehead with her palm.

Axle's eyes dart between everyone. "Well . . ." He scratches the back of his neck.

"Don't worry about it." My tone is soft. I make eye contact with Axle, and he blows out a gush of air. I don't want to make anyone feel uncomfortable when I'm the one staying in their home.

When Knox sits, his eyes latch onto mine, then they wander around my face. I give him a reassuring smile.

"There are chocolate pancakes on the first plate, blueberry and vanilla on the second plate, and banana on the third," Ava says.

"Ava's pancakes are the bomb!" Twitch says from across the table.

I grab a banana pancake, place it on my plate, and pick up the honey, drizzling it on top.

When I'm finished eating, I leave my fork and knife next to my plate. Hands come out, and it's Knox placing another pancake on my plate.

I shake my head. "No, no."

His jaw ticks. "Please." His voice is rough, but his brows are furrowed. He leans in close to me. "You need to eat."

My shoulders fall. "One more. That's it."

The tension drains from his face.

"Did you say please?" Viper asks. "I bet that tasted like acid coming from your mouth."

Knox tsks back at him.

Once finished, I stand to help the women. Knox stands with me. "I'm helping them take the cutlery and plates inside," I tell him. Viper gets up and steps to Knox, grabs his shoulders, and pushes him until he is seated.

"Thank you," I whisper to Viper.

Viper shakes Knox's shoulders again. "You need to loosen up."

I feel Knox's eyes on me as I make my way to the back door. Cash moves, opening it for me, as my hands are full. "Thanks," I mutter.

"You need some weed to chill the fuck out," says Demon.

Knox never touched drugs when I was with him, but that very well could have changed. I don't dare look back but go inside and to the kitchen. A young woman with blond hair makes her way to me with a wide smile. "Hi, I'm Candy."

I smile back. "I'm Zara. Nice to meet you."

She fidgets. "I can't believe Bomber has an ol' lady. So many women over the years have tried to hook up with him." I flinch. "He always said no, so you must be special."

"I, ahh . . ." I don't know what to say to that, so I plaster on another smile.

"Just, so you know . . . I'm with Viper."

"No, you're not," another woman calls out, then approaches us. Her shiny lips mash together.

"I nearly am," Candy responds, confidence evident in her voice.

The woman's head falls back as she laughs. Then she peers at me. "My name's Mercedez."

She's petite, like Candy, but with brown hair and a full face of glamorous makeup on.

"Hi, nice to meet you too."

Mercedez pivots on the spot and points. "That's Trixie." The woman's hands are in the sink, but she looks my way and gives me a small smile. Trixie is wearing a blue tank top that showcases the sleeve of tattoos on her left arm. She has denim short shorts on, and she has long black hair that hangs down her back.

"And that's Dolly." A smile stretches across the young woman's face. She walks to me and wraps her arms around me, so I hug her back. She's wearing a similar shirt and shorts as Trixie but has short light-pink hair in two pigtails.

"I'm bi," she says with a wicked glint in her eyes.

I chuckle. "Sorry, I'm straight." I have no judgment, it's just that I'm one hundred percent straight.

Her face scrunches. "Dang it!" She playfully bangs her hand.

"Do you need any help in here?" I ask.

"No, we're good," Trixie replies.

Elena puts the sauces in the pantry, and Ava adds more plates, knives, and forks to the pile.

I sit at the kitchen island. Axle comes out, walks toward Elena, and gives her a kiss on the cheek. "Babe, you need to communicate with me. As much as you wish I could . . . I can't read your mind."

"Babe"—she uses the same tone of voice as he did—"I don't know how many subtle hints I can give you. Maybe it's *you* who needs to learn facial expressions and body language cues."

Axle pauses and looks up, as if thinking about her comment. "Nah . . . You know I'm shit at that, so *you* will just have to tell me."

Elena subtly rolls her eyes.

Axle's eyes narrow a fraction at her. "I saw that," he says playfully. When he sees me, he steps closer. "Bomber's real intense with you."

Viper walks through the door, takes one look at us, and struts over. Elena moves closer to us as well. "Yes, he's full on . . ." Elena adds. "I had an inkling he would be protective, but he has taken it to the next level."

My body warms and I blush. "It's Knox. He's always been overprotective. He means well, though."

Axle briefly peers down. "Oh, no, it's more than that . . . He's wound up so tight over you."

"What do you mean?" I ask Axle.

"We've seen him riled up before, but with you . . ." Viper lets out a whistle then leans forward, places his hand on mine, and lowers his voice. "All I'm saying is tread carefully," he says.

"What . . . the . . . fuck . . ." A deep voice comes from the doorway.

I sit up straighter in my chair, my eyes dart to Knox. There's weight of tension in the air. A muscle tics along Knox's jawline as he glares at Viper's hand resting on mine.

Viper is the only one who isn't fazed by Knox's reaction. He lifts his hand with an easygoing expression. "We were just talking," he says in a calm but firm voice.

Viper leans into Knox, who has turned to stone, and whispers in his ear. Whatever he said seemed to work, as Viper pats him on the back and walks away. Knox's shoulders fall, his expression softening.

I walk to Knox and take his hand in mine. I tug him through the living room and out the front door, onto the porch. "Why are you so upset?"

"I don't want anyone touching you."

I can understand how that may have come across with his friend's hand over mine and the closeness between us as he leaned in to warn me about Knox, but it's not like Knox has seemed interested.

"You don't want to talk to me . . . touch me . . . if I mean so little to you, why—"

His lips are on mine, silencing me. They are soft and greedy. His tongue taking advantage, delving in deep and aggressively. I still at first, then wrap my arms around his neck, kissing him back, jerking him closer. My heart beats too fast. A moan escapes me in pure desperation. The kiss heightens sensual parts of me.

He demands possession with every sweep and twist of his tongue. His fingers dig into my hips. His other hand is on the side of my neck as his thumb caresses my throat. I raise my hand and run my fingers through his hair, then begin tugging, which grants me a drawn-out groan.

His hands wander, then squeeze my ass. A shiver travels

down my spine as I feel the rigid outline of his cock through his jeans. He swivels his hips into mine, slowly dragging it across my clit, which makes the ache turn into throbbing between my legs.

The passionate kiss lingers on. Both of us are scared of ending it. He sucks on my bottom lip before pulling away, and every inch of my body hurts without his lips on mine.

His gaze is heavy lidded. He cups my face with one hand. "I will always want to touch you," he says as he squeezes my behind with his other hand. "Kiss you." He leans in, pressing a hard kiss on my lips before pulling away. "Zara . . ." he says in a breathy plea. "You are my fucking air . . . I'm dead without you."

BEST
FRIENDS

TWELVE
BATTLE SCARS

Zara

Peering out the window, I see the sun's coming up. I've been awake most of the night, frozen in Knox's bed. I'm my own worst enemy—I get stuck in my mind, dwelling on memories of Misty. It eats me alive to know I still have no answers.

It's ten years today since Misty's disappearance, and no matter how busy I am or what I'm doing on her anniversary, I can't get away from the darkness that torments me. Some days, it feels like yesterday that she was here. Others feel like a lifetime ago.

I pull out my phone and go to Misty's name in my contacts and press on the message icon. I slide my finger up, looking at the unread texts I've written to her over the years. I start typing.

Misty

Hey bestie, Ten years since you've been gone, and it pains me to not see you. I miss your jokes and the way you made me laugh all the time. Every day you made me smile, and at the time I didn't realize how lucky I was to have you in my life. I wish you could see the work I've done at the shelter. I think you would be proud. Mom and Dad are happier now that Dad retired. I didn't think they would ever recover from not having you in their lives, but they are, like the rest of us. We are slowly learning, over the years, how to live our lives without you in it. I think I'm finally coming to the realization that, for whatever reason, you're not going to return to us. I just wish I knew why. I'm back in Crown Village to help with your vigil, though the hope of you returning is small. Mom's never given up. It's days like today that I miss your advice about how to handle Knox. As much as he tore my heart out, I still love him, but after everything, I don't think I could handle another heartbreak. I'm trying to keep my distance, but so far, I'm failing miserably. Wherever you are, please know that I'll never forget the friendship we shared, and no matter how much time passes, you're always in my mind and in my heart. *Best friends forever, Zara xxx*

Tears stream down my face. I give myself permission on this day to feel everything—the loss, the pain, the darkness but also the light of her memories. Slowly sitting up, I inch to the side of the bed, place my feet on the ground, and tread to my suitcase, where I take out my toiletry bag. I make my way to the door and open it. The slight creak of the door makes me curse. I look back to see Knox still asleep.

I walk into the bathroom, then lock it behind me. I zip open the toiletry bag and pick up the sharp object with my fingers. My throat tightens when I look down at the top of my thigh where Misty's tattoo is, along with nine neat scars underneath.

Her anniversary is the most painful and intense. The scars are punishment and reprieve. I wish I could find out what happened. I need answers so I can find peace.

My hands move to the silk-like scars on my leg and hover just below them. I rest my foot on the bathtub and lift my pajama shorts. Taking a deep breath, I push the blade into my skin, wincing at the sharp, piercing pain. I drag the blade in line with the other scars and watch the blood trickle down my leg, leaving crimson drops on the floor.

On the most painful day of the year, the cutting helps with the pain in my chest. Tension releases, almost as if the anger and emotional pain are bleeding out of the cut.

Even though the scars heal on the outside, the wounds go so much deeper. Those are the scars that don't heal, and they never fade. I lean over, grab the large Band-Aid from the bag, and stick it over the cut. I wipe my leg and begin cleaning up.

"Zara!" Knox yells.

I pull my shorts down on my hips to hide what I've just done, but it doesn't hide as much as I would like.

"Zara!"

I zip up the bag, unlock the door, and rush out. "I'm here."

Reaper and Viper's heads are poking out of their bedroom doors. Viper smirks when he sees me. Knox's face instantly relaxes, and his shoulders visibly slump as he exhales deeply. He strides toward me.

"I needed the bathroom," I say quietly to not wake anyone up, though I think Knox just did.

Viper mumbles, "Knox, ya psycho. Go back to bed." He closes his bedroom door.

Reaper studies Knox and waits. Knox lifts his chin, then Reaper shuts his bedroom door.

Knox's eyes search mine. Then, like a light switch turned

on, he stares at my thigh. His muscles tense and a deep frown curves his lips. He pulls me into his arms, where I sag into him.

Knox tenderly kisses the top of my head and lingers before he pulls away. He lowers himself into a crouch and inspects the bandage. He clears his throat. "Let me know if you need another one," he says before he stands. There's no missing the sadness in his voice.

My belly growls loudly in the silence.

His eyes widen as he peers down at my stomach and then back to my face. "Come downstairs. I'll grab you something to eat."

"I'm not hungry." His gaze sharpens. I put up my hand in a stopping motion. "Please, I can't eat. I'll throw it up."

He rubs a hand through his thick black hair, concern apparent in his eyes.

So I negotiate, yet again. "One piece of toast."

"Thank you."

After breakfast, my phone pings with a new message.

Boss

Thinking of you today.

I stare blankly at the message. I never know how to act and how to reply.

Thank you.

Ava walks into the living room, yawning.

I cringe. "I hope we didn't wake you."

She jumps, then grabs her chest when she looks at us. "Sorry, I'm still half asleep . . . I usually get up around this time to get a start on breakfast." Her body stiffens and her lips curve into a deep frown as recognition dawns. She rushes to me, bends, and puts her arms around me in a big hug. "I'm so sorry, lovely."

I wrap my arms around her. "Thank you."

"If you need anything, I'm here."

She moves to the kitchen, and it isn't long until I hear sizzling and smell bacon.

The other women appear next, looking as tired as I feel. They make their way to Ava. I go to stand to help, but Knox grabs my hand and shakes his head. "Don't worry about it . . . not today."

The men file down the stairs, one after another. I gather the smell of food has gotten them swiftly into their seats. As the women bring the dishes out and lay them on the table, I'm amused by the looks on the men's faces. A mix of appreciation and hunger.

"Fuck yeah!" I peer up to see Axle and Elena walking in, hand in hand. "I'm starved. My woman kept me up all night." His lips twist into a naughty smile, while Elena's face goes red.

"Axle, I beg of you, no details," Ava pleads.

He jerks his head. "Yes, queen."

Reaper strides toward us and leans down to kiss Ava on the cheek. When he pulls back, his eyes dart around to everyone before they pause on Knox, then land on me. He gives me a sad smile. He doesn't have to say anything. The sympathy in his eyes is unmistakable.

Reaper leaves, going toward the back of the house. I listen to the chitchat around the table until I hear "Conan!" from outside.

I stand in curiosity. Ava and Elena rush out the back door, so I follow them to see Reaper chasing Conan around the backyard. Reaper is fast, but Conan's bolting at full speed with what I presume is Reaper's shirt in his mouth.

I laugh as Ava cackles and Elena is bent over in a fit of laughter. Knox is chuckling to himself. Axle and Viper are next, bursting from the back door. We watch as Reaper leaps off to the left, missing Conan by an inch.

"Go, Conan! Go, Conan!" Axle hollers next to me, waving his arm.

Reaper stops and throws his hands up. "I give up! That dog is a pest!"

When Reaper reaches us he's still breathless. Ava gently puts her hand on his back. "I'll get you another clean shirt."

His adoring gaze is a lovely sight. "That would be great. Thank you, beautiful." He kisses her cheek.

A bit of jealousy bubbles up inside of me. *I wish I had that with Knox.*

"That was fuckin' fantastic. Conan," Viper yells, "you never disappoint!"

Conan is still gripping the shirt in his mouth, and by the looks of it, he won't be giving it up anytime soon.

Axle elbows Reaper. "Maybe next time."

Reaper shakes his head at him. "I don't know what else to do. The dog hates me."

"He'll warm up to you soon," Ava coos as we all walk back inside.

"Ha! Highly doubtful," Axle replies.

Ava's eyes narrow at Axle. He shrugs. "What? It's true."

I smile at them. They remind me of the bickering and jokes from when I was young with Knox, Misty, and Kane.

AFTER MY SHOWER, I PUT ON LIGHT MAKEUP AND CONCEALER under my eyes to hide my restless night. I spend the day in the living room watching trashy TV that the women have put on. Anything for a distraction, but it's good chilling out, spending time with everyone.

"Who do you think the father is?" Candy asks.

"Her husband's best friend for sure," Twitch replies.

Mercedez is in his lap. She turns to him, nodding. "I think so too."

I watch the TV as another man walks onto the stage. The crowd gasps and cheers. The husband stands. He gestures at the man while looking at his wife. "Who the fuck is this guy?" The woman's hand flies to her mouth.

The presenter steps toward the new guy and leans over. "Why don't you tell him and the audience who you are?"

"I'm the guy she's been fucking for the last ten years."

The crowd cheers.

Rage's hands come up in disbelief.

The husband strides toward the man, his face full of anger, though two huge security guards dressed in black-collared shirts beat him to it and hold him back. "You asshole! I can't wait until I get my hands on you!"

I stand to get fresh air. Knox tugs at my wrist, so I peer down at him. "I'm going to go outside for a bit."

He holds eye contact and slowly nods.

I remember that there's a dog outside, so I move to Ava, who glances up at me.

"The dog's name is Conan, isn't it? Does he bite?" I ask.

"Yes, that's his name." Ava smiles. "No, he's fine with women."

"Why is that?" I ask softly, not wanting to cause too much of a distraction to the others watching the TV. "Is he aggressive toward men?"

"If he senses a threat, he will react. He's wary of men at the beginning, but after a while, he's fine."

"Thanks," I mutter.

I make my way through the house and step outside. Heat

from the sun meets my skin, instantly warming me. I look over at Conan, who has lifted his head and cocked his ears. When his eyes land on me, he wags his tail. As I walk toward him, he stands. I halt and allow him to come to me. He circles me, sniffing at my legs and feet. I put my hand out. He sniffs my hand, his nose cold against my skin. Then he licks me and nuzzles his head into me.

I pat him softly, but the more I pat him, the more he leans into me. I chuckle and step toward the table and chairs. "Come on. Over here, Conan." His tail wags faster, and he follows me. As I take a seat, he positions himself in front of me, leaning in seeking more affectionate touches.

The back door opens and Knox walks out, though I'm not surprised to see him. As he makes his way to me, Conan rolls over, so I bend and pat his belly up and down in long, slow strokes.

Knox sits next to me. "I've called Kane. He'll be here soon."

I sit up. When my focus shifts to Knox, Conan whines.

"How did Kane sound on the phone?"

Knox frowns and looks away. "Like himself, though I doubt he'll be able to fake tonight, which is probably why he didn't want the vigil to take place."

"I can't say I was too thrilled about the idea either, but if Mom needs it, I'll be there. Did Kane mention whether your mom was coming tonight?"

"She is, but she won't be staying long. Kane said she'll be leaving afterward."

I briefly shake my head, wishing she was staying longer. It will please Mom that Audrey is at least coming.

"What about your dad?"

"He wouldn't miss it."

There's another whine next to me. Conan lies on his belly, looking up at me with sad eyes, as if he has never had a pat in his life. Sympathy wells up inside of me, so I slide off the seat and sit cross-legged next to him on the ground and return to patting him.

"Spoiled dog."

I smile up at Knox. "He is a little needy."

Knox puffs. "A little?" he asks, with amusement in his tone.

Conan stands and leaves a long lick of slobber up my face. "Awe." He licks again, so I put my hands over my face and giggle, but the more he licks, the more I laugh.

"That's enough, Conan." Knox's voice is stern, so Conan stops and backs away.

Knox stands and bends down to offer me his hand. I place my hand in his and he helps me up. He kisses it above where the ring is that he gave me. "Let me hold you . . . support you . . . Let me be your person today. You can go back to hating me tomorrow."

I gasp, then pull out of his hold and stand on my toes, looping my arms around his neck. "I don't hate you," I whisper into his ear as his arms come around me, holding me firm against him.

He left an imprint on me when we were only kids. That has never lessened.

I faintly hear the back door close.

"Umm . . . Bomber."

I pull away from him.

We turn our attention to Twitch. He peers at the ground, then back at us. "Uh, sorry, but your brother's out the front, waiting."

Knox and I glance at each other. "I need to grab my bag and wash my face," I tell him. He nods. I wait until Twitch leaves to say, "You can be there today, and to be honest, I'd struggle without you." He was always my safe space.

Knox gives me a stiff nod, though I notice his shoulders

fall. He follows me inside and places his hand on my lower back, making me shiver. When I get to his room, I pick up my bag from the floor, go to the bathroom to wash my face, add a little more makeup, then make my way back to Knox, who hasn't moved from the bottom of the stairs.

"Are you ready?"

My heartbeat quickens. *No*, but I reply with, "Yes."

As we move through the house, Knox stops to talk to Reaper, but I keep walking out the front door.

Kane is leaning against the limousine. When our eyes meet, I see a flash of pain in his. Like Knox said, he puts on a front, but I can tell he feels the pain like I do.

We walk to each other. My vision blurs with tears as I step into his warm embrace. When we shared this day together, he and Knox made it bearable. Sometimes, sharing the pain with someone rather than internalizing it is comforting.

We step out of the hug and I brush my tears away.

"I'm glad you're back," Kane admits.

I clear my throat. "Me too."

He tilts his head toward the idling limousine. "Let's get going."

Kane opens the door and slides across the leather seat. The front door of the clubhouse opens and Knox walks out. With his eyes on us, he swiftly moves to the limousine. I shuffle over as he sits next to me and pulls the door shut.

Kane knocks on the glass panel between us and the driver, then the car moves forward. Apart from the gravel crunching under the tires, there's a heavy silence between us. My chest pounds with the relentless beating of my heart. I lift my hand to my necklace and drag the heart charm across the chain over and over again.

Knox places his hand on my leg. He squeezes it in support. I glance at Kane. He's frozen in place. His shoulders are hunched and he's peering out the window blankly.

Arriving at the amusement park makes my pulse spike. The car pulls up at the entrance, and I look up to see the familiar large clown face that covers the entryway. Knox opens the car door and gets out first. I follow and wait for Kane. When he doesn't come, I bend down to look inside. I give him a quivery smile because I understand his hesitation.

His lips are curved into a deep frown. When I look into his eyes, his fear distorts my vision. "I get it's hard, but it's only us today. We can focus on celebrating the life we had with her. Tonight is the time we can let out all our other emotions." He stays seated, so I add, "Please, Kane, I need *you* today."

It wouldn't be the same without him, and I'd like to think today would bring him a sense of closeness to her.

He reluctantly slides across the seat and gets out. Knox threads his fingers through mine, and I grab hold of Kane's hand with my other to pull them up the stairs and toward the entry. This is what Misty and I used to do: grab their hands and pull them inside.

But this time, it's just me.

After I get the VIP passes, we walk through the entrance and toward the rides. Everything looks the same, even though I haven't been back in a long time—the smell of the food, the sound of the carnival music, and kids laughing in the background.

I look back at Kane. "Are you okay?"

His shoulders and torso loosen. "You're right . . . I'll do my best to focus on the positives."

Kane looks around, then walks toward a cotton candy cart. He talks to the man, who is wearing a navy-blue uniform. The man passes him three cotton candies, one for each of us, and Kane strolls back and hands me and Knox a stick. I pull off a piece of the pink cloud and put it in my mouth. The super-sweet cotton candy hits my tongue, and it's heavenly. Misty and I would eat this all day until we felt sick.

Kane's eyebrow rises while he watches me eat. "Good?"

"So good," I mumble, and a small smirk tugs on his lips.

We walk around the park, bypassing all the children's rides, and before I know it, my legs have taken me to the ride I see in my dreams. I can't stop staring at the carousel as I watch the young children travel around on it, smiling and laughing.

I hear a chuckle beside me and look at Kane.

"Out of all the rides, she liked this ride the best. The little kids' ride." He grins, remembering the past, and my heart warms at his smile.

My body stiffens as I spot the back of a young woman riding on the carousel. She has long, straight, blond hair. When the ride turns and she faces us, my chin dips and my shoulders drop in disappointment. It's not Misty but a woman with her young child.

Knox puts his arm around me and rubs my arm in soothing motions. I look up at him and can't stop the tears from falling down my face. I slump into him, my head resting against his shoulder. Every time I see someone who resembles Misty, I experience a surge of hope in my chest. Until I find out the truth about what happened to her, I'll always search for her.

THIRTEEN
MEMORIES BRING HER BACK

Bomber

I LET OUT A HUGE BREATH AS THE SAFETY HARNESS OF THE RIDE lifts above my head. As I slide out of the seat, when my feet land on the base of the ride, the rush fades. Zara and Kane are smiling, and I follow them off the ride and onto the ground. I stride up to them.

The thrill rides provide a short high, but being on my motorcycle, that's a real rush. Being on the rides brings me back to when we were kids, and even I can admit it's been worth it to see them both happy, even for a while, before the hell that tonight will bring.

It's late afternoon, and I want Zara to eat something decent before tonight, as she always struggled to eat when she's upset.

I tilt my head in the restaurant's direction. "Follow me." I know if I tell them about going, Zara might put the brakes on and refuse to eat.

It's only a short walk until we reach the restaurant that

overlooks the water. It's a tapas bar called the Decadent Flame, where we used to go when celebrating events and birthdays when we were kids. When we reach the entryway, I dare to glance at Zara. She stares at me with her lips pressed into a hard line, but she doesn't object, so I take that as a win.

We walk in and as we reach the hostess, the woman's eyes bulge when she looks at me. Her eyes travel from my face to my cut, and she licks her lips. "Knox, we weren't expecting you." She peers over my shoulder. When her gaze falls on Zara, her eyes widen even more.

"Zara," she says in an exasperated tone. She moves from behind the podium and steps to her, throwing her arms around Zara.

"I should have known you'd be back in Crown Village. After I finish here, I'll be going to the vigil."

"Thank you, Shelly," Zara replies. I realize we went to school with the woman.

"I'm sure some more news will come to light tonight," says Shelly.

Zara's face falls, though she answers her. "I hope so."

They pull apart, and Shelly points to a table. "I have a four-seater available. I'm glad you came now. It was very busy at lunchtime."

I'm not surprised. The place always used to be packed. As we follow her, I look around. It's been a long time since I've been here. It's been renovated. The atmosphere is intimate, with dark lighting and a mixture of plush easy chairs and tall wooden tables. The new furniture, maroon walls, and high, dangling light fixtures create an atmosphere that is both modern and luxurious.

When we sit, Shelly hands us the menus and smiles before walking back to the front of the restaurant. A waitress arrives at our table, and her eyes flick between the three of us. "Would you like a drink?"

"Crown Village whiskey with cola," Zara answers.

I look at Kane in time to see him flinch, as if her words brought him pain. Though, soon after, he gives her a heartfelt smile. "Me too."

"Make that three," I tell her.

The waitress nods. "I'll go get them for you now."

There's a comfortable silence between us. I follow Zara's eyes out the window. It's been a hot day. The sun is reflecting off the water, and the waves are lapping the shore in slow motion.

Kane picks up the menu. "I can't pronounce half the meals on this."

"Did you want anything in particular?" I ask Zara.

She scans the menu. "The fish tacos look good. So does the pork belly."

Calmness washes over me. She's hungry.

"We can get those. Kane, why don't you order a mix of dishes, and then we can all pick at them?"

Kane's lips pull up into a wicked smirk. "Absolutely."

The waitress comes back with our drinks and places them in front of us. "Are you ready to order yet?"

"We are," Kane replies.

She pulls her pad and pen out. "What would you like?"

"Come here, I'll point to them. I'm not even going to bother trying to pronounce them."

Zara smothers a laugh.

The waitress steps toward Kane, who's holding the menu and pointing to what he wants. "That one, two of that one." She nods as she scribbles them down.

Zara's eyes are on the ocean, her hand touching the glass. "I forgot how beautiful the view is from here." Instead of the view, my eyes latch onto the ring on her finger. A sliver of warmth lightens my chest that she's still wearing it after all this time.

Kane leans back in his chair and peers at Zara. "So what else have you been up to?"

"I've been really busy with work, and apart from that, I occasionally help at the local homeless shelter when I can."

Fuckkkk! We have gone on two very different paths, almost the opposite of one another.

Her eyes bounce between the two of us. "What else have you guys been up to?"

Kane looks at the ground, then rubs his chin. "Not helping at a homeless shelter, that's for sure."

"I wasn't expecting you to," she says, smirking. "How's the casino going?"

"It's always chaos. Each day, I never know what I'm going to walk in on or what drunk asshole I'm going to have to deal with."

Zara shifts, giving me her full attention. "What about you? What do you do for work?"

I don't even have to look at Kane to know he has a stupid, smug grin. When I glance at him, I see I'm right. He raises a brow, as if curious to know how I'm going to answer her.

"I don't have a day job. I'm sergeant at arms in the MC."

She squints at me. "But how do you earn a wage?"

I pause. "I can't divulge that information. It's club business."

Kane doesn't even know what we do, but he's not stupid. He knows we earn money by doing something illegal.

An awkward silence hangs heavy in the air. I can't tell her. She would have to be my ol' lady before I can give her details, and even though I've been saying to everyone that she is, she's really not. No civilian can be half in and half out. We can't afford for anyone to let slip that we grow and distribute weed.

"Are your cousins still living here?" Zara asks us.

Our cousins hung out with us during the holidays when

they came home from private school, but then we all grew up and did our own thing.

"Yeah," I answer Zara. "Alec, Lawson, and Harrison are still here. Sophie moved away a while ago."

"Are they coming tonight?" she asks.

"They are. I'm not sure about Sophie, though," Kane replies.

The waitress brings our drinks and sets them in front of us on the table. "Food won't be long."

Zara raises her glass. "To Misty." We pick up our glasses and clink them.

"To Misty," we say in unison.

Shortly after, our food arrives. There's a comfortable silence as we eat. I glance at Zara every so often to check that she's eating. When we finish the food, we chat among ourselves.

As we leave, I pull out my wallet and open it. Kane gives me a weird look. "We aren't paying."

Shelly smiles. "Yes, family is free."

Zara steps up next to me and gasps when she sees the photo section of my wallet. I watch her closely as she takes my wallet from me, bringing it closer to her face to get a better look.

"Can I take this out?"

I slowly nod, watching her expression. She slips her finger in, pinching the photos and sliding them out. There's two of them. Two of Zara, one recently and one before Misty left—before the pain tainted her.

Her brows pinch. "How long ago was this one?"

I look away, thinking. "Six months."

Her eyes widen. "You really came to see me." She frowns. "I wish you would have actually spoken to me." Her voice conveys her longing, underlined with sadness.

I clench my teeth as guilt churns my stomach. "You were better off."

"No, I wasn't." Her voice breaks.

My shoulders fall and my chest is heavy. *Did I make a mistake? Should I have gone to see her and spoken to her?*

As we walk out, my phone rings in my pocket. I pull it out to see Reaper's name. I answer it immediately. "Is everything all right?"

He lets out a deep chuckle. "Everything is fine. I was calling to tell you we just arrived."

I pull my phone away from my ear to see that it's five thirty.

"Who's that?" Kane asks.

"Reaper," I mouth to him.

"Oh . . . Tell him they should allow everyone to come in for free now for the vigil."

"Did you hear that?" I ask Reaper.

"Yes. See you soon," he replies.

"We'd better get going," Zara says, her anguish obvious. "Mom is probably already here."

Kane's shoulders fall. I wish I could take their pain away from them. I know I need to look into Misty's disappearance again, for everyone's sake. "You two go ahead. I need to make a phone call."

They pause. Zara nods. Kane searches my eyes, interested in who I'm calling.

"I'll tell you later," I say quietly. I wait until they leave, then I call Alec.

He's my cousin on my mom's side. He practically manages all his father's businesses in Crown Village, and if anyone can get the ins and outs, he can because nothing happens in this town without my uncle and Alec's say so.

"Hello, Alec speaking," he says in a professional, monotone voice.

"It's Knox."

"My apologies for today. I might be late to the vigil, but I'll get there when I can."

I'm grateful my family is coming. "I appreciate it. Can I ask a favor?"

"Anything."

"Can you investigate Misty's case for me? I'm going to try to get more answers tonight, but I want to go over everything again. Something has been missed. Someone knows more than they are letting on."

"Sure . . . It's been playing on my mind since Helen approached me about having the vigil. Ten years, I can't believe it. The vigil is all everyone's been talking about. Everyone's going, so be prepared for a crowd. All my family should be there soon to pay our respects—even Sophie traveled for it."

Having the family back together with Mom and Dad, just like old times . . . I wish it were under different circumstances.

After we hang up, I search for everyone. When I see men with cuts on huddled around the carousel, I walk toward them. They all turn to look at me when I arrive.

Reaper squeezes my shoulder. "The women and some men are getting the supplies from Zara's mom's car. What do you need from us?"

I tip my head. "Thanks, pres. When they get back, I'll ask Zara's mom, Helen."

Viper steps toward me, gives me a bear hug, and slaps my back.

"Did you want me to check the crowds?" Demon asks. "See if there's anything suspicious or watch out for anything out of the ordinary?"

"Yeah, actually." I've got my hands full with Zara. At least I have the men to fall back on. They will step up if I need them to, especially Demon. He nods and leaves us as he strolls. A woman pulls her child closer and gives Demon a wary stare when he walks around the back of them.

Rage, Cash, and Axle walk to the tables with big brown boxes in tow, women trailing.

"What's the boxes for?" Viper asks me.

"I have no idea."

The men put the boxes down and make their way to us, while the women open them. Zara pulls out a pamphlet. She studies the front of it. Her fingers trail over the image. When she opens it, she wipes away tears. I step toward her, but both women dash to her side. Elena puts her arms around her waist, pulling Zara to her, as they all peer down at the pamphlet.

I've appreciated the women helping around the clubhouse, but I've never truly valued their kindness and support until now. They're there for Zara, when they don't even know her.

"The women have got her back."

I glance up at Reaper and let out a heavy breath. I clear my voice. "It means a lot."

"That's not all. We purchased hot dogs, rolls, and some sauces, and we'll grill some hot dogs for the people attending."

"You didn't need to."

"My woman insisted. You know what she's like."

I hear a sob and peer up to see Zara holding Helen. Their arms are wrapped around each another. I look up at the sky, wondering why bad things happen to good people. Zara hugs her dad next, and I make my way to them. I peer over my shoulder to see the men following me.

When we reach them, Helen leaps into my arms. "Oh, Knox," she says, and I wrap her tight. When she pulls back, she wipes her nose with a tissue, which she then puts back in her pocket. When she lifts her eyes, they widen at the men surrounding us.

Reaper steps forward. "We're here for you. Whatever your family needs."

Helen steps to Reaper and puts her arm around him. She looks so small next to him. He puts his arms around her. "Thank you," she says, then looks around at all the men. "I'm thankful for all of your help."

Viper puts his arm around her shoulder. "Bomber's family is our family." John introduces himself to each man, shaking their hands, then Ava and Elena fuss over Helen. I've never been prouder than I am today to wear the club's vest and patches.

Kane makes his way to us and stands beside me. "Who did you call?" he asks with a raised brow.

I turn my back on everyone else and lower my voice. "Alec. I'm not settling for what we already know about Misty's disappearance anymore. I'm looking into it myself, and Alec is going to help. The police might have missed something."

Pain etches his face. "Are you sure you want to bring all of that up again? We would have found out when it happened with all the resources we had."

"Actually, I do. The Pratt family needs answers, and I'm going to do whatever it takes to find out what happened." I gesture toward the crowd. "Look at all the people here already. Her disappearance rocked our community just as much back then as it does now."

Kane lets out a deep sigh. "Okay. I'm with you, every step of the way."

My eyes land on our mom, who strides toward the Pratts. Helen lets out a squeal, and they embrace each other.

"Well, she showed up," Kane deadpans.

"Mmm . . ." I grumble.

It's not good enough. I lost all respect for her a long time ago.

Twitch steps to us. "Hey, I heard Helen mention needing to set up the sound equipment and projector." He peers over at Zara's parents. "I can do that for them."

"I'll show you where it is and help you," Kane replies.

They stride toward the hall.

Mom's eyes land on me, and I groan when she walks my way. Her arms come out for a hug, but I take a deliberate step back. She frowns and her arms fall.

"It's good to finally see you."

"Well, whose fault's that?" I reply bluntly.

My once-confident Mom breaks eye contact and looks away briefly before glancing back up at me. She used to be covered in diamonds. Her hair was always tied back in a bun, and she wore the most expensive brands. She's none of that now. Instead, she has black jeans and a long black shirt on. Her face isn't full of makeup, and her hair is back in a ponytail.

I peer around her, seeing no guards with her. "Where's all your security?"

Something flashes across her face but quickly disappears. "There was no need for them to be here."

There was never a need for them. She's just paranoid. "Is the one-million-dollar reward still applicable?"

She slowly bobs her head. "It is."

"Good."

Another motivation for people to help.

"It's been ten years. I doubt any new information will be found."

My eyes narrow at the stranger in front of me. "You don't know that."

"Where's Kane?"

I glance to the hall, where I see Kane and Twitch with their hands full. I tilt my head in their direction. "Helping with the sound equipment."

"I'm going to make myself useful."

I grab her arm as she goes to leave. "What was the private investigator's name?"

She stills momentarily. Then her mouth falls open. "Why?"

"I want to ask him some questions."

She blinks rapidly. "Knox, it was a long time ago. You can't expect me to remember."

"I need for you to look into it for me."

"Why?"

The frustration in her voice makes me grind my teeth. What a stupid question!

"Just do it. It's the least you can do."

Her eyes narrow and she pulls her arm out of my grip. "Don't talk to me like that. I'm still your mother."

I shake my head. "Nah . . . my mom died a long time ago."

Harsh but true.

She gasps and covers her mouth, but I walk away. She left when we needed her. I don't recognize who she's become.

I look around at everyone working together. Kane's setting up the sound equipment. Twitch and Helen talk while looking at a laptop on the table. Rage and Axle are off to the side, handing out the pamphlets. Elena and Ava are getting the candles out.

I see John talking to my dad. We make eye contact, and I give him a small wave. My dad smiles and waves back.

"Bomber." I shift to face Viper. His eyes are bulging. "Who's that?" He points into the crowd, but there's a lot more people here now and I can't decipher who he's talking about. "Who?"

"The blond bombshell."

The side of my mouth curves when my eyes land on her. "That's my cousin Sophie."

She's off to the side, talking with my other cousins, Harrison and Lawson.

"Do you mind if I . . .?" He gives me a suggestive brow raise.

I scratch my head. "I wouldn't."

His jaw drops. "Why?"

"She will eat you alive."

He laughs. "I fucking hope so."

I chuckle, knowing how feisty Sophie is. "Not even you are a match for her."

He groans and runs a hand down his face. "Is she into women?" He smiles. "I think I can turn her."

"She's not into women. Well, not that I know of."

Viper smiles smugly. "I think I can handle her."

"Don't whine to me when it all goes to shit." When we were younger, she left a long trail of broken hearts everywhere she went.

He whacks my back. "Sweet! How long is she going to be in Crown Village for? You'll have to introduce us."

I shake my head. *Idiot!* He can't help himself thinking he's God's gift to women. It will be entertaining to see him try and fail miserably. "I'm not too sure how long."

I search the crowd for Zara. She's talking to Iris. I go to them, and when I reach Zara, I press a kiss to her temple. She looks up at me and smiles, then I glance at Iris. "Hey."

She grabs my cut. "What's this?" She clicks her tongue.

"What do you think it is?" I ask her.

"Trouble!"

We laugh together.

"Can I see you before you go?" I ask Iris. "I want to ask you a few questions."

Zara tugs on my hand. "I'm meeting up with her tomorrow if you want to come."

My eyes flick between the two of them. "I will. If you don't mind."

"Zara!"

We turn to Helen. "It's time . . ."

Zara's breath hitches and she bows her head.

I lace our fingers together, bring her hand to my mouth, and plant a kiss above her ring. Her eyes soften, but I let her hand go so she can be with her parents. The crowd goes quiet when "Memories" by Maroon 5 plays.

The projector is showing a photo of Misty that was taken prior to her disappearance. Helen passes out roses to Zara and John, and they walk over and put them by the projector. Elena and Ava go around with their lit candle, lighting others.

When the song finishes, Twitch hands Helen the microphone. She looks out at the group. "I'd like to thank everyone for coming out tonight."

As she says a prayer, I peer at the sky. There's only a small beam of light left from the sun as it descends, and apart from her voice, it's quiet besides the rides in the background. As I glance at everyone, I see Reaper off to the side, speaking to Parker, the police officer. There's a line of my MC brothers around the back of the crowd, paying their respects.

"Please protect my baby girl, Misty," Helen says, with tears streaming down her face. "We miss her every second of every day." She chokes on her words, and even I'm having trouble keeping the tears at bay. I stride toward them, linking my hand with Zara's once more. "Did you want me to talk?"

I had no idea what I was going to say, but I hated seeing Helen breaking down.

Zara shakes her head. "No, I will . . ." She looks at me with glassy eyes. "Can you come up with me?"

I squeeze her hand in support.

"Okay . . ." she says through a breath.

We step to Zara's parents, and Zara gently takes the microphone from Helen's hands. Helen sags into John.

"Heavenly Father," Zara begins, glancing up at the sky, "protect Misty, my sister and best friend. Please watch over her and guard her from evil. Give her the courage to return to us, to reunite us . . . because she has left a hole in my family"—she looks at her parents—"in her friends"—she looks at Kane, then looks back at the crowd—"and in the community." She takes another deep breath. "Help us find out what happened to her. Grant us peace. Amen."

I wrap my arm around her waist. While holding her, I reach for the microphone. She passes it to me as she buries her face in my chest and cries, and every tear shreds me. I turn to her parents before talking into the mic. "Do you want to talk again or . . .?"

John replies, "Zara said everything that needed to be said."

I bring the microphone to my mouth. "For those who don't know me, my name is Knox. I'm a close friend of the family. Again, we would like to thank everyone who has come to pay their respects." I search the crowd and wave Parker over. "If anyone remembers anything leading up to or on the date of Misty's disappearance, no matter how small, please speak to our local police." I wait for Parker to join me. "This is Officer Parker, and he will record the information."

I'm aware no one will come forward if I ask them to talk to our MC, and at least I can get feedback from Parker.

"Don't forget there's still a million-dollar reward for information that leads to finding Misty. Now, please join us for hot dogs, provided by War Brothers Motorcycle Club."

ONCE WE GET BACK TO THE CLUBHOUSE, I WAIT FOR ZARA'S LEAD to see what she wants to do. She pulls on my hand to go up the stairs, so I follow her down the hallway and to my room. Once the door closes, she lets go of my hand and throws her arms around my neck. The pain in her eyes levels me.

"Please, Knox, just make me forget," she whispers with a breathy plea.

I pull her closer, my arms around her back. I lower my head and take her mouth with a promise of what lies ahead. I'd give her the temporary relief she needs. As our mouths open and our tongues meet, I tilt my head, tasting her with slow, deep licks.

A sexy moan leaves her. The sound of her pleasure reverberates through me, firing into a blaze that had lain dormant since I was with her last. I bring my lips to her neck, placing delicate kisses along it, the way she used to like it. She shivers, then her head falls back, giving me better access.

I've waited so long for her that my hands are shaking. There's a desire to shred her dress, but I resist and step away from her to kick my shoes off. Her breathing is quick and harsh. She watches me as I take my jeans off, then rip my shirt over my head and toss it on the floor. My boxers are next. Her gaze flits to my cock, and she doesn't hide the hunger in her eyes.

Her dress and underwear are next. The faded light from the moon and stars seeps through the blinds casting shadows over her ivory skin. Every curve, every inch of her, is just as flawless as I remember. We're breathing heavily, her chest rising and falling, and my own.

I move to her and cup her face, my eyes piercing hers. "I love you," I breathe.

Her mouth opens into an O, so I capture her lips again, not wanting to hear the rejection. I'm helpless against the way she makes me feel.

As my tongue delves into hers, I run my fingers feathery light down her throat, down her side, allowing my hands to tighten their grasp on her hips. The kiss fuels the passion inside of me. She presses into me like she needs me as much as I do her. We walk together toward the bed, never breaking apart. When the back of her legs meets the bed, she falls, and I fall with her, bracing myself with my arms to ensure I don't crush her petite frame.

Nestling my hips between her thighs, she spreads her legs wide. My lips return to hers and I ravage her mouth again. Our tongues stroke each other in feverish desperation. I kiss her, letting her feel how much I've missed her. Her perfume wafts over me, making me hungrier.

Blood rushes through my veins. The anticipation of sinking into her has me struggling to hold back the need to claim her. "Are you on the pill?"

I want to take her bareback. No, I fucking *need* it.

"Yes," she answers against my lips.

I inch back. "I want nothing between us. Are you okay with that?"

I need her consent, even though my cock is twitching to be inside her. I'm desperate to feel her around me . . . raw.

Her entire face is soft. She looks at me with hooded eyes. She nods, her tongue snaking out, wetting her lips. "Yes."

Need, sharp and painful, surges.

Grabbing my throbbing cock, I drag it through her heat. She draws a breath through those full lips. Her hand drifts between us, curling around my dick, giving it a firm squeeze, a warning.

I lift her leg up over my hip. I enter her swiftly, then slowly push myself all the way into her. Zara gasps. She is tight and hot, and she clamps down on me. *Fuck!* I stay that way, letting her adjust. Barely holding on to my control, I drive in and out. Thrusting deep and slow, I work her. Her slick wetness coats me. Seeing her nipples erect, I have to have them. I lean down, my mouth capturing the tight bud. My tongue swirls greedily, teasing, tasting.

She exhales. "Knox."

I love the way she says my name.

When I pull back, I knead her breast possessively. She looks sexy and wild. Her hair is fanned out around her head and perspiration licks her skin. As I pick up the pace, she matches my rhythm. The air pushes from my lungs in heavy spurts.

She arches her back. Her nails dig into my shoulders. I groan at the mix of pleasure and pain. She's close. I can feel little tremors along my cock. I've wanted to come inside Zara a million times over and then take her again and again. It would never be enough.

I pull out, then slam home. Zara mewls my name. Pulsing and soaking wet, she comes, and I follow her over the edge. I let the tip of my nose run up her clammy neck, and I place one more lingering kiss there, savoring her, never wanting this moment to end.

BEST
FRIENDS

SECRETS AND LIES KILL RELATIONSHIPS

Zara

Waking up, I feel the warmth of Knox's body. The weight and heat of his muscular arm around me. The throb between my thighs is a reminder of last night. *He said he loves me.* My chest tightens at the thought. More than anything, I would love to let my walls down, but I can't. I still hold a wariness with him, terrified that he could shatter my world again. I won't survive it a second time.

I gently take his wrist and pull his arm off my body, then shuffle across the bed. When I reach the end, my eyes dart between his sweatshirt and my dress as I wonder what to put on to walk to the bathroom. When my feet meet the floor, I bend down and scoop up his sweatshirt. I pull it over my head, loving its warmth and the scent of his cologne.

I step to my suitcase and fumble through my clothes until I find my jeans and a casual shirt, underwear, a bra, and my toiletry bag.

"What are you doing?" he asks, making me jolt.

I turn and look at him. His eyes are skimming over me, the smallest smile on his lips. He nods, as if happy with my selection of clothing. The blanket is dangerously low on his hips. I jerk my head away to stop myself from checking him out. *Today is a new day. Everything is to go back to how it was.*

Looking back, I ensure my eyes meet his and not his body. "Thank you for yesterday." I didn't want to be ungrateful.

He stiffens, and he grimaces like my words hurt him. "Don't go back to treating me like a stranger." He sits up and turns his legs over the edge of the bed. He runs his hand through his hair. "Stay with me . . ." His voice is thick with pain. He stands with his arms out. "Stay with me . . ."

I know I'm not dying, but my heart's bleeding out. I turn my back to him and grasp the door handle. "I can't . . . I'm sorry."

After stepping out of the room, I gently close the door behind me. I briskly walk to the bathroom, tears running down my face.

Once I've showered, I feel more awake, but my body feels cold. My breathing quickens with every step to Knox's bedroom. When I open the door, he's sitting on the edge of the bed, his head in his hands. It makes me frown, and the guilt hits me.

I did this.

I want to reach out and touch him, comfort him, though I tightly grip my clothes to keep my hands restrained.

Knox thought I was doing better without him . . . but maybe he was just saying that to be kind . . . Maybe it was the other way around. He didn't want to get involved with me again. He didn't want to have to tiptoe around me and treat me like glass or be the one to lean on.

Being a burden is a heavy weight to carry. The guilt swells, assaulting me, so I sit beside him. He lifts his face from his hands.

His sad eyes pierce mine. "I never said this, but I'm sorry," I tell him. "I was in a lot of pain with Misty when she disappeared, and even though I was broken, I never asked you how you were coping . . . how you were feeling. So thank you for being selfless, and even though we broke up, I want you to know I did and still appreciate every time you've been there for me."

His eyes soften. Even though I wanted to keep my distance, my hand moves of its own accord around his waist to hug him, as if I were granting us this moment of surrender.

His arms envelop me, pulling me into him, as he tenderly kisses my head before he says, "You bleed, I bleed . . . remember?"

"I remember," I whisper, blinking back tears. I could never forget.

During breakfast, I make an effort to thank everyone again for their support at the vigil. Afterward, we put on our helmets and head for his motorcycle. He swings his leg over it and hops on. With his hand out, he helps me get on behind him.

"Hold on tight."

Excitement shoots through me. My arms tighten around him and we pull away. I can't stop smiling as we leave, slow at first and then racing off down the road, with the roar of the motorcycle between my legs and the howl of the wind biting my skin, making my hair flutter from underneath the helmet. There's a freeing feeling to being on the back of a motorcycle.

I shift my head to the side as I look at the view once we get closer to the main street of Crown Village. There are mountains in the distance, and trees and dense shrubs cover the land. I forgot how gorgeous the scenery is here. A mix of heritage and modern businesses greet us next. Most I'm familiar with, but there're new ones as well.

We ride closer to the shore and pull into the beach parking lot.

Happiness slides away and nervousness takes its place. My heart thumps as I get off the motorcycle, and my hands shake as I struggle to get the helmet off. Knox's hands gently fold over mine and he unclasps the helmet for me, freeing the straps, making me exhale in relief.

"Thank you," I say, handing him the helmet.

He doesn't answer, but the devotion in his eyes says it all. There's an ache at the back of my throat, and I'm finding it difficult to swallow. I shift, looking away and out along the tree line, where there are picnic tables. When I squint, I see Iris sitting at the second table closest to us, so I walk to her. My stomach drops further with every step, unsure about what this conversation will bring about Misty's disappearance.

When we reach her, she stands and smiles, and I walk into her outstretched arms. When I pull back, I notice the wrinkles around her eyes she's gained over the years. I sit as she gives Knox a brief hug. She sits across from me and fans her face as her eyes gloss with fresh tears.

I try to swallow again, but it's difficult.

"Helen did a spectacular job of the vigil. It was a beautiful ceremony," says Iris.

"It was. I wish Misty could have seen how many people were there and how many miss her." My voice is strangled. I rub the bottom of my throat. "It sounded like you wanted to talk to me about something."

"Yes," she replies, but she briefly peers out at the beach. "What did you get told about me leaving?"

I find that an odd question.

"You returned to be with your family." My eyebrows furrow. "Why, was there something else?"

Tears fall down her face. "Please forgive me when I tell you this."

I freeze. Everything quietens, and I focus on Iris. Every one of my senses heightens. I don't answer her . . . I can't. Heavy silence descends on us until she speaks again.

"Early on, when it was me, Audrey, and Helen in the kitchen, we were talking about where Misty could have gone, and we were throwing out suggestions on what could have happened. I told them I thought Misty was pregnant."

My world spins and I gasp for air. Knox shuffles over, his arms coming around me, holding me. "I . . . How?" I pause. "She was still a virgin. She would have told me . . ."

The sympathy in her eyes tells me otherwise. I shift and look into Knox's eyes. His sad gaze makes me shake my head at him. "She would have told me. We didn't keep secrets from each other."

He flinches, making me think I was wrong. An unsettling feeling takes hold of me. I pull out of Knox's embrace and shuffle away from him. "You knew?" I whisper with hurt in my voice. "You never told me."

His frown deepens. He puts his hand on mine, but I pull mine away.

"I told Misty and Kane to tell you they were, but they didn't get around to and then she went missing. Kane told me they were using protection, so I thought nothing of it." His eyes narrow at Iris. "You don't know she was pregnant, and you have no proof, so why bring it up?"

There's a bite in his tone, but they *both* were hiding secrets from me.

Iris lets out a long sigh. "She was vomiting every day. She had cravings. I knew she was having sex because I caught them. It all aligned, and it made sense to me. You say he wore protection, but nothing is one hundred percent effective."

Her words saturate my mind, though they feel like barbed wire twisting, making incisions into my heart.

"There was no reason for her to leave. She would have known everyone would have supported her."

She raises a hand. "Let me finish. Helen's eyes looked the way yours do. Denial that Misty would be having sex. Audrey was quiet for the first time in her life. I thought it was strange, but the next day, she approached me with her body-guard at my home."

Iris's eyes dart between us and she visibly swallows. She takes a torturous moment, as if trying to keep herself together to continue. "Audrey had papers in her hand and asked if she could come in, so I let them. We went into the dining room, where we sat down, and she told me that my employment was terminated immediately. Your family needed time and space to be together as a family during the difficult time."

I tilt my head. "My parents told you to leave?" I needed her. *They wouldn't . . . would they?*

"I don't know if you're aware, but it was Audrey who helped me get the position. She has cleaners as well, so she had her lawyer draw up a similar contract to theirs for the Pratts that stated my terms and conditions. In that was a nondisclosure clause that Audrey reminded me about. She said to keep my opinions about Misty to myself and that they were not to be discussed with anyone or they would sue me. She was cold and clinical. I had never seen her act that way before, and it scared me. I told her I wouldn't tell anyone. I wanted to stay, but she was firm on letting me go."

"Did she explain why?" I'm quick to ask.

"She mentioned she didn't want Kane brought into the case and she didn't want her family's name tarnished because I had made up a rumor that wasn't true. She offered me a bonus for being a good and loyal employee but only on the condition I sign an updated nondisclosure agreement. I realized maybe she also thought Misty was pregnant and that she was paying me off so I wouldn't say anything, but another part of me had known Audrey for so long. I had trouble reconciling that it was a possibility."

I suck in a sharp breath that fills my lungs. *No . . . no . . . no . . .* I dare a peek at Knox. His face is pale, his eyes wide, his expression pained.

So many questions bubble up inside of me. "You took what she said as fact and didn't even see us or come say goodbye?"

"The conditions were clear. I wasn't allowed to contact any member of your family or hers. I needed the bonus payment. It was life changing. I could not pass up the opportunity to pay off my house, so I asked no more questions. I signed the documents. After months and years of reflecting, I had my suspicions she knew more than she was letting on. It was too coincidental that a day after I suggested Misty was pregnant by her son, she was at my house with an offer of a bonus in return for my silence."

"Who else did you say it to? Did Kane know?"

"No one, and I never spoke to him about it. If he knew, he didn't hear it from me."

"Why didn't you call the police?" I'm dumbfounded Iris had her suspicions but did nothing.

She shakes her head and gives Knox a pointed look. "His family is powerful, and I was scared. Her bodyguard was intimidating enough while in my house, and if I had gone to the police with only my suspicions, they would have laughed at me. Audrey's family has and always will have a direct influence on the police. I didn't know what Audrey was capable of, and I wasn't going to find out."

Her words are cutting me. It's all too much. My head pounds. I need to get away from her . . . from him . . . from everyone.

"Was there anything else you wanted to tell me?"

She reaches out to touch me.

"Don't."

I don't want her comfort. I understand, but it doesn't lessen the blow. She could have been honest a long time ago.

Tears fall down Iris's face. "No, there's not. If you need anything, even someone to talk to, please call me. My phone number is still the same."

I abruptly stand to leave. "Why tell me now?"

"Please don't bring up that I said anything, but after the vigil, I couldn't keep it to myself any longer."

"I won't. I'm leaving." I turn my back on her and walk away.

All these secrets and lies are like poison eating away at my relationships. I walk to the motorcycle in a daze. *Did I even know Misty?*

Knox grabs my wrist.

"Don't touch me!"

He flinches and his brows draw together as his hand falls to his side. "I had no idea about my mom . . . about any of it."

My eyes tighten, though I want to believe him. "How do I know that? All of you kept secrets from me! Was I delusional?" I throw my hands up. "I thought I was happy and everyone cared about me as much as I did them, but now I'm not so sure."

"I do—"

"No. I don't believe that to be true. Even Misty was keeping secrets from me. Hell, she probably knew she was pregnant too."

I pull my phone out, press on Mom's number, and bring it to my ear.

"Hi, is everything okay?"

"Are you free?" My voice comes out in a hurry.

"Sure . . . Where are you?"

I stare at Knox while I answer. "Can you pick me up from Crown Beach and take me home to get my car? I'll be waiting in the parking lot."

"Are you okay?"

I try not to cry. "Can you come now?"

"Okay, I'm leaving. I'll see you soon."

After I hang up, I tell Knox, "I'm fine. You can go."

He doesn't move. His body is rigid. "I'll wait until Helen gets here."

"No, I need space." I point to his motorcycle. "Just go."

He shoves his helmet on, swings his leg over the motorcycle, revs the engine, and peels out of the parking lot.

FIFTEEN
DANGEROUS TRUTHS

Bomber

I pull the throttle back to accelerate. My heart races.

Pain . . . Fear . . . Dread . . . One punch after another to my gut.

I'm going to be sick. Minutes later, I pull up outside the casino, throw my keys at the valet, and bolt to the garden. As I bend with my hands on my knees, vomit rises and I retch until there's nothing left. I've never been sick over my emotions, but Zara makes me feel everything.

I'm going to lose her again . . . What has Audrey done? When I stand, I take a couple of deep breaths, though my throat burns.

I walk to the glass entrance doors. They open wide, allowing me to stride inside. Two women with casino uniforms on are standing behind the stone counter.

"Hi, Knox," one says in an overly cheerful voice. I don't have time for pleasantries. I yank my phone out of my pocket and press Kane's number. When he answers, I say, "I'm at the casino. Where are you?"

"I'm in my office."

I hang up, walk to the elevator, and quickly and repeatedly press the button to call it to the ground floor.

When the doors open, a man walks out as I walk in. I swivel and press the button for the third floor, then swipe my access tag. No one but my family and managers are allowed on that level. As the elevator rises, I tap my leg. When the doors open, I step outside, march down the corridor, and yank my brother's door open. It bangs as it hits the wall.

Kane stands at his desk. "What the fuck, Knox!"

"Did you know?"

His brows furrow. "Know what?"

My chest heaves, but then a thought comes to mind. *What if he doesn't know, or what if Misty wasn't pregnant?* I choose my words carefully. "Audrey paid off Iris after Misty left. Did you know about it?"

Kane tilts his head, his eyes hardening at my accusation. "How would I know that?" He plonks down in his chair and leans back. "You're pissed off. Why? Why does it matter?"

"It matters because Iris told Helen and Audrey"—*she's not my mom anymore*—"that she thought Misty was pregnant." I focus on Kane. He gasps and stills. I watch for any tell that he knew, but he shakes his head.

"She wasn't pregnant."

"Well, Audrey turned up with her bodyguard the next day at Iris's house. Audrey said her employment with the Pratts was terminated and she was to abide by the terms and conditions of her employment, which included an NDA." The longer I speak, the paler Kane gets. "Then she offered Iris a bonus if she signed another NDA to not talk about the case to anyone and because she didn't want you,"—I point to him—"being pulled into the case."

"Don't point your finger at me, *brother*! I always wore protection. I'm telling you she wasn't pregnant."

"So there wasn't one time that you even started having sex, then put the condom on afterward? You know condoms aren't one hundred percent effective."

Uncertainty clouds his face. He shoves himself up out of his chair, which tumbles backward, hitting the wall. "It was a long time ago. I don't remember."

"You need to think real fucking hard. If there was even the slightest of chances Misty was pregnant, it changes everything. If Audrey paid Iris off, then she knew. She knew, Kane . . . all this time."

Dad walks in. "What the hell is going on?"

I pull my gaze from Kane and turn to Dad, who is standing in the doorway. "Shut the door and come in," I tell him.

Dad pauses first, his eyes darting between Kane and me. He opens his mouth, but he says nothing and gently closes the door before turning to us. In my peripheral vision, I see Kane pacing by his desk.

"Did you know?" I ask Dad.

"Uh . . . know what?"

"Misty *could have been* pregnant."

He chuckles. "What are you talking about? She wasn't pregnant. We would have known about it."

"By the sounds of it, Audrey knew, and when Iris made a comment about her thoughts that Misty was pregnant, Audrey terminated Iris's employment and paid her for keeping silent."

Dad blinks repeatedly and looks at Kane. "Is this true?"

Kane stops pacing, turns, and leans on his desk with his hands, bowing his head. "I don't know . . ." he whispers.

Dad's hands come to his face, his mouth agape. A heavy tension fills the air.

Kane raises his head. "We were having sex. I knew she was sick, but I thought she had caught some bug," he says with undeniable sadness.

It all clicks together like a puzzle. "That's why Audrey moved!" My voice booms. "She and Misty moved to our holiday home. Audrey isolated herself, remember? It's why she has never invited us over and why she kept her distance. She didn't want anyone to know."

"But why?" Dad asks. "It's been ten years. If Misty was pregnant, there's no reason to stay hidden. Something doesn't make sense. Let's go now!" He stomps his foot. "We need to demand answers."

I put my hands out. "No! If Audrey and Misty hid this long, we don't know what Audrey's capable of. She could leave the state—hell, the country—if she wanted to. As you said, something isn't right. We need a plan, and we need to execute it carefully. I don't want to spook her, and we still don't know for sure if that's what has happened."

There's a thump. Kane has collapsed. Dad and I rush to him. It's as if he fell to hold himself steady.

Tears fall down Kane's face. I haven't seen him cry since Misty left. His anguish pains me.

Dad is by his side, his hand on his shoulder. "We're here for you. We will find out the truth."

"What if she was pregnant?" Kane sobs.

It's a soul-crushing sound. I know I'll never forget it. I turn to leave.

"Where are you going?" Dad yells out.

I clench my jaw. "To find Kane some fucking answers."

With every step, the anger washes over the pain, digging in its claws, and I embrace it. My breaths come short and quick. I crack my knuckles on the way out. If what I think is true, when I find out who has helped Audrey and Misty keep their secret, they are going to pay. I'm the sergeant at arms for a reason.

AFTER GETTING ON MY MOTORCYCLE, I RIDE TO THE CROWN Resort. My cousin Alec is the CFO and also lives in the penthouse, so I'm sure he's in the building somewhere. First I go to his office and stride past the receptionist and other staff, ignoring his personal assistant, who's telling me I can't go into his office. I open the door to see my cousin in a meeting with another man.

Alec's eyes narrow, but then he studies my face. He stands and looks at the man on the other side of his desk. "Sorry, James, we will have to reschedule."

The man stands and nods, gives me a wary glance, and goes around me to leave.

"I'm sorry!" the PA says from behind me.

"It's okay, Mandy. Close the door on your way out."

When she does, I ask. "Did you look into Misty's case?"

He straightens his tie. "Take a seat."

My heart crashes against my ribs. "I can't. Tell me what you found out."

He sits, opens a drawer in his desk, then pulls out a manila folder. He puts it on his desk and opens it. "I'll warn you now. You're not going to like it." His lips tighten. "There was hardly anything on Misty's file for her disappearance. Which I thought was strange." He scatters the documents across his desk. "There were interviews with family, friends, schoolteachers, her biological family, and basic information about her case. I expected more since the case was linked to our family. Her case was on TV and Audrey had a reward out, but there was not one eyewitness after she left the Pratts'."

I rub my face. "It makes no sense, and I'm desperate for answers or even a lead."

He gives me a sharp nod. "I agree. So I did some digging. The lead investigator on the case has resigned and now lives with his wife in a house in the suburbs in Crown Village. However, it's only his wife's name on the deed of the house."

"How did they afford that?"

"I had someone look into both of their financials for me. I only got them back this morning." He looks back at the papers and grabs the sheet on top. He passes it to me, but I don't take it.

My hands are clenched by my side. I'm too wound up. "Just tell me."

His shoulders fall. "Years after Misty's disappearance, the investigator's wife purchased a house outright, so it's only her name on the deed, and then the investigator resigned."

"You think the cop got paid off . . . so they purchased the house with the money but put it in the wife's name to avoid what would look like a payoff?" I pause. "It was Audrey." It had to be.

Alec tilts his head. His hand goes to his chin. "Why do you think it was her?"

"I don't want to go into it right now. Can I have the lead investigator's address?"

He passes me the piece of paper. "It's on that. And Knox?"

"Mmm . . ."

"If Audrey had anything to do with it, tread carefully. Regardless, she's still my dad's sister. And trust me, you don't want any blowback from him or our family." He and Audrey own most of the large establishments in Crown Village. They are wealthy, and with money comes power.

I shrug, then walk out.

I don't give a shit.

WHEN I GET BACK TO THE MC, I PARK BETWEEN VIPER AND Demon. It's a sunny day, so the men are outside cleaning their motorcycles. I pull my helmet off. Viper has stopped cleaning and is staring at me with a raised brow, wipe in hand. He opens his mouth as if to say something, then slams it shut and stands.

Demon stands too. They know something is wrong. I step to Reaper. He wipes over the handlebars, but when I get close, he peers over at me and slowly stands up.

"I need a church meeting," I tell him.

He takes a second, then nods. "Church."

Everyone stops what they're doing. I feel their curious stares as I move inside. Ava is wiping down the entryway table as I walk in. She gives me a small smile and looks behind me, then frowns. "Where's Zara?"

I shake my head at her, make my way to the computer room, and peek inside. "Twitch, church."

He swivels in his chair to face me. "Yeah, coming." He stands and follows me out.

Once we've gathered the rest of the MC, we stand around the table, with Reaper at the top, me and Viper at his sides, and the rest of the club around it.

Everyone sits.

"Bomber, you have the floor," says Reaper.

"First, I'd like to say thank you to every one of my brothers for being there for me during this difficult time." Reaper leans over and puts his hand on my shoulder. "I called a meeting because I found out more information in relation to Zara's sister's missing persons case, but before I go further, before bringing all of you into this. I wanted to call a vote. This isn't club business," I say as I look around the table, "so leave now if you don't want to be involved. I won't have any hard feelings toward any of you."

I make eye contact with every single member, giving them an out, but no one leaves.

"I live for this shit!" Demon says from beside me.

I knew he would be with me. Keen to get his hands dirty.

"Zara and I contacted an ex-employee who worked at the Pratts' when Misty disappeared. Once she suggested Misty was pregnant with my brother's child, she was paid off by Audrey, my mom, and was made to sign an NDA to not speak about the case to anyone."

A mix of grunts and gasps sound around the table.

"I went to visit my father and brother, Kane, who did not know about it. Then I went to see my cousin Alec. He had done his own digging for me and said there wasn't enough done about the case. The lead investigator purchased a home outright in Crown Village. Alec and I drew the same conclusions—that he was most likely paid off. I know it was Audrey, but I wouldn't mind paying the investigator a visit."

"Yes!" Demon says beside me, rubbing his hands together.

"Why would your mother do that?" Viper asks.

"She cared about her reputation, and if she found out Misty was pregnant, I know she wouldn't have approved. I don't know what happened, but it can't be a coincidence that soon after Misty's disappearance Audrey left to go live at our holiday house in the mountains and never returned. We thought it was odd, but we put it down to her being a coward and wanting to get away from everyone's grief."

"A police officer, even in retirement, couldn't afford a home in Crown Village," Cash chimes in.

"You know," Twitch says, "I looked into the statistics of

missing persons cases, and when it comes to teenagers, acquaintance kidnapping is comparatively high for women compared to your stereotypical kidnapping where the person doesn't know the perpetrator."

Axle squints at Twitch. "Only you would look at statistics in your spare time . . . ya nerd."

I didn't even consider kidnapping as a possibility. I look at Reaper. "Did you hear from Officer Parker?"

"Yeah. There was nothing worth mentioning," Reaper answers.

"I need to work with my brother and Zara on this, so I'll have to bring them into the fold, update them on what's going on. Raise your hand if you are okay with this."

Everyone raises their hands.

"What are you going to do about your mom?" Axle asks. "Do you think Misty's there, or what's going through your mind?"

"I don't know about that part. I want to face Audrey, but she's a flight risk. I might scope out the property tonight. If I confront her, it needs to be by surprise, and I want it planned out to ensure there're no mistakes. I can't let her get away without an explanation. And on that"—I glance at Twitch—"can you get me house plans and any information on the security of her house and anything else you can think of?"

"Where's your girl?" Viper asks.

My throat gets clogged, so I shake my head.

"I'll manage all of this. You go get your woman!" Viper replies.

"Thanks," I say, appreciation clear in my tone.

"When am I visiting the pig?" asks Demon. I know he's referring to the lead investigator of the police.

I pull the piece of paper from my pocket and pass it to him. "You can watch his house. Check back and make sure he's there, but you can't go in . . . not without me."

His wicked smile dims. "Shame, how long are you going to be?"

My lip lifts at his eagerness. "Hopefully not long." I'm going to get *my woman* first.

BEST
FRIENDS

SIXTEEN
THE CUNNING PUPPET MASTER

Zara

I couldn't go inside my old home, and I didn't want my parents to see my unrest, so I drove to the lake instead. I'm in the parking lot, watching the boats and people walk along the trail on the shore. So many emotions strangle me. I'm scarcely aware of the tears falling.

I slam my hands on the steering wheel.

Why was everyone hiding the truth from me? Misty . . . Knox . . . Iris . . . Audrey . . . *Did my parents draw the same conclusion that Misty was pregnant? Did Kane know? Has Misty been hiding from me and my family all this time? How could she do this to me?* I slam my hands again as a tormented scream bursts past my lips.

My phone rings. I stare blankly at the lake. My phone pings with what's most likely a voicemail message but then rings again. I shuffle through my bag, moving my wallet out of the way to see my phone lit up with Knox's name. My thumb hovers over the cancel button but presses the answer button instead. I remain silent, waiting for him to talk.

"I'm sorry." His voice is thick with emotion.

"Tell me . . . what else do you know that I don't? No more hidden truths."

"Nothing . . . but I've been to see Kane, Dad, and Alec to get some answers."

I sit up straight in my seat and listen carefully, hanging on to every single word Knox says.

"Alec said there wasn't enough done on Misty's case, but the lead investigator somehow paid for a house in Crown Village. My senses tell me it's why Audrey moved away and paid everyone off to not look into the case. Audrey put up a million-dollar reward, and even though she has the money to back it up, she knew no one would come forward because she paid Iris off and paid off the investigator to turn a blind eye to any important information that comes their way."

I pause, allowing the news to sink in. "What about Misty? Do you think she was pregnant and they both moved away? Why would they do that? Misty loved Kane. If she was pregnant, I don't see her moving away from him. I'm hurt that Misty thought she couldn't confide in me and was hiding stuff from me, but I still have trouble grappling with the idea she left us to go with Audrey of all people. I can't say Misty was her biggest fan." Misty's carefree nature did not go down well with Audrey.

"I agree with you. Can I pick you up? I'm working on getting answers. Demon and I are visiting the lead investigator tonight, so please come back to the clubhouse."

I hesitate. "Okay," I answer softly, eager for more information but still unsure on where I stand with Knox and how I feel. "No more surprises, okay?"

"No more surprises. But there are some things I want to

talk to you about. Where are you? I'll come pick you up now."

"I need my car, so I'll drive to the clubhouse."

There's a gush of air through the phone. "When are you going to get here?"

My chest warms at his need for me. "I'll see you soon, Knox."

I drive to the clubhouse, faster than I should. I pull up off to the side of the house so that I'm not blocking any cars or motorcycles in. Knox waits for me, leaning against the pillar on the porch.

As I open the door and stand, he rushes over, stands next to the car, and pushes my door closed for me. He wraps his arms around me and pulls me to his chest. My body tenses. He pulls back and cups my chin in his hand, forcing eye contact. His stare is intense.

"The only thing I knew about was Misty and Kane sleeping together. Nothing else. I promise."

I stop resisting and embrace him, tightening our hold as he kisses the top of my head.

"I'm sorry, so sorry, precious."

I blink rapidly as I force those emotions down and pull back. "What are your plans next?"

"Me and Demon are going to see the investigator tonight. Twitch is looking into the house plans because I want to visit Audrey, to catch her off guard, but that won't be tonight. I wouldn't mind capturing her security guard. He would know what's going on or what happened."

I've noticed him calling his mom by her first name. "That security guard has been by her side for as long as I remember."

"Yeah," he answers, glancing away. "Pretty sure they were having an affair and that's why my parents split."

I rub his back. "I'm so sorry."

"I heard Dad slip up in conversation once, but there was no need to bring it up again. Dad's happier without her."

"What's with the security guard, anyway?" I ask.

"Audrey's always felt she needed one, whether it's because of our wealth or because she somehow thought she was popular enough to need one.

"Come inside." Knox tilts his head toward the clubhouse. I follow him in a daze, though catch sight of Ava and Elena by the front door, as if they're waiting for me.

Ava's lips curve up into a big smile, her eyes brightening. "Are you okay?" mouths Elena.

Their compassion and empathy makes me smile back. "I'll catch up with you two later."

Knox and I move briskly up the stairs and to his room, where he shuts the door behind us. We sit on his bed as I think back, linking Audrey as the main denominator. As if the jigsaw puzzle was slowly coming together, revealing the story. My brain zaps. "Well, I guess that's why Audrey sorted out a psychiatric center in the city for me."

His frown deepens. "She paid your fees as well," he answers.

I gape. Anger surges through my veins. He places his hand over mine. "She encouraged me to join the military and . . ." He looks away from me, before turning back with eyes full of emotion. "I believe she influenced your parents to make us break up, with the intention of sending you to the facility to keep you away from Crown Village, and from uncovering the truth."

I shift backward. "My parents asked you?" It was as soft as a whisper. "Why didn't you tell me?"

"Everyone, including myself, thought you needed it, and I told you . . . I will always put you first."

His selfless act saved and destroyed me. "If only you had told me, I would have still gone and we could have stayed together."

His eyes search mine. He doesn't look convinced. "Tell me the truth. Would you have left to go if we were still together?"

I lean back, away from him. "I guess we'll never know. You took that choice away from me." There's an undercurrent of frustration in my voice, but I deserved to have a say in our relationship. I shouldn't have had it forced on me without my knowledge.

A small, bitter laugh escapes him. "I've done *everything* in my power to protect you."

My mind scatters. "Protect me? You left me . . ."

"To save you!" He raises his voice.

I shake my head.

"You were physically harming yourself. Zara, what did you expect of me?" He stands and throws his arms up as his gaze goes directly to my thigh. "I was nineteen, trying to be there for you but then struggling to be there for Kane. He was always drunk, and then you cut yourself." He pats his chest. "I was drowning . . . failing everyone around me. I thought I wasn't enough for you . . . I couldn't be the person you needed."

My. Heart. Cracks.

I hurl myself at him, looping my arms around his stiff body. "You were exactly what I needed! You always have been." His body softens and he puts his arms around my waist.

I'm in a constant state of pushing him away and pulling him closer again. I inch back. Our gazes lock, my voice tight as I speak. "I thought you broke up with me because you didn't want me."

"It was the hardest thing I've ever done. I nearly couldn't go through with it." He chuckles, but there's no humor in it.

"I knew you were in pain, and I'm sorry for hurting you, but you needed help. You're still cutting . . ."

There was no judgment, just sadness.

I pause, thinking about how to answer him, then clear my throat as my heart constricts. I rub my thumb over the scars on my thigh. "They are my battle scars of depression . . . from the deep sadness of losing Misty. Every cut is a year of guilt and shame, like a million what-if scenarios ran through my brain. 'What if I had stayed home with her? Would she still have left? Should I have made her go to the doctor's earlier?' I could see all the shrinks in the world and understand why I do it and that it wasn't my fault, but it's not enough. It doesn't take the pain away."

He hugs me tighter and his fingers touch my arm in a soothing motion. "I love you. Never doubt that."

A rush of warmth fills my chest. I'll never get sick of him telling me that. He loves me, even knowing how damaged and broken I am.

"I love you too," I reply, my voice thick with emotion.

He nuzzles my neck and takes a deep breath, giving me goose bumps. "I'm obsessed with your perfume," he says in a raspy voice.

A smile tugs at the corner of my lips. "I'm going to go see Ava and Elena."

His shoulders fall.

I frown. "What's wrong?"

"I want to spend time with you without all this other bullshit."

I stand. "I hope that time will be soon." I bend, put my hand in his, and tug him to his feet.

We walk through the hallway and down the stairs. Knox turns and walks toward the computer room as I search for Elena and Ava. They're by the pool table.

Axle leans close to Elena. "You have to bend more," he

says. "Keep the cue near your waist . . . your waist," he reiterates. "Elena! Where's your waist?" His patience is gone.

Cash is suppressing a laugh.

Ava sees me and rushes over. Elena places the cue on the pool table. "Don't you speak to me like that. I'm not playing anymore," she mutters with her head held high. She sees me, her eyes widen, and she walks over.

"Oh, c'mon, baaaabe," Axle says. "Don't be like that!"

She peers over at him with narrowed eyes. "No! Don't *you* be like that!"

When Axle sees me, he tilts his head in greeting. "Good to have you back."

"Thank you!" I reply, noting the relief I feel being back here.

"Hey, Zara," Cash says in a friendly tone.

I give him a small smile.

Rage saunters in with a case of beer on his shoulder and walks to the bar.

"Did you get my wine?" Elena calls out to him.

He gets up from putting the beer on the floor and glances our way. He raises his head; his hair falls back out of his eyes. "Yes, I did. I got you two," he says, his eyes darting between Elena and Ava. "Four bottles between you. Is that enough?"

Axle chuckles and answers for them. "Hell yeah! I'm getting lucky."

"Yes, it is, thank you, Rage." Elena's eyes flit back to me. "Axle's a handful!"

I crack a smile and peek at Axle. "I can see that."

"I got your whiskey too." Rage says.

I look up to see his eyes on me. I swallow hard and feel a hand on my arm.

"I'm sorry. I didn't know what else you drank, so I made sure there was enough whiskey here," says Ava.

"Thank you for thinking of me."

"I know what it's like to feel out of place here," Elena says, but Ava finishes.

"We wanted to make sure you felt welcome. No matter what happens, we would love to exchange numbers with you. We don't have any real friends, and it's hard to find genuine people these days."

My hand goes to my heart. "I'm flattered. I would love to catch up again."

I've missed having friendships with other women. I have people I work with, but I've never found a bond like the one I had with Misty. I know I never will, but I need to stop comparing my friendship with her to my friendships with others. These women are here now and seem like lovely people to build one with.

"Did you want to go outside?" Elena asks. "Somewhere a bit more private."

We follow her out past the kitchen and out the back door. Conan raises his head and wags his tail when he sees us. When we step down closer to him, he stands with his long tongue hanging out. We all pat him as we walk to the table and chairs, and he trots beside us. When we sit, he sits in front of Ava.

"He's like a big gentle teddy bear," I say to them.

Ava laughs and rubs behind his ears. "Yes, he is," she replies.

Conan groans with enjoyment and leans further back into her.

"How are you?" Elena asks.

My lips press into a line. "I'm struggling, if I'm being honest."

"You don't have to tell us anything, but know that if you need to talk to someone, we're here for you."

I pull my phone from my pocket and pass it to Elena. "Can you both put your numbers in my phone?"

Elena grasps the phone and types away on it, then passes it to Ava.

"There's so much going on, but it looks like my sister and Knox's mom, Audrey, left together. Audrey now lives in their holiday home in the mountains, so we think that is where Misty is. But then again . . . I don't know how much you know about Knox's family, but they are very wealthy. Audrey could have taken Misty wherever she wanted."

"I knew the clubhouse is on Bomber's land," Ava points out.

"If I was that rich, I'd be living it up somewhere on a beach, drinking wine." Elena shakes her head. "How do you feel about the news that they left together?"

My throat tightens. "It hasn't been confirmed yet, but it hurts. I thought me and Misty were close . . . but the more information that's uncovered, the more I don't think I knew her at all. The Misty I knew would never leave her family and Kane."

"That's Bomber's brother, isn't it?"

I give Elena a sharp nod.

"All I know is the police officer managing Misty's case did a poor job and purchased a home in Crown Village, which his wife paid for in full. So we're thinking he got paid off by Audrey."

"Isn't Crown Village expensive to buy in?" Elena asks.

"Yes, it sure is. Your everyday worker wouldn't be able to afford it."

Elena's nose crinkles. "So . . . someone gave him hush money. Is that what you're saying?"

I nod sharply. "We think so."

She lets out a heavy sigh. "I'm sorry, it's a lot to take in. I can't even imagine how you must be feeling. How are you and Bomber?"

I blink a few times. "I don't think I'll ever get used to everyone calling him Bomber."

Elena bops her head. "I felt the same with Jake. Axle, like the axle on a motor vehicle, as a name sounds ridiculous."

Ava clears her throat. "No, Reaper wins hands down!"

Me and Elena laugh. "I don't know. Bomber's not that great." I look away, thinking about the rest of their names. "Demon and Rage aren't that crash-hot either." We laugh again. "Sorry, I lost track of what we were saying."

"You and Bomber," Elena answers.

"We are . . . I'm not sure. Everything's a mess. We have talked about how we feel and about the past. He told me things I never knew about. I appreciate his honesty."

"But?" Elena questions.

"What happened in the past, that pain of him leaving me . . . That wound is still fresh, even now. He told me why he left, which has made a difference—I know he still cares."

"He doesn't just care," Ava points out, "he loves you."

"I agree," Elena says.

"It's in the way he looks at you. I told Reaper a while ago that I was worried about Bomber . . . sad even that he didn't want to find a relationship with anyone."

Relief washes over me, but then Elena snorts. "True. He only paid for sex."

My eyes bulge. "What? Paid?"

Both women flinch.

"I'm sorry," says Elena. "I shouldn't have said anything."

Ava inches closer to me. "Reaper said he only paid for sex because it was a transaction, nothing more."

I sigh, knowing that I should have known he slept with others. "Don't worry about it," I tell them. "I guess I should be grateful he doesn't have a wife and kids by now."

KNOX IS BUSY TALKING TO THE MEN. BUT IN BETWEEN, NO MATTER where I am, it isn't too long until he finds me to make sure I'm okay.

After helping the women with dinner, I go upstairs with Knox for privacy. When I jump into bed and under the comforter, I stay seated. "Did you find out anything?"

He gets in beside me and lies on his side. "The investigator is still home. Demon's been keeping watch. I'll meet him there soon to find out what he knows."

Relief and anxiety clash inside of me. I want to find answers, but at what cost? "And the cop's going to freely give up that information?" Suspicion coats my voice.

"Oh, he will," he replies confidently.

I nibble on my bottom lip. "What will happen to him?"

"Don't ask questions you don't want the answer to."

Oh, what the hell! "No more secrets. What are you going to do . . . intimidate him?"

Knox grunts. "More than that."

"Hurt him?" I ask, cringing.

His eyes scan my face as he watches my reaction carefully. "We will. Does that bother you?"

My shoulders fall, my hands clench the comforter.

He sits up and puts his hand over mine. "Think of it this way. If he was a decent human being, he would have done his job and we wouldn't be where we are now. I think we would have had a much clearer picture of what was going on. You, and my brother"—he shakes his head—"could have had answers a long time ago."

"I know," I whisper. My stomach sinks. "Will you and Demon be okay? Won't the retired cop have a gun?"

"There's nothing to worry about."

He's self-assured, but I'm not. The thought of him getting hurt makes me feel physically ill.

"Is there anything else you haven't told me?" I ask him.

"Twitch has got the house plans and is working on the security system as we speak. I want to pay Audrey a visit. See if Misty is there."

"I'm coming!"

"Afterward." His tone is sharp.

I frown. "What do you mean by that?"

"Once we have the security down and any security guards taken care of. *Then* you can come inside."

"No!"

His face and body turn to stone. "Well, that's what's happening."

I shake my head. "It's not, actually. It's important to me that I'm there. I want to see Audrey's and Misty's faces when we find them."

His face softens and he releases a deep breath.

My lip curves in a victorious smirk. "I'll take that as a 'Yes, I can.'" I'm relieved there's no more pushback. "What about Kane?"

"I'll call him tonight when I get back. I don't want him getting involved yet. His emotions make him unpredictable."

I nod, then glance away, knowing Kane will be as torn up as me.

"I heard about the escorts."

His eyes widen and he frowns. "Since I've known you were in Crown Village, I haven't seen them."

Them . . . I flinch.

"Hey . . ." he says, cupping my chin. "It's always only been you."

I nod in acknowledgment. "Since we're being honest, can you tell me what you do as a job in the MC?"

"If I tell you, you're not allowed to talk to anyone about it."

My pulse skyrockets. "I promise."

"We earn money by running and managing an illegal fighting ring, here at our warehouse, and we grow and distribute pot."

My mouth twists. "Is distributing marijuana dangerous?"

"It's nothing compared to running guns or hard drugs and having to deal with the mafia or a drug lord."

"I don't like it," I blurt out.

"You don't have to like it, but you have to accept it because it's what we do to earn money, and it won't be changing anytime soon." His voice is firm.

I look around the room, considering his words. Who am I to come back into his world and tell him what he shouldn't be doing? He's a different person now. He accepts me the way I am. I should accept him as well.

"I'm sorry for judging you and the MC." The butterfly painting on the wall captures my gaze. I can't help but ask, "Why is there a butterfly painting here? It seems out of place." As I fixate on the intricate details of the artwork, a sense of awe washes over me. "It's truly extraordinary."

Looking closely, the butterfly isn't perfect. Its wings are damaged, and it's missing scales.

"I had a young local artist paint it for me."

My eyes bulge. It looks like it's from someone who has been painting all their life. "How young?"

His hand comes to his chin. "When he did this, he was in high school. His name is Jackson. He tattoos now. If you see murals around Crown Village, they're from him."

"He's gifted. But wait, why did you ask him to paint a butterfly?"

A thoughtful look crosses his face. "You don't know?"

My brows furrow. "Should I?"

"It was my reminder of you."

My lip trembles as I look at the broken wing again.

He sits up and leans in closer. I can feel his warm breath on my neck. "Beautiful . . ." He places a soft kiss on the bend of my neck, making me shiver. "Survivor . . ." Another lingering kiss. "Mine." His voice is thick with lust.

I turn to him. His expression is dark.

"Yours," I whisper. The connection we share is soul deep, and no matter how much time has passed, it hasn't changed a thing.

He cradles my face and his mouth is on mine in an instant, making my eyes lazily drift closed. His lips are soft and greedy. When I part mine, his tongue slides in, taking . . . taking and taking. Heat gathers between my legs. He leans over me. His weight pushes me down on the bed, though our lips never break away.

He rises and I whimper at the loss of contact, but then his hand goes to my shorts. He unbuttons and I lift my hips. He yanks them down, and then my thong. I'm breathless. My heart's pounding in out-of-control beats.

His hands skim my hips before he grasps my shirt and shoves it and my bra up to reveal my breasts. Desire swims through my veins, but when his mouth wraps around my nipple and sucks, the desire morphs into need, creating a deep ache below. He lifts my shirt over my head and unclasps my bra. His eyes rake over me, the heat of his gaze making me feel sexy.

When he sits up, I watch him yanking his shirt off over his head. My eyes greedily roam over every muscle and every scar. He unbuttons his jeans next. The sound of his zipper lowering fills the room alongside my beating heart and heavy breaths. He kicks his jeans off. His eyes are wild and hold no control.

I open my legs wide, welcoming him. He crawls up,

peppering kisses up body. He places two tender kisses over the scars on my thigh, then over my stomach. I embrace the heat and weight of his body pressing into mine as he moves, placing soft kisses between my breasts and up my throat. He slips his hand between us to reach my folds. A deep husky sound escapes his throat when he feels how ready I am for him.

He eagerly spreads my legs wider. The tip of his cock pushes in, forcing a harsh breath from my lips. I feel myself stretching for him, then he thrusts all the way in. He seeks my mouth and kisses me again. His tongue swirls with mine, a mixture of tenderness and passion.

He pulls out almost entirely, then drives inside of me with a guttural groan. I grip his shoulders before he thrusts again. His pace quickens.

"Say my name. Scream it for me."

The sound of slapping skin ricochets off the bedroom walls.

"Yes," I hiss through gritted teeth.

A sheen of sweat covers his skin as he mercilessly drives into me.

"Knox, harder," I beg.

My fingers dig into his shoulders as his thrusts become harder and more and more frantic. As he inches back, my eyelids flutter closed at the building pressure within me.

"Zara, open your eyes," he growls breathlessly. "Keep them open. Look at me."

I follow his command. His dark eyes sear into mine. I'm so close, so very close. Everything is buzzing and I'm gasping for air. Punishing stroke after punishing stroke, he slams into me. I hold him tighter as we approach our orgasms.

"Let go, precious," he utters against my lips.

Overwhelming heat rises through me. We cry out in unison as we come together and the warmth of him releases into me. My world turns to white. My legs quake, and I unravel as the blissful wave of pleasure washes over me.

We stay this way, catching our breath. I wind my fingers through his thick hair and gently stroke the back of his neck. It's just us in our bubble of happiness before the cruel reality of our situation filters through.

BEST
FR_ENDS

BLEEDING OUT

Zara

Knox's phone rings on the side table. He leans over and looks at the bright screen. I dare a peek and see it's Demon.

Knox answers, listens for a second, and then says, "I'm on my way."

Alarm shoots through me. He gets up and puts on black jeans and pulls on a black shirt and a plain black hoodie.

"Do you have to go?" Worry is clear in my voice.

He bends over the bed and pecks my lips. I'm tempted to grab him, pull him down to me, and not let go.

"Yes, I do. I need to find out as much as I can."

"Can't Demon just go?"

"He won't know what questions to ask, and he can get"—he cringes—"uh . . . carried away."

I swallow hard.

He points to his cut, which is on the chest of drawers. "I'm sergeant at arms. This is who I am now. My job even within the MC is to protect and defend the club, and that can get bloody, depending on the threat."

I break eye contact, hating what he does.

"We'll be back soon," he replies, his voice softening.

When he leaves, he closes the door. I lie in bed and wait for the sound of his motorcycle, but instead I hear a car.

I toss and turn as the hours drift by but can't get comfortable. I pull my phone from behind my pillow and press the home button to see that it's 12:00 a.m. It feels so much later.

I shuffle to the edge of the bed, then step to my suitcase. I pull on underwear, shorts, and a shirt. When I poke my head out the door, there's a light coming from downstairs, but no one else is around.

I quietly pad down the hallway. Deep chuckles come from downstairs. I pause, not sure whether to join them or go in the opposite direction toward the front door. I decide to walk to the men.

Cash, Axle, and Viper are drinking beers at the bar. Cash smiles and shakes his head. He shifts when he sees me and dips his beer in greeting. Viper and Axle swivel in their chairs to look at me.

"Can't sleep?" Viper asks.

"No. Unfortunately," I reply as I make my way to them.

Cash stands, pointing to his chair, offering me his seat.

"Thank you." I step up and onto the stool.

Cash walks around the bar. "Would you like a drink?"

I raise my hand. "No, I'm fine, but thank you."

My eyes flick between the three of them. "Do you know how long Knox is going to be?"

Axle lets out a low whistle. "It could be minutes . . . it could take hours."

Viper leans forward so that he can see me fully. "Do you want me to call him?"

I shake my head. I don't want to distract Knox. "It means a lot that all of you are getting involved."

"Anything for Bomber," Viper answers.

Their close bond, fills my heart with warmth. "So . . . how did all of you meet?"

"Bomber, Reaper, and I are the founders of the War Brothers MC. We met in the military," Viper replies.

I nod. "I remember Knox mentioning that."

"Me and Cash here were in the army together. We heard about the MC through some other veterans, so we thought we'd come down to check it out," Axle says, then chuckles. "And we never left."

"Just like a bad smell," Viper mutters under his breath. "Hey, Zara, do you know Bomber's cousin Sophie?" Viper asks.

I suppress a smile at the softness in his voice. "Yes, though we don't talk much anymore."

"What's she like?"

Axle slaps Viper's shoulder. "Knox said you had no chance man, give it a break."

Viper's head falls back. "I can't," he groans. "She's by far the sexiest chick I have ever laid eyes on."

"She's really smart. Did well at school, though was also a party animal," I answer Viper.

"Did you even speak to her at the vigil?" Axle asks Viper with a raised brow.

"I was going to, but . . ."

Axle laughs out loud. "Fuckin' pussy!"

Viper's eyes sharpen. He mock shoves Axle. "If she stays in Crown Village longer, I'm going to get Knox to introduce us."

Axle rolls his eyes. "What happened to you? Mr. I'm-so-confident."

"She's a challenge, but I'm up for it," Viper answers him, with apparent determination in his eyes.

Hours roll by. I get more and more impatient. I've moved from the bar to the living room, where I'm mindlessly watching the ads that play on TV this late. I grab my phone and press the home screen. Still no messages or missed calls.

A car pulls up outside. My heart races. I'm on my feet, rushing to the front of the house. I throw open the door and bolt to the garage, from which Knox and Demon are emerging.

The metallic scent of blood is in the air. My eyes travel all over his body. "Are you hurt?"

Knox pulls away from me. "No . . . I need a shower." I stand still, watching as he leaves me to go inside. My stomach churns. Something's wrong. I stride after him and rush up the stairs. I peek inside his room, but he isn't in there. The sound of water running draws me to the bathroom.

I knock on the door. "Knox, is that you?"

"Yeah."

When I open the door, he's in the shower. His head is bowed to his chest. I can see every hardened ridge of his well-defined muscles. The droplets lick his skin and cascade over each corded muscle in his body. He hurt the retired cop to get information. I'm waiting for the guilt to come for the blood that's on my hands, but it doesn't.

Knox is quiet . . . detached. He knows I'm here but won't even look at me. I open my mouth to speak, but I don't know what to say. I'm desperate, but in his current state, I don't want to push him. I turn and go in search of Demon.

I close the door and pad down the hallway, to what I think

is Demon's room. I tap on his door; he doesn't answer. I hesitate. He shouldn't be asleep—he just got home.

I tap again, a little louder this time. "Come on in," he says in an amused tone.

My hand rests on the door handle, but my curiosity and need for answers override my hesitancy to walk in. I press down and exhale through my teeth as I walk in.

"Sorry to disturb you," I say as I open the door.

His bedside lamp is on, and he's lying on the bed with just sweatpants on. A swirl of tattoos covers every inch of his skin. He's staring at the ceiling, his arms under his head. The smell of blood is in the air.

I swallow down the bile threatening to rise, but then an uncomfortable thought flows through my mind. Even though Knox said he wasn't hurt, maybe Demon is.

"Are you hurt? Do you need me to get you anything?" It's the least I could do. He helped Knox.

Demon's face twists in pain. When he looks at me, his head tilts an inch to the side. But then he shakes his head and a wicked smile curves on his lips, though there's no mistaking the vulnerability in his eyes. That grin is his mask, and my heart aches at the thought.

He chuckles and says, "I'm alllll good. Though I can't say the same for the pig."

My body freezes. "What did you find out?"

"Ask Bomber."

"Zara." I hear my name being called from the hallway. I step toward Demon's door and open it wide to see Knox. His hair is still wet from the shower. His eyes narrow. "What are you doing in there?"

"Please tell me. What did you find out?"

He moves to me, grabs my hand, and starts tugging me outside, but I hold my ground. "Please!" The torment in my voice is unmistakable. Tidal waves of dread wash over me.

His eyes glow with anguish. "It was Audrey."

I look at him with bulging eyes. Pain fills my chest as though his words stabbed my heart.

"Misty and Audrey left together," he says, his face scrunching like every word is toxic.

"How do you know?" I ask.

"There was video footage of Misty at the pharmacy where she purchased a pregnancy test. Then there was video footage from the local retail store that's close to Audrey's house showing Misty's car parked outside, then again, with them leaving shortly afterward with Audrey's security guard. The officer never added the evidence to the file."

"So Misty's okay? She left me?" I ask as my world spins.

She actually left me . . . She near killed me. I was lifeless without her . . . without Knox. She was the hand holding the knife, cutting me open, and I was bleeding out.

BEST
FR—ENDS

EIGHTEEN
STRENGTH IN NUMBERS

Zara

I STARE BLANKLY AT KNOX, WONDERING HOW IT GOT TO THIS point. "How could they do this to me?" My voice stutters at the end.

With eyes full of sympathy, he steps toward me. He wraps his arms around me, though I feel cold . . . as if no warmth would ever penetrate. "I'm sorry," he whispers, then pulls me tighter. "I'm so sorry." His voice is raw, as if he did wrong and is apologizing for it.

I have an inkling to tell him it's not his fault, but my chest feels heavy and every inch of my body is cloaked with numbness.

He pulls back, his arms falling to his sides. "I have to call Kane."

I bring my eyes to his and nod.

"You want me to get everyone up for church or do you want to wait till the morning?" Demon asks from behind me.

I faintly hear voices, then see Axle, Viper, and Cash beside Knox. Their smiles fall, seriousness taking over.

"What do you need?" Viper asks.

Knox exhales deeply. "I've got to make a call."

Axle and Cash stay. Viper trails behind Knox. Axle peers at me and frowns.

Demons stands. "I'm going to wake Reaper."

"I'll help wake the rest and get everyone downstairs," Cash adds, and they leave.

"I'll be right back," Axle says.

It's just me, afraid to think . . . afraid to feel. I stand, gazing at the white wall in a dreamlike state.

Minutes pass and then Elena rushes to me. A deep frown mars her pretty face. "How about we go downstairs?" she whispers. She links our arms together. My legs move, but I feel disconnected from my body.

As we walk down the stairs, there's someone to my right, and I look to see Ava linking her arm with my other one. She gives me a sad smile, but the kindness of both women stirs something within me. We move past the men, who have congregated around the bar. I feel their eyes on me as we go toward the kitchen, where I sit on a stool.

"Where's Zara?"

I shift and peer over my shoulder to see Knox. His eyes roam over me, and he strides to me and kisses my forehead. "I've got to talk to the men. Kane's on his way."

Kane . . . he is going to be a wreck when he finds out. "What did you tell him?"

"Everything." He leans in, pressing another kiss on my lips before he leaves.

Conversations swirl around me. I'm aware of Ava making herself busy by going over and cleaning an already clean kitchen.

My fingers keep tapping on the stone countertop as I wait for Kane. The longer I wait, the more the anxiety pushes through the numbness.

A door bangs, and I whip around to see Kane. We lock eyes. His shoulders are hunched. I swivel the stool around, jump off it, and run to him, crashing my body into him. We hold each other tightly, as if holding our bleeding hearts together. That's all it takes for my vision to blur.

"I don't understand why they left." I inch back to look at him. Droplets of pain fall down his face.

"What if Misty had a baby?" His voice is strangled with despair. "I never got to hold the child, be a father. Instead . . . I'll be a stranger. They took my future from me. I would've been by Misty's side through her pregnancy. I would've supported her, done anything for her and the baby."

Pulling back further, I suck in a sharp breath. "We will find out what happened." That, I promise him.

Tears fall down my cheeks like rain. Knowing they've taken so much from all of us breaks my heart. We stay that way until the church door opens and the men walk out. Knox strides over. His eyes glisten as he sees his brother. I pull away, allowing them to hug.

"I want to keep you two updated with what's going on. Me, Viper, and Twitch are going to stake out Audrey's home to find out the extent of the surveillance and what security guards are there. Twitch got me the house plans showing the layout. I want to confront Audrey tomorrow night."

"When are you going to look at her security?" I ask Knox.

"Now."

"I need to go too. I can't stay here," Kane blurts.

"We are going to scope out the place. We are *not* going in yet," Knox exclaims.

"I realize that," Kane answers. "I still have to go with you."

Knox, Viper, Twitch, and Kane all get in a black van and leave. I helplessly watch as the van travels down the driveway and then the road. My shoulders drop as I make my way back inside. Elena and Ava stand when I walk in.

"Come watch some TV with us," Elena says.

Only Reaper and Axle are by the bar. It looks like the others have gone to bed.

I follow Elena into the living room. She sits and pats the seat next to her on the three-seater, so I sit in the middle.

Ava grabs the TV remote and passes it to Elena. "I'll be back."

Elena flicks through the channels, then turns her head to me. "What do you want to watch?"

I shrug, not having the mental capacity to think about it.

"I'll put a comedian on then," Elena says.

Ava comes back holding a blanket. She sits next to me and drags the blanket across us. This is what Misty and I used to do . . . and as if someone clicked their fingers, I'm transported to reality. She's the reason I'm feeling this way. *She's the reason for all my pain.*

Watching comedian after comedian make jokes, I'm struggling to focus on what they are saying, but then I'm distracted by the loud snoring that has started up next to me.

Elena turns and sits forward to stare at her sister. "Jesus Christ, it's like a freight train coming through the house."

My lip curves up as I smile. We peer at Ava, whose head is back on the couch. Her mouth is wide open as she draws in air, breathes out heavily, snorts, and gargles. It makes me giggle.

I can sense Elena's eyes on me, and when I peek at her, she has a warm smile.

"Reaper," Elena calls out. "Your ol' lady is snoring her head off. You might want to take her to bed."

Reaper and Axle make their way over. Reaper smiles at

Ava adoringly. He looks back at us. "She's been exhausted lately."

Axle bursts out laughing, his shoulders shaking. "She's got some pipes on her."

"She doesn't believe me that she snores," Reaper tells us.

"These women, I tell you what. They act all sweet and innocent at first . . . a couple of months later, it's all farts and burps, or, in your case"—he looks back at Ava—"snoring."

Elena gasps. "When have I ever farted in front of you?" she asks, sounding offended.

He raises a brow. "Are you serious, babe?" I'm not sure whether he's joking or not. "You literally *blow me away* in your sleep!"

I peek back at Elena. Her face is red. "You lie!" she spits.

Axle shakes his head, chuckling. "Nah, it's like you hold it in all day, then wait till we're in bed and then you just let it riiippppp. You're way too comfortable if you ask me. You think Ava sounds like a freight train, you sound like foghorn."

I feel immature, but I can't stop a laugh escaping.

"Well . . . I didn't ask you." She crosses her arms. "I call bullshit."

Axle puts his hand on Reaper's shoulder and looks up at him. "I think we are going to have to start videoing them."

Reaper chuckles and shakes his head. "No, Ava will be embarrassed. I'll take her to bed." He lifts the blanket from her and passes it to me. With an arm around her back and one under her legs, he lifts her and they leave.

I shuffle over, allowing Axle to sit between us so that he's next to Elena. He gives me a smile and sits.

"Do I really fart that much in my sleep?" Elena asks.

"I was exaggerating. You've done it twice."

She slaps his shoulder. "Why do you always have to embarrass me?"

He shrugs. "Because it's funny . . . and I love seeing you squirm."

Elena huffs. "Unbelievable."

Axle bats his eyelashes. "Yes, I am, baby," he purrs, putting his arm across her shoulders and pulling her to his side.

Another two hours roll by. Elena and Axle fall asleep on the couch. I'm wide awake, left wondering what the men are doing . . . and what they've seen.

Finally, a car pulls up. I'm on my feet and bolting to the front door.

Twitch is first inside, followed by Viper, who gives me a tight smile. Then Knox and Kane. I study their faces. Knox flinches when he lays eyes on me. Knox's and Kane's bodies radiate tension, making my stomach roll.

"I'm off to bed," Twitch says when he's halfway up the stairs. "Me too," Viper says, walking toward Axle and Elena. He wakes them up, gently shaking their shoulders, and they look at us.

"We will talk tomorrow," Knox says.

Axle yawns while nodding his head. He and Elena hold hands and walk up the stairs toward their room. I follow Knox and Kane to the living room. We all take a seat.

My heart races. I peer up at Knox. "What's going on?"

He releases a long deep breath. "There were no security guards out the front. Twitch could hack into her security, so he can disable it before we go tomorrow night."

"That was quick!"

"He's smart. He had a drone fly over and there was no movement within the property. Demon and Twitch are going to go there again tomorrow to see if there are any other security guards or anything we didn't catch tonight. I want tomorrow to go off with no issues."

I look at Kane, who looks disengaged. I don't even know if he's listening to us.

Knox puts his arm around my waist, bringing me close to his body. "It will all be over soon. You'll finally have your answers," he whispers in a reassuring tone.

BEST
FRIENDS

NINETEEN
CONFESSIONS

Zara

Laying in bed my eyes wander over Knox's face. His whiskey-colored eyes reflect my own, with puffiness and dark circles underneath. We haven't slept; we lay together in silence.

"Should I call my parents?"

"No," he replies gruffly. "We can't talk to your parents until it's all sorted with the police, and it depends on what we find. Once there are no threats present, me, you, and Kane will approach Audrey and Misty, if she's there. If we need to inform the police, I'll call Parker, our contact at the police station. I can't have any of this falling back on the MC, so we can't tell anyone."

I jerk my head in a nod, feeling overwhelmed.

He leans in closer to me. "I need you to promise you won't say anything. The club is important to me."

"I promise." I wouldn't risk it. The MC is like family to

him, and he's loyal. The MC has become important to me too, especially the women.

THE DAY AND AFTERNOON DRAG ON. EVERY MINUTE IS TORTURE. I wish I could turn my mind off. I stretch out my sore arms, hoping for a reprieve. Every muscle aches from suppressing the dozens of emotions that keep crashing around inside of me.

At least it's now dark outside. "Are you coming with us tonight?" I ask Kane, making small talk, knowing the answer.

"You're coming?" he asks, surprised. "Knox is letting you go?"

I wrinkle my nose. "Yes, I'm coming, and Knox isn't my keeper."

"Have you asked him?"

My eyes narrow. "Kane," I warn. "I need to be there."

He looks away. "I know . . . I do too." His voice is heavy with heartache.

My eyes linger on the closed wooden doors to church. I wish I was in there with them, going through all the final details of tonight, but Knox said it's for patched members only.

"So you haven't said anything to your dad yet?"

Kane shakes his head. "Knox said I can't."

Silence descends. "Do you think he knew anything about Misty?"

"Our parents were fighting like hell for a while before the divorce, and that was before Misty went missing. They avoided each other at all costs. Dad's always been real with us. He would have told us."

He drifts off before speaking. "I'm questioning everything I ever knew about Misty. What was a lie? What was real?"

"What do you mean by that?" I ask him.

"I thought I knew her, but with every passing day . . . it's like I never truly did."

"Whatever the outcome, the relationship you had with her was real." I lean toward him. "You know it . . . you feel it here." I place my hand over his heart.

His Adam's apple bobs.

I drop my hands and sit up straighter in my seat. "There's no proof Misty's living there. Audrey could have helped her travel anywhere around the world. Regardless of the truth, there's still this part of me that can't believe Misty would leave us . . . that she would willingly cause us this much pain."

Kane's hands clench. "I'll forgive *no one* that was involved."

Doors open, and the men file out of church. Knox walks to us holding black vests. When he's close, he hands them to us. "They're bulletproof."

I open my mouth to speak, but he's quick to say, "Neither of you are coming unless you wear them. Go get changed into comfortable clothes and shoes you can run in."

It's finally happening . . . I feel like I'm going to vomit.

Both vans stop only minutes away from the property, out of sight of security cameras. Tension buzzes as we wait in the car. Everyone's dressed in black clothes. My stomach tightens at what's coming.

"Twitch, do it now," Knox tells him.

Twitch turns to us from the front passenger side. "It's done. The security has been disabled. I'll monitor it and keep you updated."

Knox nods, then talks into the walkie-talkie. "Demon, you there?"

"Sure am," Demon replies. He's in the van behind us with Cash, Axle, Viper, and Rage.

"Make sure none of the men leave the van without their masks."

"Will do," Demon's voice comes through again.

Knox hands us black masks. I grab mine from him with a shaky hand. "Leave them on till I say otherwise," he says.

Knox taps Reaper's shoulder. Reaper, who's driving, accelerates fast, making me slip further into my seat.

My pulse thrashes against my skin as I pull the mask over my head. My heart pounds on my ribcage like it's trying to break free. As we get to a clearing, lights glint from a mansion on a hillside. The mansion is surrounded by a vast wall.

"Are you sure that security is off, Twitch?" Knox asks.

"One hundred percent—I've got your back. Don't forget the electricity circuit on the right side of the house, if you want the electricity off. And ensure the generator isn't linked to the house."

The van veers off the road and drives up the hill, along the wall. Kane leans over and slides the van door open. Everything is tingling.

"Pass me the gun in the center console," Knox asks Reaper.

As I'm stepping out onto the ground, the other van pulls up behind us. I look up at the wall and see security cameras on top. I hope Twitch knows what he's doing.

Knox grips my arms. His eyes pierce mine. "Are you sure you want to come inside? You can wait here with Twitch."

"No, I want to come. I want to look her in the eye and find out why."

All the men stand around us waiting for instructions. Faint screamy music plays. One man has an earpiece in one of his ears. I peer at his eyes and glance down. The tattoos on his hands indicate it's Demon.

Knox's eyes land on Kane, and he steps toward him, places his hand on his shoulder, and squeezes it. "If you're thinking about going off by yourself or doing anything that can put any of us in danger, you can sit your ass back down in the car." The warning hangs heavy in the air.

"As long as you get me my answers," Kane replies through gritted teeth.

"Trust me to handle this."

Kane gives the slightest nod, so Knox hands him the gun.

"Are the guns necessary?" I ask.

Knox tilts his head an inch to the side. "We always carry them on us."

Viper and Cash get the ladder off the roof of the van, and Knox goes to Reaper's side and whispers something to him. Reaper looks at me while they're talking.

Reaper looks back at Knox and nods. We follow the men to the wall.

With the few lights on the property, I can see that it's a three-level mansion, modern in shape, dark, with large, black-tinted windows.

Knox turns to me. "Stay with Reaper." His eyes flick to Kane. "You are to go behind them. Stay with us. Don't go anywhere by yourself and do not shoot anyone unless it's necessary."

Adrenaline kicks in as they place the ladder against the wall. Knox is the first one to go over. I go to step forward, but Reaper gently tugs on my arm, holding me back.

"Demon is next, then Viper, me, then you." There is no negotiation in Reaper's tone.

I shuffle my feet, my heart beating in my ears. Demon travels up the rungs with ease, then Viper. My breathing is out of control, short and quick. Reaper is next. Then I move and grab the sides of the ladder.

Axle holds the ladder for me as I climb on shaky legs,

putting one foot above the other. As I get to the top, the house lights go off and we are plunged into darkness. At the top of the wall, the edging is wide enough that I can stand on it.

A light shines below. "Jump, I've got you," Reaper's voice rumbles. Nothing is stopping me from going inside, so I close my eyes and jump. I let out a breath of relief when I land in two arms and then my feet are placed on the ground.

I scan the yard, though I can't see much. The stars in the sky provide little light, but enough to see objects in front of me.

When the rest of the men get over the wall, we dash to Viper and Knox. Reaper is by my side as we move in a line and hurry toward the back of the house.

Demon moves ahead to the door, and when I shuffle to the side, I can see him picking the lock. The door opens with ease, making me wonder just how many times he has done it.

Before we step inside, Knox says, "The bedrooms are on the top level." Once in, I stay in the middle of the pack with Reaper and Kane while the others clear every room before we reach the stairs to the next level.

"We must separate. There's too much ground to cover, and we don't know how long the security will be disabled for. Cash, Rage, Axle, and Viper, you go through this level and let me know if there's anyone there. Afterward, all of you get out of here," Knox says to the group.

There's a round of grunts, but Viper leads them away and Knox directs us up another set of stairs. The sounds of boots against the steps makes my stomach twist.

Demon heads past us to go step in stride with Knox, both with their hands on their guns, which have flashlights attached to them. As we move down the hallway, I see bedrooms to the left and right.

Knox and Demon move ahead. I step toward them, but Reaper tells me and Kane, "Us three stay here."

Demon opens the first door wide, and Knox walks in with his gun pointed forward. "Clear," Knox says softly. After going through another bedroom, Demon and Knox move to either side of another door. Knox whispers, "This is the main bedroom." He looks at Demon. "You open the door," he mouths to him. "Three. Two. One."

Demon opens the door and they go inside. "Hands up! Hands up!" Knox booms.

I rush forward, but Reaper's got me by the vest. He reaches out for Kane, but Kane shoves past him until he's in the room with Knox and Demon.

There's a high-pitched scream. "Where's Misty?" Kane demands, his tone harsh.

"Please, please, let me go in, Reaper," I screech as adrenaline courses through me. Desperation of knowing who's in that room consumes me. I pull forward, but Reaper's grip keeps me in my spot.

A slap echoes. "What was that?" I'm on edge, listening intently.

Audrey and Kane walk out of the room, Knox's light shining on Audrey. She's wearing a white night gown and holds one hand over her heart as she breathes out heavily, wide eyed. "Let go of me!"

Demon and Knox walk out behind them.

"Where are you taking me? What's this about?" Audrey screeches.

Kane rips his mask off, then raises his gun, aiming it at Audrey. "Where is Misty?"

Horror flashes across Audrey's face. "Kane?" she whispers. Her shoulders fall. Then she looks at Knox. He takes his mask off. Her eyes dart to the bedroom they just came out of. "You didn't have to hurt him."

"Your bodyguard is only unconscious, but don't think we won't harm him if we need to," Knox threatens.

"Tell me now!" Kane's voice is deadly, making me think he might go through with it—he might kill Audrey.

Anger strikes me too. I yank the mask off my face and glare at her. "You saw Misty last, you lying bitch! Answer him!"

Tears line Audrey's eyes.

Footsteps sound behind us. It's the rest of the MC's men. Audrey takes a step back. Reaper's hand comes out in a stopping motion and the men pause.

"Have you got this?" Reaper asks Knox.

"All of you can go."

Reaper answers. "I'll wait outside. Do you want the electricity back on?"

"Yes," Knox replies.

Reaper walks to the men.

Demon points to the bedroom. "Do you want me to take the bodyguard?"

"No!" Audrey shrieks.

"I'll take him, if need be," Knox answers him.

Demon's shoulders sink.

I watch as the men walk down the hallway and then turn my attention back to Audrey. Silence crackles between us.

Knox shifts, turning. "Do I have to break some of the security guard's bones to get you to talk?" He steps toward the room.

"It was an accident. Misty and I fought for a gun, and it went off," Audrey blurts out. A burst of air escapes my lips.

"What did you just say? Are you saying she's dead?" Kane asks softly, sounding afraid of her answer.

Tears flood Audrey's face. She nods sharply.

The agony that flashes across Kane's face breaks my heart. The wound from Misty's disappearance has just been sliced open again. My head pounds, my heart aches, and my vision blurs.

"Tell us everything!" Kane screams at her. "Now!" He brings the gun closer to her, only an inch from her head.

Audrey swallows hard, her eyes on the floor. "Misty came over that day and was waiting for you," she says, making eye contact with Kane. "She told me she was pregnant with your baby. Could you imagine the scandal we would have had with her being pregnant, with you as the father? The both of you were too irresponsible and young. You could never have raised a child at that age."

His lip curls. "I didn't ask for your opinion. I asked what happened to her," he roars.

Audrey flinches. "I suggested that she have an abortion, but she refused, though she was ashamed of the baby and didn't want to disappoint her family and you," she says as she stares at Kane. "I thought there was one option left, and that was to give birth to the baby in secrecy and put it up for adoption. So, before you came home, I told Misty we had a holiday house she could stay at."

The pieces fall together. "Everything was a lie. You played everyone!"

She looks at me with tears and remorse in her eyes. "We ended up getting rid of Misty's phone and car. Misty and I came up with a plan that she supposedly came to break up with Kane and left because she needed some space but would be back. I was supposed to tell everyone that she told me instead, because Kane wasn't home, but I didn't say anything to anyone, and after that the lies kept on piling up."

"What did you do to Misty?" I ask, shocked.

"Misty ended up wanting to keep the baby and go home, but I couldn't let her expose everything we had done. Then, one night, she got her hands on the security guard's gun. Me and her fought over it, then the gun went off. It was an accident." She sobs harder, struggling to breathe.

Kane's hands shake while holding the gun. Audrey closes her eyes, ready to meet her maker.

Knox slowly raises his hand and puts the other over Kane's gun. "We have her. Don't do this. Now, put the gun down and let me notify Parker, our contact at the police station."

Kane shakes his head, pushing the gun into her forehead, making her let out a brief scream. "It's not enough," Kane yells, fat tears rolling down his face. "She'll get out. You know she has money and connections."

"No, she won't. Kidnapping and manslaughter—she will do time. Let her live . . . let her suffer."

Kane's eyes are trained on his mother. "She deserves to die," Kane reiterates.

"She does, but she also deserves to rot in a cell. Death will be an easy way out for her," Knox replies, desperately trying to stop Kane from doing something he'll regret.

Lights flick on. Kane's shoulders slump in defeat as Knox helps him lower the gun.

"Nanny."

I turn to the softly spoken voice, and nothing could have prepared me for what I see next.

BEST
FRIENDS

TWENTY
DISCOVERY

Zara

A girl glances between everyone. Her eyes return to Audrey. "Why is everyone being so loud? Nanny, why are you crying?"

Audrey rubs her eyes and her face. She clears her throat. "Everything is all right," she replies.

The girl walks toward us. When I get a better look at her, the wind is knocked out of me, as if I'm dreaming I'm on the merry-go-round. It's going round and round faster and faster, and all I see is Misty's face at that age, smiling back at me. The room spins. My knees hit the ground.

My world halts. Misty's face morphs into the girl's. She looks like Misty did when she was younger, except for Kane and Knox's whiskey-colored eyes. This is a dream. It can't be real. I didn't think she was alive.

"What's your name?" I ask her in a small voice.

"Avyanna."

"That's a beautiful and unusual name."

She peers up at Audrey. "Nanny said my mom gave it to me. It means strong and beautiful."

I breathe out a long breath at the mention of Misty. It's such a perfect and fitting name. I look up at Kane, who is frozen in place. He looks over every inch of her. His hands tremble, and tears fall.

I bring my eyes back to Avyanna. "I'm your auntie and he," I say as I glance at Kane, "is your father."

She peers back at Audrey for reassurance. She nods to Avyanna. "It's your dad."

Avyanna stills, her eyes darting between all of us. "It's okay," Audrey says softly. A slow smile paints Avyanna's face as she runs to Kane and leaps into his arms. He goes from frozen to melting into his daughter's embrace. He cradles her against his chest and kisses the top of her head as more tears stream down his cheeks.

Knox leans down to me and helps me stand on unsteady legs.

Kane keeps looking over Avyanna, checking that she's real, and then pulls her back into a tighter hug. She giggles. The sound makes my chest constrict.

When Kane puts Avyanna down, Knox steps toward her. He bends down until he's at her height. "I'm Knox, your uncle. Nice to meet you," he says as they shake hands.

She smiles. "I have an uncle too!" She peers up at Audrey. "Did you hear that, Nanny?"

She blinks furiously. "I did, dear," Audrey replies.

"Did you get to meet your mom?" I ask Avyanna.

She shakes her head and frowns. "Nanny said she went to heaven when I was a baby."

My heart splinters at her words, and it takes everything in me to contain myself and not lash out at Audrey. She stole so many moments from everyone. "I knew your mother. She was my best friend, and my sister."

Avyanna's eyes widen. "What was she like?"

"She would have been an exceptional mother to you. I'm sorry you didn't get to spend time with her. She looked out for me, and I always envied how strong she was." I grab a lock of Avyanna's hair and twist it between my fingers. "And you look just like her, but you have your dad's eyes."

"I'm going to call Parker," Knox says to me, then peers at Audrey. "Say your goodbyes now."

Audrey makes her way to Avyanna while Kane glowers at her. She bends down, grabbing Avyanna's hands. "I've got to go away for a while, so you're going to stay with your dad."

She frowns. "How long are you going away for?"

She sniffles, and when I glance at Audrey, she's crying. "I'm not too sure yet. But I will see you. Now you better go with your dad so you can get your bags packed."

Knox walks back. "The police are on their way."

"Show me to your room?" Kane asks Avyanna. She puts her hand in his and they wander down the hallway.

Knox lifts his walkie-talkie to his mouth. "Hey, you still there?"

"Yeah, man," Twitch replies.

"Police are on their way. You and Reaper get out of here, but pick us up in about half an hour. I don't want any of you here when the cops get here."

"Downstairs, now," Knox says to Audrey.

He follows closely behind her through the hallway and down the stairs and out the front door. Police sirens wail.

"This will be the last freedom you will have for a while," says Knox.

"I didn't mean to kill Misty. You have to believe me."

Knox chuckles darkly. "You were so obsessed with your image that you jeopardized any chance for Avyanna to have a mother in her life, and you've selfishly taken all those years away from your own son."

Blue-and-red lights flicker, and I watch as a sedan and two cop cars make their way to the mansion.

Dread slithers up, gripping my throat. I grab Audrey's arm. "Where's Misty buried?"

"There's a plaque in the backyard with her name on it. It's surrounded by flowers. Exactly the way Avyanna wanted it."

"We're ready!" I drop my arm and peek over Audrey's shoulder to see Kane and Avyanna walking toward us. With one hand Kane's dragging a large hot-pink suitcase with a large tote bag on top. He's holding Avyanna's hand with the other.

AFTER TALKING TO THE POLICE, WE DROP KANE AND AVYANNA off at Kane's house. As much as I want to spend time with her, the sun would be up soon and she should stay with Kane.

When we walk inside the clubhouse, all the men are awake and seated at the bar. Everyone stops talking and all eyes are on us, but it's me who speaks. "I'd like to thank everyone again. With your help, we could find answers that have been haunting our families for over ten years." There's a round of cheers and claps. "I'm both happy and sad to report that my sister had passed away, but her daughter Avyanna is alive and well and is with her father, Kane, now."

There are gasps and a mix of feelings on everyone's faces.

I peer back at Knox. "I'm going to go to bed. I'm exhausted. You can stay up with the men."

He shakes his head and links our fingers together. "I'm coming with you."

"Night, everyone," Knox calls out. Hand in hand, we go up the stairs and to Knox's room. Once inside, I pull the comforter back and sit on the edge of the bed. I take my sneakers off, then lie down.

Knox's phone rings. He pulls it out of his pocket, looks at the screen, then places it on the side table. "Who is it?"

"My uncle. I presume Audrey has called the family lawyer to represent her. I'm sure my uncle wants to know everything."

"Aren't you going to answer it?"

"I'll talk to him when we wake up." He kicks his shoes off and shuffles in next to me. He folds his arm over me, pulls my back flush against him, and covers my hand with his. "All I need now is you."

"You have me."

Forever . . . I have nothing to run from anymore. My life is here with Knox, Kane, Avyanna, and my parents. Soon we'll be faced with the heartbreaking duty of informing my parents about the tragic events that unfolded.

BEST
FR ENDS

TWENTY-ONE
UNTIL WE MEET AGAIN

Zara

TWO WEEKS HAVE PASSED SINCE THAT NIGHT. WE'VE GIVEN OUR statements to the police. Audrey is in jail being held without bail. Her security guard provided details of the kidnapping and confirmed Audrey's story for a lesser sentence.

I rub my leg, anxiousness taking hold. Kane is pacing in front of me, wearing marks into the carpet. Mom has a blank stare. She was always the one who had hope, even when I told her that Audrey said Misty had passed away. Mom refused to accept it.

There's a knock on the door. Knox goes to stand, but his dad, David, puts his hand out to stop him and stands instead. "No, son, I'll get it. You stay with Zara."

I give him a sad smile. He's been visiting all of us most days. I see the heavy burden that Audrey's actions have placed on all the men in the Hart family.

Officer Parker walks in with David. Kane halts when he sees him, and Parker gives us a tight smile.

"Well?" Kane asks, cutting to the chase.

Parker holds my stare as he brings his hand out to me and places a necklace into my palm, the best friend one Misty and I shared. A painful scream tears from Mom's throat. Dad is by her side, holding her.

"No . . . no . . . no. Not my baby," she sobs.

Knox wraps me in his arms.

"We found this with the body. Do you recognize it?" Parker asks.

I nod briefly, unable to talk because of the constriction in my throat.

"What is it?" Kane asks.

I clear my throat and show him the necklace. "It was hers," I whisper. I bring hers against my own, showing how the two parts link to form a single heart.

Kane's body droops as he sits back down, his head in his hands. David squeezes Kane's shoulders as tears fall down his face.

"We'll confirm her identity with you once the DNA results come in."

"Thank you." Knox speaks for all of us.

"It's okay. I can see myself out."

"Has there been an update about the charges laid against Audrey?" I ask Parker before he leaves.

"There's a strong legal case. She's facing charges for murder, kidnapping, and the imprisonment of Avyanna."

So she should.

"Thank you."

After he leaves, I turn to my mom and put my arm around her. "We still have a piece of Misty with us. Avyanna is our little miracle," I say out loud to everyone, hoping to ease their pain.

Everything is a blur until we receive the results confirming that the body is indeed Misty's. We find the perfect cemetery for her close by, one overlooking the water.

A feeling of peace has cloaked me since finding the truth. Kane and Mom are still struggling, but having Avyanna gives them something to be grateful for, even under these circumstances.

When we lay her to rest, after everyone has said goodbye, I stay behind. I slowly walk over and place a single sunflower on her casket as I smile down at her. "You finally got the send-off you deserved," I say as I touch the smooth-grained wood of the casket. "I've missed you so much. It's hard to believe it's been so long since you've been gone. I wish you were here, but I know you're smiling down at us."

I release a ragged breath. "I'll try my best to help Kane raise your beautiful daughter. I hope we make you proud. She's been in my life for a short while, but I don't know what life would be like without her in it."

A little giggle escapes me. "She looks exactly like you, and I'm sure you're amused that she has your sass and attitude already and has her daddy and grandparents wrapped around her little finger. No one can say no to her because she deserves the world . . . and so much more."

I peer over at Knox. He's too far away to hear me, but he's still watching closely—always watching me. "I want you to know that I'm happy with Knox. He is everything I ever needed. He loves me for me, even with all my battle scars."

I kiss my fingers and press them to the casket. "Best friends forever," I whisper. "Until we meet again."

BEST
FRIENDS

TWENTY-TWO
NEW BEGINNINGS

Three months later

Zara

Kɴᴏx ᴀɴᴅ I ʟᴇꜰᴛ ᴀ ᴄᴏᴜᴘʟᴇ ᴏꜰ ᴅᴀʏꜱ ᴀꜰᴛᴇʀ ᴛʜᴇ ꜰᴜɴᴇʀᴀʟ ᴛᴏ ɢᴇᴛ my belongings from my home in the city. I spoke to my manager to hand in my resignation. It was sad leaving her and my colleagues—and the women's shelter where I put my heart and soul into helping other people, though I know it's in good hands.

As I'm tossing the salad, I gaze at the newest members of my family. I'm blown away every day by how much Avyanna reminds me of Misty, even though they never truly met.

"How's that mac and cheese coming along, Avyanna?" Ava asks as she peeks into the oven.

Avyanna spoons a small scoop into her mouth, then her lips curve into a blinding smile. "Yum!"

"Don't put the spoon back in. Put it in the sink." My words hurry out before she contaminates the food.

"I saw that!" Twitch grumbles. He looks at Ava with one brow raised. "How come she gets to eat it?"

Ava waves him off. "She's a child. You're a grown adult. She can try it."

"Is he really an adult, though? He acts like a child." Elena's voice is full of amusement.

Axle points a finger at Twitch. "Ha! Take that!"

Elena whips around to face Axle. "Don't you talk. You are just as bad as him, if not worse."

Twitch's lips rise into a victorious smile as he looks at Axle with mocking eyes.

"Babe, me and you," Axle says as his finger flicks between the two of them, "are supposed to be a team and ahh . . . you aren't pulling your weight."

Ava opens the oven, steam rises. She uses tea towels to pull out a huge chicken with baked vegetables. The smell saturates the air, making my stomach grumble.

I look at Ava. "Salad's done. Do you want cling film over it?"

"Yes, please," Ava replies.

Reaper walks into the busy kitchen from the living room. "Would you like some help?"

Ava nods. "Ham is in the fridge, and I need someone to take the cookies." She tilts her head toward the large container with the blue lid on the counter.

Knox stands from the stool. "On it."

"Twitch, can you take the fried rice that's beside me?"

"Yep," Twitch answers.

"This is a test run . . . I hope everyone likes it and that it's good enough," Ava says, then nibbles on her bottom lip.

My eyes tear up. "Of course they will. You'll never grasp

how much they will appreciate it. To have a people be there for them means the world."

She tilts her head back and blinks furiously, then she scans the room, looking at all of us. "I know exactly what that feels like."

I look around at everyone, at the women and men who have been by our sides and offered their assistance and support. "I know too," I answer.

"So what are we doing again?" Avyanna asks, though her eyes are still locked onto the mac and cheese.

"It's a surprise," I blurt out, not wanting to give anything away. She doesn't know. Hell, Mom and Dad and Kane don't know. We have been good at keeping this secret from them. Avyanna heard us talking about cooking food for a surprise occasion, so she wanted to help.

"Are the guys finished and ready for everyone to see? Knox, can you call them to check?"

He shoots me a smile, and it lessens the nervousness. "They will be fine. Now, are we ready to go?"

"Yes," I answer, dying to see what the place looks like finished.

We pile into the vans and truck.

Fifteen minutes later, I pull up to a redbrick hall that the Crown family owned but gave to us because we needed a place. The van's side door slides across, and I'm out first, with a large bowl of salad in hand.

"It's perfect." I rush forward, goose bumps traveling across my skin. The front lawn is a lush green, with a cream-colored paved path to the entrance door. On the side is a blanket covering what I know to be a large plaque that says "Misty's Safe Haven."

After we buried Misty, I was determined to ensure that her death wasn't in vain. I wanted to help others who are going through traumatic experiences. With the help of family and friends, I created a charity called Misty's Safe Haven.

The charity will also have a hotline women and children can call if they feel they are in danger. The Harts and the MC have offered to assist by removing the victims from the situation and bringing them to the charity, which will provide free meals, shelter, and other necessities.

After my mom, dad, and Kane see it, I plan to contact local professionals like counselors and lawyers who can help victims get back on their feet. I've managed a shelter before, so I can use my skills and assist with getting the victims jobs and accommodation.

Ava has been cooking up ridiculous amounts of food, ensuring she masters every dish before the shelter opens. I'm so proud of what we've achieved, and I couldn't have done it without the help of the MC.

Viper greets me at the door. He gives me one of his easy smiles. He reaches out and grasps the salad. "I'll take that. Come check it out. Turned out better than I imagined."

I want to . . . so bad. "No, I want it to be a surprise with Mom, Dad, and Kane."

"How long till they get here?"

"Shouldn't be long."

Seeing the smiles and excitement radiating from the men truly touches my soul and warms my heart. Allowing them to help, to be a part of something that's important and special, has brought out how amazing this group really is. I helped with the layout of the shelter and ordered what we needed, but they have spent late nights renovating, painting, and putting furniture and beds together.

"Can I tell you one thing?" He's bursting at the seams like a little child at Christmas.

I chuckle at his excitement. "Okay, what?"

"We've put together a playground for the kids," he blurts

out. "Demon has outdone himself. The kids are going to love it." He hurries off.

I step outside and wait on the front lawn for everyone to walk inside. I hear gasps and squeals. I shuffle from one foot to the other, holding myself back from going inside.

I squint as a familiar car turns up the street. I dash to the door. "Everyone, they are here! Quick, quick!" I yell.

I hear footsteps as I hurry back to the grass. The car pulls up to the curb in front of me and I nervously wait until they get out.

David knows about it, so I've had him distracting them this morning. He gives me a knowing smile. Mom, Dad, and Kane step out of the car looking confused. Avyanna darts out to Kane.

I wipe my clammy hands on my jeans before I step closer to Mom and kiss her cheek. "I've got a surprise for the three of you." I move to the front of the hall and usher them over until they are close. "Welcome to . . ." I pull the blanket down, and as it falls, it reveals a silver plaque engraved with "Misty's Safe Haven."

Mom's shaky hands go to her mouth as Dad's lip trembles.

"It's a safe haven for women and children where we'll provide them with the resources they need to get their lives back on track."

It's Dad who rushes to me and hugs me tight. "I'm so very proud of you," he whispers into my ear. He sniffles and pulls back, wiping his now glassy eyes.

"That's Mom's name," Avyanna says as she inspects it. She steps closer, looking at the smaller writing at the bottom. "In loving memory of Misty Pratt, a sister, a daughter, a mother, and a best friend. Her life a beautiful memory that will never be forgotten," she reads out, then peers up at me. "This is for Mom?"

"Yes, we created this to honor her." Maybe, if Misty had something like this to turn to, to get anonymous advice or help, things would have been different.

Viper appears. "Everything is ready."

"Thank you," I reply.

"Dad, Dad," Avyanna says. "Are you okay? Don't cry." She wraps her arms around her dad.

He mouths "Thank you" to me. I smile back, glad that they're happy.

I grasp Mom's hand in mine. "Let's take the tour. Viper, did you want to do the honors?"

His face, if possible, brightens more. He gestures broadly at the center. "Welcome, follow me . . ."

BEST
FRIENDS

TWENTY-THREE
THE BRIGHTEST STAR

Eight months later

Zara

It's Misty's anniversary again, and it's bittersweet. We go to visit her often, but today is different. I walk into the house with a bunch of bright-yellow sunflowers and put my keys and bag down on the table by the entrance.

This anniversary differs from others. No more lies, no more nightmares, no more cuts. When she visits me in my dreams, I still see her face and her beautiful blond hair and zest for life, which I see in her daughter too.

When I go out into the backyard, the sight before me makes me laugh. Viper and Avyanna are dancing to "You Can Do It" by Ice Cube. They roll their bodies from left to right in unison with the lyrics and I smile in amusement, thinking Misty would do the same with them if she were here.

When Avyanna looks up at me, she beams, "Viper's teaching me the dance."

"Is he now?" I dare a peek at Kane, who rolls his eyes, but there's a smirk on his lips.

"She has potential," Viper chimes in.

"Since when are you a dance teacher?" Axle yells out.

Noting the swearing and offensive language of the song, I ask, "Where can I change the music?"

"It's connected to my phone," Twitch answers, phone in hand.

"Can you change it . . . to something more appropriate," I say as I look at Avyanna.

Viper scoffs. "Oh please, she hears swearing all the time."

I try my best to stifle a laugh while two arms come around me, hugging me and pulling me into a broad chest. I turn to see Knox giving me one of his devastating smiles.

"He has a point," he says into my ear.

Avyanna runs to me and puts her arms around my waist so that I'm sandwiched between the two of them. I have to lift the flowers above Avyanna's head so they don't get crushed.

"It's a good song, Aunty Zara." I smile back at Avyanna as her eyes widen at the flowers. "Are those for Mom?" she asks.

"They sure are."

"When are we going?"

"Now, because we're going to see your mom first and then we're going to Crown Village Amusement Park."

"Yes!" she says, excited. "Can I come back here afterward?"

Kane walks to us and peers down at Avyanna. "We'll be back tomorrow for lunch. Nan and Pop will be here as well."

Knox, Avyanna, Kane, and I go together to Misty's grave before setting out for the amusement park.

Avyanna gets to go on her mom's favorite rides, which are now her favorite rides too—no surprises there. Now that I know the truth and have accepted it, I don't look for Misty in the crowds anymore.

We stay for hours, sharing stories with Avyanna about her mother, one being the time Misty cheekily smashed the ice cream in Kane's face. I smile at all the precious memories we share. No one can take those away from us.

After we get off the bumper cars, Kane says, "We'd better get going."

Avyanna groans, making me chuckle.

"We can come back another time," Kane tells her.

"Fine," she grumbles. He has got his hands full with her. Kane shakes his head with a smile.

A hand tugs on my wrist. I peer back at Knox. He drops to one knee.

I gasp as my heartbeat quickens. He looks up at me with that smile that's reserved for me. He opens the navy case to reveal an elegant engagement ring with a pear-shaped diamond stone.

"Zara, I know what it's like to live without you, and I could never do that again. You are everything to me, and I'm nothing without you. As you know, life is short, and I can't wait another second without us being bound in every way possible. Be my wife, and I promise to make you happy for the rest of your life."

"Yes, of course," I answer with a shaky voice.

His whole face transforms into sheer happiness. I'm holding back tears.

Knox stands and puts the ring on my finger. He holds my face in his hands as he bends down and touches his lips to mine in a lingering kiss.

"I love you so much," he says, his eyes flashing with so many emotions.

"I love you too," I whisper back.

Kane comes over to us. "Congratulations! You two deserve to be happy."

My eyes glisten. "So do you," I say back to him.

Kane pats Knox on the back.

Avyanna jumps to me, all excited, her mother's best-friends necklace bouncing from side to side around her neck. She looks at my ring. "That's really pretty."

"It is," I answer.

We walk back to the car. The night is dark, apart from the moon lighting up the sky and the stars shining brightly. Avyanna skips up to me and puts her hand in mine. I look down at her and notice she's looking up at the stars.

"Which one do you think is Mommy?" she asks.

I close my eyes briefly, then look at Kane as he steps up to Avyanna and takes her other hand in his.

"The brightest star in the sky, baby girl."

After we get back to the clubhouse, I walk through the front door, but I don't get far as Elena and Ava dive on me, grabbing my hand.

"Oh, it's beautiful," Ava says and kisses my cheek. "Congratulations!"

Elena gives me a tight hug. "Congratulations."

My eyes flick between the two of them. "How do you know already?"

"Bomber told Reaper and Viper. Viper told Axle." Elena cringes. "And Axle told everyone."

As we walk further inside, Cash, Rage, Reaper, and Twitch crowd around Bomber. I hear a round of congratulations coming from them.

Axle makes his way to me and pulls me into his arms. "Congratulations and good luck."

I pull back with a smirk. "What do you mean good luck?"

"Having to deal with that cranky bastard for the rest of your life."

I laugh out loud.

Viper's next. He puts his arms around my shoulders. "Congrats!" He peers up at the men. "Bomber." Knox turns to him. "I shotgun organizing the bachelor party!"

"Fuck yeah!" Axle is the first to yell out. Elena glares at him. "Oh . . . I meant boooo!"

"No strippers!" Elena warns sternly.

"I'm not having strippers," Knox tells Elena. She looks relieved. I feel a bit of relief as well.

"We will have a joint party. There's no need for a bachelorette party," says Knox.

Viper chuckles, then peers down at me. "He just doesn't want *you* to have any strippers."

"You're boring, Knox!" Viper yells out in amusement. "Wait . . . will Bomber's cousin be invited?" Viper asks me.

"Yes," I reply, knowing that they will want to be there.

"Can you introduce me to Sophie?" he asks softly, so that only I can hear.

"Sure," I reply with a grin. He doesn't know what he's in for.

BEST
FR-ENDS

TWENTY-FOUR
PEACE

Zara

"Hey, Mom." I smile brightly as she walks into my arms. When we pull back, I lift my hand up.

She grasps my hand and her mouth gapes open. "He didn't!"

I giggle. "He did!"

"John, your daughter's getting married."

Dad shakes Knox's hand and smiles. "That's wonderful news." Dad steps to me and leans in, giving me a kiss on the cheek.

"Follow me inside. Everyone is out the back," I say to them.

"There's quite a few people here," Mom points out as she looks at the parked motorcycles and cars.

"No, not really. Don't forget that a lot of people live here."

When we step inside, her eyes widen. She walks slowly as she inspects the clubhouse. "Are you two going to buy your own house now?"

I shake my head. "In the future . . . I actually enjoy living here. It's like an extended home."

When Mom moves to where all the men's police mug shots are displayed on the wall, she clicks her tongue. "Knox Hart." She emphasizes both his names. "What did you do?"

Knox puts his hands on her back, ushering her toward the rear of the house. "Oh, look, it's Elena," he says.

"Nice save," I mutter under my breath to Knox.

Mom throws her arms around Elena, and Elena hugs her back with a huge grin. "Mrs. Pratt, it's so good to see you again."

"You too, and please call me Helen." Seeing how well my parents get along with the ol' ladies and all the men from the MC makes me happy because I can have everyone together at once.

Ava comes running in through the back door and past us with her hands covering her mouth. My eyes flick back to Mom and Dad. "Kane and Avyanna are outside. You go sit. I'll check on Ava."

I follow Elena, and we rush to her. Ava's bent over the toilet, vomiting. I cringe at the sound of it, but also feel bad for her.

"Are you okay?" Elena asks. "Did you want me to go get Milly?"

Ava stands and presses the flush button. "No, I'm fine, really."

I know the signs. "You're pregnant!"

Elena squeals. Ava goes bright red. Elena points her finger at Ava. "You are!"

"We only found out a couple of days ago. Please keep it quiet . . . Reaper and I weren't going to tell anyone until I safely passed the twelve-week mark."

Elena squeals again and jumps up and down on the spot. I

grab Ava, giving her a tight hug. "I'm so excited for the two of you."

"I can't believe it. I'm going to be an aunty. I can't wait to go baby shopping!" Elena beams.

Ava's eyes stretch wide. "Shhh! No one can find out," she whispers. "With my endometriosis, I'm worried something bad could happen."

Elena raises her hands. "I'm sure everything is going to be fine. I won't say anything. I promise."

"I won't say anything either," I tell Ava. My heart fills with joy at the thought of her having a baby. She's such a loving person, she will be the perfect mother.

When we step outside, there's music playing in the background, but by the table there's chatter and laughter. As I take my seat beside Knox, his lips curve up into an affectionate smile, making my heart strum. He folds his hand over mine and I lean into him. I'm the one who gets to see every side of him . . . his love . . . his compassion . . . his devotion.

Reaper's frowning. He and Ava talk in hushed tones. I peer around the table of friends and family and see only a few people I don't know. "Who's the attractive woman sitting next to Twitch?"

The woman's head falls back as she laughs, her hand going to Twitch's leg.

"Reaper's sister, Milly. She's a doctor."

Twitch smiles back at her. They hold eye contact.

"Are they together?"

"No."

I look up at Knox. "They look like they're a couple."

Knox's shakes his head. "It's not going to happen. It's Reaper's sister. They just flirt."

I keep my mouth closed, but I have a feeling, by the way they are looking at each other, it might be more than just *friends.*

"Oh dear lord," Mom calls out in a high-pitched voice. She's sitting on the other side of me. Her eyes are on Conan.

"He's friendly, Mom."

She sits up straighter in her chair. "He certainly doesn't look like it." Conan's sitting next to the barbecue, massive strands of drool hanging from both sides of his mouth. Avyanna runs to Conan and Mom yells "No!" but Avyanna doesn't listen and pats Conan on the head.

"See, Nan, he's a friendly dog." Conan licks her hand and she giggles.

Mom's shoulders fall in relief and an adoring smile lights up her face as she watches Avyanna. As I peek around the table, Kane and Knox share the same smile as Mom, and my chest could burst from happiness.

Knox

Later that night

"Are you sure about this?" I ask Kane, one more time, allowing him the opportunity to back out, because once it's done, he can't come back from this.

Kane's lips press into a hard line. "I've never been so sure about anything in my life. Burn it down to the ground."

I stare at Audrey's mansion that held Avyanna and Misty captive. I press the detonator and brace for impact. The blast shoots bright yellow flames and scatters debris through the sky. A rush of air hits my face. We're far enough away to not be hit by the explosion. The destruction of the structure provides an odd feeling of satisfaction, enjoyment even, that the house that held years of pain and secrets is gone forever.

I pull the burner phone from my back pocket, press the

number for Harrison—my cousin who's a firefighter—and bring the phone to my face.

"Hello," he answers in a croaky voice.

"You didn't hear it from me, but Audrey's place just exploded."

There's shuffling. "You just blew up her house?"

I chuckle. "Yeah, we did."

There's a breath. "Fuck, man . . . Honestly, I don't blame you. House of horrors. Is it just the house or has it started fires outside the walls?"

"Not that I can see."

"We're on our way," he says.

"Focus on ensuring the fire doesn't extend to outside the home, but let the house burn for a while. We want nothing to be left there."

"I'll do my best," he answers.

Kane, Zara, and I get into the van and drive away. I watch in the side mirror as the flames dance in the sky's darkness.

I place my hand on top of hers. She looks at me and smiles. I'm in awe of her fearlessness and passion to help others. Hell, she brought the men in our MC closer together. Like being in the military, we are honored to help women and children in the community and are once again proud of ourselves and what we have accomplished.

"This is what freedom feels like," Zara says in the passenger seat next to me.

I glance at her; she has a small smile. I know she's referring to Audrey's house—the last painful piece of the past has been eliminated—but for me, it's not just that. My freedom comes from Zara returning to me. She broke the chains that had stopped me from living.

Zara is the very essence of my being, the life that runs through my veins, the heartbeat of my existence, and the one who completes me in every way.

The end.

If you want to see Zara and Knox's celebratory combined bachelorette and bachelor party, view the sneak peek of Viper.

Did you want to go into the draw to win a *free paperback*? Sign up for my mailing list. Simply opening my newsletter emails enters you to win any paperback.

If you love my books, please leave a *review* or *rating* on your purchased retailer or your favorite platform. It encourages other readers to take a chance on me. It truly makes a difference and provides crucial feedback.

SNEAK PEEK AT VIPER

Viper

"Shots! Shots! Shots!" Axle, my MC brother, hollers as he walks toward us with a tray of shots.

I rub my hands together "Fuck yeah!" I reply enthusiastically. My mission is celebrating Bomber and Zara's soon-to-be marriage, but I also want to sleep with Bomber's cousin Sophie. I don't want to get too drunk because if I can get her in the sheets, I want to remember every curve of her body, her taste, her scent—everything about her. I'm aware I'll be lucky to ever sleep with someone as classy as her again.

I've caught a glimpse of Sophie a few times, while she's been back. If it were a different woman, I would have at least chatted her up. I shake my head. Well… tonight's my chance.

When I pick up the overfilled shot glass, the liquid trickles down and onto my hand. I wait until everyone has a shot in their hand, and then I raise mine. "To Bomber and Zara," I yell.

Everyone cheers, "To Bomber and Zara."

We clink our shot glasses together, then I toss the shot

down my throat, feeling the burn. I'm left with a sweet taste in my mouth, but I enjoy it better than the last shot.

"What's the name of that one?" I ask Axle, having to raise my voice over the music.

His grin widens. "Wet pusssyyyyyy," he replies, making me laugh.

"No wonder I like the taste of it then," I say with a wink, then turn my attention to Ava. "Aren't you having any shots tonight?" She hasn't touched one that's been brought out.

Her eyes widen, but then she smiles. "No, thank you. I'm happy with my cocktail."

My brows lift. I bet it's a mocktail. I peer at her, then Reaper, who is her partner and the president of the MC. He subtly shakes his head at me, as in telling me to leave the topic. How stupid do they think I am? She's pregnant. I have no doubt about it. I'm patiently waiting for them to tell everyone.

Alec did an awesome job organizing Bomber and Zara's party. We got VIP access to this exclusive nightclub called Envy, so we didn't have to line up, and he got us a VIP table. But the best part is Alec set up a tab, so we don't have to pay for a drink all night.

The second floor is classier. Everything from the furniture to the lighting to the VIP bar. I settle back in my seat. I'm stoked that the sweet butts didn't come. Candy is a cool chick and all… but she's getting way too clingy. We have sex, that's it. I'm not interested in anything more. Having casual sex with her is convenient. I've told her time and time again what the deal is between us.

I lean over, putting my empty glass on the table. I peer around at the couples surrounding me. It feels like everyone is settling down. Axle and Elena, Reaper and Ava, now Bomber and Zara. The men will be attached to the women's hips tonight, never allowing them to go too far away. Possessive psychos. Though I don't blame them—I'd trust no man outside the club.

There's a twinge of jealousy I haven't experienced before. Seeing all the couples together and how well everyone gets along has me wondering if I want more than just hookups. I clear my throat... I can't believe that crossed my mind. Bomber and Zara's engagement and their promise of a happily ever after is messing with my head.

There's me, Twitch, Demon, Cash, and Rage, the last men standing, though I'm sure someone will be next. Twitch might sleep with Mercedez, one of the MC's sweet butts, but he's not interested in a relationship with her. And as much as he pines over Reaper's sister, Milly, he's got no chance. Rage is in his early twenties, still too young for anything serious, and I could laugh at Demon ever getting a woman. Perhaps it will be Cash, but according to the men, he still hasn't moved on from his past relationship.

I walk by our table and to the balcony that leads over to the first floor. The lights are dim where we are, with different colored flashing lights coming from the main stage. My shoulders move to the beat of techno music. Steve Aoki is killing it tonight. The first level is packed with people dancing.

There's a squeal, so I turn to see Zara standing, hugging Sophie. Harrison, Alec, and Lawson are off to the side, shaking hands with the MC men. Their family is beyond wealthy—like generational, old-money wealthy. Sophie looks incredible in a red dress that shows off her long legs. As I turn my gaze to the side to get a better sight of her, the slit in her dress reveals the creamy skin of her thigh. She should model for Victoria's Secret because she's an absolute bombshell.

I lean back on the edge of the balcony, drinking her in. I first saw her at Zara's sister's vigil, and I've never been so taken by a woman. I couldn't even go and talk to her, so I sussed her out, asking Zara and Bomber to give me the lowdown. Sophie used to be close to them when they were young, but they haven't kept in touch since she finished school, then moved away to New York.

Sophie is devoted. Coming home when her family and friends need her. She had a career on a silver platter because of all the businesses her family owns but moved away instead to pursue her own dreams. Sophie isn't just a beauty, she seems to be so much more, and that has piqued my interest. I've never wanted to spend more than one wild night with a woman, but I want to get to know her.

That we do business with her father should be reason not to go there because it could cause problems, but right now I'm living in the present. I can worry about all the other nonsense later.

When the men have shaken Bomber's cousins' hands, I step forward. I grasp Alec's hand in a firm handshake. He's a nice guy and all, but he looks like a tool being in a club with a suit on… though maybe that's his game. Showing women that he's loaded, because the Crowns are the richest people I've ever met.

Lawson's next, and we shake hands. "Hey," I say to him. He's a sexy son of a bitch, I'll give him that. My eyes drift over the family. They all are a good-looking bunch.

I pull back on seeing Harrison. His smile is wide. "Hey, man, how are you doing?" I ask him. He always says hi to me even though we don't know him well. He's dressed in a casual shirt and jeans, like the rest of us.

"Awesome… now." He glances around the club. "I haven't been back to Vegas in so long."

"I haven't either. The clubs are insane," I reply. I'm used to the parties back home in the MC clubhouse or at our local bar.

Harrison looks around, then tilts his head. "I'm going to the bar; do you want anything?"

I nod. "A beer, thanks."

"What type?"

"Anything will do."

He nods, then makes his way over to the bar as Sophie walks over to me. My pulse thrums. I scold myself for acting like a pussy. I can't stop my eyes from wandering down her breasts to the curve of her hips, to those long legs that I hope to be spreading tonight.

"Viper, is it?" she says, and I like the way my name rolls off her tongue a little too much. I'm getting a semi.

I inch back, giving her an indecent grin. "Sure is, darlin'."

I swear to God, I saw her mouth the word "delicious," but with the damn music up so loud, I can't hear shit. She pulls me in for a hug, which startles me for a second, but then I hug her back, appreciating her body against mine.

I take a deep breath and say, "You smell heavenly…" Mouth-watering and appetizing.

She leans back, giving me a seductive smile. "So do you… like coconut and lime."

Now I have a raging hard-on. She's giving me the eyes already, and I just met her. "Do you come to Vegas often?" I ask.

"No, but I'm in the clubbing scene," she says as she peers down at the crowd.

"It's a pretty good setup here," I say.

She arches a perfectly shaped brow. "Mine's better."

"Yours? What do you mean?"

She grins. "I own a club in New York."

I knew she left Crown Village for her modeling career, but I didn't know she owned a club. Beauty and brains. What a dangerous combination. "Businesswoman, hey… I'm impressed." She gives me a funny look I can't quite make out. "You model too, don't you?"

"Yes, but I'm not doing as many shows anymore. I want to focus on running my club."

"Fair enough." A successful, sexy, rich woman would intimidate most men. Not me—I think running a business just makes her more appealing. It's a nice change to hang out with a woman who's driven and motivated to do something with her life. I want to know everything about her and what makes her tick.

"What do you do?" she asks.

I point to the patch on my vest. "Vice president of the best motorcycle club in the US."

She smiles. "I know that, but what else do you do as a job?"

My shoulders tense. Her father, Garrett, and brother Alec know we grow, distribute, and sell large amounts of pot and aren't licensed. Hell, they said we could. Nothing goes on in the town without her father's say-so, but I don't know how much she knows, so I decide to talk about the charity.

"We help with Zara's charity, at the women and children's safe house."

Her face lights up. "It's unbelievable. Zara has done such a good job. After everything she's been through, she's turned a devastating outcome into something positive. So… what's your role in it?"

"We renovated the property and building where the charity houses the women and children. We help the victims, like picking them up and taking them away from dangerous situations they're in and bringing them to the charity." I think back to the frightened woman and children we picked up last week. "It's really brought the club together, everyone working together to help others. We're honored to assist, and the town's response to us has been positive." People now smile and praise us for helping rather than fearing us.

She steps closer to me and searches my eyes. "You're doing such a great job. I'm proud of you and everyone who's helped Zara."

She's proud of me? I don't think anyone has said that to me before. I give her one of my panty-dropping smiles.

She lifts her hands and grabs each side of my leather cut. "You look sexy in leather."

I'm the one who's supposed to be dishing out compliments. Maybe… just maybe… I'm in over my head with her.

I slip my arms out of my cut and hold it out for her, and without hesitation, she slides the leather vest on over her red dress. My mouth goes dry. Fuck meeeeeee! "Hmm… Temptress, you look better." My voice is husky and my hard-on is achingly uncomfortable against my jeans. An ol' lady property patch with my name on it would be even better.

I glance at the men to see if anyone noticed. Bomber's shaking his head at me and Axle's jaw is gaping. We don't let just anyone wear our club colors. No man outside the MC is allowed to wear our patch, and only the women we're serious about—our ol' ladies—get to wear a property patch with their man's name on it. By letting Sophie wear my cut, I know Axle is going to give me shit later for it.

I lean toward Sophie, pulling her blond wavy hair from under my cut and allowing it to fall down her back, while she gives me a slow once-over.

Harrison appears next to us and hands me my beer. "Thanks," I say, wishing I hadn't asked for it now.

"Where's my drink?" Sophie asks Harrison.

"Sorry, sis, you should have told me beforehand."

"Well… I might go over and order a cocktail. I'll be back soon," she says as she makes her way over to the bar, swaying those sexy hips. I stare at her, captivated.

Harrison's laugh brings my eyes back to him. "I almost feel bad for you."

I frown. "What do you mean?"

"It looks like Sophie's got her eye on you."

I chuckle. "I'm stoked with that." I peek at her again. She's at the bar and is flanked by a man on either side, undoubtedly trying to buy her a drink. Annoyance flares up inside of me. She's *mine* for tonight.

"I thought you were a one-night-stand type of guy."

I am, apart from Candy. "Why do you say that?" I ask.

"Well… you're looking at my sister like you want to be her knight in shining armor. Sophie can more than handle herself with men, but proceed with caution. Every man has wanted to bang her, and after one night, every one of them has wanted more from her. But she doesn't have any more to give, and if she sees you getting jealous or needy"—he looks at her, then at me, and I assume he means the way I'm acting now—"she will run. She's a player."

"What makes you think I want anything other than sex?"

He mocks me with his laughter.

"What?" I ask him.

"She's wearing your cut. She's already got you by the balls."

I chuckle but don't reply because Sophie comes over to us.

She tugs at my arm. "Come have a shot with me."

I smile back at her. "Sure, darlin'."

Harrison gives me an I-told-you-so grin.

I follow Sophie to the bar, where the barman ignores all the other patrons only talking to Sophie. "Your cocktail is being made now." He tilts his head to the lady mixing a blue drink in a fancy glass beside him. "Do you want anything else?" he asks, then licks his lips, his eyes flicking to her breasts, then back to her face.

I itch to say something, but I want Sophie in my bed badly, so I don't want to screw it up.

She gives him a naughty smile. "Two tequila shots, please." The man pulls out the shot glasses, pours the clear liquid into them, and puts the glasses in front of us. "Can we have lime and salt?" she asks. The barman obliges.

"Give me your hand," my little temptress demands. I follow her command. She dips her fingers into a drink and dabs tequila on the part of my hand between my thumb and index finger.

I watch as she shakes salt onto my wet skin. *She's not, is she...* Sophie bends down and runs her soft tongue along the edge of my hand, taking the salt with her, then she tosses her drink back. The movement is erotic.

Sophie places the lime between my lips, making my heart pound. She leans toward me, and her mouth presses against mine as she sucks the lime. My mouth waters—it's intoxicating. She seductively licks her lips. I swiftly down my shot, feeling the warmth of the alcohol, but my attention stays fixed on Sophie.

The barwoman places the cocktail in front of her. "Can I have two more tequila shots?" I ask. She gives me the once-over and then a flirty smile, so I smile back. As soon as the barwoman pours one shot, I take Sophie's hand in mine, dab my fingers into the liquid and dampen her hand, then shake the salt. My body hums in anticipation.

I bring her hand to my lips, and sensually lick the salt while maintaining eye contact. I delight in watching her eyes heat and those luscious lips part. I bring the glass to my lips and finish the shot, but instead of the lime, my hand goes to Sophie's chin. I lean down, sealing my mouth over hers. Sophie's lips are soft. I apply a gentle pressure to begin with and she kisses me back. As my tongue dips inside, I taste her with long, leisurely licks.

Her hands rise, looping over my shoulders until she's running her fingers through my hair. My heartbeat is surging as the kiss deepens. I press my lips against hers harder but try to rein in my wild passion. My hands slip to her hips, then the curve of her ass. The club evaporates, and all that's left is us. I break the kiss, then yank her hips toward mine. I slowly grind my pelvis against hers so that she can feel my hard-on.

Hunger burns in her eyes, proof that I'm not the only one who's turned on. I lean over and run my nose up her throat to her ear, noticing her breathing quicken. I place two kisses on her neck. "I can't wait to fuck you," I tell her, my voice rough.

She squirms. Goosebumps travel along her arms. *She likes the dirty talk.* My fingers dig into her sides. I want her now… to explore every inch of her. She slips her hand between us and grabs my dick through my jeans. I jerk and a hiss escapes me. She slowly rubs up and down, making my eyes roll back.

She bites down on her plump red bottom lip. "I'm ready for round one now," she purrs, and I let out a drawn-out groan. No shyness… just a woman who knows what she wants. I want to brand my name on her pretty little flesh and keep her all for myself.

"Four more shots of tequila," I say to the bartender. I'm already having fun with her. I don't want this night to end. With the two of us drunk together, the night is going to be wild.

I can't believe a man hasn't put a ring on her finger yet. She's the ultimate catch. I wonder what it would take for her to stay at the clubhouse with me and get to know me. Hell, if given the chance, I could show her I'm a decent guy and maybe, just maybe, I'd be worthy.

Grab your copy of <u>Viper</u> now.

RESOURCES

One Australian dollar of every paperback book purchase from Bianca's website will go to the LifeLine charity.

If you are struggling with your mental health, contact Life-Line. LifeLine is available in many countries and offers help for people experiencing emotional distress. They provide confidential crisis support, and in most instances, you can call, chat online, or text.

Please visit https://lifeline-intl.com/our-network/ for more information.

If you are seeking help with a drinking problem, contact Alcoholics Anonymous. AA is an informal society that operates in many countries and offers peer support for recovery from alcoholism.

Please visit https://www.aa.org/find-aa/world for more information.

ABOUT THE AUTHOR

Bianca Lee Ward is an Australian romance author with a love of culinary adventures and a playlist for every mood. She enjoys exploring themes of identity, personal growth, and resilience in her work—with a little spice on the side. When she isn't lost in storytelling or absorbed in her latest read, Bianca can be found watching true crime stories and documentaries.

You can connect with Bianca online at:
Website: www.biancaleeward.com
Email: info@biancaleeward.com
Instagram: https://www.instagram.com/biancaleeward
Facebook: https://www.facebook.com/biancaleeward
Spotify: Bianca Lee Ward
Goodreads: https://www.goodreads.com/author/show/30477361.Bianca_Lee_Ward
BookBub: https://www.bookbub.com/authors/bianca-lee-ward

Don't forget to sign up to Bianca's mailing list, where you'll get *huge* discounts, *exclusive* giveaways, and new release alerts!

9 781763 780293